Nancy

A Novel

by

Rhoda Broughton

Double9
BOOKS

Nancy

A Novel
by Rhoda Broughton

ISBN: 978-93-63051-10-2

Published by

DOUBLE 9 BOOKS

2/13-B, Ansari Road
Daryaganj, New Delhi – 110002
info@double9books.com
www.double9books.com
Tel. 011-40042856

ABOUT THE AUTHOR

Rhoda Broughton was a Welsh novelist and short-story writer. Her early works were known for their sensationalism, thus critics often overlooked her later, stronger work, despite her being dubbed the "queen of the circulating libraries." Her novel Dear Faustina (1897) is known for its homoeroticism. Her novel Lavinia (1902) portrays a supposedly "unmanly" young man who wishes he had been born a woman. Broughton was a granddaughter of the 8th baronet, hence she descended from the Broughton family. She was Sheridan le Fanu's niece, and he helped her begin her literary career. Rhoda Broughton was born on November 29, 1840, in Denbigh, North Wales, the daughter of the Rev. Delves Broughton, youngest son of the Rev. Sir Henry Delves-Broughton, 8th baronet, and Jane Bennett, daughter of George Bennett, a prominent Irish barrister. Her aunt, Susanna Bennett, married the renowned fiction writer Sheridan le Fanu. Rhoda Broughton acquired an interest in reading as a young girl, particularly poetry. She was influenced by William Shakespeare, as seen by the frequent citations and allusions in her works. Presumably, after reading Anne Isabella Thackeray Ritchie's The Story of Elizabeth, she decided to test her own talent. Broughton, in turn, introduced Mary Cholmondeley to her publishers in 1887.

CONTENTS

CHAPTER I

"Put into a small preserving pan three ounces of fresh butter, and, as soon as it is just melted, add one pound of brown sugar of moderate quality—"

"Not moderate; the browner the better," interpolates Algy.

"Cannot say I agree with you. I hate brown sugar—filthy stuff!" says Bobby, contradictiously.

"Not half so *filthy* as white, if you come to that," retorts Algy, loftily, looking up from the lemon he is grating to extinguish his brother. "They clear white sugar with but—"

"Keep these stirred gently over a clear fire for about fifteen minutes," interrupt I, beginning to read again very fast, in a loud, dull recitative, to hinder further argument, "or until a little of the mixture dipped into cold water breaks clear between the teeth without sticking to them. When it is boiled to this point, it must be poured out immediately or it will burn."

Having galloped jovially along, scorning stops, I here pause out of breath. We are a large family, we Greys, and we are *all* making taffy. Yes, every one of us. It would take all the fingers of one hand, and the thumb of the other, to count us, O reader. Six! Yes, six. A Frenchman might well hold up his hands in astonished horror at the insane prolificness—the foolhardy fertility—of British householders. We come very *improbably* close together, except Tou Tou, who was an after-thought. There are no two of us, I am proud to say, exactly simultaneous, but we have come tumbling on each other's heels into the world in so hot a hurry that we evidently expect to find it a pleasant place when we get there. Perhaps we do—perhaps we do not; friends, you will hear and judge for yourselves.

A few years ago when we were little, people used to say that we were quite a pretty sight, like little steps one above another. We are big steps now, and no one any longer hazards the suggestion of our being pretty. On the other hand, nobody denies that we are each as well furnished with legs, arms, and other etceteras, as our neighbors, nor can affirm that we are notably more deficient in wits than those of our friends who have arrived in twos and threes.

We are in the school-room, the big bare school-room, that has seen us all—that is still seeing some of us—unwillingly dragged, and painfully goaded up the steep slopes of book-learning. Outside, the March wind is roughly hustling the dry, brown trees and pinching the diffident green shoots, while the round and rayless sun of late afternoon is staring, from behind the elm-twigs in at the long maps on the wall, in at the high chairs—tall of back, cruelly tiny of seat, off whose rungs we have kicked all the paint—in at the green baize table, richly freaked with splashes. Hardly less red than the sun's, are our burnt faces gathered about the fire.

This fire has no flame—only a glowing, ruddy heart, on which the bright brass saucepan sits; and kneeling before it, stirring the mess with a long iron spoon, is Barbara. Algy, as I have before remarked, is grating a lemon. Bobby is buttering soup-plates. The Brat—the Brat always takes his ease if he can—is peeling almonds, fishing delicately for them in a cup of hot water with his finger and thumb; and I, Nancy, am reading aloud the receipt at the top of my voice, out of a greasy, dog's-eared cookery-book, which, since it came into our hands, has been the innocent father of many a hideous compound. Tou Tou alone, in consideration of her youth, is allowed to be a spectator. She sits on the edge of the table, swinging her thin legs, and kicking her feet together.

Certainly we deteriorate in looks as we go downward. In Barbara we made an excellent start: few families a better one, though we say it that should not. Although in Algy there was a slight falling off, it was not much to complain of. But I am sensibly uglier than Algy (as indeed he has, on several occasions, dispassionately remarked to me); the Brat than me; Bobby than the Brat; and so steadily on, till we reach our nadir of unhandsomeness in Tou Tou. Tou Tou is our climax, and we certainly defy our neighbors and acquaintances to outdo her.

Hapless young Tou Tou! made up of the thinnest legs, the widest mouth, the invisiblest nose, and over-visiblest ears, that ever went to the composition of a child of twelve years.

"Keep stirring always! You must take care that it does not stick to the bottom!" say I, closing the receipt-book, and speaking on my own account, but still as one having authority.

"All very well to say 'Keep stirring always,'" answers Barbara, turning round a face unavoidably pretty, even though at the present moment deeply flame-colored; eyes still sweetly laughing with gay good-humor, even though half burnt out of her head, to answer me; "but if you had been stirring as long as I have, you would wonder that you had any arm left to stir with, however feebly. Here, one of you boys, take a turn! You Brat, you never do any thing for your living!"

The Brat complies, though not with eagerness. They change occupations: the Brat stirs, and she fishes for almonds. Ten minutes pass: the taffy is done, and what is more it really is taffy. The upshot of our cookery is in general so startlingly indifferent from what we had intended, that the result in the present case takes us by surprise. We all prove practically that, in the words of the receipt-book, it "breaks clear between the teeth without sticking to them." It is poured into Bobby's soup-plate, and we have thrown up the window-sashes, and set it on the ledge to cool. The searching wind blows in dry and biting. Now it is rushing in a violent current through the room, for the door has opened. Mother enters.

"To what may we attribute the honor of this visit?" says Algy, turning away from the window to meet her, and setting her a chair. Bobby gives her a kiss, and the Brat a lump of taffy, concerning which it would be invidious to predicate which were the stickier; so exceedingly adhesive are both.

"Your father says," begins she, sitting down. She is interrupted by a loud and universal groan.

"Says what? Something unpleasant of course, who is it now? Who has done any thing now? I do hope it is the Brat," cries Bobby, viciously; "it is quite his turn; he has been good boy of the family for the last week."

"I dare say it is," replies the Brat, resignedly; "one can't expect such prosperity as mine to last forever."

"Of course it is *I*," says Algy, rather bitterly, "it is always I. I have never been good boy since I was ploughed; and, please God, I never will be again."

"But what is it? what is it? About how bad is it? Is it to be one of our worst rows?"

We are all speaking together at the top of our voices; indeed, we rarely employ a lower key.   ⁓

"It is no one; no one has done any thing," replies mother, when, at last, we allow her to make herself heard, "only your father sends you a message that, as Sir Roger Tempest is coming here to-day, he hopes you will make less noise this evening in here than you did last night: he says he could hardly hear the sound of his own voice."

"Ahem!" "Very likely!" "I dare say!" in different tones of angry incredulity.

"He begs you to see that the swing-door is shut, as he does not wish his friend to imagine that he keeps a private lunatic asylum."

A universal snort of indignation.

"If we are bedlamites, we know who made us so. We will tell old Roger if he asks," etc.

"For my part," say I, resolutely pinching my lips together as I kneel on the carpet, and violently hammer the now cold and hard taffy with the handle of the poker, which in its day has been put to many uses vile, "I can tell you that I shall not dine with you to-night: I should infallibly say something to father—something unfortunate—I feel it rising; and it would be unseemly to have one of our *émeutes* before this old gentleman, would not it?"

"They are nice breezy things when you are used to them," says Barbara, laughing; "but one requires to be brought up to them."

"Do not you dine either, Brat," say I, looking up, and waving the poker with suave command at him, "and we will broil bones for tea, and roast potatoes on the shovel."

"Some of you must dine," says poor mother, rather wearily, "or your father—"

"He cannot complain if we send our two specimen ones," say I, again looking up, and indicating Barbara and Algy with my weapon, "our sample figs: if Sir Robert—Sir Robin—Sir Roger—what is he?—does not see the rest of us, he may perhaps imagine that we are all equally presentable, which would be more to your credit, mother, than if Bobby and Tou Tou and I were to be submitted to the poor old thing's notice."

Mother looks rather at sea.

"What are you talking about? What poor old thing? Oh! I understand."

"He will have to see us," says Tou Tou, rather lugubriously, "he cannot help it—at prayers."

Tou Tou has descended from the table, and is standing propped against mother's knee, twisting one leg with ingenious grace round the other.

"Bless your heart," says the Brat, comfortingly, "he will never find out that we are there: do you suppose that his blear old eyes will see all across that big room, economically lit up by one pair of candles?"

Mother smiles.

"Wait till you see whether he has blear eyes!"

"He must be very ancient," says Algy, in all the insolence of twenty, leaning his flat back against the mantel-shelf, "as he was at school with father."

"Father has not blear eyes," remarks Bobby, dryly. "Would God he had! For then perhaps he would not see our little vices quite so clearly with them as he does."

"But then father has not been in India," retorts Algy, stretching. "India plays the deuce with one's organs and appurtenances."

"I wish you joy of him," say I, rising flushed and untidy from my knees, having successfully smashed the taffy into little bits; "from soup to walnuts, you will have to undergo a ceaseless tyranny of tales about hitmaghars and dak bungalows and Choto Lazery: which of us has not suffered in our day from the horrible monotony of ideas of an old Indian?"

"Never you mind, Barbara!" cries the Brat, giving her a sounding brotherly pat on the back. "Pay no attention to her."

"'What great events from trivial causes spring!' as the poet says: you may live to bless the day that old Roger crossed our doors."

"As how?" says Barbara, laughing, and rocking herself backward and forward in a veteran American rocking-chair which, at different periods of our history, has served most of us the dirty turn of tipping us over, and presenting us reversed to the eyes of our family.

"Never you mind," repeats the Brat, oracularly; "truth is stranger than fiction! odd things happen: I read in the paper the other day of a man who pulled up the window for an old woman in the train, and she died at once—I do not mean on the spot, but very soon after, and when she died—listen, please, all of you—" (speaking very slowly and impressively)—"she left him *two thousand pounds* a year."

"I wish I saw the application," answers Barbara, still rocking and sighing.

"Mind that you set a stool for his gouty foot," says Algy, feeling for his faint mustache, "and run and search for his spectacle-case, when he has mislaid it."

"Seriously," say I, "what a grand thing it would be for the family if he were to adopt you, Barbara!"

"Or me," suggests the Brat, standing before the fire with his coat-tails under his arm. "Why not *me*? My manners to the aged are always considered particularly happy."

"Here he is!" cries Tou Tou from the window, whither she has retired, and now stands, like a heron, on one leg, leaning her elbow on the sill. "Here is the dog-cart turning the corner!"

We all make a rush to the casement.

"Yes, there he is! sure enough! our future benefactor!" says Algy, looking over the rest of our heads, and making a counterfeit greeting.—"Welcome, welcome, good old man!"

"And father, all affability, pointing out the house," supplements Bobby.

We laugh grimly.

"But who is it he has in the fly?" say I, as the second vehicle follows the first. "His harem, I suppose! half a dozen old Wampoos."

"His valet, to be sure," replies the Brat, chidingly, "with his stays, and his evening wig, and the calves of his legs."

CHAPTER II

The wind is even colder than it was, stronger and more withering now that the sun's faint warmth is withdrawn, and that the small and chilly stars possess the sky. Nevertheless, both the school-room windows are open. We are all huddled shivering round the hearth, yet no one talks of closing them. The fact is, that amateur cooking, though a graceful accomplishment, has its penalties, and that at the present moment the smell of broiled bones and fried potatoes that fills our place of learning is something appalling. Why may not it penetrate beneath the swing-door, through the passages, and reach the drawing-room? Such a thing has happened once or twice before. At the bare thought we all quake. I am in the pleasant situation, just at present, of owning a chilled body and a blazing face.

Chiefest among the cooks have I been, and now I am sitting trying to fan my red cheeks and redder nose, with the back of an old atlas, gutted in some ancient broil, trying, in deference to Sir Roger, to cool down my appearance a little against prayer-time. Alas! that epoch is nearer than I think. Ting! tang! the loud bell is ringing through the house. My hair is loosened and tumbled with stooping over the fire, and I have burnt a hole right in the fore front of my gown, by letting a hot cinder fall from the grate upon it. There is, however, now no time to repair these dilapidations. We issue from our lair, and *en route* meet the long string of servants filing from their distant regions. How is it that the cook's face is so much, *much* less red than mine? Prayers are held in the justicing-room, and thither we are all repairing. The accustomed scene bursts on my eye. At one end the long, straight row of the servants, immovably devout, staring at the wall, with their backs to us. In the middle of the room, facing them, father, kneeling upon a chair with his hands clutched, and his eyes closed, repeating the church prayers, as if he were rather angry with them than otherwise. Mother, kneeling on the carpet beside him, like the faithful, ruffed, and farthingaled wife on a fifteenth-century tomb. Behind them, again, at some little distance, we and our visitor. With the best will in the world to do so, I can get but a meagre view of the latter. The room is altogether rather dark, it being one of our manners and customs not to throw much light on prayers, and he has chosen the darkest corner of it. I only vaguely see the outline of a kneeling figure, evidently neither bulky nor obese, of a flat back and vigorous shoulders. His face is generally hidden in his hands, but once or twice he lifts it to scan the proportions of my late grandfather's preposterously fat cob, whose portrait hangs on the wall above his head.

There is no doubt that on some days the devil reigns with a more potent sway over people than on others. To-night he has certainly entered into the boys. He often does a little, but this evening he is holding a great and mighty carnival among them. While father's strong, hard voice vibrates in a loud, dull monotone through the silent room, they are engaged in a hundred dumb yet ungodly antics behind his back.

Algernon has thrust his head far out between the rungs of his chair-back, and affects to be unable to withdraw it again, making movements of simulated suffocation. The Brat is stealthily walking on his knees across the space that intervenes between them to Barbara, with intent, as I too well know, of unseemly pinchings. If father unbutton his eyes, or move his head one barley-corn, we are all dead men. I hold my breath in a nervous agony. Thank Heaven! the harsh recitation still flows on with equable loud slowness. In happy ignorance of his offspring's antics, father is still asking, or rather ordering, the Almighty (for there is more of command than entreaty in his tone) to prosper the High Court of Parliament. Also the Brat is now returning to his place, travelling with surprising noiseless rapidity over the Turkey carpet, dragging his shins and his feet after him. I draw a long breath of relief, and drop my hot face into my spread hands. My peace, however, is not of long duration. I am aroused again by a sort of choking snort from Tou Tou, who is beside me—a snort that seems compounded of mingled laughter and pain, and, looking up, detect Bobby in the act of deftly puncturing one of her long bare legs with a long brass pin, which he has found straying, after the vagabond manner of pins, over the carpet.

I raise myself, and lean over Tou Tou, to give the offender a silent buffet of admonition, and, lifting my eyes apprehensively to see if I am noticed, I meet the blear eyes of Sir Roger fixed upon mine. He has turned his face quite toward me, and a ray from the candles falls full upon it. *Blear!* Well, if his eyes are blear, then henceforth blear must bear a different signification from the unhandsome one it has hitherto worn. Henceforth it must mean blue as steel: it must mean clear as a glass of spring water; keen as a well-tempered knife; kindly as the early sunshine.

I am so astonished at my discovery, that I remain for full two minutes staring blankly at the object of it, while he also looks stealthily at me; then, recollecting my manners, I burrow my face into my chair-bottom, and so remain until mother's gentle Amen, and a noise of shuffling and scrambling to their feet on the part of the congregation, tell me that the end has come.

We all go up to father, and coldly and stiffly kiss him. While I am waiting for my turn to receive our parent's chilly salute, I steal a second glance at our guest. Yes, he is old certainly. Despite the youth of his eyes, despite the uprightness, the utter freedom from superfluous flesh—from the ugly shaky bulkiness of age—in his tall and stalwart figure, still he is old—old in the eyes of nineteen—as old as father, perhaps—though in much better preservation—forty-eight or forty-nine; for is not his hair iron-gray, and his heavy mustache, and the thick and silky beard that falls on his broad breast, are they not iron-gray too? I have dropped my small and unwilling kiss on father's forehead—and said "good-night" in a tone as suppressedly hostile as his own. Now I may go. We may all go. I am the last, or I think I am, to pass through the swing-door. I hurry along the passage to join the rest in the school-room. I upbraid the boys for the rash impiety of their demeanor. I feel a foot on my garments behind, and hear a long cracking sound that I too, too well know to mean *gathers*.

"You beast!" cried I, in good nervous English, turning sharply round with my hand raised in act to strike, "that is the third time this week that you have torn out my—"

I stop dumfounded. If I mean to box the offender's ears, I must raise my hand considerably higher than it is at present. Angels and ministers of grace! what has happened? I have called General Sir Roger Tempest a *beast*, and offered to cuff him. For a moment, I am dumfounded. Then, for shyness has never been my besetting sin, and something in the genial laughter of his eyes reassures me.

I hold out the injured portion of my raiment, and say:

"Look! when you see what you have done, I am sure you will forgive me; but of course I meant it for Bobby. I never dreamt it was you."

He takes hold of one end of the rent, I of the other, and we both examine it.

"How exceedingly clumsy of me! how could it have happened? I beg your pardon ten thousand times."

In his words there is polite remorse and solicitude; in his face only a friendly mirth. He is old, that is clear. Had he been young, he would have said, with that variety and suitability of epithets so characteristic of this generation:

"I am awfully sorry! how awfully stupid of me! what an awful duffer I am!"

The gas is shining in its garish yellow brightness full down upon us, as we stand together, illuminating my plain, scorched face, the slatternly looseness of my hair, and the burnt hole in my gown.

"You will have to give me another," I say, looking up at him and smiling. I should not have thought of saying it if he had been a young man, but with a *vieux papa* one may be at one's ease.

"There is nothing in the world I should like better," he says, with a sort of hurry and eagerness, not very suggestive of a *vieux papa*; "but really—" (seeing me look rather ashamed of my proposition)—"is it *quite* hopeless? the damage quite irremediable?"

"On the contrary," reply I, tucking my gathers in, with a graceful movement, at the band of my gown, "five minutes will make it as good as new—at least" (casting a disparaging eye over its frayed and taffy-marked surface), "as good as it ever will be in this world."

A little pause.

"I suppose I have lost my way," he says, thinking, I fancy, that I look rather eager to be gone. "I am never very good at the geography of a strange house."

"Yes," say I, promptly; "you came through *our* door, instead of your own; shall I show you the way back?"

"Since I have come so far, may not I come a little farther?" he asks, glancing rather longingly at the half-open school-room door, whence sounds of pious mirth are again beginning to reissue.

"Do you mean *really*?" ask I, with a highly-dissuasive inflection of voice. "Please not to-night; we are all higgledy-piggledy—at sixes and sevens! To tell you the truth, we have been *cooking*. I wonder you did not smell it in the drawing-room."

Again he looks amused.

"May not I cook too? I *can*, though you look disbelieving; there are few people that can beat me at an Irish stew when I set my mind to it."

A head (Bobby's) appears round the school-room door.

"I say, Nancy, who are you colloquing with out there? I believe you have got hold of our future benefact—"

An "oh!" of utter discomfiture, and the head is withdrawn.

"I am keeping you," Sir Roger says. "Well, I will say good-night. You will shake hands, won't you, to show that you bear no malice?"

"That I will," reply I, heartily stretching out my right hand, and giving his a cordial shake. For was not he at school with father?

CHAPTER III

Day has followed night. The broiled smell has at length evacuated the school-room, but a good deal of taffy, spilt in the pouring out, still adheres to the carpet, making it nice and sticky. The wind is still running roughly about over the earth, and the yellow crocuses, in the dark-brown garden-borders, opened to their widest extent, are staring up at the sun. How *can* they stare so straight up at him without blinking? I have been trying to emulate them—trying to stare, too, up at him, through the pane, as he rides laughing, aloft in the faint far sky; and my presumptuous eyes have rained down tears in consequence. I am trying now to read; but a hundred thousand things distract me: the sun shining warm on my shoulder, as I lean against the window; the divine morning clamor of the birds; their invitations to come out that will take no nay; and last, but oh! not, *not* least, the importunate voices of Barbara and Tou Tou. Every morning at this hour they have a weary tussle with the verb "aimer," "to love." It is hard that they should have pitched upon so tender-hearted a verb for the battle-field of so grim a struggle:

J'aime, I love.

Tu aimes, Thou lovest.

Il aime, He loves.

Nous aimons, We love.

Vous aimez, You love.

Ils aiment, They love.

This, with endless variations of ingenious and hideous inaccuracies—this, interspersed with foolish laughter and bitter tears, is what I have daily been audience to, for the last two months. The day before yesterday a great stride was taken; the present tense was pronounced vanquished, and Barbara and her pupil passed on in triumph to the imperfect, "j'aimais, I loved, or was loving." To-day, in order to be quite on the safe side, a return has been made to "j'aime," and it has been discovered that it has utterly disappeared from our young sister's memory. "J'aimais, I loved, or was loving," has entirely routed and dispersed his elder brother, "j'aime, I love." The old strain is, therefore, desperately resumed:

J'aime, I love.

Tu aimes, Thou lovest.

Il aime, He loves, etc.

It is making me drowsy. Ten minutes more, and I shall be asleep in the sun, with my head down-dropped on the window-sill. I get up, and, putting on my out-door garments, stray out into the sun, leaving Barbara— her pretty forehead puckered with ineffectual wrath, and Tou Tou blurred with grimy tears, to their death-struggle with the restive verb "to love." It is the end of March, and when one can hide round a corner from the wind, one has a foretaste of summer, in the sun's warm strength. I gaze lovingly at the rich brown earth, so lately freed from the frost's grasp, through which the blunt green buds are gently forcing themselves. I look down the flaming crocus throats—the imperial purple goblets with powdery gold stamens— and at the modest little pink faces of the hepaticas. All over our wood there is a faint yet certain purply shade, forerunner of the summer green, and the loud and sweet-voiced birds are abroad. O Spring! Spring! with all your searching east winds, with your late, shriveling frosts, with your occasional untimely sleets and snows, you are yet as much better than summer as hope is better than fruition.

J'aime, I love.

Tu aimes, Thou lovest.

Il aime, He loves.

It runs in my head like some silly refrain. I meet Bobby. I also meet Vick, my little shivering, smooth, white terrier. They both join me. The one wriggles herself into the shape of a trembling comma, and, foolishly chasing herself, rolls over on her back, to demonstrate her joy at my advent. The other says:

"Come into the kitchen-garden, and see whether the apricot-flowers are out on the south wall."

We pace along the broad and even gravel walk among the red cabbages and the sea-kale, basking in the sun, whose heat we feel undiminished by the influence of any bitter blast, in the prison of these four high walls, against which the long tree-branches are pinioned. In one place, the pinioning has failed. A long, flower-laden arm has burst from its bonds, and is dangling loosely down. There is a ladder against the wall, set for the gardener to replace it.

"Is it difficult to get up a ladder, Bobby?" ask I, standing still.

"Difficult! Bless your heart, no! Why?"

"One can see nothing here," I answer. "I should like to climb up and sit on the top of the wall, where one can look about one."

My wish is easy of gratification. Bobby holds the ladder, and I climb cautiously, rung by rung. Having reached the summit, I sit at ease, with my legs loosely dangling. There is no broken glass, there are no painful bottoms of bottles to disturb my ruminant quiet. The air bites a little, but I am warmly clad, and young. Bobby sits beside me, whistling and kicking the bricks with his heels. There is the indistinctness of fine weather over the chain of low round hills that bound our horizon, giving them a dignity that, on clearer days, they lack. As I sit, many small and pleasant noises visit my ears, sometimes distinct, sometimes mixed together; the brook's noise, as it runs, quick and brown, between the flat, dry March fields; the gray geese's noise, as they screech all together from the farm-yard; the church-bells' noise, as they ring out from the distant town, whose roofs and vanes are shining and glinting in the morning sun.

"Do you hear the bells?" say I. "Some one has been married this morning."

"Do not you wish it was you?" asks Bobby, with a brotherly grin.

"I should not mind," reply I, picking out a morsel of mortar with my finger and thumb. "It is about time for one of us to move off, is not it? And Barbara has made such a signal failure hitherto, that I think it is but fair that I should try my little possible."

"All I ask of you is," says Bobby, gravely, "not to take a fellow who has not got any shooting."

"I will make it a *sine qua non*," I answer, seriously.

A louder screech than ever from the geese, accompanied with wing-flappings. How unanimous they are! There is not a voice wanting.

"I wonder how long Sir Roger will stay?" I say presently.

"What connection of ideas made you think of him?" asks Bobby, curiously. "Do you suppose that he has any shooting?"

I break into a laugh.

"I do not know, I am sure. I do not think it matters much whether he has or not."

"I dare say that there are a good many women—old ones, you know— who would take him, old as he is," says Bobby, with liberality.

"I dare say," I answer. "I do not know. I am not old, but I am not sure that I would not rather marry him than be an old maid."

A pause. Again I laugh—this time a laugh of recollection.

"What a fool you did look last night!" I say with sisterly candor, "when you put your head round the school-room door, and found that you had been witty about him to his face!"

Bobby reddens, and aims a bit of mortar at a round-eyed robin that has perched near us.

"At all events, I did not call him a *beast*."

"Well, never mind; do not get angry! What did it matter?" say I, comfortingly. "You did not mention his name. How could he tell that he was our benefactor? He did not even know that he was to be; and I begin to have misgivings about it myself."

"I cannot say that I see much sign of his putting his hand into his breeches-pocket," says Bobby, vulgarly.

There is the click of a lifted latch. We both look in the direction whence comes the sound. He of whom we speak is entering the garden by a distant door.

"Get down, Bobby!" cry I, hurriedly, "and help me down. Make haste! quick! I would not have him find me perched up here for *worlds*."

Bobby gets down as nimbly as a monkey. I prepare to do likewise.

"Hold it steady!" I cry nervously, and, so saying, begin to turn round and to stretch out one leg, with the intention of making a graceful descent backward.

"Stop!" cries Bobby from the bottom, with a diabolical chuckle. "I think you observed just now that I looked a fool last night! perhaps you will not mind trying how it feels!"

So saying, he seizes the ladder—a light and short one—and makes off with it. I cry, "Bobby! Bobby!" suppressedly, several times, but I need hardly say that my appeal is addressed to deaf ears. I remain sitting on the wall-top, trying to look as if I did not mind, while grave misgivings possess my soul as to the extent of strong boot and ankle that my unusual situation leaves visible. Once the desperate idea of jumping presents itself to my mind, but the ground looks so distant, and the height so great, that my heart fails me.

From my watch-tower I trace the progress of Sir Roger between the fruit-trees. As yet, he has not seen me. Perhaps he will turn into another walk, and leave the garden by an opposite door, I remaining undiscovered. No! he is coming toward me. He is walking slowly along, a cigar in his mouth, and his eyes on the ground, evidently in deep meditation. Perhaps he will pass me without looking up. Nearer and nearer he comes, I hold my breath, and sit as still as stone, when, as ill-luck will have it, just as he is approaching quite close to me, utterly innocent of my proximity, a nasty, teasing tickle visits my nose, and I sneeze loudly and irrepressibly. Atcha! atcha! He starts, and not perceiving at first whence comes the unexpected sound, looks about him in a bewildered way. Then his eyes turn toward the wall. Hope and fear are alike at an end. I am discovered. Like Angelina, I—

.... "stand confessed,
A maid in all my charms."

"How—on—earth—did you get up there?" he asks, in an accent of slow and marked astonishment, not unmixed with admiration.

As he speaks, he throws away his cigar, and takes his hat off.

"How on earth am I to get down again? is more to the purpose," I answer, bluntly.

"I could not have believed that any thing but a cat could have been so agile," he says, beginning to laugh. "Would you mind telling me how *did* you get up?"

"By the ladder," reply I, laconically, reddening, and, under the influence of that same insupportable doubt concerning my ankles, trying to tuck away my legs under me, a manœuvre which all but succeeds in toppling me over.

"The *ladder!*" (looking round). "Are you quite sure? Then where has it disappeared to?"

"I said something that vexed Bobby," reply I, driven to the humiliating explanation, "and he went off with it. Never mind! once I am down, I will be even with him!"

He looks entertained.

"What will you do? What will you say? Will you make use of the same excellently terse expression that you applied to me last night?"

"I should not wonder," reply I, bursting out into uncomfortable laughter; "but it is no use talking of what I shall do when I am down: I am not down yet; I wish I were."

"It is no great distance from the ground," he says, coming nearer the wall, standing close to where the apricot is showering down her white and pinky petals. "Are you afraid to jump? Surely not! Try! If you will, I will promise that you shall come to no hurt."

"But supposing that I knock you down?" say I, doubtfully. "I really am a good weight—heavier than you would think to look at me—and coming from such a height, I shall come with great force."

He smiles.

"I am willing to risk it; if you do knock me down, I can but get up again."

I require no warmer invitation. With arms extended, like the sails of a windmill, I hurl myself into the embrace of Sir Roger Tempest. The next moment I am standing beside him on the gravel-walk, red and breathless, but safe.

"I hope I did not hurt you much," I say with concern, turning toward him to make my acknowledgments, "but I really am very much obliged to you; I believe that, if you had not come by, I should have been left there till bedtime."

"It must have been a very unpleasant speech that you made to deserve so severe a punishment," he says, looking back at me, with a kindly and amused curiosity.

I do not gratify his inquisitiveness.

"It was something not quite polite," I answer, shortly.

We walk on in silence, side by side. My temper is ruffled. I am planning five distinct and lengthy vengeances against Bobby.

"I dare say," says my companion presently, "that you are wondering what brought me in here now—what attraction a kitchen-garden could have for me, at a time of year when not the most sanguine mind could expect to find any thing good to eat in it."

"At least, it is sheltered," I answer, shivering, thrusting my hands a little farther into the warm depths of my muff.

"I was thinking of old days," he says, with a hazy, wistful smile. "Ah! you have not come to the time of life for doing that yet. Do you know, I have not been here since your father and I were lads of eleven and twelve together?"

"*You* were eleven, and *he* was twelve, I am sure," say I, emphatically.

"Why?"

"You look *so much* younger than he," I answer, looking frankly and unembarrassedly up into his face.

"Do I?" (with a pleased smile). "It is clear, then, that one cannot judge of one's self; on the rare occasions when I look in the glass it seems to me that, in the course of the last five years, I have grown into a *very* old fogy."

"He looks as if he had been so much oftener vexed, and so much seldomer pleased than you do," continued I, mentally comparing the smooth though weather-beaten benignity of the straight-cut features beside me, with the austere and frown-puckered gravity of my father's.

"Does he?" he answers, with an air of half-surprised interest, as if the subject had never struck him in that light before. "Poor fellow! I am sorry if it is so. Ah, you see"—with a smile—"he has *six* more reasons for wrinkles than I have."

"You mean us, I suppose," I answer matter-of-factly. "As to that, I think he draws quite as many wrinkles on our faces as we do on his." Then, rather ashamed of my over-candor, I add, with hurried bluntness, "You have never been married, I suppose?"

He half turns away his head.

"No—not yet! I have not yet had that good fortune."

I am inwardly amused at the power of his denial. Surely, surely he might say in the words of Lancelot:

"Had I chosen to wed,
I had been wedded earlier, sweet Elaine."

"And you?" he asks, turning with an accent of playfulness toward me.

"Not yet," I answer, laughing, "and most likely I shall have to answer 'not yet' to that question as often as it is put to me till the end of the chapter."

"Why so?"

I shrug my shoulders.

"In moments of depression it strikes Barbara and me, that me and Tou Tou shall end by being three old cats together."

"Are you so anxious to be married?" he asks with an air of wonder, "in such a hurry to leave so happy a home?"

"Every one knows best where his own shoe pinches," I answer vernacularly. "I am afraid that it does not sound very lady-like, but since you ask me the question, I *am* rather anxious. Barbara is not: I am."

A shade of I cannot exactly say what emotion—it *looks* like disappointment, but surely it cannot be that—passes across the sunshine of his face.

"All my plans hinge on my marrying," I continue, feeling drawn, I do not know how or why, into confidential communication to this almost total stranger, "and what is more, on my marrying a rich man."

"And what are your plans?" he asks, with an air of benevolent interest, but that unexplained shade is still there.

"Their name is Legion," I answer; "you will be very tired before I get to the end of them."

"Try me."

"Firstly then," say I, narratively, "my husband must have a great deal of interest in several professions—the army, the navy, the bar—so as to give the boys a helping hand; then he must have some shooting—good shooting for them; for them all, that is, except Bobby! *never* shall *he* fire a gun in my preserves!"

My mind again wanders away to my vengeances, and I break off.

"Well!"

"He must also keep two or three horses for them to hunt: Algy *loves* hunting, but he hardly ever gets a day. He is so big, poor dear old boy, that nobody ever gives him a mount—"

"Yes?"

"Well, then, I should like to be able to have some nice parties—dancing and theatricals, and that sort of thing, for Barbara—father will never hardly let us have a soul here—and to buy her some pretty dresses to set off her beauty—"

"Yes?"

"And then I should like to have a nice, large, cheerful house, where mother could come and stay with me, for two or three months at a time, and get *clear* away from the worries of house-keeping and—" the tyranny of father, I am about to add, but pull myself up with a jerk, and substitute lamely and stammeringly "and—and—others."

"Any thing else?"

"I should not at all mind a donkey-carriage for Tou Tou, but I shall not *insist* upon that."

He is smiling broadly now. The shade has fled away, and only sunshine remains.

"And what for yourself? you seem to have forgotten yourself!"

"For myself!" I echo, in surprise, "I have been telling you—you cannot have been listening—all these things are for myself."

Again he has turned his face half away.

"I hope you will get your wish," he says shortly and yet heartily.

I laugh. "That is so probable, is not it? I am so likely to fall in with a rich young man of weak intellect who is willing to marry all the whole six of us, for that is what he would have to do, and so I should explain to him."

Sir Roger is looking at me again with an odd smile—not disagreeable in any way—not at all hold-cheap, or as if he were sneering at me for a simpleton, but merely *odd*.

"And you think," he says, "that when he hears what is expected of him he will withdraw?"

Again I laugh heartily and rather loudly, for the idea tickles me, and, in a large family, one gets into the habit of raising one's voice, else one is not heard.

"I am so sadly sure that he will never come forward, that I have never taken the trouble to speculate as to whether, if he did, my greediness would make him retire again."

No answer.

"Now that I come to think of it, though," continue I, after a pause, "I have no manner of doubt that he would."

Apparently Sir Roger is tired of the subject of my future prospects, for he drops it. We have left the kitchen-garden—have passed through the flower-garden—have reached the hall-door. I am irresolutely walking up the stone steps that mount to it, not being able to make up my mind as to whether or no I should make some sort of farewell observation to my companion, when his voice follows me. It seems to me to have a dissuasive inflection.

"Are you going in?"

"Well, yes," I answer uncertainly, "I suppose so."

He looks at his watch.

"It is quite early yet—not near luncheon-time—would it bore you very much to take a turn in the park? I think" (with a smile) "that you are quite honest enough to say so if it would: or, if you did not, I should read it on your face."

"Would you?" say I, a little piqued. "I do not think you would: I assure you that my face can tell stories, at a pinch, as well as its neighbor."

"Well, *would* it bore you?"

"Not at all! not at all!" reply I briskly, beginning to descend again; "but one thing is very certain, and that is that it will bore *you*."

"Why should it?"

"If I say what I was going to say you will think that it is on purpose to be contradicted," I answer, unlatching the gate in the fence, and entering the park.

"And if I do, much you will mind," he answers, smiling.

"Well, then," say I, candidly, looking down at my feet as they trip quickly along through the limp winter grass, "there is no use blinking the fact that I have no conversation—none of us have. We can gabble away among ourselves like a lot of young rooks, about all sorts of silly home jokes, that nobody but us would see any fun in; but when it comes to real talk—"

I pause expressively.

"I do not care for *real talk*," he says, looking amused; "I like *gabble* far, far better. I wish you would gabble a little now."

But the request naturally ties my tongue tight up.

"This is the tree that they planted when father was born," I say, presently, in a stiff, *cicerone* manner, pointing to a straight and strong young oak, which is lifting its branchy head, and the fine net-work of its brown twigs, to the cold, pale sky.

Sir Roger leans his arms on the top of the palings that surround the tree.

"Ah! eight-and-forty years ago! eight-and-forty years ago!" he repeats to himself with musing slowness. "Hard upon half a century!"

I turn over in my own mind whether I should do well to make some observation of a trite and copy-book nature on the much greater duration of trees than men, but reflecting that the application of the remark may be painful to a person so elderly as the gentleman beside me, I abstain. However, he does something of the kind himself.

"To think that it should be such a stripling," he says, looking with a half-pensive smile at the straight young trunk, "hardly out of the petticoat age, and *we*—he and I—such a couple of old wrecks!"

It never occurs to me that it would be polite, and even natural, to contradict him. Why should not he call himself an old wreck, if it amuses him? I suppose he only means to express a gentleman decidedly in the decline of life, which, in my eyes, he is; so I say kindly and acquiescingly—

"Yes, it *is* rather hard, is it not?"

"Forty-one—forty-two—yes, forty-two years since I first saw him," he continues, reflectively, "running about in short, stiff, white petticoats and bare legs, and going bawling to his mother, because he tumbled up those steps to the hall-door, and cut his nose open."

I lift my face out of my muff, in which, for the sake of warmth, I have been hiding it, and, opening my mouth, give vent to a hearty and undutiful roar of laughter.

"Cut his nose open!" repeat I, indistinctly. "How pleased he must have been, and what sort of a nose was it? already hooked? It never *could* have been the conventional button, *that* I am sure of; *yours* was, I dare say, but *his*— *never*. Good Heavens!" (with a sudden change of tone, and disappearance of mirth) "here he is! Come to look for you, no doubt! I—I—think I may go now, may not I?"

"Go!" repeats he, looking at me with unfeigned wonder. "Why? It is more likely *you* that he has missed, *you*, who are no doubt his daily companion."

"Not quite daily," I answer, with a fine shake of irony, which, by reason of his small acquaintance with me, is lost on my friend. "Two, you know, is company, and three none. Yes, if you do not mind, I think it must be getting near luncheon-time. I will go."

So I disappear through the dry, knotted tussocks of the park grass.

CHAPTER IV

"Friends, Romans, and countrymen!" say I, on that same afternoon, strutting into the school-room, with my left hand thrust oratorically into the breast of my frock, and my right loftily waving, "I wish to collect your suffrages on a certain subject. Tell me," sitting down on a hard chair, and suddenly declining into a familiar and colloquial tone, "have you seen any signs of derangement in father lately?"

"None more than usual," answers Algy, sarcastically, lifting his pretty, disdainful nose out of his novel. "If, as the Eton Latin Grammar says, *ira* is a *brevis furor* you, will agree with me that he is pretty often out of his mind, in fact, a good deal oftener than he is in it."

"No, but *really*?"

"Of course not. What do you mean?"

"Put down all your books!" say I, impressively. "Listen attentively. Bobby, stop see-sawing that chair, it makes me feel deadly sick. Ah! my young friend, *you* will rue the day when you kept me sitting on the top of that wall—"

I break off.

"Go on! go on!" in five different voices of impatience.

"Well, then, father has sent a message by mother to the effect that *I* am to dine with them to-night—*I*, if you please—*I!*—you must own" (lengthening my neck as I speak, and throwing up my untidy flax head) "that sweet Nancies are looking up in the world."

A silence of stupefaction falls on the assembly. After a pause—

"YOU?"

"Yes, *I!*"

"And how do you account for it?"

"I believe," reply I, simpering, "that our future benefac—, no! I really must give up calling him that, or I shall come out with it to his face, as

Bobby did last night. Well, then, Sir Roger asked me why I did not appear yesterday. I suppose he thought that I looked so *very* grown up, that they must be keeping me in pinafores by force."

Algy has risen. He is coming toward me. He has pulled me off my chair. He has taken me by the shoulders, and is turning me round to face the others.

"Allow me!" he says, bowing, and making me bow, too, "to introduce you to the future legatee!—Barbara, my child, you and I are *nowhere*. This depraved old man has clearly no feeling for symmetry of form or face; a long career of Begums has utterly vitiated his taste. To-morrow he will probably be clamoring for Tou Tou's company."

"Brat!" says Barbara, laughing, "where has the analogy between me and the man who pulled up the window in the train for the old woman gone to?"

"Mother said I was to look as nice as I could," say I, casting a rueful glance at the tea-board, at the large plum loaf, at the preparations for temperate conviviality. I have sat down on the threadbare blue-and-red hearth-rug, and am shading my face with a pair of cold pink hands, from the clear, quick blaze. "What *am* I to wear?" I say, gloomily. "None of my frocks are ironed, and there is no time now. I shall look as if I came out of the dirty clothes-basket! Barbara, dear, will you lend me your blue sash? Last time I wore mine the Brat upset the gum-bottle over my ends."

"Let us each have the melancholy pleasure of contributing something toward the decking of our victim," says Algy, with a grin; "have my mess-jacket!"

"Have as many beads as you can about you," puts in Bobby. "Begums always have plenty of beads."

A little pause, while the shifting flame-light makes small pictures of us on the deep-bodied teapot's sides, and throws shadowy profiles of us on the wall.

"Mother said, too, that I was to try and not say any of my unlucky things!" I remark, presently.

"Do not tell him," says Bobby, ill-naturedly, "as you told poor Captain Saunders the other day, that 'they always put the fool of the family into the army.'"

"I did not say so of myself," cry I, angrily. "I only told it him as a quotation."

"Abstain from quotations, then," retorts Bobby, dryly; "for you know in conversation one does not see the inverted commas."

"What *shall* I talk about?" say I, dropping my shielding hand into my lap, and letting the full fire-warmth blaze on eyes, nose, and cheeks. "Barbara, what *did* you talk about?"

"Whatever I talked about," replies Barbara, gayly, "they clearly were not successful topics, so I will not reveal what they were."

Barbara is standing by the tea-table, thin and willowy, a tea-caddy in one hand, and a spoon in the other, ladling tea into the deep-bodied pot—a spoonful for each person and one for the pot.

"I will draw you up a list of subjects to be avoided," says Algy, drawing his chair to the table, and pulling a pencil out of his waistcoat-pocket. "Here, Tou Tou, tear a leaf out of your copy-book—imprimis, *old age*."

"You are wrong there," cry I, triumphantly, "*quite* wrong; he is rather fond of talking of his age, harps upon it a good deal. He said to-day that he was an *old wreck!*"

"Of course he meant you to contradict him!" says Bobby, cackling, "and, from the little I know of you, I am morally certain that you did not—*did* you, now?"

"Well, no!" reply I, rather crestfallen; "I certainly did not. I would, though, in a minute, if I had thought that he wanted it."

"I wish," says Barbara, shutting the caddy with a snap, "that Providence had willed to send the dear old fellow into the world twenty years later than it did. In that case I should not at all have minded trying to be a comfort to him."

"He must have been very good-looking, must not he?" say I, pensively, staring at the red fire-caverns. "Very—before his hair turned gray. I wonder what color it was?"

Visions of gold yellow, of sunshiny brown, of warm chestnut locks, travel in succession before my mind's eye, and try in turn to adjust themselves to the good and goodly weather-worn face, and wide blue eyes of my new old friend.

"It is so nice and curly even now," I go on, "twice as curly as Algy's."

"Tongs," replies Algy, with short contempt, looking up from his list of prohibitions.

"*Very* good-looking!" repeat I, dogmatically, entirely ignoring the last suggestion.

"Perhaps when this planet was young!" retorts he, with the superb impertinence of twenty.

"You talk as if he were eighty years old," cry I, with an unaccountably *personal* feeling of annoyance. "He is *only* forty-seven!"

"*Only* forty-seven!"

And they all laugh.

"Well, I must be going, I suppose," cry I, leisurely rising, stretching, sighing, and beginning to collect the various articles of my wardrobe, scattered over the furniture. "Good-by, dear teapot! good-by, dear plum loaf! *how* I wish I was going to stay with you! It really is ten minutes past dressing-time, and father is always so pleased when one keeps him waiting for his soup."

"He would not say any thing to you to-day if you *were* late," says Bobby, astutely. "You might tumble over his gouty foot, and he would smile! Are we not the most united family in Christendom—*when we have company?*"

After all, I need not have disquieted myself; I am in very good time. When I open the drawing-room door, and make my entrance in the borrowed splendor of Barbara's broad blue-sash tails, and the white virginity of my own muslin frock, I find that neither of my parents have as yet made their appearance. Sir Roger has the hearth-rug to himself; at least he only shares it with Vick, and she is asleep; sitting very upright, it is true, with her thin tail round her toes, like a cat's, her head and whole body swaying from side to side in indisputable slumber. At sight of the chaste and modest apparition that the opened door yields to his gaze, an exclamation of pleasure escapes him—at least it sounds like pleasure.

"Ah! this is all right! You are here to-night at all events; but, by-the-by, what became of you yesterday?"

"What always becomes of me?" reply I, bluntly, lifting my grave gray eyes to his face, and to the hair which sweeps thick and waved above his broad brown forehead. (Tongs indeed!)

"I remember that you told me you had been *cooking*, but you cannot cook *every* night."

"Not quite," reply I, with a short smile, stretching my hands to the blaze.

"But do not you dine generally?"

"Never when I can possibly help it," I reply, with emphasis. And no sooner are the words out of my mouth than I see that I have already transgressed my mother's commands, and given vent to one of "my unlucky things." I stand silent and ashamed, reflecting that no after-tinkering will mend my unfortunate speech.

"And to-night you could not help it?" he asks, after a slight, hardly perceptible pause.

I look up to answer him. He is forty-seven years old. He is a general, and a sir, and has been in every known land; has killed big and little beasts, and known big and little people, and I am nineteen and nobody, and have rarely been beyond our own park and parish, and my acquaintance is confined to half a dozen turnipy squires and their wives; and yet he is looking snubbed, and it is I that have snubbed him. Well, I cannot help it. Truth is truth; and so I answer, in a low voice:

"No, father said I was to."

"And you look upon it as a great penance?" he says, still with that half-disappointed accent.

"To be sure I do," reply I, briskly. "So does Barbara. Ask her if she does not. So would you, if you were I."

"And why?"

"Hush!" say I, hearing a certain heavy, well-known, slow footfall. "He is coming! I will tell you by-and-by—when we are by ourselves."

After all, how convenient an elderly man is! I could not have said that to any of the young squires!

His blue eyes are smiling in the fire-light, as, leaning one strong shoulder against the mantel-piece, he turns to face me more fully.

"And when are we likely to be by ourselves?"

"Oh, I do not know," reply I, indifferently. "Any time."

And then father enters, and I am dumb. Presently, dinner is announced, and we walk in; I on father's arm. He addresses me several times with great *bonhomie* and I respond with nervous monosyllables. Father is always suavity itself to us, when we have guests; but, when one is not in the habit of being treated with affability, it is difficult to enter into the spirit of the joke. Several times I catch our guest's frank eyes, watching me with inquiring wonder, as I respond with brief and low-voiced hurry to some of my parent's friendly and fatherly queries as to the disposition of my day. And I sit tongue-tied and hungry—for, thank God, I have always had a large appetite—dumb as the butler and footman—dumb as the racing-cups on the sideboard—dumber than Vick, who, being a privileged person, is standing—very tall—on her hind-legs, and pawing Sir Roger's coat-sleeve, with a small, impatient whine.

"Why, Nancy, child!" says father, helping himself to sweetbread, and smiling, "what made you in such a hurry to get away this morning out of the park?"

(Why can't he always speak in that voice? always smile?—even his nose looks a different shape.)

"Near—luncheon-time," reply I, indistinctly, with my head bent so low that my nose nearly touches the little square of bare neck that my muslin frock leaves exposed.

"Not a bit of it—half an hour off.—Why, Roger, I am afraid you had not been making yourself agreeable! eh, Nancy?"

"No," say I, mumbling, "that is—yes—quite so."

"I was *very* agreeable, as it happened—rather more brilliant than usual, if possible, was not I? And, to clear my character, and prove that you thought so, you will take me out for another walk, some day, will not you?"

At the sound of his voice so evidently addressing me, I look up—look at him.

"Yes! with pleasure! when you like!" I answer heartily, and I neither mumble nor stutter, nor do I feel any disposition to drop my eyes. I *like* to look at him. For the rest of dinner I am absolutely mute, I make only one other remark, and that is a request to one of the footmen to give me some water. The evening passes. It is but a short one—at least, as regards the company of the gentlemen, for they sit late; father's port, I am told, not being to be lightly left for any female frippery. I retire to the school-room, and regale my brethren with lively representations of father's unexampled benignity. I also resume with Algy the argument about *tongs*, at the very point where I had dropped it. It lasts till prayer-time; and its monotony is relieved by personalities. The devil in the boys is fairly quiescent to-night, and our evening devotions pass over with tolerable peace; the only *contretemps* being that the Brat, having fallen asleep, remains on his knees when "Amen" raises the rest of the company from theirs, and has to be privily and heavily kicked to save him from discovery and ruin. Having administered the regulation embrace to father, and heartily kissed mother—not but what I shall see her again; she always comes, as she came when we were little, to kiss us in bed—I turn to find Sir Roger holding open the swing-door for us.

"Are you quite sure about it to-night?" I say, stretching out my hand to him to bid him good-night. "*Ours* on the right—*yours* on the left—do you see?"

"*Yours* on the right—*mine* on the left," he repeats, "Yes—I see—I shall make no more mistakes—unless I make one on purpose."

"Do not come without telling us beforehand!" I cry, earnestly. "I mean *really*: if you hold a vague threat of paying us a visit over our heads, you will keep us in a state of unnatural tidiness for days."

I make a move toward retiring, but he still has hold of my hand.

"And about our walk?"

The others—boys and girls—have passed us: the servants have melted out of sight; so has mother; father is speaking to the butler in the passage—we are alone.

"Yes? what about it?" I ask, my eyes calmly resting on his.

"You will not forget it?"

"Not I!" reply I, lightly. "I want to hear the end of the anecdote about father's nose! I cannot get over the idea of him in a stiff white petticoat: I thought of it at dinner, whenever I looked at him!"

At the mention of father, his face falls a little.

"Nancy," he says, abruptly, taking possession of my other hand also, "why did you answer your father so shortly to-day? Why did you look so scared when he tried to joke with you?"

"Ah, why?" reply I, laughing awkwardly.

"You are not *afraid* of him, surely?"

"Oh, no—not at all!"

"Why do you speak in that sneering voice? It is not your own voice; I have known you only twenty-four hours, and yet I can tell that."

"I will not answer any more questions," reply I, recovering both hands with a sudden snatch: "and if you ask me any more, I will not take you out walking! there!"

So I make off, laughing.

CHAPTER V

"A peck of March dust is worth a king's ransom," say I slowly next morning, as I stand by the window, trying to see clearly through the dimmed and tearful pane. "The king would have to do without his ransom to-day."

It is raining *mightily*; strong, straight, earnest rain, that harshly lashes the meek earth, that sends angry runlets down the gravel walks, that muddies the gold goblets of the closed crocuses.

"And you without your walk!" says Barbara, lifting her face from her stitching. "Poor Miss Nancy!"

"There is not enough blue sky to make a cat a pair of breeches!" cries Bobby, despondently, and with his usual vulgarity.

Sometimes I am tempted to fear that Bobby is hopelessly ungenteel — ungenteel for life. He has now taken possession of another window, and is consulting the eastern sky.

"A ransomless king, and a trouserless cat! That is about the state of the case!" say I, turning away from the window with a grin.

After all, now I come to think of it, I am nearly as vulgar as Bobby. But I am right. Through the day, through the long, light, cold evening, the posture of the weather changes not. To-day, Barbara, Algy, and I, are all constrained to dine; for have not we a dinner-party, or rather a mild simulation of one? — a squire or two, a squiress or two, a curate or two — such odd-come-shorts as can be got together in a scattered country neighborhood at briefest notice. Barbara and I, as it happens, are both late. It is five minutes past eight, when with the minor details of our toilets a good deal slurred, with a paucity of bracelets and lack of necessary pins, we hurriedly and sneakingly enter the drawing-room, and find all our guests already come together. Mother gives us an almost imperceptible glance of gentle reproach, but father is so occupied in bantering a strange miss — banter in which the gallant and the fatherly happily join to make that manner which is the envy and admiration of the neighborhood — that he seems unconscious of our entrance. An intuition, however, tells us that this is not the case, but that he is making a note of it. This depresses us so much that, until song and sherry have comforted and emboldened us, we have not spirits to make any effort toward the entertainment of our neighbors. We have been paired with a couple of curates. Mine is a strong-handed, ingenuous Ishmael, who tells everybody that he hates his trade, and that he thinks it is very hard that he may not get out of it, now that his elder brother is dead. I am thankful to say that his appetite is as vast as his shoulders; so, after I have told him that I *love* raw oysters, and that Barbara cannot sit in the room with a roast hare; and have heard in return that he does not care about brill, but worships John Dory, we slide into a gluttonous silence, and abide in it. Barbara's man of God is in a wholly different pattern to mine. He is a macerated little saint, with the eyes of a ferret and the heart of a mouse. As the courses pass by, in savory order, I, myself unemployed, watch my sister gradually reassuring, comforting, heartening him, as is her way with all weakly, maimed, and unhandsome creatures. She has succeeded in thawing him into a thin trickle of parochial talk, when mother bends her laced and feathered head in distant signal from the table-top, and off we go. We drink coffee, we drink tea, we pick clever little holes in our absent neighbors, in brisk duet and tortuous solo we hammer the blameless spinnet, we sing affecting songs about "fair doves," and "cleansing fires," and people "far away," and still our deliverers come not. They *must* hear our appealing melodies clearly through the walls and doors, but still they come not. Sunk in sloth and old port, still they come not. I seem to have said every possible thing that is to be said on every known subject to the young woman beside me, and now I am falling asleep. I feel it. Lulled by the warm glow diffused through the room, by the smell of the jonquils, lilies of the valley and daphnes, by the low even talk, I am slipping into slumber. The door opens, and I jump into wakefulness; Sir Roger to the rescue. I am afraid that I look at him with something not unlike invitation in my eyes, for he makes straight toward me.

"Wish me good-morning," say I, rubbing my eyes, "for I have been sweetly asleep. I fell asleep wondering which of you would come first—somehow I thought it would be you. Are you going to sit here? Oh! that is all right!" as he subsides into the next division of the ottoman to mine. "What have you been talking about?" I continue, with a contented, chatty feeling, leaning my elbow on the blue-satin ottoman-top; "any thing pleasant? Did not you hear our screams for help through the wall?"

"Have not we come in answer to them?"

Yes; they are all here now, at last; all, from father down to the curates; some sitting resolutely down, some standing uncertainly up. Barbara's *protégé*, with frightened stealth, is edging round the furniture to where she sits on a little chair alone. Barbara is locketless, braceletless, chainless, head-dressless! such was our unparalleled haste to abscond. Ornaments has she none but those that God has given her: a sweep of blond hair, a long, cool throat, and two smooth arms that lie bare and white as any milk on her lap. As he nervously draws near, she lifts her eyes with a lovely friendliness to his face. He is poor, slightly thought of, sickly, not over-clever; probably she will talk to him all the evening.

"Look at Barbara!" say I, with deep admiration, familiarly laying my hand on Sir Roger's coat-sleeve, to make sure of engaging his attention, "that is always her way! Did you ever see any thing so cruelly shy as that poor little man is? See! he is wriggling all over like an eel! He came to call the other day, and while he was talking to mother I watched him. He tore a pair of quite new tea-green gloves into thin strips, like little thongs! He must find it rather expensive work, if he makes many morning calls, must he not?"

"Rather!"

"I am sure that you and Barbara would get on," continue I, loquaciously, leaning my head on my hand, and talking in that low, comfortable voice that our proximity warrants; "I cannot understand how it was that you did not make great friends that first night! I suppose that you are not poor and ugly and depressed enough for her to make much of you! Shall I make a sign to her to come over and talk to us?"

Sir Roger does not accept my proposal with the alacrity I had expected.

"Do not you think that she looks very comfortable where she is?" he asks, rather doubtfully.

I am a little disappointed.

"I am sure she would like you," I say, with a dogmatic shake of the head. "I told her that you were—well, that *I* got on with you, and we always like the same people."

"That must be awkward sometimes?"

"What do you mean? Oh! not in *that* way—" (with an unblushing heart-whole laugh). "Lucky for me that we do not."

"Lucky for *you*?" (interrogatively).

"Why *will* you make me say things that sound mock-modest?" cry I, reddening a little this time. "You know perfectly well what I mean—it is not likely that any one would *look* at me when Barbara was by—you can have no notion," continue I, speaking very fast to avoid contradiction, "how well she looks when she is dancing—never gets hot, or flushed, or *mottled*, as so many people do."

"And *you*? how do *you* look?"

"I grow purple," I answer, laughing—"a rich imperial purple, all over. If you had once seen me, you would never forget me."

"Go on: tell me something more about Barbara!"

He has settled himself with an air of extreme repose and enjoyment. We really *are* very comfortable.

"Well," say I, nothing loath, for I have always dearly loved the sound of my own voice, "do you see that man on the hearth-rug?—do not look at him this very minute, or he will know that we are speaking of him. I cannot imagine why father has asked him here to-night—he wants to marry Barbara; he has never said it, but I know he does: the boys—we all, indeed—call him *Toothless Jack!* he is not old *really*, I suppose—not more than fifty, that is; but for Barbara!—"

I think that Sir Roger is beginning to find me rather tiresome: evidently he is not listening: he has even turned away his head.

There is a movement among the guests, the first detachment are bidding good-night, the rest speedily do the like. Father follows his favorite miss into the hall, cloaks her with gallant care, and through the door I hear him playfully firing off parting jests at her as she drives away. Then he returns to the drawing-room. Sir Roger has gone to put on his smoking-coat, I suppose. Father is alone with his wife and his two lovely daughters. We make a faint movement toward effacing ourselves, but our steps are speedily checked.

"Barbara! Nancy!"

"Yes, father" (in a couple of very small voices).

"May I ask what induced you to keep my guests waiting half an hour for their dinner to-night?"

No manner of answer. *How* hooked his nose looks! how fearfully like a hawk he has grown all in a minute!

"When you have houses of your own," he continues with iced politeness, "you may of course treat your visitors to what vagaries you please, but as long as you deign to honor *my* roof with your presence, you will be good enough to behave to my guests with decent civility, do you hear?"

"Well, Roger, how is the glass? up or down? What is it doing? Are we to have a fine day to-morrow?"

For Roger apparently has got quickly into his smoking-coat: at least he is here: he has heard all. Barbara and I *crawl* away with no more spring or backbone in us than a couple of torpid, wintery flies.

Five minutes later, "Do you wonder that we hate him?" cry I, with flaming cheeks, holding a japanned candlestick in one hand, and Sir Roger's right hand in the other.

"I do not care if he *does* hear me!—yes, I do, though" (giving a great jump as a door bangs close to me).

Sir Roger is looking down at me with an expression of most thorough discomfiture and silent pain in his face.

"He did not mean it, Nancy!" he says, hesitatingly, and with a sort of look of shamed wonder in his friendly eyes.

"*Did* not he?" (ironically).

A little pause, the position of the japanned candlestick and of Sir Roger's hand still remaining the same. "*How* I wish that *you* were my father instead!" I say with a sort of sob. He does not, as I fully expect, say, "So do I!" and I go to bed, feeling rather small, as one who has *gushed*, and whose gush has not been welcome to the recipient.

CHAPTER VI

A fortnight has passed. Two Sundays, two Mondays, two Tuesdays, etc. Fourteen times have I sleepily laid head on pillow. Fourteen times have I yawningly raised it from my pillow. Fourteen times have I hungrily eaten my dinner, since the night when I stood in the hall with Sir Roger's hand in mine, raging against my parent. And Sir Roger is here still. After all, there is nothing like the tenacity of boyish friendship, is there?

I suppose that, to Sir Roger, father is still the manly, debonair youth that he remembers thirty years ago. In happy ignorance he slurs over the thirty intervening years of moroseness, and goes back to that blest epoch in which I have so much difficulty in believing, and about which he, walking beside me now and again through the tender, springing grass of the meadows, has told me many a tale. For our promised walk has come off, and so has many others like it.

He *must* be dotingly fond of father. It is the 15th of April. I dare say, O reader, that it seems to you much like any other date, but to me, through every back-coming year, it seems to gain fresh significance—the date that marks the most important day—take it for all in all—of my life, though, whether for good or ill, who shall say, until I am dead, and my life's sum reckoned up. I awake on that morning with no forecast of what is coming? I tear myself from my morning dreams with as sleepy unwillingness as usual. I eat my bread-and-butter with as stolidly healthy an appetite. I run with as scampering feet, as evenly-beating a heart as is my wont, with little Vick along the garden-walks, in the royal morning sun. For one of God's own days has come—one that must have lost his way, and strayed from paradise.

It has the steady heat of June, though we are only in mid-April, and the freshness of the prune. The leaves on the trees are but tender and tiny, and through them the sun sends his might. The tulips are all a-blaze and a-stare, making one blink with the dazzle of their odorless beauty: the frolicsome young wind is shaking out their balm from the hyacinth-bells, and the sweet Nancies—my flowers—blowing all together, are swaying and *congéeing* to the morning airs.

O wise men, who know all things, do you know this? Can you tell it me? Where does the flower hide her scent? From what full cup of hidden sweets does one suck it?

It is one of those days when one feels most convinced of being immortal—when the spirits of men stretch out longing arms toward the All-Good, the Altogether Beautiful—when souls thirst for God, yearn most deeply for the well of his unfathomed truth—when, to those who have lost, their dead come back in most pleasant, gentle guise. As for me, I have lost nothing and no one as yet. All my treasures are still about me; I can stretch out live hands, and touch *them* alive; none of my dear names are yet to be spoken sparingly with bated breath, as too holy for common talk. And yet I, too, as I walk and bask, and bend to smell the hyacinth-blooms, feel that same vague and most unnamed yearning—a delicate pain that he who has it would barter for no boisterous joy. The clocks tick out the scented hours, and with loud singing of happy birds, with pomp of flowers and bees, and freaked butterflies, God's day treads royally past.

It is afternoon, and the morning wind, heaving with too much fragrance, has lain down to sleep. A great warm stillness is on the garden and house. The sweet Nancies no longer bow. They stand straight up, all a-row, making the whole place honeyed. The school-room is one great nosegay. Every vase and jug, and cup, and pot and pan and pipkin that we can command, is crammed with heavy-headed daffodils, with pale-cheeked primroses, with wine-colored gilly-flowers, every thing that spring has thrust most plentifully into our eager hands.

The boys have been out fishing.

Algy and Bobby have been humorously trying to drown the Brat.

He looks small and cold in consequence, and his little pert nose is tinged with a chilly pink. Half an hour ago, mother called me away to a private conference, exciting thereby a mighty curiosity not unmixed with envy in my brethren.

Our colloquy is ended now, and I am reëntering the school-room.

"Well, what was it? out with it," cries Algy, almost before I am inside the door again. Algy is sitting more than half—more than three-quarters out of the window, balancing himself with great nicety on the sill. He is in the elegant *négligé* of a decrepit shooting-jacket, no waistcoat, and no collar.

"What have you been doing to your face?" says Bobby, drawing nigh, and peering with artless interest into the details of my appearance; "it is the color of this" (pointing to a branch of red rhibes, which is hanging its drooped flowers, and joining its potent spice to the other flower-scents).

"Is it?" I answer, putting both hands to my cheeks, to feel their temperature. "I dare say! so would yours be, perhaps, if you had, like me, been having a—" I stop suddenly.

"Having a *what*?"

"I will not say what I was going to say," I cry, emphatically, "it was nonsensical!"

"But what *has* she told you, Nancy?" asks Barbara, who, enervated by the first hot day, is languishing in the rocking-chair, slowly see-sawing. "What could it have been that she might not as well have said before us all?"

"You had better try and guess," I reply, darkly.

"I will not, for one," says Bobby, doggedly, "I never made out a conundrum in my life, except, 'What is most like a hen stealing?'"

"It is not much like that," say I, demurely, "and, in fact, when one comes to think of it, it can hardly be called a conundrum at all!"

"I do not believe it is any thing worth hearing," remarks the Brat, skeptically, "or you would have come out with it long ago! you never could have kept in to yourself!"

"Not worth hearing!" cry I, triumphantly raising my voice, "is not it? That is all *you* know about it!"

"Do not wrangle, children," says Algy from the window; "but, Nancy, if you have not told us before the clock gets to the quarter" (looking impressively at the slowly-traveling hands), "I shall think it right to—"

What awful threats would have followed will never now be certainly known, for I interrupt.

"I *will* tell you! I *mean* to tell you!" I cry, excitedly, covering my face with my hands, and turning my back to them all; "only do not *look* at me! look the other way, or I *cannot* tell you."

A little pause.

"You have only three minutes, Nancy."

"Will you *promise*," cry I, with indistinct emphasis from under my hands, "none of you to *laugh*—none, even Bobby!"

"Yes!"—"Yes!"—"Yes!"

"Will you *swear*?"

"What is the use of swearing?—you have only half a minute now. Well, I dare say it is nothing very funny. Yes, we will swear!"

"Well, then, Sir Roger—I *hear* Bobby laughing!"

"He is not!"—"He is not!"—"I am not!—I am only beginning to sneeze!"

"Well, then, Sir Roger—"

I come to a dead stop.

"Sir Roger? What about him? There is not a smile on one of our faces: if you do not believe, look for yourself!—What about our future benefactor?"

"He *is* not our future benefactor," cry I, energetically, whisking swiftly round to face them again, and dropping my hands, "he *never* will be!—he does not *want* to be! He wants to—to—to marry me! there!"

The murder is out. The match is set to the gunpowder train. Now for the explosion!

The clock-hand reaches the quarter—passes it; but in all the assembly there is no sound. The westering sun shines in on four open mouths (the youthful Tou Tou is absent), on four pairs of stupidly-staring eyes. The rocking-chair has ceased rocking. Bobby's sneeze has stopped half-way. There is a petrified silence.

At length, *"Marry you!"* says the Brat, in a deeply-accented tone of low and awed disbelief. "Why, he was at school with father!"

"I wish to heavens that he had never been at school anywhere!" cry I, in a fury. "I am sick to death of hearing that he was at school with father. Will no one ever forget it?"

"He is for-ty-sev-en!" says Algy, at last closing his mouth, and speaking with slow impressiveness. "Nineteen from forty-seven! how many years older than you?"

"Do not count!" cry I, pettishly; "what is the use? not all the counting in the world will make him any younger."

"It is not true!" cries Bobby, with boisterous skepticism, jumping up from his seat, and making a plunge at me; "it is a *hoax!* she has been taking us all in! Really, Nancy, for a beginner, you did not do it badly!"

"It is *not* a hoax!" cry I, scornfully, standing scarlet and deeply ashamed, facing them all; "it is real, plain, downright, simple truth."

Another pause. No sound but the monotonous, unemotional clock, and the woodpecker's fluty laugh from the orchard.

"And so you *really* have a lover at last, Nancy?" says Algy, the corners of his mouth beginning to twitch in a way which looks badly for the keeping of his oath.

"Yes!" say I, beginning to laugh violently, but quite uncomfortably; "are you surprised? you know I always told you that if you half shut your eyes, and looked at me from a great way off, I really was not so bad-looking."

"You have distanced the Begums!" cries the young fellow, joining in my mirth, but with a good deal more enjoyment than I can boast.

"So I have!" I answer; and my sense of the ludicrous overcoming all other considerations, I begin to giggle with a good-will.

"Let us look at you, Nancy!" says the Brat, taking hold of me by both arms, and bringing the minute impertinence of his face into close neighborhood to mine. "I begin to think that there must be more in you than we have yet discovered! we never looked upon you as one of our most favorable specimens, did we?"

"Do not you remember old Aunt Williams?" reply I, merrily; "how she used to say 'I was not pretty, my dears, but I was a pleasant little devil!' perhaps I am a pleasant little devil!"

"*Poor—dear—*old fellow!" says Barbara, in an accent of the profoundest, delicatest, womanliest pity, "*how* sorry I am for him! Nancy, how will you break it to him most kindly? I am afraid he will be sadly hurt! will you speak to him, or do it by letter?"

Barbara has risen. We are all standing up, more or less; it is impossible to sit through such news; Barbara's garden-hat is in her hand. The warm and mellow sun that is making Africa's dreary expanse in the map on the wall, one broad fine sheet, is enkindling, too, the silk of her hair, the flower-petals of her cheeks, the blue compassion of her eyes. My pretty, tall Barbara! Let them say what they like, I am sure that somewhere—*somewhere*—you are pretty now!

"If you write," says Algy, still laughing, but with more moderation, "I should advise you to depute me to make a fair copy of the letter; else, from the extreme ambiguity of your handwriting, he will most likely mistake your drift, and imagine that you are saying yes."

"How do you know that I am not going to say yes?" I ask, abruptly.

Rivers of additional scarlet are racing to my cheeks, over my forehead—in among the roots of my hair—all around and about my throat, but I stand, looking the assembled multitude full in the face, fairly, well, and boldly.

"Listen!" I continue, holding up my right hand in deprecation, "let me speak!—do not interrupt me!—Bobby, I know that he was at school with father—Algy, I know that he is forty-seven—all of you, I know that his hair is gray, and that there are crows'-feet about his eyes—but still—but still—"

"Do you mean to say that you are *in love* with him?" breaks in Bobby, impressively.

Instances of enamored humanity have been rare in Bobby's experience. With the exception of Toothless Jack, he has never had a near and familiar view of an authentic specimen. I therefore see him now regarding me with a reverent interest, not unmixed with awe.

"I mean nothing so silly!" I answer, with lofty petulance. "I am a great deal too old for any such nonsense!"

"There I go with you," says Algy, not without grandeur. "I believe that it is the greatest humbug out, and that it rarely occurs between the ages of sixteen and sixty."

"Father's and mother's was a love-match," says Bobby, gravely. "Did not Aunt Williams tell us that they used always to sit hand-in-hand before they were married?"

A shout of laughter at our parents' expense greets this piece of information.

"*All* married people grow to hate one another after a bit," say I, comprehensively; "it is only a question of time."

"But if you do not love him *now*, and if you are sure that you will hate him by-and-by," says Barbara, looking rather puzzled, "what makes you think of taking him?"

"It would be such a fine thing for all the family: I could give all the boys such a shove," say I, with homely shrewdness.

"They killed seven hundred head of game on his big day last year; I heard him tell father so," says Bobby, with his mouth watering.

"He has a moor in Scotland," throws in the Brat.

"He must ride a stone heavier than I do," says Algy, thoughtfully, "his horses would certainly carry me: I wonder would he give me a mount now and then?"

"I would have you *all* staying with me *always*," I cry, warming with my theme, and beginning to dance, "all except father: he should come once a year for a week, if he was good, and *not at all*, if he was not."

"What will you call him, Nancy?" asks the Brat, inquisitively. "What shall *we* call him?"

"He will be Tou Tou's *brother*," cries Bobby, with a yell of delight.

"Hush!" says Barbara, apprehensively, "he will hear you."

"No he will not," I answer, composedly. "A person would have to bawl even louder than Bobby does, to make him hear: he has gone away for a week; he said he did not wish me to decide in a hurry: he has given me till this day week; I wish it were this day ten years—"

"This day week, then," says Algy, walking about with his hands in his pockets, and smiling to himself, "we may hope to see him return in triumph in a blue frock-coat, with the ring and the parson: at that age one has no time to lose."

"Haste to the wedding!" cries the Brat at the top of his voice, seizing me by both hands, and forcing me to execute an uncouth war-dance, in unwilling celebration of my approaching nuptials.

"I hope that there will be lots of almonds in the cake!" says Bobby, gluttonously.

CHAPTER VII

The week's reprieve has ended; my Judgment Day has come. Never, never, surely, did seven days race so madly past, tumbling over each other's heels. Even Sunday—Sunday, which mostly contains at least forty-eight hours—has gone like a flash. Morning service, afternoon service, good looks, sermon to the servants, supper, they all run into one another like dissolving views. For the first time in my life, my sleep is broken. I fall asleep in a fever of irresolution. I awake in one. I walk about in one. I feed the jackdaw in one. I box Bobby's ears in one. My appetite (oh, portent!) flags. In intense excitement, who can eat yards of bread-and-butter, pounds of oatmeal-porridge, as has ever been my bucolic habit? Shall I marry Sir Roger, or shall I not? The birds, the crowing cocks, the church-bells, the gong for dinner, the old pony whinnying in the park, they all seem to say this. It seems written on the sailing clouds, on the pages of every book that I open. Armies of *pros* wage battle against legions of *cons*, and every day the issue of the fight seems even more and more doubtful.

The morning of the day has arrived, and I am still undecided. I dress in a perfect storm of doubts and questionings. I put on my gown, without the faintest idea of whether it is inside out, or the reverse. I go slowly down-stairs, every banister marked by a fresh decision. I open the dining-room door. Father's voice is the first thing that I hear; father's voice, raised and rasping. He is standing up, and has a letter in his hand; from the engaging blue of its color, and the harmony of its shape, too evidently a bill.

"I regret to have to hurt your feelings," he is saying, in that awful civil voice, at which we all—small and great—quake, "but the next time that *this* occurs" (pointing to the bill), "I must request you to find accommodation for yourself elsewhere, as really my poor house is not a fit place for a young gentleman with such princely views on the subject of expenditure."

The object of this pleasant harangue is Algy, who, also standing, with his face very white, his lips very much compressed, and his eyes flashing with a furious light, is fronting his parent on the hearth-rug.

Behind the tea-urn, mother is mingling her drink with tears, and making little covert signs to Algy, at all rates to hold his tongue.

My mind is made up, never to be unmade again. I will marry Sir Roger. He shall pay all Algy's debts, and forever dry mother's sad, wet eyes.

The weather of paradise is gone back to paradise. This day is very earthly. There has been a sharp, cold shower, and there is still a strong rain-wind, which has snapped a score of tulip-heads. Poor, brave *Jour ne sols*! Prone they lie on the garden-beds, defiled, dispetalled. Even the survivors are stained and dashed, and the sweet Nancies look pinched and small. If you were to go down on your knees to them, they could not give you any scent. I am walking up and down the room, in a state of the utmost agitation. My heart is beating so as to make me feel quite sick. My fingers are very hot, but hardly so hot as my face.

"For Heaven's sake do not make me laugh! do not!" cry I, nervously, "it would be *too* dreadful if I were to receive his overtures with a broad grin, would not it? There! is it gone? Do I look quite grave?"

I take half a dozen hurried turns along the floor, and try to think of all our most depressing family themes—father; Algy's college-bills; Tou Tou's shrunk face and thin legs; nothing will do. When I stop before the glass and consult it, that hysterical smile is there still.

"Do you remember the day, when we were children, that we all went to the dentist?" says the Brat, chuckling, "and father gave Bobby a New Testament because he had his eye-tooth out? Does to-day at all remind you of it, Nancy?"

"I had far rather have *both* my eye-teeth out, and several of my double ones, too," reply I, sincerely.

A little pause.

"I must not keep him waiting any longer," cry I, desperately. "Tell me!" (appealing piteously to them all), "do I look all right? do I look pretty natural?"

"You do not look *middle-aged* enough," says Bobby, bluntly.

"Put on your bonnet," suggests Algy. "You look twenty years older in that, particularly when you cock it well over your nose, as you did last Sunday."

"You are all very unkind!" say I, in a whimpering voice, walking toward the door.

"And if he becomes too demonstrative," says the Brat, overtaking me with a rush before I reach it, "say—

'Unhand me, graybeard loon!'"

Then I go. As I know perfectly well, that if I give myself time to think, I shall stand with the drawing-room door-handle in my grasp for half an hour, before I can make up my mind to enter, I take the bull by the horns, and whisking in suddenly and noisily, find myself *tête-à-tête* with my lover.

Certainly, I never felt such a fool in my life. How *awful* it will be if I burst out laughing in his face! It is quite as likely as not that I shall do it out of sheer hysterical fright. Oh, how different! how much nicer it was when we last parted! I had taken him to see the jackdaw, and the little bear that Bobby brought from foreign parts; and jacky had bitten his finger so humorously, and we had been so merry, and I had told him again how much I wished that he could change places with father. And now! I *feel*—more than see—that he is drawing nigh me. Through my eyelids—for I am very sure that I never lift my eyes—I get an idea of his appearance.

Under his present aspect I am much more disposed to be critical, and to pick holes in him, than I was under his former one. Any attempt at youthfulness, any effort at *smartness*, will not escape my vigilant reprobation—down-eyed and red-cheeked as I appear to be. But none such do I find. There is no false juvenility—there is no trace of dandyism in the plain and quiet clothes, in the hair sparsely sprinkled with snow, in the mature and goodly face.

An iron-gray, middle-aged gentleman stands before me, more vigorous, more full of healthy life than two-thirds of the puny youth, nourished on sherry and bitters, of the present small generation, but with no wish, no smallest effort to take away one from the burden of years that God has laid on his strong shoulders.

There is no doubt that I shall not speak first, so for a moment there is a profound silence. Then I find my hot hand in Sir Roger's where it has so often and so familiarly lain before, and I hear Sir Roger's voice addressing me.

"I am an old fool, Nancy, and you have come to tell me so?"

Somehow I know that the bronze of his face is a little paled by emotion, but there is no sawny sentiment in his tone, none of the lover's whine. It is the same voice—as manly, as sustained—that made comments on Bobby's little bear. And yet, for the moment, I am physically unable to answer him. Who *can* answer the simplest question ever put with a lump the size of a cocoa-nut in their throat? My eyelids are still hopelessly drooped over my eyes, but, by some sense that is not eyesight, I am aware that there is a sort of shyness in his face, a diffidence in his address.

"Nancy, have I come back too soon? am I hurrying you?"

I raise my eyes for an instant, and then let them fall.

"No, thank you," I say, demurely, "not at all. I have had plenty of time!"

And then, somehow, there seems to me something so ludicrous in the sound of my own speech, that I tremble on the verge of a burst of loud and unwilling laughter.

"Speak out all your thought to me, whatever it is," he says, in a tone of grave entreaty, moved and tender, yet manly withal. "Look at me with the same friendly, fearless eyes that you did last week! I know, my dear, that you always think of others more than yourself, and I dare say that *now* you are afraid of hurting me! Indeed, you need not be! I am tough and well-seasoned; I have known what pain is before now—it would be very odd, at my time of life, if I had not! I can well bear a little more, and be the better for it, perhaps."

I stand stupidly silent. One's outer man or woman often does an injustice to one's inner feelings. As he speaks, my heart goes out to him, but I can find no words in which to dress my thought.

"Nancy!" in a tone of thorough distress. "I can bear any thing but seeing you shrink and shiver away from me, as I have seen you do from your father."

"You *never* will see that," reply I, laconically, gathering bravery enough to look him in the face, as I deliver this encouraging remark.

"Do you think," he says, beginning to walk restlessly about the room—(long ago he dropped my limp hand)—"that all this week I have had much hope? Every time that I have caught a glimpse of myself in the glass, I have said, 'Is this a face likely to take a child's fancy? Do you bear much resemblance to the hero of her storybooks?' My dear"—(stopping before me)—"you cannot think my presumption more absurd than I do myself."

"I do not think it at all absurd," reply I, beginning to speak quite stoutly, and to be rather diffuse than otherwise. "Perhaps I did, just at first, when they were all laughing, and saying about your having been at school with father; but *now* I do not in the least—I do not care what the boys say—I do not, really. I am not joking."

At my words he half stretches out his hand to take mine; but, as if repressing some strong impulse, withdraws it again, and speaks quietly, with a rather sober smile.

"I am afraid that one's soul ages more slowly than one's body, Nancy! Even at my age it has seemed difficult to me to be brought into hourly companionship with all that was most fresh and womanly, and spirited, and pretty."

"Pretty!" think I. "I wish the boys could hear him! they will never believe me if I tell them."

"And not wish to have it for my own, to take and make much of. I that have never had any thing very lovely or lovable in my life. And then, dear, it was all your good-nature, you did not know what you were doing; you seemed to find some little pleasure in my society—even chose it by preference now and then. My talk did not weary you, as I should have thought it would have done, and so I grew to think—to think—Bah!" (with a movement of impatience) "it was a foolish thought! what can there be in common between me and a child like you?"

"I think that there is a great deal," reply I, speaking very steadily, and so saying, I stretch out my hand and of my own accord put it in his again. He cannot well return it to me, so he keeps it.

"And yet it is impossible?" he says, with hesitating interrogation, while his steel-blue eyes look anxiously into mine.

"Is it?" say I, a wily smile beginning to creep over my features. "If it is, what was the use of asking me?" I have the grace to grow extremely red as I make this observation.

"Nancy!" seizing my other hand, too, and speaking in a hurried, low voice that slightly shakes with the force of his emotion, "what are you saying? You do not know what you are implying."

"Yes I do," reply I, firmly. "I know perfectly. And it is *not* impossible. Not at all, I should say."

Upon this explicit declaration an ordinary lover would have had me in his arms and smothered me with kisses before you could look round, but my lover is abnormal. He does nothing of the kind.

"Are you sure," he says, with an earnest gravity and imploring emphasis, "that you understand what you are doing? Are you certain, Nancy, that if we had not been friends, if you had not been loath to pain me, that you would not have answered differently? Think, child! think well of it! this is not a matter of months or even years, but of your whole long young life."

"Yes," say I, gravely, looking down. "I know it is."

And put thus solemnly before me, the idea of the marriage state seems to me, hardly less weightily oppressive than the idea of eternity.

"How should I feel," he continues (he has put a hand on each of my shoulders, and is looking at me with a serious yet tender fixity), "if, by-and-by, in the years ahead of us, you came and told me that by my selfishness, taking advantage of your youth, I had destroyed your life?"

"And do you think," say I, with a flash of indignation, "that even if you had done it, I should come and tell you?"

"Are you *quite* sure that among all the men of your acquaintance, men nearer you in age, more akin in tastes, men *not* gray-haired, *not* weather-beaten, *not* past their best years—there is not one with whom you would more willingly spend your life than with me? If it is so, I *beseech* you to tell me, as you would tell your mother!"

"If there were," reply I, smiling broadly, a smile which greatly widens my mouth, and would show my dimples if I had any, "I should *indeed* be susceptible! The two curates that you saw the other night—the one who tore his gloves into strips, you know, and the other who ate so much—Toothless Jack—these are the sort of men among whom my lines have lain. Do you think I am likely to be very much in love with any of *them*?"

My speech does not seem so altogether reassuring as I had expected.

"I am very suspicious," he says, half apologetically, "but you have seen so little of the world, you have led such a nun's life! how can you answer for it that hereafter out in the world you may not meet some one more to your liking? You are a dear little, kindly, tender-hearted sort, and you do not tell me so, but you do not like me *much*, Nancy! Indeed, dear, I could far better do without you now, than see you by-and-by wishing me away and yet be unable to rid you of me."

"People can help falling in love," say I, with matter-of-fact common-sense. "If I belonged to you, of course I should never think of any one else in that way."

"Are you sure—?"

"I wish that you would not ask me any more questions," say I, interrupting him with a pout. "I am quite sure of every thing you can possibly think of."

"I will only ask *one* more—are you quite sure that it is not for your brothers' and sisters' sakes—not your own—that you are doing this? Do you remember" (with a smile half playful, half sad) "what you told me about your views of marriage on that first day when I found you in the kitchen-garden?"

"I hope to Heaven that you did not think I was *hinting*," say I, growing crimson; "it certainly sounded very like it, but I really and truly was not. I was thinking of a *young* man! I assure you" (speaking with great earnestness) "that I had as much idea of marrying you as of marrying *father*!"

Looking back with mature reflection at this speech, I think that it may be safely reckoned among my unlucky things.

"No," he says, wincing a little, a very little. "I know you had not; but—you have not answered my question."

For a moment I look down irresolute, then, through some fixed belief in him, I look up and tell him the plain, bare truth.

"I *did* think that it would be a nice thing for the boys," I say, "and so it will, there is no doubt; you will be as good as a fa—, as a brother to them; but—I like you *myself* besides, you may believe it or not as you please, but it is quite, *quite*, quite true."

As I speak, the tears steal into my eyes.

"And *I* like *you!*" he answers very simply, and so saying, stoops, and with a sort of diffidence, kisses me.

"Well, how did it go off?" cries Bobby, curiously, when I next rejoin my compeers. "Did you laugh?"

"*Laugh!*" I echo, with lofty anger, "I do not know what you mean! I never felt in the least inclined." Then seeing my brethren look rather aghast at this sudden change in the wind, I add gayly: "Bobby, you must never again breathe a word about Sir Roger's having been at school with father; let it be supposed that he did without education."

CHAPTER VIII

This is my wooing: thus I am disposed of. Without a shadow of previous flirtation with any man born of woman—without any of the ups and downs, the ins and outs of an ordinary love-affair, I place my fate in Sir Roger's hands. Henceforth I must have done with all girlish speculations, as to the manner of man who is to drop from the clouds to be my wooer. Well, I have not many day-dreams to relinquish. When I have built Spanish castles—in a large family, one has not time for many—a lover for myself has been less the theme of my aspirations than a benefactor for the family. One, who will exercise a wholesomely repressive influence over father, has been more than any thing the theme of my longings; on the unlikely hypothesis of my marrying at all. For, O friends, it has seemed to me *most* unlikely; I dare say that I might not have been over-difficult—might have thankfully and heartily loved some one not quite a Bayard, but one cannot love *any thing*—any odd and end—and, say what you will, the choice of a country girl, with a little dowry and a plain face, is but small. For—do not dislike me for it if you can help—I *am* plain. I know it by the joint and honest testimony of all my brethren. I have had no trouble in gathering the truth from them. A hundred times they have volunteered it, with that healthy disregard of any sickly sensitiveness which arms one against blows to one's vanity through all after-life. Yes: I am plain; not offensively so, not largely, fatly, staringly plain, but in a small, blond, harmless way. However, Sir Roger thinks me pretty. Did not he say so, in unmistakable English? I have tried darkly to hint this to the boys, but have been so decisively pooh-poohed that I resolve not to allude to the subject again. Not only am I plain now, but I shall remain plain to my life's end. Unlike the generality of ugly heroines, you will not see me develop and effloresce into beauty toward the end of my story.

The interval between my betrothal and my marriage is but short. On April 22d, I put my hand into Sir Roger's. On May 20th, I am to put it into his for good. When the bridegroom is forty-seven, and the bride one of six, why should there be any delay? Why should a man keep and lodge his daughter any longer than he can help, when he has found some one else willing to do it for him? This, I think, is father's view. And, meanwhile, father himself is more like an *angel* than a man. Not once do we hear the terrible polite voice that chills the marrow of our bones. Not once is his nose more than becomingly hooked. Not once does he look like a hawk. *Another* long bill comes in for Algy, and is dismissed with the benevolent comment that you cannot put gray heads upon green shoulders. I dine every day now; and father and I converse agreeably upon indifferent topics. Once— oh, prodigious!—we take a walk round the Home Farm together, and he consults me about the Berkshire pigs. Then comes a mad rush for clothes. I am involved in a whirlwind of haberdashery, Brussels lace, diamonds. It feels very odd—the becoming possessed of a great number of stately garments, to which Barbara has no fellows—Barbara and I, who hitherto have been always stitch for stitch alike. And meanwhile I see next to nothing of my future husband. This is chiefly my own doing.

"You will not mind," I say, standing before him one day in the drawing-room window, and speaking rather bashfully—somehow I do not feel so comfortably easy and outspoken with him as I did before the catastrophe— "you will not mind if I do not see much of you—do not go out walking—do not talk to you very much till—till *it* is over!"

"And why am I not to mind?" he asks, half jestingly, and yet a little gravely, too.

"You will have quite enough—*too much* of me afterward," I say, with a shy laugh, "and *they*—they will never have much of me again—never so much, at least—and" (with rather a tremble in my voice) "we have had *such* fun together!"

And so Sir Roger keeps away. Whether his self-denial costs him much, I cannot say. It never occurs to me at the time that it does. He may think me a very nice little girl, and that I shall be a great comfort to him, but he cannot care much about having any very long conversations with me—he that has seen so many lands, and known so many great and clever people, and read so many books. He has always been *most* undemonstrative to me. At *his* age, no doubt, he does not care much for the foolish endearments of lovers; so, with an easy conscience, I devote myself, for my short space, to the boys, to Barbara, to Vick, and the jackdaw. Once, indeed—just once—I have a little talk with him, and afterward I almost wish that I had not had it. We are sitting under a horse-chestnut-tree in the garden—a tree that, under the handling of the warm air, is breaking into a thousand tender faces. We did not begin by being *tête-à-tête*; indeed, several lately-occupied chairs intervene between us, but first one and then another has slipped away, and we are alone.

"Nancy!" says Sir Roger, his eyes following the Brat, who is lightly tripping up the stone steps, looking very small and agile in his white-flannel cricketing things, "what is that boy's real name? Why do you call him 'the Brat'?"

"Because he *is* such a *Brat*," reply I, fondly, picking up from the grass a green chestnut-bud that the squirrels or the rooks have untimely nipped. "Did you ever see any thing so little, so white and pert? He has sadly mistaken his vocation in life: he ought to have been a street Arab."

"One gets rather sick of one's surname," says my companion. "Except your father, hardly any one calls me Roger now! I should be glad to answer to it again."

He turns and looks at me with a kind of appeal as he says this. If he were not forty-seven and a man, I should say that he was coloring a little. After all, blushing is confined to no age. I have seen a veteran of sixty-five redden violently.

"Do you mean to say," cry I, looking rather aghast, and speaking, as usual, without thinking, "that you mean *me* to call you *Roger*! indeed, I could not think of such a thing! it would sound so—so *disrespectful*! I should as soon think of calling my father *James*."

"Should you?" he answers, turning away his face toward the garden-beds, where the blue forget-me-not is unrolling her sky-colored sheet, and the double daisies are stiffly parading their tight pink buttons. "Then call me what you like!"

I am not learned in the variations of his voice, as I am in those of father and Algy, in either of which I can at once detect each fine inflection of anger, contest, or pain; but, comparatively unversed as I am in it, there sounds to me a slight, carefully smothered, yet still perceptible, intonation of disappointment—mortification. I wish that the air would give me back my words; but that it never yet was known to do.

"I will try if you like," say I, cheerfully, but a little shyly, as, like the March Hare and the Hatter in the "Mad Sea Party," I move up past the empty chairs to the one next him. "I do not see, after all, why I should not get quite used to it in time! Roger! Roger! it is a name I have always been very partial to until" (laughing a little) "the Claimant threw discredit on all Rogers!"

He is looking at me again. After all, I must have been mistaken. There is no shadow of disappointment or mortification near him. He is smiling with some friendliness.

"You must never mind what *I* say," I continue, dragging my wicker chair along the shortly-shorn sward a little nearer to him. "*Never!* nobody ever does; I am a proverb and a by-word for my malapropos speeches. Mother always *trembles* when she hears me talking to a stranger. The first day that I dined after you came, Algy made me a list of things that I was not to talk about to you."

"A list of sore subjects?" says my lover, laughing. "But how did the boy know what *were* my sore subjects? What were they, Nancy?"

"Oh, I do not know! I have forgotten," reply I, in some confusion. "I've made some very bad shots."

And so we slip away from the subject; but, all the same, I wish that I had not said it.

We have come to the day before the wedding. My spirits, which held up bravely during the first two weeks of my engagement, have now fallen— fallen, like a wind at sundown. I am as limp, lachrymose, and lamentable, a young woman as you would find between the three seas. I have cried with loud publicity in full school-room conclave; I have cried with silent privacy in bed. I have cried over the jackdaw. I have cried over the bear. I have not cried over Vick, as I am to take her with me. To-day we have *all* cried— boys and all; and have moistened the bun-loaf and the gooseberry-jam at tea with our tears. Our spirits being now temporarily revived, I am undergoing the operation of trying my wedding-dress. I am having a private rehearsal, in fact, in mother's boudoir, with only mother, Barbara, and the maid, for audience.

"Mine is the most hopeless kind of ugliness," say I, with an admirable dispassionateness, as if I were talking of some one else, as, armed in full panoply, I stand staring at my white reflection in a long mirror let into the wall—staring at myself from top to toe—from the highest jasmine star of my wreath to the lowest edge of my Brussels flounce. "If I were very fat, I might fine down; if I were very thin, I might plump up; if I were very red, I might grow pale; if I were—hush! here are the boys. I would not for worlds that they should see me!"

So saying, I run behind the folding-screen—the screen which, through so many winter evenings, we have adorned with gay and ingenious pictures, and which, after having worked openly at it under her nose for a year and a half, we presented to mother *as a surprise*, on her last birthday.

"Come out, ostrich!" cries Algy, laughing. "Do you suppose that you are hidden? Did it never occur to you that we could see your reflection in the glass?"

Thus adjured, I reissue forth.

"Did you ever see such a fool as I look?" say I, feeling very sneaky, and going through a few uncouth antics to disguise my confusion.

"Talk of *me* being a Brat," cries the Brat, triumphantly. "I am not half such a brat as you are! You look about ten years old!"

"Mark my words!" cries Bobby. "Wherever you go, on the Continent, you will be taken for a good little girl making a tour with her grandpapa!"

Bobby is speaking at the top of his voice; as, indeed, we have all of us rather a bad habit of doing. Bobby has the most excuse for it, as, being a sailor, I suppose that he has to bellow a good deal at the blue-jackets. In the present case, he has *one* more listener than he thinks. Sir Roger is among us. The door has been left ajar, and he, hearing the merry clamor, and having always the *entrée* to mother's room, has entered. By the pained smile on his face, I can see that he has heard.

"You are right, my boy," he says, quite gently, looking kindly at the unfortunate Bobby; "she *does* look very—*very* young!"

"I shall mend of that!" cry I, briskly, putting my arm through his, in anxious amends for Bobby's hapless speech. "We are a family who age particularly early. I have a cousin whose hair was gray at five-and-twenty, and I am sure that any one who did not know father, would say that he was sixty, if he was a day—would not they, mother?"

CHAPTER IX

The preparations are ended; the guests are come; no great number. A few unavoidable Tempests, a few necessary Greys (I have told you, have not I, that my name is Grey?). The heels have been amputated from a large number of white satin slippers, preparatory to their being thrown after us. The school-children have had their last practice at the marriage-hymn.

I have resolved to rise at five o'clock on my wedding-morning, so as to make a last gloomy progress round every bird and beast and gooseberry-bush on the premises. I have exacted—binding her by many stringent oaths—a solemn promise from Barbara to make me, if I do not do so of my own accord, at the appointed hour. I am sunk in heavy sleep, and wake only very gradually, to find her, in conformity with her engagements, giving my shoulder reluctant and gentle pushes, and softly calling me.

"Is it five?" say I, sitting up and yawning. Then as the recollection of my position flashes across my mind, "I will *not* be married!" I cry, turning round, and burying all my face in my pillow again. "Nobody shall induce me! Let some one go and tell Sir Roger so."

"Sir Roger is not awake," replied Barbara, laughing rather sleepily, "you forget that."

And by the time he is awake, I have come to a saner mind. We dress, for the last time, *alike*. The thought that never again shall I have a holland frock like Barbara's is nearly too much for us both. We run quietly down-stairs, and out into as August a morning as God ever gave his poor pensioners.

We walk along soberly and silently, hand-in-hand, as we used to do when we were little children. My heart is very, *very* full. I may be going to be happy in my new life. I fully expect to be. At nineteen, happiness seems one's right, one's matter of course; but it will not be in the same way. *This* chapter of my life is ended, and it has been *such* a good chapter, so full of love, of healthy, strong affection, of interchanged, kind offices, and little glad self-denials, so abounding in good jokes and riotous laughter, in little pleasures that—looked back on—seem great; in little wholesome pains that—in retrospect—seem joys. And, as we walk, the birds

"Prefer soft anthems to the ears of men
To woo them from their beds, still murmuring
That men can sleep while they their matins sing.
Most divine service, whose so early lay
Prevents the eyelids of the blushing day."

The old singers have said many a fine and lovely thing about lusty spring. From their pages there seems to come a whiff of clean and healthy perfume from many dead Mays. In sweet and matterful verse they have sung their praises; but, oh! no singer, old or new—none, at least, that was but human—none but a God-intoxicated man could tell the glories of that serenely shining and suave morn.

One so seldom sees the best part of a summer day! Buried in swinish slumber, with window-curtains heedfully drawn, and shutters closely fastened, between us and it, we know nothing of the stately pageant spread outside our doors.

It is wasted; nay, not wasted, for the birds have it. It is so early, that the gardening-men are not yet come to their work. Every thing is as wet as though there had been a shower, but there has been none.

Talk of the earth moving round the sun—he himself the while stupidly stock-still—let *them* believe it who like; is not he now placidly sailing through the turquoise sea? Below, the earth is unfolding all her freshened meadows, bravely pied with rainbow flowers. There is a very small soft wind, that comes in honeyed puffs and little sighs, that wags the lilac-heads, and the long droop of the laburnum-blooms. The grass is so wet—so wet—as we swish through it, every blade a separate green sparkle. The young daisies give our feet little friendly knocks as we pass.

All round the old flowering thorn there is a small carpet, milk-white and rose-red, of strewn petals. Every flower that has a cup, is holding it brimful of cool dew. Vick is sitting on the top of the stone steps, her ears pricked, and her little black nose working mysteriously as she sniffs the morning air.

On the bright gravel walk stands the jackdaw, looking rather a funereal object in his black suit, on this gaudy-colored day; his gray head very much on one side, his round, sly eyes turned upward in dishonest meditation. A worse bird than Jacky does not hop. His life is one long course of larceny, and I know that if he had the gift of speech, he would also be a consummate liar. I kneel on the walk, and, holding out a bit of cake, call him softly and clearly, "Jacky! Jacky!" He snatches it rudely, with a short hoarse caw, puts one black foot on it, and begins to peck.

"Jacky! Jacky!" say I, sorrowfully, "I am going to be married! Oh, you know that? You may thank your stars that you are not."

As I speak, my tears fall on his sleek black wings and his dear gray head. I try to kiss him; but he makes such a spiteful peck at my nose, that I have to give up the idea. Thus one of my good-byes is over. By the time that they are all ended, and we have returned to the house, I am drowned in tears, and my appearance for the day is irretrievably damaged. My nose is certainly *very* red. It surprises even myself, who have known its capabilities of old. Bobby, always prosaic, suggests that I shall hold it in the steam of boiling water, to reduce the inflammation. But I have not the heart to try this remedy. It may be sky blue, for all I care. Nose or no nose, I am dressed now.

Instead of the costly artificial wreath that Madame Elise sent me, Barbara has made a little natural garland of my own flowers—my Nancies. I smell them all the time that I am being married. I have no female friends—Barbara has always been friend enough for me—so I have stipulated that I shall have no other bridesmaids but her and Tou Tou. They are not much to brag of in the way of a match. Algy indeed suggested that in order to bring them into greater harmony, Tou Tou shall clothe her thin legs with long petticoats, or Barbara abridge her garments to Tou Tou's length; but the proposition has met with as little favor in the family's eyes as did Squire Thornhill's proposal, that every gentleman should sit on a lady's lap, in the Vicar of Wakefield.

The guests are all off to the church. I follow with my parents. Mother is inclined to cry, until snubbed and withered into dry-eyedness by her consort. He is, however, all benignity to me. I catch myself wondering whether I *can* be his own daughter; whether I am not one of the train of neighboring misses who have sometimes made me the depository of their raptures about him.

We reach the church. I am walking up the aisle on red cloth: the wedding-hymn is in my ears, gayly and briskly sung, though it *is* a hymn, and not an *Epithalamium*: a vague idea of many people is in my head. I am standing before the altar—the altar smothered in flowers. The old vicar who christened me is to marry me. I have declined the intervention of all strange bishops and curates whatsoever. He is a clergyman of the old school, and spares us not a word of the ritual.

Truly in no squeamish age was the marriage-service composed! I know—that is, I could have told you if you had asked me—that I am standing beside a large and stately person, to whom, if neither God nor man interpose to prevent it, I shall, within five minutes, be lawfully wed; but I do not in the least degree realize it.

Now and again a strong sense of the ludicrous rushes over me. There seems to me something acutely ridiculous in the idea of myself standing here, so finely dressed—of the boys, demure and prim in their tall hats and Sunday coats, gathered to see *me* married—*me* of all people!

Like lightning-flash there darts into my head the recollection of the *last time that I was married*! when, long ago we were little children, one wet Sunday afternoon, for want of a job, I had espoused Bobby; and Algy, standing on a chair, with his night-gown on for a surplice, had married us. It is over now. I am aware that several persons of different genders have kissed me. I have signed my name. I am walking down the church-yard path, the bells jangling gayly above my head, drowning the sweet thrushes; and the school-children flinging bountiful garden flowers before my feet. It seems to me a sin to tread upon them. It goes to my heart. We reach the house. Vick comes out to meet us in a crawling, groveling manner, which owes its birth to the *shame* caused in her mind by the huge favor which my maid has tied round her little neck. We go into breakfast and feed—the *women* with easy minds; the *men*, with such appetites as the fear of impending speeches, of horrible shattered commonplaces leaves them.

I suppose that, despite my change of name, I cannot yet be wholly a Tempest; for, while I remain perfectly serene and calm during Sir Roger's few plain words, I am one red misery while Algy is returning thanks for the bridesmaids, which he does in so appallingly lame, stammering, and altogether agonizing a manner, that I have serious thoughts of slipping from my bridegroom's side under the friendly shade of the table, among its sheltering legs.

Thank God it is over, and I am gone to put on my traveling-dress! The odious parting moment has come. The carriage is at the door: the maid and valet are in the dickey. What a pity that they are not bride and bridegroom too! Vick has jumped in—alert and self-respecting again now that she has bitten off her favor.

I have begun my voluminous farewells. I have kissed them all round once, and am beginning again. How can one make up one's mind where to stop? with whom to end?

"Never you marry, Barbara!" say I, in a sobbing whisper, as I clasp her in my last embrace, greatly distorting my new bonnot, "it is *so* disagreeable!"

We are off, followed by a tornado of shoes—one, aimed with dexterous violence by that unlucky Bobby, goes nigh to cut the bridegroom's left eye open, as he waves his good-byes.

As we trot smartly away, I turn round in the carriage and look at them through my tears. There they all are! After all, what a nice-looking family! Even Tou Tou! there is something pretty about her, and standing as she is now, her legs look quite nice and thick.

We reach Dover before dinner-time. Sir Roger has gone out to speak to the courier who meets us there. I am left alone in our great stiff sitting-room at the Lord Warden. Instantly I rush to the writing-materials.

"What, writing already?" says my husband, reëntering, and coming over with a smile toward me. "Have you forgotten any of your finery?"

"No, no!" cry I, impulsively, spreading both hands over the sheet; "do not look! you must not look!"

"Do you think I *should*?" he says, reproachfully, turning quickly away.

"But you may," cry I, with one of my sudden useless remorses, holding out the note to him. "Do! I should like you to!—I do not know why I said it!—I was only sending them a line, just to tell them how *dreadfully* I missed them all!"

CHAPTER X

I have been married a week. A *week* indeed! a week in the sense in which the creation of the world occupied a week!—seven geological ages, perhaps, but *not* seven days. We have been to Brussels, to Antwerp, to Cologne. We have seen—(with the penetrating incense odor in our nostrils, and the kneeling peasants at our feet)—the Descent from the Cross, the Elevation of the Cross—dead Christs manifold. Can it be possible that the brush which worthily painted Christ's agony, can be the same that descended to eternize redundant red fishwives, and call them goddesses? We have given ourselves cricks in the necks, staring up at the divine incompleteness of Cologne Cathedral. And all through Crucifixions, cathedrals, table d'hôtes, I have been deadly, *deadly* homesick—homesick as none but one that has been a member of a large family and has been out into the world on his or her own account, for the first time, can understand. When first I drove away through the park, my sensations were something like those that we all used to experience, on the rare occasions when father, as a treat, took one or other of us out on an excursion with him—the *honor* great, but the *pleasure* small.

It seems to myself, as if I had not laughed once since we set off!—yes— *once* I did, at the recollection of an old joke of Bobby's, that we all thought very silly at the time, but that strikes me as irresistibly funny now that it recurs to me in the midst of strange scenes, and of jokeless foreigners.

After forty, people do not laugh at absolutely *nothing*. They may be very easily moved to mirth, as, indeed, to do him justice, Sir Roger is; but they do not laugh for the pure physical pleasure of grinning. The weight of the absolute *tête-à-tête* of a honey-moon, which has proved trying to a more violent love than mine, is oppressing me.

At home, if I grew tired of talking to one, I could talk to another. If I waxed weary of Bobby's sea-tales, I might refresh myself with listening to the Brat's braggings about Oxford—with Tou Tou's murdered French lesson:

J'aime, I love.
Tu aimes, Thou lovest.
Il aime, He loves.

How many thousand years ago, the labored conjugation of that verb seems to me!

Now, if I do not converse with Sir Roger, I must remain silent. And, somehow, I cannot talk to him now as fluently as I used. Before—during our short previous acquaintance—where I used to pester the poor man with filial aspirations that he could not reciprocate, there seemed no end to the things I had to say to him. I felt as if I could have told him any thing. I bubbled over with silly jests.

It never occurred to me to think whether I pleased him or not; but *now—now*, the sense of my mental inferiority—of the gulf of years and inequalities that yawns between us—weighs like a lump of lead upon me.

I am in constant fear of falling below his estimate of me. Before I speak, I think whether what I am going to say will be worth saying, and, as very few of my remarks come up to this standard, I become extremely silent. Oh, if we could meet some one we knew—even if it were some one that we rather disliked than otherwise: some one that would laugh and have as few wits as I, and be *young*.

But it is too early in the year for many people to be yet abroad, and, so far, we have fallen upon no acquaintances. Once, indeed, at Antwerp, I see in the distance a man whose figure bears a striking resemblance to that of "Toothless Jack," and my heart leaps—detestable as I have always thought Barbara's aspirant; but on coming nearer the likeness disappears, and I relapse into depression.

Long ago, I had told my husband—on the first day I had made his acquaintance indeed—that I had no conversation, and now he is proving experimentally the truth of my confession. At home, our talk has always been made up of allusions, half-words, petrified witticisms, that have become part of our language. Each sentence would require a dictionary of explanation to any strange hearer. *Now*, if I wish to be understood, I must say my meaning in plain English, and very laborious I find it.

To-day, we are on our way from Cologne to Dresden; sixteen hours and a half at a stretch. This of itself is enough to throw the equablest mind off its balance.

We have a *coupé* to ourselves. This is quite opposed to my wishes, nor is it Sir Roger's doing, but Schmidt, the courier, knowing what is seemly on those occasions—what he has always done for all former freshly-wed couples whom he has escorted—secured it before we could prevent him. As for me, it would have amused me to see the people come in and out, to air my timid German in little remarks about the weather; albeit I have thus early discovered that the German, which we have been exhorted to talk among ourselves in the school-room, to perfect us in that tongue, bears no very pronounced likeness to the language as talked by the indigenous inhabitants. They *will* talk so fast, and they never say any thing in the least like Ollendorff.

Sixteen hours and a half of a *tête-à-tête* more complete and unbroken than any we have yet enjoyed. All day I watch the endless, treeless, hedgeless German flats fly past; the straight-lopped poplars, the spread of tall green wheat, the blaze of rape-fields — the villages and towns, with two-towered German churches, over and over, and over again. Oh, for a hill, were it no bigger than a molehill! Oh, for a broad-armed English oak!

At Minden we stop to lunch. The whole train pushes and jostles into the refreshment-room, and, in ten galloping minutes, we devour three filthy *plats*; a nauseous potage, a terrible dish of sickly veal, and a ragged Braten. Then a rush and tumble off again.

The day rolls past, dustily, samely, wearily. There have been flying thunder-storms — lightning-flashes past the windows. I hide my face in my dusty gloves to avoid seeing the quick red forks, and leave a smear on each grimy cheek. Every moment, I am a rape-field — a corn-field, a bean-field, farther from Barbara, farther from the Brat, farther from the jackdaw.

"This is rather a long day for you, child!" says Sir Roger, kindly, perceiving, I suppose, the joviality of the expression with which I am eying the German landscape. "The most tedious railway-journey you ever took, I suppose?"

"Yes," reply I, "far! It seems like three Sundays rolled into one, does not it? What time is it now?"

He takes out his watch and looks.

"Twenty past five."

"*Seven* hours more!" say I, with a burst of desperateness.

"I am so sorry for you, Nancy! what can one do for you?" says my husband, looking thoroughly discomfited, concerned, and helpless. "Would you care to have a book?"

"I cannot read in a train," reply I, dolorously, "it makes me *sick*!" Then feeling rather ashamed of my peevishness — "Never mind me!" I say, with a dusty smile; "I am quite happy! I — I — like looking out."

The day falls, the night comes. On, on, on! There is a bit of looking-glass opposite me. I can no longer see any thing outside. I have to sit staring at my own plain, grimed, bored face. In a sudden fury, I draw the little red silk curtain across my own image. Thank God! I can no longer see myself. Sir Roger ceases to try his eyes with the print of the *Westminster*, and closes it.

"I wonder," say I, pouring some eau-de-cologne on my pocket-handkerchief, and trying to cleanse my face therewith, but only succeeding in making it a muddy instead of a dusty smudge—"I wonder whether we shall meet any one we know at Dresden?"

"I should not wonder," replies Sir Roger, cheerfully.

"Is the Hôtel de Saxe the place where most English go?" inquire I, anxiously. "Ah, you do not know! I must ask Schmidt."

"Yes, do."

"I hope we shall," say I, straining my eyes to make out the objects in the dark outside. "We have been very unlucky so far, have not we?"

"Are you so anxious to meet people? are you so dull already, Nancy?" he asks, in that voice of peculiar gentleness which I have already learned to know hides inward pain.

"Oh, no, no!" cry I, with quick remorse. "Not at all! I have always *longed* to travel! At one time Barbara and I were always talking about it, making plans, you know, of where we would go. I enjoy it, of all things, especially the pictures—but do not you think it would be amusing to have some one to talk to at the *tables d'hôte*, some one English, to laugh at the people with?"

"Yes," he answers, readily, "of course it would. It is quite natural that you should wish it. I heartily hope we shall. We will go wherever it is most likely."

After long, *long* hours of dark rushing, Dresden at last. We drive in an open carriage through an unknown town, moonlit, silent, and asleep. German towns go to bed early. We cross the Elbe, in which a second moon, big and clear as the one in heaven, lies quivering, waving with the water's wave; then through dim, ghostly streets, and at last—at last—we pull up at the door of the Hôtel de Saxe, and the sleepy porter comes out disheveled.

"There is no doubt," say I, aloud, when I find myself alone in my bedroom, Sir Roger not having yet come up, and the maid having gone to bed—addressing the remark to the hot water in which I have been bathing my face, stiff with dirt, and haggard with fatigue. "There is no use denying it, I *hate* being married!"

CHAPTER XI

We have been in Dresden three whole days, and as yet my aspirations have not met their fulfillment. We have met no one we know. We have borrowed the Visitors' Book from the porter, and diligently searched it. We have expectantly examined the guests at the *tables d'hôte* every day, but with no result. It is too early in the year. The hotel is not half full. Of its inmates one half are American, a quarter German, and the other quarter English, such as not the most rabidly social mind can wish to forgather with. At the discovery of our ill-success, Sir Roger looks so honestly crestfallen that my heart smites me.

"How eager you are!" I say, laying my hand on his, with a smile. "You are far more anxious about it than I am! I begin to think that you are growing tired of me already! As for me," continue I, nonchalantly, seeing his face brighten at my words, "I think I have changed my mind. Perhaps it would be rather a *bore* to meet any acquaintance, and—and—we do very well as we are, do not we?"

"Is that true, Nancy?" he says, eagerly. "I have been bothering my head rather with the notion that I was but poor company for a little young thing like you; that you must be wearying for some of your own friends."

"I never had a friend," reply I, "*never*—that is—except *you*! The boys" — (with a little stealing smile)—"always used to call you my friend—always from the first, from the days I used to take you out walking, and keep wishing that you were my father, and be rather hurt because I never could get you to echo the wish."

"And you are not much disappointed *really*?" he says, with a wistful persistence, as if he but half believed the words my lips made. "If you are, mind you tell me, child—tell me every thing that vexes you—*always*!"

"I will tell you every thing that happens to me, bad and good," reply I, quite gayly, "and all the unlucky things I say—there, that is a large promise, I can tell you!"

I am no longer dusty and grimy; quite spick and span, on the contrary; so freshly and prettily dressed, indeed, that the thought *will* occur to me that it is a pity there are not more people to see me. However, no doubt some one will turn up by-and-by. The weather is serenely, evenly fine. It seems as if no rain *could* come from such a high blue sky. It is late afternoon or early evening. Since dinner is over—dinner at the godless hour of half-past four—I suppose we must call it evening. Sir Roger and I are driving out in an open carriage beyond the town, across the Elbe, up the shady road to Weisserhoisch. The calm of coming night is falling with silky softness upon every thing. The acacias stand on each side of the highway, with the delicate abundance of their airy flowers, faintly yet most definitely sweet on the evening air.

I look up and see the crowded blooms drooping in pensive beauty above my head. The guelder-rose's summer snow-balls, and the mock-orange with its penetrating odor, whiten the still gardens as we pass. The billowy meadow-grass, the tall red sorrel, the untidy, ragged robin, all the yearly-recurring May miracles! What can I say, O my friends, to set them fairly before you?

Under the trees the townsfolk are walking, chatting low and friendly. A soldier has his arm round a fat-faced Mädchen's waist, an attention which she takes with the stolidity engendered by long habit. Dear, willing, panting dogs, are laboriously dragging the washer-women's little carts up-hill.

"Vick," say I, gravely, "how would you like to drag a little cart to the wash?"

Vick does not answer verbally, but she stretches her small neck over the carriage-side, and gives a disdainful yet inquisitive *smell* at her low brethren. No words could express a fuller contempt for a dog that earns his own living.

The driver is taking his horses along very easily, but we do not care to hurry him. I have not felt so happy, so at ease, so gay, since I was wed.

"This *is* nice," say I, making a frantic snatch at a long acacia-droop; "*how* I wish they were *all* here!"

Sir Roger laughs a little, and raises his eyebrows slightly.

"Do you mean *with us—now—in the carriage*? Should not we be rather a tight fit?"

"Rather," say I, laughing too. "We should be puzzled how to pack them all, should not we? We would be like the animals in a Noah's ark."

A little pause.

"General," say I, impulsively, "it has just occurred to me, are not you sometimes deadly, *deadly* tired of hearing about the boys? I am sure I should be, if I were you. Confess! I will try not to be any angrier with you than I can help; but do not you sometimes wish that Algy and Bobby, and the Brat—not to speak of Tou Tou—were drowned in the Red Sea, or in the horse-pond, at home?"

"At least you gave me fair warning," he says, with a smile. "Do you remember telling me that whoever married you would have to marry all six?"

"I wish you would not remind me of that," say I, reddening.

It was quite the broadest hint any one ever gave. The evening is deepening. We have reached Weisserhoisch. Now our faces are turned homeward again. As we pass the entrance to the Gardens of the Linnisches Bad, we see the lamps springing into light, and the people gayly yet quietly trooping in, while on the soft evening air comes the swell of merry music.

"Stop! stop!" cry I, springing up, excitedly. "Let us go in. I *love* a band! It is almost as good as a circus. May we, general? Do you mind? Would it bore you?"

Five minutes more, and we are sitting at a little round table, each with a tall green glass of Mai-Trank before us, and a brisk Uhlanenritt in our ears. I look round with a pleasant sense of dissipation. The still, green trees; the cluster of oval lamps, like great bright ostrich-eggs; the countless little tables like our own; the happy social groups; the waiters running madly about with bif-tecks; the great-lidded goblets of amber-colored Bohemian beer; the young Bavarian officers, in light-blue uniforms, at the next table to us—stalwart, fair-haired boys—I should not altogether mind knowing a few of them; and, over all, the arch of suave, dark, evening sky.

"What shall we have for supper?" cry I, vivaciously. "I never can see anybody eating without longing to eat too. *Blutwurst!* That means black-pudding, I suppose—certainly not *that*—how they do call a spade a spade in German! By-the-by, what are the soldiers having? Can you see? I think I saw a vision of *prawns!* I saw things sticking out like their legs. I *must* find out!"

I rise, on pretense of getting a little wooden stool from under an unoccupied table close to the object of my curiosity, and, as I stoop to pick it up, I fraudulently glance over the nearest warrior's shoulder. My sin finds me out. He turns and catches me in the act, and at the same time a young man—*not* a warrior, at least not in uniform, but in loose gray British clothes—turns, too, and fixes me with a stony, British stare. I am returning in some confusion, having moreover incidentally discovered that they were *not* prawns, when to my extreme surprise, I hear my husband addressing the young gentleman in gray.

"Why, Frank, my dear boy, is that you? Who would have thought of seeing *you* here?"

"As to that," replies the young man, stretching out a ready right hand, "who would have thought of seeing *you*? What on earth has brought *you* here?"

Sir Roger laughs, but with a sort of shyness.

"Like the man in the parable, I have married a wife," he says; then, putting his hand kindly on the young fellow's shoulder—"Nancy, you have been wishing that we might meet some one we knew, have not you? Well, here is some one. I suppose that I must introduce you formally to each other. Lady Tempest—Mr. Musgrave."

Despite the searching, and, I should have thought, exhaustive examination of my appearance, that my new friend has already indulged in, he thinks good to look at me again, as he bows, and this time with a sort of undisguisable surprise in his great dark eyes.

"I must apologize," he says, taking off his hat. "I had heard that you were going to be married, but I am so behind the time, have been so out of the way of hearing news, that I did not know that it had come off yet."

He says this with a little of that doubtful stiffness, which sometimes owes its birth to shyness, and sometimes to self-consciousness; but he seems in no hurry to return to his friends, the big, blond soldiers. On the contrary, he draws a chair up to our table.

"Do they ever get *prawns* here?" say I, with apparent irrelevancy, not being able to disengage my mind from the thought of shell-fish, "or is it too far inland? I am *so* fond of them, and I fancied that these gentlemen—" (slightly indicating the broad, blue warrior-backs)—"were eating some."

His mouth curves into a sudden smile.

"Was that why you came to look?"

I laugh.

"I did not mean to be seen: that person must have had eyes in the back of his head."

I relapse into silence, and fish for the sprigs of woodruff floating in my Mai-Trank, while the talk passes to Sir Roger. Presently I become aware that the stranger is addressing me by that new title which makes me disposed to laugh.

"Lady Tempest, have you seen those lamps that they have here, in the shape of flowers? Cockney sort of things, but they are rather pretty."

"No," say I, eagerly, dropping my spoon and looking up; "*in the shape of flowers?* Where?"

"You cannot see them from here," he answers; "they are over there, nearer the river."

"I should like to see them," say I, decisively; "shall we, general?"

"Will you spare Lady Tempest for five minutes?" says the young man, addressing my husband; "it is not a hundred yards off."

At *my* words Sir Roger had made a slight movement toward rising; but, at the stranger's, he resettles himself in his chair.

"Will you not come, too? Do!" say I, pleadingly; and, as I speak, I half stretch out my hand to lay it on his arm; then hastily draw it back, afraid and ashamed of vexing him by public demonstrations.

He looks up at me with a smile, but shakes his head.

"I think I am lazy," he says; "I will wait for you here."

We set off; I with a strongish, but unexplained feeling of resentment against my companion.

"Where are they?" I ask, pettishly; "not far off, I hope! I do not fancy I shall care about them!"

"I did not suppose that you would," he replies, in an extremely happy tone; "would you like us to go back?"

"No," reply I, carelessly, "it would not be worth while now we have started."

We march on in solemn silence, not particularly pleased with each other. I am staring about me, with as greedily wondering eyes as if I were a young nun let loose for the first time. We pass a score—twoscore, threescore, perhaps—of happy parties, soldiers again, a *bourgeois* family of three generations, the old grandmother with a mushroom-hat tied over her cap—soldiers and Fräuleins *coketteering*. The air comes to our faces, dry, warm, and elastic, yet freshened by the river, far down in whose quiet heart all the lamps are burning again.

"Have you been here long?" says Mr. Musgrave, presently, in a formal voice, from which I see that resentment is not yet absent.

"Yes," say I, having on the other hand fully recovered my good-humor, "a good while—that is, not very long—three, four, three whole days."

"Do you call that a *good while?*"

"It seems more," reply I, looking frankly back at him in the lamplight, and thinking that he cannot be much older than Algy, and that, in consequence, it is rather a comfort not to be obliged to feel the slightest respect for him.

"And how long have you been abroad altogether?"

We have reached the flower-lamps. We are standing by the bed in which they are supposed to grow. There are half a dozen of them: a fuchsia, a convolvulus, lilies.

"I do not think much of them," say I, disparagingly, kneeling down to examine them. "What a villainous rose! It is like an *artichoke*!"

"I told you you would not like them," he says, not looking at the flowers, but switching a little stick nonchalantly about; then, after a moment: "How long did you say you had been abroad?"

"You asked me that before," reply I, sharply, rising from my knees, and discovering that the evening grass has left a disfiguring green trace on my smart *trousseau* gown.

"Yes, and you did not give me any answer," he replies, with equal sharpness.

"Because I cannot for the life of me recollect," reply I, looking up for inspiration to the stars, which the great bright lamps make look small and pale. "I must do a sum: what day of the month is this?—the 31st? Oh, thanks, so it is; and we were married on the 20th. It is ten days, then. Oh, it *must* be more—it seems like ten *months*."

I am looking him full in the face as I say this, and I see a curious, and to me *puzzling*, expression of inquiry and laughter in the shady darkness of his eyes.

"Has the time seemed so long to you, then?"

"No," reply I, reddening with vexation at my own *bêtise*; "that is—yes—because we have been to so many places, and seen so many things—any one would understand *that*."

"And when do you go home?"

"In less than three weeks now," I reply, in an alert, or rather joyful tone; "at least I hope so—I mean" (again correcting myself)—"I *think* so."

Somehow I feel dissatisfied with my own explanations, and recommence:

"The boys—that is, my brothers—will soon be scattered to the ends of the earth; Algy has got his commission, and Bobby will soon be sent to a foreign station—he is in the navy, you will understand; and so we all want to be together once again before they go."

"You are not going home *really*, then?" inquires my companion, with a slight shade of disappointment in his tone; "not to *Tempest*—that is?"

"What a number of questions you do ask!" say I, impatiently. "Of what possible interest can it be to you where we are going?"

"Only that I shall be your nearest neighbor," replies he, stiffly; "and, as Sir Roger has hardly ever been down hitherto, I am rather tired of living next an empty house."

"Our nearest neighbor!" cry I, with animation, opening my eyes. "Not *really*? Well, I am rather glad! Only yesterday I was asking Sir Roger whether there were many young people about. And *how* near are you? *Very* near?"

"About as near as I well can be," answers he, dryly. "My lodge exactly faces yours."

"Too close," say I, shaking my head. "We shall quarrel."

"And do you mean to say," in a tone of attempted lightness that but badly disguises a good deal of hurt conceit, "that you never heard my name before?"

Again I shake my head.

"Never! and, what is more, I do not think I know what it is now: I suppose I did not listen very attentively, but I do not think I caught it."

"And your tone says" (with a very considerable accession of huffiness) "that you are supremely indifferent as to whether you *ever* catch it."

I laugh.

"*Catch* it! you talk as if it were a *disease*. Well" (speaking demurely), "perhaps on the whole it *would* be more convenient if I were to know it."

Silence.

"Well! what is it?"

No answer.

"I shall have to ask at your lodge!"

"Who *can* pronounce his *own* name in cold blood?" he says, reddening a little. "I, for one, cannot—there—if you do not mind looking at this card—"

He takes one out of his pocket, and I stop—we are slowly strolling back—under a lamp, to read it:

Mr. MR. FRANCIS MUSGRAVE,
MUSGRAVE ABBEY.

"Oh, thanks—*Musgrave*—yes."

"And Sir Roger has never mentioned me to you *really?*" he says, recurring with persistent hurt vanity to the topic. "How very odd of him!"

"Not in the least odd!" reply I, brusquely. "Why should he? He knew that I was not aware of your existence, and that therefore you would not be a very interesting subject to me; no doubt"—(smiling a little)—"I shall hear all about you from him now."

He is silent.

"And do you live *here* at this abbey"—(pointing to the card I still hold in my hand)—"*all by yourself?*"

"Do you mean without a *wife?*" he asks, with a half-sneering smile. "Yes—I have that misfortune."

"I was not thinking of a *wife*," say I, rather angrily. "It never occurred to me that you could have one! you are too young—a great deal too young!"

"*Too young*, am I? At what age, then, may one be supposed to deserve that blessing? forty? fifty? sixty?"

I feel rather offended, but cannot exactly grasp in my own mind the ground of offense.

"I meant, of course, had you any father? any mother?"

"Neither. I am that most affecting spectacle—an orphan-boy."

"You have no brothers and sisters, I am *sure*," say I, confidently.

"I have not, but why you should be *sure* of it, I am at a loss to imagine."

"You seem to take offense rather easily," I say, ingenuously. "You looked quite cross when I said I did not think much of the flowers—and again when I said I had forgotten your name—and again when I told you, you were too young to have a wife: now, you know, in a large family, one has all that sort of nonsense knocked out of one."

"Has one?" (rather shortly).

"Nobody would mind whether one were huffy or not," continue I; "they would only laugh at one."

"What a pleasant, civil-spoken thing a large family must be!" he says, dryly.

We have reached Sir Roger. I had set off on my little expedition feeling rather out of conceit with my young friend, and I return with those dispositions somewhat aggravated. We find my husband sitting where we left him, placidly smoking and listening to the band.

"Four-and-twenty fiddlers all in a row!"

They have long finished the Uhlanenritt, and are now clashing out a brisk Hussarenritt, in which one plainly hears the hussars' thundering gallop, while the conductor madly waves his arms, as he has been doing unintermittingly for the last two hours.

"You were quite wise," say I, laying my hand on the back of his chair; "you had much the best of it! they were a great imposture!"

"Were they?" he says, taking his cigar out of his mouth, and lifting his handsome and severe iron-gray eyes to mine. "They were farther off than you thought, were not they? I began to think you had not been able to find them."

"Have we been so long?" I say, surprised. "It did not *seem* long! I suppose we dawdled. We began to talk—bah! it is growing chill! let us go home!"

Mr. Musgrave accompanies us to the entrance to the gardens.

"Good-night, Frank!" cries Sir Roger, as he follows me into the carriage.

As soon as I am in, I recollect that I have ungratefully forgotten to shake hands with my late escort.

"Good-night!" cry I, too, stretching out a compunctious hand, over Sir Roger and the carriage-side. "I am so sorry! I forgot all about you!"

"What hotel are you at?" asks Sir Roger, closing the carriage-door after him. "The Victoria? Oh, yes. We are at the Saxe. You must come and look us up when you have nothing better to do. Our rooms are number—what is it, Nancy? I never can recollect."

"No. 5," reply I. "But, indeed, it is not much use any one coming to call upon us, is it? For we are always out—morning, noon, and night."

With this parting encouragement on my part, we drive off, and leave our young friend trying, with only moderate success, to combine a gracious smile to Sir Roger, with a resentful scowl at me, under a lamp-post. We roll along quickly and easily, through the soft, cool, lamplit night.

"Well, how did you get on with him, Nancy?" asks Sir Roger. "Good-looking fellow, is not he?"

"Is he?" say I, carelessly. "Yes, I suppose he is, only that I never *can* admire *dark* men: I am so glad that all the boys are fair—I should have hated a *black* brother."

"How do you know that my hair was not coal-black before it turned gray?" he asks, with a smile. "It may have been the hue of the carrion-crow for all you know."

"I am *sure* it was not," reply I, stoutly; then, after a little pause, "I do not think that I *did* get on well with him—not what *I* call getting on—he seems rather a touchy young gentleman."

"You must not quarrel with him, Nancy," says Sir Roger, laughing. "He lives not a stone's-throw from us."

"So he told me!"

"Poor fellow!" with an accent of compassion. "He has never had much of a chance; he has been his own master almost ever since he was born—a bad thing for any boy—he has no parents, you know."

"So he told me."

"Neither has he any brothers or sisters."

"So he told me!"

"He seems to have told you a great many things."

"Yes," reply I, "but then I asked him a great many questions: our conversation was rather like the catechism: the moment I stopped asking *him* questions, he began asking me!"

CHAPTER XII

Three long days—all blue and gold—blue sky and gold sunshine—roll away. If Schmidt, the courier, *has* a fault, it is over-driving us. We visit the Grüne Gewölbe, the Japanese Palace, the Zwinger—and we visit them *alone*. Dresden is not a very large place, yet in no part of it, in none of its bright streets—in neither its old nor its new market, in none of its public places, do I catch a glimpse of my new acquaintance. Neither does he come to call. This last fact surprises me a little, and disappoints me a good deal. Our walk at the Linnisches Bad in the gay lamplight, his character, his conversation, even his appearance, begin to undergo a transformation in my mind. After all, he was not *really* dark—not one of those black men, against whom Barbara and I have always lifted up our testimonies; by daylight, I think his eyes would have been hazel. He certainly was very easy to talk to. One had not to pump up conversation for him, and I do not suppose that, *as men go*, he was *really* very touchy. One cannot expect everybody to be so jest-hardened and robustly good-tempered as the boys. Often before now I have only been able to gauge the unfortunateness of my speeches to men, by the rasping effect they have had on their tempers, and which has often taken me honestly by surprise.

"*Again*, Mr. Musgrave has not been to call," say I, one afternoon, on returning from a long and rather grilling drive, speaking in a slightly annoyed tone.

"Did you expect that he would?" asks Sir Roger, with a smile. "I think that, after the searching snub you gave him, he would have been a bolder man than I take him for, if he had risked his head in the lion's mouth."

"*Am* I such a lion?" say I, with an accent of vexation. "*Did* I snub him? I am sure I had no more idea of snubbing him than I had of snubbing *you*; that is the way in which I always cut my own throat!"

I draw a chair into the balcony, where he has already established himself with his cigar, and sit down beside him.

"I foresee," say I, beginning to laugh rather grimly, "that a desert will spread all round our house! your friends will disappear before my tongue, like morning mist."

"Let them!"

After a pause, edging a little nearer to him, and, regardless of the hay-carts in the market below—laying my fair-haired head on his shoulder:

"What *could* have made you marry such a *shrew*? I believe it was the purest philanthropy."

"That was it!" he answers, fondly. "To save any other poor fellow from such an infliction!"

"Quite unnecessary!" rejoin I, shaking my head. "If you had not married me, it is very certain that nobody else would!"

Another day has come. It is hot afternoon. Sir Roger is reading the *Times* in our balcony, and I am strolling along the dazzling streets by myself. What can equal the white glare of a foreign town? I am strolling along by myself under a big sun-shade. My progress is slow, as my nose has a disposition to flatten itself against every shop-window—saving, perhaps, the cigar ones. A grave problem is engaging my mind. What present am I to take to father? It is this question which moiders our young brains as often as his birthday recurs. My thoughts are trailing back over all our former gifts to him. This year we gave him a spectacle-case (he is short-sighted); last year a pocket-book; the year before, an inkstand. What is there left to give him? A cigar-case? He does not smoke. A hunting-flask? He has half a dozen. A Norwegian stove? He does not approve of them, but says that men ought to be satisfied with sandwiches out shooting. A telescope? He never lifts his eyes high enough above our delinquencies to look at the stars. I cannot arrive at any approximation to a decision. As I issue from a china-shop, with a brown-paper parcel under my arm, and out on the hot and glaring flags, I see a young man come stepping down the street, with a long, loose, British stride; a young man, pale and comely, and a good deal worn out by the flies, that have also eaten most of me.

"How are you?" cry I, hastily shifting my umbrella to the other hand, so as to have my right one ready to offer him. "Are not these streets blinding? I am blinking like an owl in daylight!—so you never came to see us, after all!"

"It was so likely that I should!" he answers, with his nose in the air.

"Very likely!" reply I, taking him literally; "so likely that I have been expecting you every day."

"You seem to forget—confound these flies!"—(as a stout blue-bottle blunders into one flashing eye)—"you seem to forget that you told me, in so many words, to stay away."

"You *were* huffy, then!" say I, with an accent of incredulity. "Sir Roger was right! he said you were, and I could not believe it; he was quite sorry for you. He said I had snubbed you so."

"*Snubbed* me!" reddening self-consciously, and drawing himself up as if he did not much relish the application of the word. "I do not often give any one the chance of doing that *twice*!"

"You are not going to be offended *again*, I suppose," say I, apprehensively; "it must be with Sir Roger this time, if you are! it was he that was sorry for you, not *I*."

We look at each other under my green sun-shade (his eyes *are* hazel, by daylight), and then we both burst into a duet of foolish friendly laughter.

"I want you to give me your advice," say I, as we toddle amicably along, side by side. "What would be a nice present for a gentleman—an elderly gentleman—at least *rather* elderly, who *has* a spectacle-case, a pocket-book, an inkstand, six Church services, and who does not smoke."

"But he *does* smoke," says Mr. Musgrave, correcting me. "I *saw* him the other day."

"Saw *whom*? What—do you mean?"

"Are not you talking of Sir Roger?" he asks, with an accent of surprise.

"*Sir Roger!*" (indignantly). "No, indeed! do you think *he* wants spectacles? No! I was talking of my father."

"*Your father?* You are not, like me, a poor misguided orphan, then; you have a father."

"I should think I *had*," reply I, expressively.

"Any brothers? Oh, yes, by-the-by, I know you have! you held them up for my imitation the other day—half a dozen fellows who never take offense at any thing."

"No more they do!" cry I, firing up. "If I tell them when I go home, as I certainly shall, if I remember, that you were out of humor and bore malice for *three* whole days, because I happened to say that we were generally out-of-doors most of the day—they will not believe it—simply they will not."

"And have you also six sisters?" asks the young man, dexterously shifting the conversation a little.

"No, two."

"And are they *all* to have presents?—six and two is eight, and your father nine, and—I suppose you have a mother, too?"

"Yes."

"Nine and one is ten—ten brown-paper parcels, each as large as the one you now have under your arm—by-the-by, would you like me to carry it? *What* a lot you will have to pay for extra luggage!"

His offer to carry my parcel is so slightly and incidentally made, and is so unaccompanied by any gesture suited to the words, that I decline the attention. The people pass to and fro in the sun as we pace leisurely along.

"Have you nearly done your shopping?" asks my companion, presently.

"Very nearly."

"What do you say to taking a tour through the gallery?" he says, "or are you sick of the pictures?"

"Far from it," say I, briskly, "but, all the same, I cannot do it; I am going back at once to Sir Roger; we are to drive to Loschwitz: I only came out for a little prowl by myself, to think about father's present! Sir Roger cannot help me at all," I continue, marching off again into the theme which is uppermost in my thoughts. "*He* suggested a traveling-bag, but I know that father would *hate* that."

"To *drive*! this time of day!" cried Mr. Musgrave, in a tone of extreme disapprobation; "will not you get well baked?"

"I dare say," I answer, absently; then, in a low tone to myself, "*why* does not he smoke? it would be so easy then—a smoking-cap, a tobacco-pouch, a cigar-holder, a hundred things!"

"Is it *quite* settled about Loschwitz?" asks the young man, with an air of indifference.

"Quite," say I, still not thinking of what I am saying. "That is, no—not quite—nearly—a bag *is* useful, you know."

"I passed the Saxe just now," he says, giving his hat a little tilt over his nose, "and saw Sir Roger sitting in the balcony, with his cigar and his *Times*, and he looked so luxuriously comfortable that it seemed a sin to disturb him. Do not you think, taking the dust and the blue-bottles into consideration, that it would be kinder to leave him in peace in his arm-chair?"

"No, I do not," reply I, flatly. "I suppose he knows best what he likes himself; and why a strong, hearty man in the prime of life should be supposed to wish to spend a whole summer afternoon nodding in an arm-chair, any more than you would wish it yourself, I am at a loss to inquire!" The suggestion has irritated me so much that for the moment I forget the traveling-bag.

"When I am as old as he," replies the young man, coldly, shaking the ash off his cigar, "if I ever am, which I doubt, and have knocked about the world for as many years, and imperiled my liver in as many climates, and sent as many Russians, and Chinamen, and Sikhs to glory as he has, I shall think myself entitled to sit in an arm-chair—yes, and sleep in it too—all day, if I feel inclined."

I do not answer, partly because I am exasperated, partly because at this moment my eye is caught by an object in a shop-window—a traveling-bag, with its mouth invitingly open, displaying all manner of manly conveniences. I hastily furl my green umbrella, and step in. My squire does not follow me. I hardly notice the fact, but suppose that he is standing outside in the sun. However, when I reissue forth, I find that he has disappeared. I look up the street, down the street. There is no trace of him. I walk away, feeling a little mortified. I go into a few more shops: I dawdle over some china. Then I turn my steps homeward.

At a narrow street-corner, in the grateful shade cast by some tall houses, I come face to face with him again.

"Did not you wonder where I had disappeared to?" he asks; "or perhaps you never noticed that I had?"

He is panting a little, as if he had been running, or walking fast.

"I thought that most likely you had taken offense again," reply I, with a laugh, "and that I had lost sight of you for three more days."

"I have been to the Hôtel de Saxe," he replies, with a rather triumphant smile on his handsome mustacheless lips. "I thought I would find out about Loschwitz."

"Find out *what?*" cry I, standing still, raising my voice a little, and growing even redder than the sun, the flies, the brown-paper parcel, and the heavy umbrella, have already made me. "There was nothing to find out! I wish you would leave things alone; I wish you would let me manage my own business."

The smile disappears rather rapidly.

"You have not been telling the general," continue I, in a tone of rapid apprehension, "that I did not want to go with him? because, if you have, it was a great, great *mistake.*"

"I told him nothing of the kind," replies Mr. Musgrave, looking, like me, fierce, but—unlike me—cool and pale. "I was not so inventive. I merely suggested that sunstroke would most likely be your portion if you went now, and that it would be quite as easy, and a great deal pleasanter, to go three hours later."

"Yes? and he said—what?"

"He was foolish enough to agree with me."

We are standing in a little quiet street, all shade and dark shops. There are very few passers-by. I feel rather ashamed of myself, and my angry eyes peruse the pavement. Neither does he speak. Presently I look up at him rather shyly.

"How about the gallery? the pictures?"

"Do you wish to go there?" he asks, with rather the air of a polite martyr. "I shall be happy to take you if you like."

"Do!" say I, heartily, "and let us try to be friends, and to spend five minutes without quarreling!"

We have spent more than five, a great deal more—thirty, forty, perhaps, and our harmony is still unbroken, *uncracked* even. We have sat in awed and chastened silence before the divine meekness of the Sistine Madonna. We have turned away in disgust from Jordain's brutish "Triumphs of Silenus," and tiresome repetitions of Hercules in drink. We have admired the exuberance of St. Mary of Egypt's locks, and irreverently compared them to the effects of Mrs. Allen's "World-wide Hair Restorer." We have observed that the forehead of Holbein's great Virgin is too high to please *us*, and made many other connoisseur-like remarks. I have pointed out to Mr. Musgrave the Saint Catherine which has a look of Barbara, and we have both grown rather tired of St. Sebastian, stuck as full of darts as a pin-cushion of pins. Now we are sitting down resting our eyes and our strained powers of criticism, and have fallen into easy talk.

"I am glad you are coming to dine at our *table d'hôte* to-night," say I, in a friendly tone. "It will be nice for the general to have an Englishman to talk to. I hope you will sit by him; he has been so much used to men all his life that he must get rather sick of having nothing but the chatter of one woman to depend upon."

"At least he has no one but himself to blame for that," replies the young fellow, laughing. "I suppose it was his own doing."

"How do you know that?" cry I, gayly, and then the recollection of my *hint* to Sir Roger—a remembrance that always makes me rather hot—comes over me, and causes me to turn my head quickly away with a red blush. "It certainly *has* a look of Barbara," I say, glancing toward the Saint Catherine, and rushing quickly into another subject.

"Has it?" he says, apparently unaware of the rapidity of my transition. "Then I wish I knew Barbara."

I laugh.

"I dare say you do."

"She is not much like you, I suppose?" he says, turning from the saint's straight and strict Greek profile to the engaging irregularity of mine.

"Not exactly," say I, with emphasis. "Ah!" (in a tone of prospective triumph), "wait till you see her!"

"I am afraid that I shall have to wait some time."

"The Brat—that is one of my brothers, you know—is the one like me," I say, becoming diffuse, as I always do, when the theme of my family is started; "we *are* like! We can see it ourselves."

"Is he one of the thick-skinned six that you told me about?"

"There are *not* six," cry I, impatiently. "I do not know what put it into your head that there were *six*; there are only *three*."

"You certainly told me there were six."

"I am *he* in petticoats," say I, resuming the thread of my own narrative; "everybody sees the likeness. One day when he was three or four years younger, we dressed him up in my things—my gown and bonnet, you know—and all the servants took him for me; they only found him out because he held up his gown so awkwardly high, and gave it such great kicks to keep it out of his way, that they saw his great nailed boots! Sir Roger thought we were twins the first time he saw us."

"Sir Roger!" repeats the young man, as if reminded by the name of something he had meant to say. "Oh, by-the-by, if you will not think me impertinent for asking, where did you first fall in with Sir Roger? I should have thought that he was rather out of your beat; you do not hail from his part of the world, do you?"

"No," reply I, my thoughts traveling back to the day when we made taffy, and tumbled over each other, hot and sticky to the window, to see the dog-cart bearing the stranger roll up the drive. "I never saw him till this last March, when he came to stay with us."

"To stay with you?"

"Yes," reply I, thinking of our godless jokes about his wig and his false calves, and smiling gently to myself; "he was an old friend of father's."

"A contemporary, I suppose?" (a little inquisitively).

"Yes, he was at school with father," I answer; and the moment I have given utterance to the abhorred formula I repent.

"At school with him?" (speaking rather slowly, and looking at me, with a sort of flickering smile in lips and eyes). "Oh, I see!"

"What do you see?" cry I, sharply.

"Nothing, nothing! I only meant to say I understand, I comprehend."

"There is nothing to understand," reply I, brusquely, and rising. "I am tired—I shall go home!"

We walk back rather silently; there is nothing so trying to eyes and mind as picture-seeing, and I am fagged, and also indefinitely, yet certainly, cross. As we reach the door of the Saxe, I hold out my hand.

"Now that we have come to the end of our walk," say I, "and that you cannot think that I am *hinting* to you, I will tell you that I think it was very ill-mannered and selfish of you not to *insist* on carrying *this*" (holding out the brown-paper parcel); "there is not *one* of the boys—not even Bobby, whom we always call so rough, who would have *dreamed* of letting a lady carry a parcel for herself, when he was by to take it. There! I am better now! I *had* to tell you; I wish you good-day!"

CHAPTER XIII

"If he does not like it," say I, setting it on the floor, and regarding it from a little distance, with my head on one side, while friendly criticism and admiration meet in happy wedlock in my eyes, "I can give it to you; I had much rather make you a present than *him*."

"Then Heaven grant that it may find disfavor in his sight!" says Sir Roger, piously.

We are talking of the traveling-bag, which at last, in despair of any thing suitable occurring to my mind, I have bought, and now regard with a sort of apprehensive joy. The blinds are half lowered for the heat, but, through them and under them, the broad gold sunshine is streaming and pushing itself, washing the careful twists of my flax hair, the bag's stout red leather sides, and Sir Roger's nose, as he leans over it, with manly distrust, trying the clasp by many searching snappings.

"I never gave you a present in my life—never—did I?" say I, squatting down on the floor beside him, crumpling my nice crisp muslin frock with the recklessness of a woman who knows that there are many more such frocks in the cupboard, and to whom this knowledge has but newly come; "never mind! next birthday I will give you one—a really nice, handsome, rather expensive one—all bought with your own money, too—there!"

This is on the morning of our last day in Dresden. Yes! *to-morrow* we set off homeward. Our wedding-tour is nearly ended: tyrant Custom, which sent us off, permits us to rejoin our fellows. Well, it really has not been so bad! I do not know that I should care to have it over again—that is, just immediately; but it has gone off very well altogether—quite as well as most other people's, I fancy. These are my thoughts in the afternoon, as (Sir Roger having gone to the post-office, and I having made myself very hot by superintending the packing of the presents—most of them of a brittle, *crackable* nature) I am leaning, to cool myself, over our balcony, and idly watching the little events that are happening under my nose. The omnibus stands, as usual, in the middle of the square, about to start for Blasewitz. Mysterious 'bus! always about to start—always full of patient passengers, and that yet was never seen by mortal man to set off. As I watch it with the wondering admiration with which I have daily regarded it, I hear the door of our sitting-room open, and Vick give a little shrewish shrill bark, speedily changed into an apologetic and friendly whiffling and whoffling.

"Is that you?" cry I, holding on by the balcony, and leaning back to peep over my own shoulder into the interior. "Come out here, if it is."

"Sir Roger is out," I say, a second later, putting my hand into that of Mr. Musgrave (for it is he), as he comes stepping, in his usual unsmiling, discontented beauty, to meet me.

"I know he is! I met him!"

"I am seeing the people start for Blasewitz for the last time! it makes me quite low!" I say, replacing my arms on the balcony, and speaking with an irrepressibly jovial broad smile on my face that rather contradicts my words.

"You *look* low," he answers, ironically, standing beside me, and looking rather provoked at my urbanity.

"This time to-morrow we shall be off," say I, beginning to laugh out of pure light-heartedness, though there is no joke within a mile of me, and to count on my fingers; "this time the day after to-morrow we shall be at Cologne—this time the day after *that* we shall be getting toward Brussels—this time the day after *that*, we shall be getting toward Dover—this time the day after *that*—"

"You will all be rushing higgledy-piggledy, helter-skelter, into each other's arms," interrupts my companion, looking at me with a lowering eye.

"Yes," say I, my eyes dancing. "You are quite right."

"Algy, and the Brat, and—what is the other fellow's name?—Dicky?—Jacky?—Jemmy?—"

"Bobby," say I, correcting him. "But you are not quite right; the Brat will not be there!—worse luck—he is in Paris!"

"Well, Barbara will not be in Paris," says the young man, still in the same discontented, pettish voice. "*She* will be there, no doubt—well to the front—in the thickest of the osculations."

"*That* she will!" cry I, heartily. "But you must give up calling her Barbara; that is not at all pretty manners."

"We will make a bargain," he says, beginning to smile a little, but rather as if it were against his will and intention. "I will allow her to call me 'Frank,' if she will allow me to call her 'Barbara.'"

"I dare say you will" (laughing).

A little pause. Another person has got into the omnibus; it is growing extremely full.

"I *hate* last days," says my companion, hitting viciously at the iron balcony rails with his stick, and scowling.

"'The Last Days of Pompeii,'" say I, stupidly, and yet laughing again; not because I think my witticism good, which no human being could do, but because I *must* laugh for very gladness. Another longer pause. (Shall I present the bag the night we arrive, or wait till next day?)

"I have got a riddle to ask you," says Frank, abruptly, and firing the observation off somewhat like a bomb-shell.

"Have you?" say I, absently. "I hope it is a good one."

"Of course, *you* must judge of that—'*Mon premier*—'"

"It is in *French!*" cry I, with an accent of disgust.

"Well, why should not it be?" (rather tartly).

"No reason whatever, only that I warn you beforehand I shall not understand it: I always *shiver* when people tell me a French anecdote; I never know when the point has arrived: I always laugh too soon or too late."

He says nothing, but looks black.

"Go on!" say I, laughing. "We will try, if you like."

"*Mon—premier—est—le—premier—de tout,*" he says, pronouncing each word very separately and distinctly. "Do you understand *that?*"

I nod. "My first is the first of all—yes."

"*Mon second n'a pas de second.*"

"My second has no second—yes."

"*Mon tout*"—(turning his long, sleepy eyes sentimentally toward me)—"*je ne saurai vous le dire.*"

"My whole—I cannot tell it you!—then why on earth did you ask me?" cry I, breaking out into hearty, wholesome laughter.

Again he blackens.

"Well, have you guessed it?"

"Guessed it!" I echo, recovering my gravity. "Not I!—my first is the first of all—my second has no second—my whole, I cannot tell it you!—I do not believe it is a riddle at all! it is a hoax—a take-in, like 'Why does a miller wear a white hat?'"

"It is nothing of the kind," he answers, looking thoroughly annoyed. "Must I tell you the answer?"

"I shall certainly never arrive at it by my unassisted genius," I reply, yawning. "Ah! there is M. Dom going out riding! Alas! never again shall I see him mount that peacocking steed!"

"It is 'Adieu!'" says my companion, blurting it out in a rage, seeing that I *will* not be interested in or excited by it.

"*Adieu!*" repeat I, standing with my mouth wide open, looking perfectly blank. "*How?*"

"You do not see?" he says. (His face has grown scarlet.) "Well, you must excuse me for saying that you are rather—" He breaks off and begins again, very fast this time. "My first is the first of all—is not *A* the first letter in the alphabet? My second has no second—has God (*Dieu*) any second? My whole—I cannot say it to you—*Adieu!*"

The contrast between the sentimentality of the words, and the brusque and defiant anger of his tone, is so abrupt, that I am sorry to say, I laugh again: indeed, I retire from the balcony into the saloon inside, throw myself into a chair, and, covering my face with my handkerchief, roar—

"It is very good," say I, in a choked voice; "very—so civil and pretty—but it is not very *funny*, is it?"

I receive no answer. I am still in my pocket-handkerchief, and he might be gone, but that I hear his quick, angry breathing, and know, by instinct, that he is standing over me, looking like a handsome thunder-cloud. I dare not look up at him, lest another mad cachinnation, such as sometimes overtakes one for the punishment of one's sins in church, should again lay violent hands upon me.

"I think I like 'Why was Balaam like a Life-Guardsman?' better, *on the whole*," I say, presently, peeping through my fingers, and speaking with a suspicious tremble in my voice.

"I have no doubt it is far superior," he answers, in a fierce and sulky tone, that he in vain tries to make sound playful. "'*Balaam like a Life-Guardsman?*' and why was he, may I ask? Something humorous about his donkey, I suppose."

"Because he had a queer ass (cuirass)," reply I, again exploding, and hiding my face in the back of the chair.

"A *queer ass!*" (in a tone of the profoundest contempt); "you have no more sentiment in you than *this table!*" smiting it with his bare hand.

"I know I have not," say I, sitting up, and holding my hand to my side to ease the pain my excessive mirth has caused; "they always said so at home. Oh, here is the general! we will make *him* umpire, which is funniest, yours or mine!"

Sir Roger enters, and glances in some surprise from Frank's crimson face to my convulsed one.

"Oh, general, do we not look as if we had been having an affecting parting?" cry I, jumping up and running to him. "Do not I look as if I had been crying? Quite the contrary, I assure you. But Musgrave and I have been asking each other such amusing riddles—would you like to hear them? *Mine* is good, plain, vulgar English, but his is French, so we will begin with it—'Mon premier—'"

I stop suddenly, for Mr. Musgrave is looking at me with an expression simply *murderous*.

"Well, what are you stopping for? I am on the horns of expectation—'Mon premier—'"

"After all, it is not so funny as I thought," I answer, brusquely. "I think we will keep it for some wet Sunday afternoon, when we are short of something to do."

CHAPTER XIV

The day of departure has really come. We have eaten our last bif-teck *aux pommes frites*, and drank our last cup of coffee in the Saxe. I have had my last look at the familiar square, at the great dome of the Frauen Kirchen, at the high houses with their dormer-windows, at the ugly big statue standing with its stiff black back rudely turned to the hotel, at the piled hay-carts. We are really and truly off. Our faces are set Barbara-ward, Bobby-ward, jackdaw-ward. I am in such rampaging spirits, that I literally do not know what to do with myself. I feel that I should like to tuck my tail, if I had one, between my legs, like Vick, and race round and round in an insane and unmeaning circle, as she does on the lawn at home, when oppressed by the overflow of her own gayety.

It seems to me as if there never had been such a day. I look at the sky as we drive along to the station. Call it sapphire, turquoise—indeed! What dull stone that ever lived darkling in a mine is fit to be named even in metaphor with this pale yet brilliant arch that so softly leans above us? It seems to me as if all the people we meet were handsome and well-featured—as if the Elbe were the noblest river that ever ran, carrying the sunlight in flakes of gold and diamond on its breast—as if all life were one long and kindly jest.

As we reach the station I see Mr. Musgrave standing on the pavement awaiting us, with a sort of mixed and compound look on his face.

"Here is Mr. Musgrave come to see us off!" I cry, jocundly. "Come to say '*Adieu!*' ha! ha! I must not forget to ask him whether he has any more riddles."

"For Heaven's sake do not!" cries Sir Roger, smiling in spite of himself, yet seriously and earnestly desirous of checking my wit. "Let the poor boy have a little peace! He no more understands chaff than I understand Parsee."

I hop out of the carriage like a parched pea, scorning equally the step and Frank's hand extended to help me. I feel to-day as if I need only stand on tiptoe, and stretch out my arms in order to be able to fly.

"So you have come to see the last of us," I say, trying to pull a long face, and walking with him into the waiting-room.

"Yes; rather a mistake, is not it?" he says, somewhat gloomily, but loading himself at once, with ostentatious haste (in memory of my former reproof), with my bag, parasol, and novel.

"The day after—the day after—the day after to-morrow," say I, smiling cheerfully up in his dismal face. "You may fancy us just turning in at the park-gates—by-the-by, have you any message to send to the boys, to Barbara?"

"None to the boys," he answers, half smiling, too. "I hate boys: you may give my love to Barbara if you like, and if you are quite sure that she is like the St. Catherine."

"Wait till you see her," say I, oracularly.

"But when *shall* I see her?" he asks, roused into an eagerness which I think promises admirably for Barbara; "when are you coming home, really?"

"Keep a good lookout at your lodge," I say, gayly, "and you will no doubt see us arrive some fine day, looking very foolish, most probably—crawling along like snails, dragged by our tenants."

"Were you *ever* known to answer a plain question plainly since you were born?" he cries, petulantly. "When are you likely to come *really*?"

"'I know not! What avails to know?'" reply I, pompously spouting a line out of some forgotten poem that has lurked in my memory, and now struts out, to the anger and discomfiture of Mr. Musgrave.

"Ah! here are the doors opening."

Everybody pours out on to the platform, and into the empty and expectant train.

Sir Roger and I get into a carriage—*not* a *coupé* this time—and dispose our myriad parcels above our heads, under our feet. Trucks roll, and porters bawl past; luggage is violently shot into vans. The last belated, panting passenger has got in. The doors are slammed-to. Off we go! The train is already in motion when the young man jumps on the step and thrusts in his hand for one parting shake.

"*Mon tout*," say I, screwing up my face into a crying shape, and speaking in a squeaky, pseudo-tearful voice, "*je ne saurai vous le dire!*"

Then he is hustled off by an indignant guard and three porters, and we see him no more. I throw myself back into my corner laughing.

"General," say I, "I think your young friend is nearly as soft-hearted as the girl in Tennyson who was

'Tender over drowning flies.'

He looked as if he were going to *weep*, did not he? and what on earth about?"

CHAPTER XV

"How mother, when we used to stun
Her head wi' all our noisy fun,
Did wish us all a-gone from home;
But now that some be dead and some
Be gone, and, oh, the place is dumb,
How she do wish wi' useless tears
To have again about her ears
The voices that be gone!"

We have passed Cologne; have passed Brussels; have passed Calais and Dover; have passed London; we are drawing near home. How refreshing sounds the broad voice of the porters at Dover! Squeamish as I am, after an hour and three-quarters of a nice, short, chopping sea, the sight of the dear green-fustian jackets, instead of the slovenly blue blouses across-Channel, goes nigh to revive me. Adieu, O neatly aquiline, broad-shaved French faces! Welcome, O bearded Britons, with your rough-hewn noses!

To avoid the heat of the day, we go down from London by a late afternoon train. It is evening when, almost *before* the train has stopped, I insist on jumping out at our station. Imagine if through some accident we were carried on to the next by mistake!

Such a thing has never happened in the annals of history, but still it *might*.

Sir Roger has some considerable difficulty in hindering me from shaking hands with the whole staff of officials. One veteran porter, who has been here ever since I was born, has a polite but improbable trick of addressing *every* female passenger as "my lady." Well, with regard to *me*, at least, he is right now. I *am* "my lady." Ha! ha! I have not nearly got over the ridiculousness of this fact yet, though I have been in possession of it now these *four* whole weeks.

It has been a hot, parching summer day, and now that the night draws on all the flagging flowers in the cottage-borders are straightening themselves anew, and lifting their leaves to the dews. The pale bean-flowers, in the broad bean-fields, as we pass, send their delicate scent over the hedge to me, as if it were some fair and courteous speech. To me it seems as if they were saying, as plainly as may be, "Welcome home, Nancy!"

The sky that has been all of one hue during the live-long day—wherever you looked, nothing but pale, *pale* azure—is now like the palette of some God-painter splashed and freaked with all manner of great and noble colors—a most regal blaze of gold—wide plains of crimson, as if all heaven were flashing at some high thought—little feathery cloud-islands of tenderest rose-pink. We are coming very near now. There, down below, set round its hips with tall rushes, is our pool, all blood-red in the sunset! Can *that* be colorless water—that great carmine fire? There are our elms, with their heads in the sunset, too.

"General," say I, very softly, putting my hand through his arm, and speaking in a small tone of unutterable content, "I should like to kiss everybody in the world."

"Perhaps you would not mind beginning with *me*," returns he, gayly; then—for I look quite capable of it—glancing slightly over his shoulder at the vigilant couple in the dickey.

"No, I did not mean *really*."

We are trotting alongside of the park-paling. I stand up and try to catch a glimpse between the coachman and footman, of the gate, to see whether they have come to meet me.

We are slackening our speed; we are going to turn in; the lodge-keeper runs out to open the gate; but no, it is needless. It is already open. I could have told *her* that. Here they all are!—Barbara, Algy, Bobby, Tou Tou.

"Here they are!" cry I, in a fidgety rapture. "Oh, general, just look how Tou Tou has grown; her frock is nearly up to her knees!"

"Do you think she *can* have grown that much in four weeks?" asks he, not contradictiously, but a little *doubtfully*, as Don Quixote may have asked the Princess Micomicona her reasons for landing at Ossime. "But pray, madam," says he, "why did your ladyship land at Ossime, seeing that it is not a seaport town?"

"I suppose not," I reply, a little disappointed. "I suppose that her frock must have run up in the washing."

To this day I have not the faintest idea how I got out of the carriage. My impression is that I *flew* over the side with wings which came to my aid in that one emergency, and then for evermore disappeared.

I do not know *this* time *where* I begin, or whom I end with. I seemed to be kissing them *all* at once. All their arms seem to be round *my* neck, and mine round all of theirs at the same moment. The only wonder is that, at the end of our greetings, we have a feature left among us. When at length they are ended—

"Well," say I, studiedly, with a long sigh of content, staring from one countenance to another, with a broad grin on my own. "Well!" and though I have been away *four* weeks, and been to foreign parts, and dined at *table d'hôtes* and seen Crucifixions and Madonnas, and seem to have more to tell than could be crowded into a closely-packed twelvemonth of talk, this is all I can find to say.

"Well," reply they, nor do they seem to be much richer in conversation than I.

Bobby is the first to regain the use of his tongue. He says, "My eye!" (oh, dear and familiar expletive, for a whole calendar month I have not heard you!)—"my eye! what a swell you are!"

Meanwhile Sir Roger stands aloof. If he *ever* thought of himself, he might be reasonably and equitably huffy at being so entirely neglected, for I will do them the justice to say that I think they have all utterly forgotten his existence: but, as he never does, I suppose he is not; at least there is only a friendly entertainment, and no hurt dignity, in the gentle strength of his face.

In the exuberance of my happiness, I have given him free leave to kiss Barbara and Tou Tou, but the poor man does not seem to be likely to have the chance.

"Are not you going to speak to the general?" I say, nudging Barbara. "You have never said 'How do you do?' to him."

Thus admonished, they recover their presence of mind and turn to salute him. There are no kissings, however, only some rather formal hand-shakings; and then Algy, as being possessed of the nearest approach to manners of the family, walks on with him. The other three adhere to me.

"Well," say I, for the third time, holding Barbara by one hand, and resting the other on Bobby's stout arm, dressed in cricketing-flannel, while Tou Tou *backs* before us with easy grace. "Well, and how is everybody? How is mother?"

"She is all right!"

"And HE? Is anybody in disgrace now? At least of course *somebody* is, but *who*?"

"In disgrace!" cries Bobby, briskly. "Bless your heart, no! we are

'Like the young lambs,
A sporting about *by* the side of their dams.'

In disgrace, indeed! we are 'Barbara, child,' and 'Algy, my dear fellow,' and 'Bobby, love.'"

"Bobby!" cries Tou Tou, in a high key of indignation at this monstrously palpable instance of unveracity, and nearly capsizing, as she speaks, into a rabbit-hole, which, in her backward progress—we are crossing the park—she has not perceived.

"Well," replies Bobby, candidly, "that last yarn may not be *quite* a fact, I own *that*; but I appeal to *you*, Barbara, is not it true *i' the main*? Are not we all 'good fellows,' and 'dear boys?'"

"I am thankful to say that we are," replies Barbara, laughing; "but how long we shall remain so is quite another thing."

"I have brought a present for him," say I, rather nervously; "do you think he will be pleased?"

"He will say that he very much regrets that you should have taken the trouble to waste your money upon *him*, as he did last birthday, when we exerted ourselves to lay out ten shillings and sixpence on that spectacle-case," answers Bobby, cheerfully.

"But what is it?"

"What is it?" cry Barbara and Tou Tou in a breath.

"It is a—a *traveling-bag*," reply I, with a little hesitation, looking imploringly from Barbara to Bobby. "Do you think he will like it?"

"A *traveling-bag!*" echoes Bobby; then, a little bluntly, "but he never travels!"

"No more he does!" reply I, feeling a good deal crestfallen. "I thought of that myself; it was not quite my own idea—it was the general's suggestion!"

"The general!" says Bobby, "whew—w!" (with a long whistle of intelligence)—"well, *he* ought to know what he likes and dislikes, ought not he? He ought to understand his tastes, being the same age, and having been at schoo—"

"Look!" cry I, hastily, breaking into the midst of these soothing facts, which are daily becoming more distasteful to me, and pointing to the windows of the house, which are all blazing in the sunset, each pane sending forth a sheaf of fire, as if some great and mighty feast were being held within. "I see you are having an illumination in honor of us."

"Yes," answers Bobby, kindly entering into my humor, "and the reason why father did not come to meet you at the gate was that he was busy lighting the candles."

My spirits are so dashed by the more implied than expressed disapproval of my brethren, that I resolve to defer the presentation of the bag till to-morrow, or perhaps—to-morrow being Sunday, always rather a dark day in the paternal calendar—till Monday.

Dinner is over, and, as it is clearly impossible to stay in-doors on such a night, we are all out again. The three elders—father, mother, and husband—sitting sedately on three rustic chairs on the dry gravel-walk, and we young ones lying about in different attitudes of restful ease, on rugs and cloaks that we have spread upon the dewy grass. We are not far off from the others, but just so far as that our talk should be out of ear-shot. In my own mind, I am not aware that Sir Roger would far rather be with *us*, listening to our quick gabble, and laughing with us at our threadbare jests, which are rewarded with mirth so disproportioned to their size, than interchanging sober talk with the friend of his infancy. Once or twice I see his gray eyes straying a little wistfully toward us, but he makes no slightest movement toward joining us. I should like, if I had my own way, to ask him to come to us, to ask him to sit on the rugs and make jokes too, but some sort of false shame, some sneaky shyness before the boys, hinders me. I am leaning my elbow on the soft fur of the rug, and my head on my hand, and am staring up at the stars, cool and throbbing, so like little stiletto-holes pricked in heaven's floor, as they steal out in systems and constellations on the night.

"There is dear old Charles Wain," say I, affectionately; "I never knew where to look for him in Dresden; *how* nice it is to be at home again!"

"Nancy!" says Algy, gravely, "do you know I have counted, and that is the *sixteenth* time that you have made that ejaculation since your arrival! Do you know—I am sorry to have to say it—that it sounds as if you had not enjoyed your honey-moon very much?"

"It sounds quite wrong, then," cry I, coming down from the stars, and speaking rather sharply. "I enjoyed it immensely; yes, *immensely!*"

I say this with an emphasis which is calculated to convince not only everybody else, but even myself.

"Come, now," cries Bobby, who is farthest off from me, and, to remedy this disadvantage, begins to travel quickly, in a sitting posture, along the rugs toward me, "tell the truth—*gospel* truth, mind!—the truth, the whole truth, and nothing but the truth, so help you, God. Would you like to be setting off on it over again, to-morrow morning?"

"Of course not," reply I, angrily; "what a silly question! Would *any* one like to begin *any thing* over again, just the very minute that they had finished it? You might as well ask me would I like to have dinner over again, and begin upon a fresh plate of soup."

No one is convinced.

"When *I* marry," continues Bobby, lying flat on his back, with his hands clasped under his head (we all laugh)—"when *I* marry, no one shall succeed in packing *me* off to foreign parts, with my young woman. I shall take her straight home, as if I was not ashamed of her, and we will have a *dance*, and make a clean sweep of our own cake."

"Nancy!" cries Tou Tou, innocently, joining in the conversation for the first time, "*did* any one take him for your *grandfather*, as the Brat said they would?"

"Of course not!" cry I, crossly, making a spiteful lunge, as I speak, at a *startle-de-buz*, which has lumbered booming into my face. "Who on earth supposed they would *really*?"

Tou Tou collapses, with a hazy impression of having been snubbed, and there is a moment's silence. A faint, fire-like flush still lingers in the west—all that is left of the dazzling pageant that the heavens sent to welcome me home. I am looking toward it—away from my brothers and sisters—away from everybody—across the indistinct garden-beds—across the misty park, and the dark tree-tops, when a voice suddenly brings me back.

"Nancy, child!" it says, "is not it rather damp for you? Would you mind putting *this* on?"

I look up in a hurry, and see Sir Roger stooping over me, with an outspread cloak in his hands.

"Oh, thank you!" cry I, hurriedly, reddening—I do not quite know why—and with that same sort of sneaky feeling, as if the boys were laughing; "I am not one much apt to catch cold—none of us are—but I will, if you like."

So saying, I drew it round my shoulders. Then he goes, *in a minute*, without a second's lingering, back to the gravel-walk, to his wicker-chair, to grave, dry talk, to the friend of his infancy! I have an uncomfortable feeling that there is a silent and hidden laugh among the family.

"Barbara, my treasure!" says Algy, presently, in a mocking voice, "*might* I be allowed to offer you our umbrella, and a pair of goloshes to defend you from the evening dews?"

"Hush!" cries Barbara, gently pushing him away, and stretching out her hand to me. She is the only one that understands. (Oh, why, *why* did I ever laugh at him with them? What is there to laugh at in him?)

"My poor Barbara!" continues Algy, in a tone of affected solicitude. "If you had not a tender brother to look after you, your young limbs might be cramped with rheumatism, and twitched with palsy, before any one would think of bringing *you* a cloak."

"Wait a bit!" say I, recovering my good-humor with an effort, reflecting that it is no use to be vexed—that they *mean* nothing—and that, lastly, *I have brought it on myself!*

"Wait for *what?*" asks Barbara, laughing. "Till Toothless Jack has grown used to his new teeth?"

"By-the-by," cries Bobby, eagerly, "that was since you went away, Nancy: he has set up a stock of *new* teeth—*beauties*—like Orient pearl—he wore them in church last Sunday for the first time. We tell Barbara that he has bought them on purpose to propose in. Now, do not you think it looks *promising?*"

"We do not mean, however," says Algy, lighting a cigar, "to let Barbara go *cheap!* Now that we have disposed of you so advantageously, we are beginning to be rather ambitious even for *Tou Tou.*"

"We think," says Bobby, giving a friendly but severe pull to our youngest sister's outspread yellow locks, "that Tou Tou would adorn the *Church*. Bishops have mostly *thin* legs, so it is to be presumed that they admire them: we destine Tou Tou for a bishop's lady!"

Hereupon follows a lively fire of argument between Bobby and his sister; she protesting that she will *not* espouse a bishop, and he asseverating that she shall. It lasts the best part of a quarter of an hour, and ends by reducing Tou Tou to tears.

"But come," says Algy, taking his cigar out of his mouth, throwing his head back, and blowing two columns of smoke out of his nose, "let us take up our subject again where we dropped it. I should be really glad if I could get you to own that you and *he*"—(indicating my husband by a jerk of his head)—"grew rather sick of each other! Whether you own it or not, I know you *did*; and it would give me pleasure to hear it. You need not take it personally. I assure you that it is no slur upon him—*everybody* does. I have talked to lots of fellows who have gone through it, and they all say the same."

"Nancy!" says Bobby, abandoning, at length, his persecution of Tou Tou, and pretending not to hear her last persevering assertion of her determination not to be episcopally wed—"tell the truth, and shame the devil. It would be different if we were strangers, but *we* that have sported with you since you wore frilled trousers and a bib—come now—did you, or did you not, kneel three times a day, like the prophet Daniel, looking eastward or westward, or whichever way it *did* look, and yearn for us, and Jacky, and the bun-loaf—come, now?"

"Well, yes," say I, reluctantly making the admission. "I do not say that I did not! Of course, after having been used to you all my life, it would have been very odd if I had not missed you rather badly; but that is a very different thing from being *sick of him!*"

"Well, we will not say *sick,*" returns Algy, with the air of one who is making a handsome concession, "it is a disagreeable, bilious expression, but it would be useless to try and convince me that *any* human affection could stand the wear and tear of twenty-eight whole days of an absolute duet and not be rather the worse for it!"

"But it was *not* an absolute duet," cry I, raising my voice a little, and speaking with some excitement; "you are talking about what you do not know! you are quite wrong."

"Well, it is not the first time in my life that I have been that," he says, philosophically; "but come—who did you the Christian office of interrupting it? tell us."

"I told you in my letters," say I, rather petulantly. "I certainly mentioned—yes, I know I did—we happened at Dresden to fall in with a friend of the general's—at least, a person he knew."

"A person he knew? What kind of a person? Man or woman?"

"Man."

"Old or young?"

"Young."

"Ugly or pretty?"

"Pretty," answer I, laughing. "Ah! what a rage he would be in, if he could hear such an epithet applied to him!"

"A young, well-looking, man-friend!" says Algy, slowly recapitulating all my admissions as he lies gently puffing on the rug beside me. "Well?"

"*Well!*" echo I, rather snappishly. "Nothing! only that I wanted to show you that it was not quite such a *duet* as you imagined! Of course—Dresden is not a big place—of course we met very often, and went here and there together."

"And where was Sir Roger meanwhile?"

"Sir Roger was there, too, of course," reply I, still a little crossly, "except once or twice—certainly not more than twice—he said he did not feel inclined to come, and so we went without him."

"You left him at home, in fact!" says Algy, with a rather malicious smile, "out of harm's way, while you and the young friend marauded about the town together; it must have been very lively for him, poor man! Oh, fie! Nancy, fie!"

"We did not do any thing of the kind," cry I, now thoroughly vexed and uncomfortable. "I wish you would not misunderstand things on purpose! there is not any fun in it! *Both* times I *wanted* him to come! I *asked* him particularly!"

"And, if I may make so bold as to inquire," asks Bobby, striking in, "how did the young friend call himself? What was his name?"

"Musgrave," reply I, shortly. "Frank Musgrave!" for the stream of my conversation seems dried.

"Was he *nice*? Should *we* like him?" ask Tou Tou, who has recovered her equanimity, dried her tears, and forgotten the bishop.

"He was nice *to look at!*" reply I cautiously.

"That is a very different thing!" says Barbara, laughing. "But was he nice in himself?"

I reflect.

"No," say I, "I do not think he was: at least, he wanted a great deal of alteration."

"As I have no doubt that you told him," says Algy, with a smile.

"I dare say I did," reply I, distantly, for I am not pleased with Algy.

A little pause.

"I think he *was* nice, too, *in a way*," say I, rather compunctiously. "I used to tell him about all of you, and—I dare say it was pretense—but he *seemed* to like to hear about you! When I came away, he sent his love to Barbara; he would not send any messages to you boys—he said he hated boys!"

"Humph!"

Another short silence. The elders have gone in to tea. Through the windows, I see the lamplight shining on the tea-cups.

"Algy!" say I, in a rather low voice, edging a little nearer to where he lies gracefully outspread, "you did not mean it, *really*? You do not think I—I—I—*neglected* the general, do you?—you do not think I—I—*liked* to be away from him?"

"My lady!" replies he, teasingly, "I *think* nothing! I only know what your ladyship was good enough to tell me!"

Then we all get up, shoulder our rugs, and walk in.

CHAPTER XVI

Well, no one will deny that Sunday comes after Saturday; and it was Saturday evening, when the heavens painted themselves with fire, and the sun lit up all the house-windows to welcome us home. Sunday is not usually one of our blandest days, but we must hope for the best.

"General," say I, standing before him, dressed for morning church, after having previously turned slowly round on the point of my toes, to favor him with the back view of as delightful a bonnet, and as airily fresh and fine a muslin gown, as ever young woman said her prayers in—"by-the-by, do you like my calling you general?"

"At least I understand who you mean by it," he says, a little evasively; "which, after all, is the great thing, is not it?"

"It is my own invention," say I, rather proudly; "nobody put it into my head, and nobody else calls you by it, do they?"

"Not now."

"*Not now?*" cry I, surprised; "but did they ever?"

"Yes," he says, "for about a year, most people did; I was general a year before my brother died."

"*Your brother died?*" cry I, again repeating his words, and arching my eyebrows, which have not naturally the slightest tendency toward describing a semicircle. "What! *you* had a brother, too, had you? I never knew that before."

"Did you think *you* had a monopoly of them?" laughing a little.

"So you were not 'Sir' always?"

"No more than *you* are," he answers, smiling. "No, I was not born in the purple; for thirty-seven years of my life I earned my own bread—and rather dry bread too."

"You do not say so!" cry I, in some astonishment.

"If I had come here seven years ago," he says, taking both my pale yellow hands in his light gray ones, and looking at me with eyes which seem

darker and deeper than usual under the shade of the brim of his tall hat—
"by-the-by, you would have been a little girl then—as little as Tou Tou—"

"Yes," interrupt I, breaking in hastily; "but, indeed, I never was a bit like her, never. I *never* had such legs—ask the boys if I had!"

"I did not suppose that you had," he answers, bursting into a hearty and most unfeigned laugh! "but" (growing grave again), "Nancy, suppose that I had come here then! I should have had no shooting to offer the boys—no horses to mount Algy—no house worth asking Barbara to—"

"No more you would!" say I, too much impressed with surprise at this new light on Sir Roger's past life to notice the sort of wistfulness and inquiry that lurks in his last words; then, after a second, perceiving it: "And you think," say I, loosing my hands from his, and growing as pink as the delicate China rose-bud that is peeping round the corner of the trellis in at the window, "that there would not have been as much inducement *then* for me to propose to you, as there was in the present state of things!"

I am laughing awkwardly as I speak; then, eagerly changing the conversation, and rushing into another subject: "By-the-by, I had something to say to you—something quite important—before we digressed."

"Yes?"

"O general!" taking hold of the lapel of his coat, and looking up at him with appealing earnestness, "do you know that I have made up my mind to give *him* the *bag* to-day! it is no use putting off the evil day—it *must* come, after supper—they all say *after supper!*"

"Yes?"

"Well, I want you to talk to him *all day*, and get him into a good-humor by then, if you can, that is all!"

"*That is all!*" repeats my husband, with the slightest possible ironical accent. Then we go to church. It is too near to drive, so we all walk. The church-yard elms are out in fullest leaf above our heads. There are so many leaves, and they are so close together, that they hide the great brown rooks' nests. They do not hide the rooks themselves. It would take a good deal to do that. Dear pleasant-spoken rooks, talking so loudly and irreverently about their own secular themes—out-cawing the church-bells, as we pace by, devout and smart, to our prayers. Last time I walked up this path, it was hidden with red cloth, and flowers were tumbling under my feet. Ah! red cloth comes but once in a lifetime. It is only the queen who lives in an atmosphere of red cloth and cut flowers.

We are in church now. The service is in progress. Can it be only *five* Sundays ago that I was standing here as I am now, watching all the little well-known incidents? Father standing up in frock-coat and spectacles, keeping a sharp lookout over the top of his prayer-book, to see *how* late the servants are. The ill-behaved charity-boys emulously trying who shall make the hind-legs of his chair squeak the loudest on the stone floor. Toothless Jack leering distantly at Barbara from the side aisle. Something apparently is amusing him. He is smiling a little. I see his teeth. They, at least, are new. *They* were not here five weeks ago. The little starved curate—the one who tore his gloves into strips—loses his place in the second lesson, and madly plunges at three different wrong verses in succession, before he regains the thread of his narrative.

We have come to the sermon. The text is, "I have married a wife, and therefore I cannot come." No sooner is it given out than Algy, Bobby, and Tou Tou, all look at me and grin; but father, who has a wily way of establishing himself in the corner of the pew, so as to have a bird's-eye view of all our demeanors, speedily frowns them down into a preternatural gravity. Ah, why *to-day*, of all days, did they laugh? and why *to-day*, of all days, did the servants file noisily in, numerous and out of breath, in the middle of the psalms? I tremble when I think of the bag.

Well, who will may laugh again now: we are out in the sunshine, with the church-yard grass bowing and swaying in the wind, and the little cloud-shadows flying across the half-effaced names of the forgotten dead, who lie under their lichen-grown tombs.

"Did you see his *teeth*?" asks Tou Tou, joining me with a leap, almost before I am outside the church-porch.

"They are not comfortable yet," remarks Bobby, gravely, as he walks beside me carrying my prayer-book. "I could see that: he was taking them out, and putting them in again, with his tongue all through the Litany."

"When once he has secured Barbara, I expect that they will go back with the box for good and all—eh, Barbara?" say I, laughing, as I speak; but Barbara is out of ear-shot. She is lingering behind to shake hands with the curate, and ask all the poor old people after their diseases. *I* never can recollect clearly *who* has *what*. I always apportion the rheumatism wrongly, but *she* never does. There she stands just by the church-gate, with the little sunny lights running up and down upon her snow-white gown, shaking each grimy old hand with a kind and friendly equality.

The day rolls by; afternoon service; walk round the grounds; early dinner (we always embitter our lives on Sundays by dining at *six*, which does the servants no good, and sours the tempers of the whole family); then prayers. Prayers are always immediately followed by that light refection which we call supper.

As the time approaches, my heart sinks imperceptibly lower in my system than the place where it usually resides.

"Be ready, Sister Nancy,
For the time is drawing nigh,"

says Algy, solemnly, putting his arm round my shoulders, as, the prayer-bell having rung, we set off for the wonted justicing-room.

"Have a pull at my flask," suggests Bobby, seriously; "there is some cognac left in it since the day we fished the pool. It would do you all the good in the world, and, if you took *enough*, you would feel able to give him *ten* bags, or, indeed, throw them at his head at a pinch."

"Have you got it?" say I, faintly, to the general, who at this moment joins us.

"Yes, here it is."

"But what will you do with it *meanwhile*?" cry I, anxiously; "he must not see it *first*."

"Sit upon it," suggests Algy, flippantly.

"Hang it round his neck while he is at prayers," bursts out Bobby, with the air of a person who has had an illumination; "you know he always pretends to have his eyes shut."

"And at 'Amen,' he would awake to find himself famous," says Algy, pseudo-pompously.

But this suggestion, although I cannot help looking upon it as ingenious, I do not adopt.

Prayers on Sunday are a much *finer* and larger ceremonial than they are on week-days. In the first place, instead of a few of the church prayers quickly pattered, which are ended in five minutes, we have a whole long sermon, which lasts twenty. In the second place, the congregation is so much greater. On week-days it is only the in-door servants; on Sundays it is the whole staff—coachman, grooms, stablemen. I think myself that it is more in the nature of a *parade*, to insure that none of the establishment are out *sweethearting*, than of a religious exercise. Usually I am delighted when the sermon is ended. Even Barrow or Jeremy Taylor would sound dull and stale if fired off in a flat, fierce monotone, without emphasis or modulation. To-night, at every page that turns, my heart declines lower and lower down. It is ended now; so is the short prayer that follows it. We all rise, and father stands with his hawk-eyes fixed on the servants, as they march out, *counting* them. The upper servants are all right; so are the housemaids, cookmaids, and lesser scullions. Alas! alas! there is a helper wanting.

Having listened to and *disbelieved* the explanation of his absence, father leads the way into supper, but the little incident has taken the bloom off his suavity.

Sir Roger has deposited the bag—still wrapped in its paper coverings—on a chair, in a modest and unobtrusive corner of the dining-room, ready for presentation. He did this just before prayers. As we enter the room, father's eyes fall on it.

"What is *that*?" he cries, pointing with his forefinger, and turning severely to the boys. "How many times have I told you that I will not have parcels left about, littering the whole place? Off with it!"

"If you please, father," say I, in a very small and starved voice, "it is not the boys', it is *mine*."

"*Yours*, is it?" with a sudden change of tone, and return to amenity. "Oh, all right!" (Then, with a little accent of sudden jocosity)—"One of your foreign purchases, eh?"

We sit round the snowy table, in the pleasant light of the shaded lamps, eating chicken-salad, and abasing and rifling the great red pyramids of strawberries and raspberries, but talking not much. We young ones never *can* talk out loud before father. He has never heard our voices raised much above a whisper. I do not think he has an idea what fine, loud, Billingsgate voices his children *really* have. He has said grace—we always have a longer, *gratefuller* grace than usual on Sundays—and has risen to go.

"Now for it!" cries Bobby, wildly excited, and giving me an awful dig in the ribs with his elbow.

"Shall I get it?" asks the general, in an encouraging whisper. "Cheer up, Nancy! do not look so *white*! it is all right."

He rises and fetches it, slips it quickly out of its coverings, and puts it into my hand. Father has reached the door, I run after him.

"Father!" cry I, in a choked and trembling voice. "Stop!"

He turns with the handle in his grasp, and looks at me in some surprise.

"Father!" cry I, beginning again, and holding my gift out nervously toward him, "here's—here's—here's a *bag*!"

This is my address of presentation. I hear the boys tittering at the table behind me—a sound which, telling me how ill I am speeding, makes my confusion tenfold worse. I murmur, helplessly and indistinctly, something about his never traveling, and my knowing that fact—and having been always sure that he would hate it—and then I glance helplessly round with a wild idea of flight. But at the same moment an arm of friendly strength comes round my shoulders—a friendly voice sounds in my buzzing ears.

"James," it says, simply and directly, "she has brought you a present, and she is afraid that you will not care about it."

"A *present!*" echoes my father, the meaning of the inexplicable object which has suddenly been thrust into his grasp beginning to dawn upon him. "Oh, I see! I am sure, my dear Nancy"—with a sort of embarrassed stiffness that yet means to be gracious—"that I am extremely obliged to you, extremely; and though I regret that you should have wasted your money on me—yet—yet—I assure you, I shall always prize it very highly."

Then he goes out rather hastily. I return to the supper-table.

"Shake hands!" cries Algy, pouring me out a glass of claret. "*Now*, perhaps, you have some faint idea of what *I* felt when I had to return thanks for the bridesmaids."

"Nancy!" cries Bobby, holding out the fruit to which he alludes, and speaking in a wobbly, quivering voice, with a painfully *literal* imitation of my late address, "here's—here's—here's a *peach!*"

But I am burying my face in Sir Roger's shoulder, like a shy child.

"I *like* you!" I say, creeping up quite close to him. "You were the only one that came to help me. If it had not been for *you*, I should be there still!"

CHAPTER XVII

The bag-affair is quite an old one now—a fortnight old. The bag itself has, I believe, retired into the decent privacy of a cupboard, nor is it much more likely to reissue thence than was one of the frail nuns built into the wall in the old times likely to come stepping out again. Bobby has at length ceased to offer me every object which it devolves upon him to hand me, with a quavering voice and a prolonged stammer, since, though I was at first excellently vulnerable by this weapon of offense, I am now becoming *hornily* hard and indifferent to it. We have stepped over the boundaries of June into July.

Yes, June has gone to look for all its dead brothers, wherever—since they say nothing is ever really lost—they lie with their stored sweets. To me, this has been as merry and good a June as any one of my nineteen.

Sir Roger is beginning to talk of going home—*his* home, that is—but rather diffidently and tentatively, as if not quite sure whether the proposal will meet with favor in my eyes. He need not be nervous on this point. I, too, am rather anxious and eager to see my house—*my* house, if you please!—I, who have never hitherto possessed any larger residence than a doll's house, whose whole front wall opened at once, giving one an improbably simultaneous view of kitchen-range, best four-poster, and drawing-room chairs. I have, it is true, seen photographs of my new house, photographs of its east front, of its west front—photographs, in its park, of the great old cedar; in its gardens, of its woody pool—but, to tell you the truth, I want to see *it*. I have already planned a house-warming, and invited them all to it, a house-warming in which—oh, absurd!—*I* shall sit at the head of the table, and father and mother only at the sides—*I* shall tell the people who they are to take in to dinner, and nod my head from the top when dessert is ended.

To-day I am going to write and secure the Brat's company—that is, later in the day—but now it is quite, *quite* early, even the letters have not come in. We have all—viz., the boys, the girls, and I—risen (in pursuance of a plan made overnight) preternaturally early, almost as early as I did on my wedding-morning, and are going out to gather mushrooms in the meadow, by the river. Indignation against the inhabitants of the neighboring town is what has torn us from our morning dreams, the greedy townsfolk, by whom, on every previous occasion, we have found our meadow rifled before we could reach it. To-day we shall, at least, meet them on equal terms. We are all rather gapy at first, more especially Algy, who has deferred the making of the greater part of his toilet till his return, looks disheveled, and sounds grumbling. But before long both gapes and grumbles depart.

Who would see the day when he is old, and stale, and shabby, when, like us, they could come out to meet him as he walks across the meadow with a mantle of dew wrapped round him, and a garland of paling rose-clouds, that an hour ago were crimson, about his head?

The place toward which we tend is at some little distance, and our road thither leads through all manner of comely rustic places, flowered fields, where the buttercups crowd their little varnished cups, and the vigilant ox-eyes are already wakefully staring up from among the grass-spears; a little wood; a deep and ruddy-colored lane, along whose unpruned hedges straggle the riches of the wild-rose, most delicately flushed, as if God in passing had called her very good, and she had reddened at his praise; where the honey-suckle, too, is holding stilly aloft the open cream-colored trumpets and closed red trumpet-buds of her heaven-sweet crown.

In an instant Tou Tou is scrawling and scrambling like a great spider up the steep bank: in an instant more she is tugging, tearing, devastating; while the faint petals that no mightiest king can restore, but that any infant with a touch can destroy, are showering in scented ruin around her. It gives me a pain to see it, as if I saw some sentient thing in agony. I think I feel, with Walter Savage Landor—

> "I never pluck the rose; the violet's head
> Hath shaken with my breath upon its bank
> And not reproached me: the ever-sacred cup
> Of the pure lily hath between my hands
> Felt safe, unsoiled, nor lost one grain of gold."

"You will have your basket filled before we get there," I say, remonstrating, but she does not heed me.

Hot and scratched—at least I am glad that in their death-pain they were able to scratch her—she still tugs and mauls. I walk on. We reach the meadow. Well, at least *to-day* we are in time. It has the silence and solitude of the dawn of Creation's first still day, broken only by the sheep that are cropping

> "The slant grass, and daisies pale."

The slow, smooth river washes by, sucking in among the rushes. Our footsteps show plainly shaped as we step along through the hoary dew.

We separate—going one this way, one that—and, in silence and gravity, pace with bent heads and down-turned eyes through the fine, short grass. Excitement and emulation keep us dumb, for let who will—*blasé* and used up—deny it, but there is an excitement, wholesome and hearty, in *seeking*, and a joy pure and unadulterated in finding, mushrooms in a probable field in the hopeful morning; whether the mushroom be a patriarch whose gills are browned with age, and who is big enough to be an umbrella for the fairy people, or a little milk-white button, half hidden in daisies and trefoil. Sometimes a cry of rage and anguish bursts from one or other of us who has been the dupe of a puff-ball family, and who is satiating his or her revenge by stamping on the deceiver's head, and reducing its fair, round proportions to a flat and fleshy pulp. We search long and diligently, and our efforts are blessed with an unwonted success. By the time that the sun has attained height enough in the heavens to make his power tyrannically felt, our baskets are filled. Tou Tou has to throw away her wild-roses, limp and flaccid, into the dust of the lane. We walk home, singing, and making poor jokes, as is our wont. As we draw near the house with joyful foretastes of breakfast in our minds, with redly-flushed cheeks and merry eyes, I see Sir Roger leaning on the stone balustrade of the terrace, looking as if he were watching for us, and, indeed, no sooner does he catch sight of us, than he comes toward us.

"Do you like mushrooms?" cry I, at the top of my voice, long before I have reached him, holding up my basket triumphantly. "See, I have got the most of anybody, except Tou Tou!"

I have met him by the end of this sentence.

"Do you like mushrooms?" I repeat, lifting the lid, and giving him a peep into the creamy and pink-colored treasures inside, "oh, you *must*! if you do not, I shall have a *divorce*! I could not bear a difference of opinion upon such a subject."

I have never given him time to speak, and now I look with appealing laughter into his silent face.

"Why, what is the matter?" I cry, with an abrupt change of tone. "What has happened? How odd you look!"

"Nothing has happened," he answers, trying to smile, but I see that it is quite against the grain, "only that I have had some not very pleasant news."

"It is not any thing about—about the *Brat*!" cry I, stopping suddenly, seizing his arm with both hands, and turning, as I feel, extremely pale, while my thoughts fly to the only one of my beloveds that is out of my sight.

"About the *Brat*!" he echoes in surprise, "oh, dear no! nothing!"

"Then I do not much care *who* is dead?" I answer, unfeelingly, drawing a long breath; "he is the only person *out* of this house whose death would afflict me much, and I do not think that there is any one besides *us* that *you* are very devoted to, is there?"

"Why are you so determined that some one is *dead*?" he asks, smiling again, but this time a little more naturally; "is there nothing vexatious in the world but *death*?"

"Yes," say I, laughing, despite myself, as my thoughts revert to my late employment, "there are *puff-balls*!" — then, ashamed of having been flippant, and afraid of having been unsympathetic, I add hastily: "I wish you would tell me what it is! I am sure, *when I hear*, I shall be vexed too; but you see as long as I do not know what it is, I cannot, can I?"

"There is no time now," he says, glancing toward father, whose head appears through the dining-room windows. "See! they are going to breakfast!—afterward I will tell you—afterward—and child—" (putting his hands on my shoulders, and essaying to look at me with an altogether cheered and careless face,) "do not you worry your head about it!—eat your breakfast with an easy mind; after all, it is nothing very bad!—it could not be any thing *very* bad, as long as—." He stops abruptly, and adds hastily, "let us have a look at your mushrooms! well, you *have* a quantity!"

"Yes, have not I?" say I, triumphantly, "more than any of them, except Tou Tou—." Then, not quite satisfied with the impression our late talk has left upon me: "General!" say I, lowering my face and reddening, "I hope you do not think that I am *quite* a baby because I like childish things—gathering mushrooms—running about with the boys—talking to Jacky. I can understand serious things *too*, I assure you. I think I could enter into your trouble—I think, if you gave me the chance, that you would find that I could!"

Then a sort of idiotic false shame overtakes me, and without waiting for his answer I disappear.

CHAPTER XVIII

I meet Bobby retiring to the kitchen to cook his mushrooms himself. He invites me to join him, but I refuse. It is the first time in the annals of history that I was ever known to say no to such an offer. Bobby regards me with reproachful anger, and makes a muffled remark, the drift of which I understand to be that, though I may *pretend* not to be, I *am* grown fine, as he always said I should. To-day it seems to me as if breakfast would *never* end. It is one of our fixed laws that no one shall leave the table until father gives the signal by saying grace. Sometimes, when he is in one of his unfortunate moods, he keeps us all staring at our empty cups and platters for half an hour. To-day I watch with warm anxiety the progress downward of the tea in his cup. At last he has come to the grounds. He lays down the *Times*. We all joyfully half bow our heads, in expectation of the wonted "For what we have received," etc., but speedily and disappointedly raise them again.

"Jane, can you spare me another cup?" and reburies himself in a long leader. Behind the shelter of the great sheet, I make a hideous contortion across the table at Sir Roger, who has fallen with great docility into our ways, and is looking back at me now with that gentle, steadfast serenity which is the leading characteristic of his face, but which this morning is, I cannot help thinking, a good deal disturbed, hard as he is trying to hide it. There are, thank Heaven, no more false starts. Next time that he lays down the paper, we are all afraid to bend our heads, for fear that the movement shall break the charm, and induce him to send for a fourth cup—he has already had *three*—but no! release has come at last.

"For what we have received the Lord make us truly thankful!"

Almost before we have reached "thankful," there is a noise of several chairs pushed back. Before you could say "knife!" we are all out of the room. All but Sir Roger! In deference, I suppose, to the feelings of the friend of his infancy, and not to appear *too* anxious to leave him—Sir Roger ought to have married Barbara, they two are always thinking of other people's feelings—he delays a little, and indeed they emerge together and find me sitting on one of the uncomfortable, stiff hall-chairs, on which nobody ever sits. To my dismay, I hear father say something about the chestnut colt's legs, and I know that another delay is in store for me. Sir Roger comes over to me, and takes his wide-awake from the stand beside me.

"We are going to the stables," he says, patting my shoulder.

I make a second hideous face. Often have I been complimented by the boys, on the flexibility of my features.

"I shall be back in ten minutes," he says, in a low voice; "will you wait for me in the morning-room?"

"I suppose I must," say I, reluctantly, with a disgusted and disappointed drawing down of the corners of my mouth.

Ten minutes pass; twenty, five-and-twenty! Still he has not come back. I walk up and down the room; I look out the window at the gardeners rolling the grass; I rend a large and comely rose into tatters, while all manner of unpleasant possibilities stalk along in order before my mind's eye. Perhaps Tempest is burnt down. Perhaps some bank, in which he has put all his money, has broken. Perhaps he has found out that his brother is not *really* dead after all! I dismiss this last *worst* suggestion as improbable. The door opens, and he enters.

"Here you are!" I cry, making a joyous rush at him. "I thought you were never coming! Please, is *that* your idea of ten minutes?"

"I could not help it," he answers; "he kept me talking; I could not get away any sooner."

"Why did you go?" say I, dutifully. "Why did not you say, when he asked you, 'No, I will not?' He would have done it to you as soon as look at you."

"That would have been so polite to one's host and father-in-law, would not it?" he answers, a little ironically. "After all, Nancy, where is the use of vexing people for nothing?"

"Not *people* generally," reply I, still chafed; "but I *should* like some one who was not his child, and in whom it would not be disrespectful, to pay him out for keeping us all as he did this morning; he knew as well as possible that we were dying to be off; *that* was why he had that last cup: he did not *want* it any more than I did. He did not drink it; did not you see? he left three-quarters of it."

Sir Roger does not answer, unless a slight shrug and a passing his hand across his face with a rather dispirited gesture be an answer. I feel ashamed of my petulance.

"Do you feel inclined to tell me about your ill news?" I say, gently, going over to him, and putting my hand on his shoulder. "I have been making so many guesses as to what it can be?"

"Have you?" he says, looking up. "I dare say. Well, I will tell you. Do you remember—I dare say you do not—my once mentioning to you that I had some property in the West Indies—in Antigua?"

I nod.

"To be sure I do; I recollect I had not an idea where Antigua was, and I looked out for it at once in Tou Tou's atlas."

"Well, a fortnight—three weeks ago—it was when we were in Dresden, I had a letter telling me of the death of my agent out there. I knew nothing about him personally—had never seen him—but he had long been in my poor brother's employment, and was very highly thought of by him."

"*Poor* brother!" think I; "well, thank Heaven! at least *he* has not revived; he would not be 'poor' if he had," but I say only, "Yes?" with a delicately interrogative accent.

"And to-day comes this letter"—(pulling one out of his pocket)—"telling me that now that his affairs have been looked into, they are found to be in the greatest confusion—that he has died bankrupt, in fact; and not only *that*, but that he has been cheating me right and left for years and years, appropriating the money which ought to have been spent on the estate to his own uses; and, as misfortunes never come single, I also hear"—(unfolding the sheet, and glancing rather disconsolately over it)—"that there has been a hurricane, which has destroyed nearly all the sugar-canes."

The thought of *Job* and his successive misfortunes instantly occurs to me—the Sabeans, the Chaldeans, the great wind from the wilderness—but being a little doubtful as to his example having a very consoling effect, with some difficulty, and at the cost of a great pressure exercised on myself, I abstain from mentioning him.

"To make a long story short," continues Sir Roger, "and not to bother you with unnecessary details—"

"But indeed they would not bother me," interrupt I, eagerly, putting my hand through his arm, and turning my face anxiously up to him; "I should *enjoy* hearing them. I wish you would not think that all sensible, sober things *bother* me."

"My dear," he says, gently pinching my cheek, "I think nothing of the kind, but I know that not all the explanations in the world will alter the result, which is, that I shall not get a farthing from the property *this* year, and very likely not *next* either."

"You do not say so!" cry I, trying to impart a tragic tone to my voice, and only hoping that my face *looks* more distressed and aghast than it feels.

To tell you the truth, I am mightily relieved. At this period of my history, money troubles seem to me the lightest and airiest of all afflictions. I have sat down, and Sir Roger is walking up and down, with a restlessness unlike his usual repose; on his face there is a vexed and thwarted look, that is unfamiliar to me. The old parrot sits in the sun, outside his cage, scratching his head, and chuckling to himself. Tou Tou's voice comes ringing from the garden. It has a tone of mingled laughter and pain, which tells me that she is undergoing severe and searching discipline at the hands of Bobby.

"I suppose," say I, presently, speaking with some diffidence, "that *that* is *all*. Of course I do not mean to say that it is not very bad, but is there nothing *worse*?"

"Is not it *bad enough*?" he asks, half laughing. "What did you expect?"

"You know," say I, still hesitatingly, "I have not an idea *how* well off you are; I mean, how much a year you have. Mercenary as I am" — (laughing nervously) — "I never thought of asking you; but I suppose, even if the earth were to open and swallow Antigua — even if there were no such things as West Indies — we should still have money enough to buy us bread and cheese, should not we?"

"Well, it is to be hoped so," he answers, a gleam of amusement flashing like a little sunshiny arrow across his vexation; "it would be a bad lookout for you and me, would not it, considering the size of our appetites, if we should not?"

A little pause. Tou Tou's voice again. The anguish has conquered the laughter, and is now mixed with a shrill treble wrath. Polly is alternately barking like Vick, and laughing with a quiet amusement at his own performance.

"Do you think," say I, still airing my opinion with timidity, as one that has no great opinion of their worth, "that it does one much good to be rich beyond a certain point? — that a large establishment, for instance, gives one much pleasure? I am sure it does not in *our* case; if you were to know the number of nails that the servants and their iniquities have knocked into mother's coffin — yes, and father's, too."

"Have they?" (a little absently). He is still pacing up and down restlessly — to and fro — along and across — he that is usually so innocent of fidget or fuss. "Nancy," he says, half seriously, half in rueful jest, "if you want a thing done, do yourself: mind that, all your life. I am a standing instance of the disadvantage of having let other people do it for me. The fact is, I ought to have gone out there long ago, to look after things myself."

"If you *had* been there, you could not have stopped the hurricane coming, any more than Canute could stop the waves," say I, filching a piece of history from "Little Arthur," and pushing it to the front.

He smiles.

"Not the hurricane—no; but the hurricane was the lesser evil. I might have done something to avert, or, at least, lessen the greater one. To tell the truth, I meant to have gone out there this spring—had, indeed, almost fixed upon a day for starting, when—*you* stopped me."

"*I!*"

"Yes," he says, pausing in his walk in front of me, and looking at me with a face full of sunshine, content, and laughter; a face whence hurricanes, West Indies, and agents have altogether fled; "you called me a '*beast*', and the expression startled me so much—I suppose from not being used to it—that it sent the West Indies, yes, and the East ones too, clean out of my head."

"I hope," say I, anxiously, "that you will never tell any one that I said *that*. They would think that I was in the habit of calling people '*beasts*', and indeed—*indeed*, I very seldom use so strong a word, *even* to Bobby."

"Well," he says, not heeding my request, not, I am sure, hearing it, and resuming his walk, "what is done cannot be undone, so there is no use whining about it, Nancy" (again stopping before me, and this time taking my face in his two hands). "Will you mind much, or will you not?—do you ever mind *any thing much*, I wonder?" (eagerly and wistfully scanning my face, as if trying to read my character through the mask of my pale skin, and small and unremarkable features). "Well, there is no help for it—as I did not go then, I must go now."

"Go!" repeat I, panting in horrid surprise, "go where?—to Antigua?"

"Yes, to Antigua."

No need now to dress my voice in the tones of factitious tragedy—no need to lengthen my face artificially. It feels all of a sudden quite a yard and a half long. Polly has stopped barking: he is now calling, "Barb'ra! Barb'ra!" in father's voice, and he hits off the pompous severity of his tone with such awful accuracy, that did not my eyes assure me to the contrary, I could swear that my parent was in the room.

After a moment I rise, throw my arms round Sir Roger, and lay my head on his breast—a most unwonted caress on my part, for we are not a couple by any means given to endearments.

"Do not go!" I say in a coaxing whisper, "do nothing of the kind!—stay at home!"

"And will *you* go instead of me?" he asks with a gentle irony, stroking, the while, my plaits as delicately as if he were afraid that they would *come off*, which indeed, *indeed*, they would not.

"By myself," say I, laughing, but not raising my head. "Oh! of course; nothing I should like better, and I should be so invaluable in mending the sugar-canes, and keeping the new agent on his P's and Q's, should not I?"

He laughs.

"Stay!" say I, again whispering, as being more persuasive; "where would be the use of going *now*? It would be shutting the stable-door after the steed was stolen, and—" (this in a still lower voice)—"we are beginning to get on so nicely, too."

"Beginning!" he echoes, with a half-melancholy smile, "only *beginning*? have not we always got on nicely?"

"And if we are poorer," continue I, insinuatingly, "I believe we shall get on better still. I am sure that poor people are fonder of one another than rich ones—they have less to distract them from each other."

I have now raised my head, and perceive that Sir Roger does not look very much convinced.

"But granting that poverty *is* better than riches, do you believe that it *is*, Nancy?—for my part I doubt it—for myself I will own to you that I have found it pleasant not to be obliged to look at sixpence upon both sides; but *that*," he says with straightforward simplicity, "is perhaps because I have not long been used to it—because once, long ago, I wanted money badly—I would have given my right hand for it, and could not get it!"

"What did you want it for?" cry I, curiously, pricking my ears, and for a moment forgetting my private troubles in the hope of a forthcoming anecdote.

"Ah! would not you like to know?" he says, playfully, but he does not explain: instead, he goes on: "Even granting that it is so, do you think it would be very manly to let a fine estate run to ruin, because one was too lazy to look after it? Do you think it would be quite *honest*—quite fair to those that will come after us?"

"*Those that will come after us!*" cry I, scornfully, making a face for the third and last time this morning. "And who are they, pray? Some sixteenth cousin of yours, I suppose?"

"Nancy," he says, gravely, but in a tone whose gentleness takes all harshness from the words, "you are talking nonsense, and you know as well as I do that you are!"

Then I know that I may as well be silent. After a pause:

"And when," say I, in as lamentable a voice as King Darius sent down among the lions in search of Daniel—"how soon, I mean, are we to set off?"

"*We!*" he cries, a sudden light springing into his eyes, and an accent of keen pleasure into his voice. "Do you mean to say that *you* thought of coming too?"

I look up in surprise.

"Do not wives generally go with their husbands?"

"But would you *like* to come?" he asks, seizing my hands, and pressing them with such unconscious eagerness, that my wedding-ring makes a red print in its neighbor-finger.

O friends, I wish to Heaven that I had told a lie! It would have been, I am sure, one of the cases in which a lie would have been justifiable—nay, praiseworthy, too. But, standing there, under the truth of his eyes, I have to be true, too.

"Like!" say I, evasively, casting down my eyes, and fiddling uneasily with one of the buttons of his coat, "it is hardly a question of '*like*,' is it? I do not imagine that you *like* it much yourself?—one cannot always be thinking of what one likes."

The pressure of his fingers on mine slackens; and, though, thanks to my wedding-ring, it was painful, I am sorry. After a minute:

"But you have not," say I, trying to speak in a tone of light and airy cheerfulness, "answered my question yet—how soon we must set off? You know what a woman always thinks of first—her *clothes*, and I must be seeing to my packing."

"The sooner the better," he answers, with a preoccupied look. "Not later than ten days hence!"

"*Ten days!*"

Again my jaw falls. He has altogether loosed my hands now, and resumed his walk. I sit down by the table, lean my elbows on it, and push my fingers through my hair in most dejected musing. Polly has been dressing himself; turning his head over his shoulder, and arranging his feathers with his aquiline nose. He has finished now, and has just given vent, in a matter-of-fact, unemotional voice, to an awful oath! There is the sound of brisk feet on the sunny gravel outside. Bobby's face looks in at the window—broad, sunburnt, and laughing.

"Well! what is up now?" cries he, catching a glimpse of my disconsolate attitude. "You look as if the fungi had disagreed with you!"

"Then appearances are deceitful," reply I, trying to be merry, "for they have not."

He has only glanced in upon us in passing: he is gone again now. I rebury my hands in my locks, which, instead of a highly-cultivated garden, I am rapidly making into a wilderness.

"I suppose," say I, in a tone which fitly matches the length of my face, "that Bobby will have got a ship before I come back; I hope they will not send him to any very unhealthy station—Hong-Kong, or the Gold Coast."

"I hope not."

"What port shall we sail from?"

"Southampton."

"And how long—about how long will the voyage be?"

"About seventeen days to Antigua."

"And how long"—(still in the same wretched and resignedly melancholy voice)—"shall we have to stay there?"

"It depends upon the state in which I find things?"

A good long pause. My elbows are growing quite painful, from the length of time during which they have been digging into the hard *marqueterie* table, and my hair is as wild as a red Indian's. *Ten* days! ten little galloping days, and then *seventeen* long, slow, monstrous ones! *Seventeen* days at sea! seventeen days and seventeen nights, too—do not let us forget that—of that deadly nausea, of that unspeakable sinking of all one's inside to the very depths of creation—of the smell of boiling oil, and the hot, sick, throbbing of engines!

"I hope," say I, in a voice so small that I hardly recognize it for my own, "that I shall not be *quite* as ill all the way as I was crossing from Calais to Dover; and the steward," continue I, in miserable meditation, "kept telling me all the while what a fine passage we were having, too!"

"So we were!"

Another pause. I am still thinking of the horrid theme; living over again my nearly-forgotten agonies.

"Do you remember," say I, presently, "hearing about that Lady Somebody—I forget her name—but she was the wife of one Governor-

General of India, and she always suffered so much from sea-sickness that she thought she should suffer less in a sailing-vessel, and so returned from India in one, and just as she came in sight of the shores of England *she died!*"

As I reach this awful climax, I open my eyes very wide, and sink my voice to a tragic depth.

"The moral is—" says Sir Roger, stopping beside me, laying his hand on my chair back, and regarding me with a mixture of pain and diversion in his eyes, "stick to steam!"

CHAPTER XIX

A heavy foot along the passage, a hand upon the door, a hatted head looking in.

"Roger," says father, in that laboriously amiable voice in which he always addresses his son-in-law, "sorry to interrupt you, but could you come here for a minute—will not keep you long."

"All right!" cries Sir Roger, promptly.

(How *can* he speak in that flippantly cheerful voice, with the prospect of seventeen days' sea before him?)

"Now, where did I put my hat, Nancy? did you happen to notice?"

"It is here," say I, picking it up from the window-seat, and handing it to him with lugubrious solemnity.

As he reaches the door, following father, he turns and nods to me with a half-humorous smile.

"Cheer up," he says, "it shall not be a sailing-vessel."

He is gone, and I return to my former position, and my former occupation, only that now—the check of Sir Roger's presence being removed—I indulge in two or three good hearty groans. To think how the look of all things is changed since this morning!

As we came home through the fields singing, if any one had given me three wishes, I should have been puzzled what to ask—and *now*! All the good things I am going to lose march in gloomy procession before my mind. *No house-warming!* It will have to be put off till we come back, and, by the time that we come back, Bobby will almost certainly have been sent to some foreign station for three or four years. And who knows what may happen before he returns? Perhaps—for I am in the mood when all adversities seem antecedently probable—he will *never* come back. Perhaps never again shall I be the willing victim of his buffets, never again shall I buffet him in return.

And the *sea*! It is all very fine for Sir Roger to take it so easily, to laugh and make unfeeling jokes at my expense! *He* does not lie on the flat of his back, surrounded by the horrid paraphernalia of sea-sickness. *He* walks up and down, with his hands in his pockets, smoking a cigar, and talking to the captain. *He* cares nothing for the heaving planks. The taste of the salt air gives *him* an appetite. An *appetite!* Oh, prodigious! I must say I think he might have been a *little* more feeling, might have expressed himself a *little* more sympathetically.

By dint of thinking over Sir Roger's iniquities on this head, I gradually work myself up into such a state of righteous indignation and injury against him, that when, after a longish interval, the door again opens to readmit him, I affect neither to see nor hear him, nor be in any way conscious of his presence. Through the chinks of my fingers, dolorously spread over my face, I see that he has sat down on the other side of the table, just opposite me, and that he is smiling in the same unmirthful, gently sarcastic way, as he was when he left me.

"Nancy," he says, "I have been thinking what a pity it is that I have not a *yacht!* We might have taken our own time then, and done it enjoyably—made quite a pleasure-trip of it."

I drop my hands into my lap.

"People's ideas of pleasure differ," I say, with trite snappishness.

"Yes," he answers, a little sadly, "no two people look at any thing in *quite* the same way, do they?—not even husband and wife."

"I suppose not," say I, still thinking of the steward.

"Do you know," he says, leaning his arms and his crossed hands on the table between us, and steadfastly regarding me, "that I never saw you look miserable before, never? I did not even know that you *could!*"

"I am not *miserable*," I answer, rather ashamed of myself, "that is far too strong a word! Of course I am a little disappointed." Then I mumble off into an indistinctness, whence the nouns "House—warming," "Bobby," "Gold Coast," crop out audibly.

"After all," he says, still regarding me, and speaking kindly, yet a little coldly too, "you need not look so woebegone. They say second thoughts are best, do not they? Well, I have been thinking second thoughts, and—I have altered my mind."

"You are going to stay at home?" cry I, at the top of my voice, jumping up in an ecstasy, and beginning to clap my hands.

"No," he says, gently, "not quite *that*, as I explained to you before, that is impossible: but—do not be downcast—something nearly as good. I am going to leave *you* at home!"

To leave me at home! My first feeling is one of irrepressible relief. No sea! no steward! no courtesying ship! no swaying waves after all! Then comes a quick and strong revulsion, shame, mortification, and pain.

"To—leave—me—at home!" I repeat slowly, hardly yet grasping the idea, "to—go—*without*—me!—by yourself?"

"By myself," he answers, gently. "You see, it is no *new* thing to me. I have been by myself for forty-seven years."

A quick, remorseful pain runs through my heart.

"But you are not by yourself any longer," I cry, eagerly. "Why do you talk as if you were? Do you count *me* for nothing?"

"For nothing?" he answers, smiling quietly. "I am glad of an excuse to be rid of you for a bit—that is it!"

"But *is* that it?" cry I, excitedly, rising and running round to him. "If you are sure of that—if you will *swear* it to me—I will not say another word. I will hold my tongue, and try to bear as well as I can, your having grown tired of me so soon—but—" speaking more slowly, and hesitating, "if—if—it is that you fancied—you thought—you imagined—that I did not *want* to come with you—"

"My dear," he says, laughing not at all bitterly, but with a genuine amusement, "I should have been even less bright than I am, if I had not gathered that much."

I sink down on a chair, and cover my face with my hands. My *attitude* is the same as it was ten minutes ago, but oh, how different are my feelings! What bitter repentance, what acute self-contempt, invade my soul! As I so sit, I feel an arm round my waist.

"Nancy," says Sir Roger, "it was ill-naturedly said; do not fret about it; you were not in the least to blame. I should not like you half so much—should not think nearly so well of you, if you had been willing to give up all your own people, to throw them lightly over, all of a sudden, for a comparative stranger, treble your age, too"—(with a sigh)—"like me."

He generously ignores the selfish fear of sea-sickness, of *personal* suffering, which had occupied the fore-front of my mind.

"It will be much, *much* better, and a far more sensible plan for both of us," he continues, cheerfully. "Where would be the use of exposing you to the discomfort and misery of what you hate most on earth for no possible profit? I shall not be long away, shall be back almost before you realize that I am gone, and meanwhile I should be far happier thinking of you merry, and enjoying yourself with your brothers and sisters at Tempest, than I should be seeing you bored and suffering, with no one but me to amuse you—you know, dear—" (smiling pensively); "do not be angry with me, it was no fault of yours; but you *did* grow rather tired of me at Dresden."

"I did not! I did not!" cry I, bursting into a passion of tears, and asseverating all the more violently because I feel, with a sting of remorse, that there is a tiny grain of truth—not so large a one as he thinks, but still a *grain* in his accusations. "It seemed rather *quiet* at first—I had always been used to such a noisy house, and I missed the boys' chatter a little, perhaps; but *indeed*, INDEED, that was all!"

"Was it? I dare say! I dare say!" he says, soothingly.

"You shall *not* leave me behind," say I, still weeping with stormy bitterness. "I *will not* be left behind! What business have you to go without me? Am I to be only a fair-weather wife to you? to go shares in all your pleasant things, and then—when any thing hard or disagreeable comes—to be left out. I tell you" (looking up at him with streaming eyes) "that I *will not*! I WILL NOT!"

"My darling!" he says, looking most thoroughly concerned, I do not fancy that crying women have formed a large part of his life-experience—"you misunderstand me! I will own to you, that five minutes ago I did you an injustice; but *now* I know, I am thoroughly convinced, that you would follow me without a murmur or a sulky look to the world's end—and" (laughing) "be frightfully sea-sick all the way; but" (kindly patting my heaving shoulder) "do you think that I want to be hampered with a little invalid? and, supposing that I took you with me, whom should I have to look after things at Tempest, and keep them straight for me against I come home?"

"I know what it is," I cry, passionately clinging round his neck, "you think I do not like you! I *see* it! twenty times a day, in a hundred things that you do and leave undone! but indeed, *indeed*, you never were more mistaken in all your life! I will own to you that I did not care *very* much about you at first. I thought you good, and kind, and excellent, but I was not *fond* of you; but *now*, every day, every hour that I live, I like you better! Ask Barbara, ask the boys if I do not! I like you ten thousand times better than I did the day I married you!"

"*Like* me!" he repeats a little dreamily, looking with a strong and bitter yearning into my eyes; then, seeing that I am going to asseverate, "for God's sake, child," he says, hastily, "do not tell me that you *love* me, for I know it is not true! you can no more help it than I can help caring for you in the idiotic, mad way, that I do! Perhaps, on some blessed, far-off day, you may be able to say so, and I to believe it, but not now!—*not now!*"

CHAPTER XX

With feet as heavy and slowly-dragging as those of some unwieldy old person, with drooped figure, and stained and swollen face, I enter the school-room an hour later to tell my ill-news.

"Enter a young mourner!" says Algy, facetiously, in unkind allusion to the gloom of my appearance, which is perhaps heightened by the black-silk gown I wear.

"What *is* up?" cries Bobby, advancing toward me with an overpowering curiosity, not unmixed with admiration, legible on his burnt face; "what *has* summoned those glorious sunset tints into your eyes and nose?"

"Which of Turner's pictures," says Algy, putting up his hand in the shape of a spy-glass to one eye, and critically regarding me through it, "is she so like in coloring? the 'Founding of Carthage,' or 'The Fighting Temeraire?'"

"Shame! shame!" cries Bobby, in a mock hortatory tone, trying to swell himself out to the shape and bulk of our fat rector, and to speak in his wheezy tone, "that a young woman so richly dowered with the good things of this life; a young woman with a husband and a deer-park in possession, and a house-warming in prospect—"

"But I have not," interrupt I, speaking for the first time, and with a snuffliness of tone engendered by much crying.

"Have not? have not *what*?"

"Have not a house-warming in prospect," reply I, with distinct malignity. A moment's silence. My bomb-shell has worked quite as much havoc as I expected.

"But where has it gone to since this morning?" asks Algy, looking rather blank.

"What do you mean?" cries Tou Tou, shrilly; "it was only last night that you were asking me for the Brat's address that you might invite him."

"And tell him to bring a judiciously-selected assortment of undergraduate friends with him," supplements Bobby, loudly.

"Yes," say I, sighing, "I know I did; but last night was last night."

"That throws a great deal of light on the matter, does it not?" says Algy, ironically.

"Nancy!" cries Bobby, seizing both my hands, and looking me in the face with an air of irritated determination, "if you do not *this moment* stop sighing like a windmill and tell us what is up, I will go to Sir Roger, hanged if I will not, and ask him what he means by making you cry yourself to a *jelly*!"

At this bold metaphor applied to my own appearance, the tears begin again to start to my eyes.

"Do not!" cry I, eagerly, catching at his wrists in detention, "it was not his fault! he could not help it; but" (mopping first one eye and then the other, and finishing by a dolorous blast on my nose) "but I am so disappointed, every thing is *so* changed, and I know I shall miss him *so* much!" I end with a break in my voice, and a long whimper.

"*Miss him!* miss whom?"

"The ge-general!" reply I, indistinctly, from the recesses of a drenched pocket-handkerchief.

"But what is going to happen to him? where is he going to? I wish that you would be a little more intelligible," cry they all, impatiently.

"He is going to the West Indies, to Antigua," reply I, lifting my face and speaking with a slow dejection.

"*To Antigua!*" cries Algy; "but what in the world is going to take him there?"

"Perhaps," says Bobby, in a loud aside to Tou Tou, "perhaps he has got another wife out there—a *black* one—and he thinks it is *her* turn now!"

Barbara says, "Hush!" and Tou Tou is beginning to embark on a long argument to prove that a man *cannot* have more than one wife at a time, when she is summarily *hustled* into silence, for I speak again.

"He has some property in the West Indies—I knew he had before—" (with a passing flash of pride in my superior information)—"I dare say you did not—and he has to go out there to look after it."

"*By himself?*"

"By himself, worse luck!" reply I, despondently, reinterring my countenance in my pocket-handkerchief.

"And you decline to accompany him? Well, I think you are about right!" says Algy, rising, lounging over to the empty hearth, and looking at his face with a glance of serious fondness in the glass that hangs above the mantel-shelf.

"I do nothing of the kind!" cry I, indignantly, "I have not the chance! he will not take me!"

I am not looking at him, nor, indeed, in his direction at all; but I am aware that Bobby is giving Tou Tou a private and severe nudge, which means "Attend! here is confirmation of my theory for you!" and that the idea of the hypothetical black lady is again traversing his ingenuous mind.

"I hope he will bring us some Jamaica ginger," he says, presently.

"I wish you would mention it, Nancy! the suggestion would come best from *you*, would not it?"

"And you are to be left *alone* at Tempest? Is that the plan?" asks Algy, turning his eyes from his own face, and fixing them on the less interesting object of mine.

It may be my imagination, but I cannot help fancying that there is a tone of slight and repressed exultation in his voice; and also that a look of hope and bright expectation is passing from one to another of the faces round me. All but Barbara's! Barbara always understands.

"*All alone?*" cries Tou Tou, opening her ugly little eyes to their widest stretch. "Nobody but the servants in the house with you? Will not you be very much afraid of *ghosts*?"

"She need never be alone, unless she chooses," says Bobby, winking with dexterous slightness at the others; "there is the beauty of having three kind little brothers!"

"The moment you feel *at all* lonely," says Algy, emphasizing his remarks by benevolent but emphatic strokes with his flat hand on my shoulder, "*send for us*! one of us is sure to be handy! If it will be any comfort to Sir Roger, I shall be most happy to promise him that I will keep *all* his horses in exercise next winter!"

"I am sorrier than I was before," says Bobby, reflectively, "that the heavy rains have drowned so many of the young birds."

"O Nancy!" cries Tou Tou, ecstatically clasping her hands, "*have* a Christmas-tree!"

"And a dance after it!" adds Bobby, beginning to whistle a waltz-tune.

"And Sir Roger's not being at home will be a good excuse for not asking father," cries Algy, catching the prevailing excitement.

"I will not have *one* of you!" cry I, rising with a face pale, as I feel with anger—with flashing eyes and a trembling voice, "not *one* of you shall enter his doors, except Barbara!—I *hate* you *all!*—you are all g—g—*glad* that he is going, and I—I never was so sorry for any thing in my life before!"

I end in a passion of tears. There is a silence of consternation on the late so jubilant assembly.

"'Times is changed,' says the dog's-meat man,"

remarks Bobby, presently, veiling his discomfiture in vulgarity, and launching into uncouth and low-lived rhyme:

"'Lights is riz,' says the dog's-meat man!"

CHAPTER XXI

However, not all the hot tears in the world—not all the swelled noses and boiled-gooseberry eyes avail to alter the case. Not even all my righteous wrath against the boys profits—and I do keep Bobby at arms'-length for a day and a half. No one who does not know Bobby understands how difficult such a course of proceeding is; for he is one of those people who ignore the finer shades of displeasure. The more delicately dignified and civilly frosty one is to him, the more grossly familiar and hopelessly, obtusely friendly is he. I have made several more efforts to change Sir Roger's decision, but in vain. He makes the case more difficult by laying his refusal chiefly on his own convenience; dilating on the much greater speed and ease with which he will be able to transact his business, if *alone*, than if weighted by a woman, and a woman's paraphernalia, and also on the desirability of having in me a *locum tenens* for himself at Tempest. But, in my soul, I know that both these are hollow pretenses to lighten the weight on my conscience.

"But," say I, with discontented demurring, "you have been away often before! how did Tempest get on *then*?"

He laughs.

"Very middling, indeed! last time I was away the servants gave a ball in the new ballroom—so my friends told me afterward, and the time before, the butler took the housekeeper a driving-tour in my T.-cart. I should not have minded *that* much—but I suppose he was not a very good whip, and so he threw down one of my best horses, and broke his knees!"

"Well, they *shall not* give a ball!" say I, resolutely, "but"—(in a tone of melancholy helplessness)—"they may throw down *all* the horses, for any thing *I* can do to prevent them! A horse's knees would have to be *very much broken* before I should perceive that they were!"

"You must get Algy to help you," he says, kindly. "It is an ill wind that blows nobody good, is not it? Poor boy!"—(laughing)—"You must not expect *him* to be very keen about my speedy return."

As he speaks, an arrow of animosity toward Algy shoots through my heart.

We are at Tempest—Sir Roger and I. It has been his wish to establish me there before his departure; and now it is the gray of the evening before his setting off, and we are strolling through the still park. Vick is racing, with idiotic ardor, through the tall green bracken, after the mottled deer, yelping with shrill insanity, and vainly imagining that she is going to overtake them. The gray rabbits are scuttling across the grass rides in the pale light: as I see them popping in and out of their holes, I cannot help thinking of Bobby. Apparently, Sir Roger also is reminded of him.

"Nancy," he says, looking down at me with a smile of recollected entertainment, "have you forgiven Bobby yet for leaving you sitting on the wall? I remember, in the first blaze of your indignation, you vowed that never should he fire a gun in your preserves!—do you still stick to it, or have you forgiven him?"

"*That* I have not!" cry I, heartily. "None of them shall shoot any thing! Why should they? Every thing shall be kept for you against you come back!"

He raises his eyebrows a little.

"Rabbits and all?"

"Rabbits and all!" reply I, firmly.

"And what will the farmers say?" asks Sir Roger, smiling.

I have not considered this aspect of the question, so remain silent. We walk on without speaking for some moments. The deer, in lofty pity for Vick, have stopped to allow her to get nearer to them. With their fine noses in the air, and their proud necks compassionately turned toward her, they are waiting, while she pushes, panting and shrieking, through the stout fern-stems; then, leap cruelly away in airy bounds.

"If I am not back by Christmas—" says Sir Roger, presently.

"By *Christmas*!" interrupt I, aghast, "one, two, three, four, *five* months— but you *must*!—you MUST!" clasping both hands on his arm.

"I hope I shall, certainly," replies he; "but one never knows what may happen! If I am *not*—"

"But you *must*," repeat I urgently, and apparently resolved that he shall never reach the end of his sentence; "if you are not—I warn you—you may not like it—I dare say you will not—but—I shall come to look for you!"

"In a *sailing-vessel*, like the governor-general's wife?" asks he with a smile.

And now he is gone! gone in the first freshness of the morning! This year, I seem fated to witness the childhood of many summer days. The carriage that bears him away is lost to sight—dwindled away to nothing among the park-trees. Five minutes ago, my arms were clinging with a tightness of a clasp that a bear might have admired round his neck. I was too choked with tears to say much, and kept repeating with the persistence of a guinea-fowl, but without the distinctness, "Come back! come back!"

"Good-by, my Nancy!" he says, holding me a little from him, that he may the better consider my face, "be quite—*quite* happy, while I am away—*indeed*, that will be the way to please me best, and be a little glad to see me when I come back!"

And now he is gone; and I am left standing at the hall-door with level hand shading my eyes from the red sun—with a smeared face—with the butler and two footmen respectfully regarding my affliction—(they do not like to disappear, till they have shut the door—*I* do not like to ask them to retire, and I do not like to lose the last glimpse) so there I remain—nineteen—a grass widow, and—ALONE! I shall not, however, be alone for long; for this evening Barbara is coming. Algy is to bring her, and to stay a few days on his way to Aldershott. All day long, I wander with restless aimlessness about the house, my big house—so empty, so orderly in its stateliness—so frightfully silent! Ah! the doll's house whose whole front came out at once was a better companion—much more friendly, and not half so oppressive. In almost every room, I cry profusely—disagreeable tears of shame and remorse and grief—only, O friends! I will tell you *now*, what I would not tell myself then, that the grief, though true, was not so great as either of the other feelings. I lunch in the great dining-room, with tall full-length Tempests eying me with constant placidity from the walls; with the butler and footman still trying respectfully to ignore my swelled nose and bunged-up eyes.

As evening draws on—evening that is to bring some voices, some sound of steps to me and my great dumb house—I revive a little. If it were Bobby that were coming, my mind would be weighted by the thought of the repression his spirits would need, but Algy's mirth is several shades less violent, and Barbara is never jarringly joyful. So I change my dress, bathe my face, make my maid retwist my hair, and prepare to be chastenedly and moderately glad to see them.

At least there will be some one to occupy two more of these numberless chairs; two more for the stolid family portraits to eye; two voices, nay *three*, for *I* shall speak then, to drown the sounding silence.

It is time they should be here. The carriage went to the station more than an hour ago. I sit down in a window-seat that commands the park, and look along the drive by which the general went this morning.

Dear Roger! I will practise calling him "Roger" when I am by myself, and then perhaps I may be able to address him by it when he comes home. I will say, "How are you, Roger?"

I have fallen into a pleasant reverie, with my head leaned against the curtain, in which I see myself giving glib utterance to this formula, as I stand in a blue gown—Roger likes me in blue—and a blue cap—I look older in a cap—while he precipitates himself madly—

My reverie breaks off. Some one has entered, and is standing by me. It is a footman, with a telegram on a salver. Albeit I know the trivial causes for which people employ the telegraph-wires nowadays, I never can get over my primal deadly fear of those yellow envelopes, that seem emblems and messengers of battle, murder, and sudden death. As I tear it open, a hundred horrible impossible possibilities flash across my brain. Algy and Barbara have both been killed in a railway-accident, and have telegraphed to tell me so; the same fate has happened to Roger, and he has adopted the same course.

"*Algernon Grey to Lady Tempest.*

"Cannot come: not allowed. *He* has turned nasty."

The paper drops into my lap, as I draw a long breath of mingled relief and disappointment. A whole long evening—long night of this solitude before me! perhaps much more, for they do not even say that they will come to-morrow! I *must* utter my disappointment to somebody, even if it is only the footman.

"They are not coming!" say I, plaintively; then, recollecting and explaining myself, "I mean, they need not send in dinner! I will not have any!" I *cannot* stand another repast—three times longer than the last too—for one *can* abridge luncheon, seated in lorn dignity between the staring dead on the walls, and the obsequious living.

As soon as the man is fairly out of the room, I cry again. Yes, though my hair is readjusted, though I spent more than a quarter of an hour in bathing my eyes, and restoring some semblance of white to their lids, though I had resolved—and without much difficulty, too, hitherto—to be dry-eyed for the rest of the evening. What does it matter what color my eyelids are? what size my nose is? or how beblubbered my cheeks? Not a soul will see them, except my maid, and I am naturally indifferent as to the effect I produce upon her. I look at the clock on the mantel-piece. It has stopped—ornamental clocks mostly do—but even this trivial circumstance adds to my affliction. I instantly take out my pocket-handkerchief, and begin to cry again. Then I look at my watch; a quarter-past seven only—and my watch always gains!

Two hours and three-quarters before I can, with the smallest semblance of decency, go to bed. Meanwhile I am hungry. Though my husband has deserted me, though my brother and sister have failed me, my appetite has done neither.

Faithful friend! never yet was it known to quit me, and here it is! I decide to have *tea* in my own boudoir. Tea is informal, and one need not be waited on at it. When it comes, I try to dawdle over it as much as possible, to sip my tea with labored slowness, and bite each mouthful with conscientious care. When I have finished, I think with satisfaction that I cannot have occupied less than half an hour. Again I consult my watch. Exactly twelve minutes. It is now five minutes to eight; two hours and five minutes more! I sigh loudly, and putting on my hat stroll out into the wide and silent garden. It is as yet unfamiliar to me. I do not know where half the walks lead. I have no favorite haunts, no chosen spot of solitude and greenery, where old and pleasant thoughts meet me. Many such have I at home, but none here. I wander objectlessly, pleasurelessly about with Vick—apparently sharing my depression—trotting subduedly, with tail half-mast high, at my heels, and at length sit down on a bench under a mulberry-tree. The scentless flame of the geraniums and calceolarias fills, without satisfying my eyes; the gnats' officious hum offends my ears; and thoughts in comparison of which the calceolarias are sweet and the gnats melodious, occupy my mind.

Sir Roger will most likely be drowned on his voyage out. Bobby will almost certainly be sent to Hong-Kong, and, as a natural consequence, die of a putrid fever. Algy has just entered the army; there can be no two opinions as to our going to war immediately with either Russia or America. Algy will probably be among the first to fall, and will die, grasping his colors, and shouting "Victory!" or "Westminster Abbey!" or perhaps both.

I have not yet decided what he shall be shouting, when the current of my thoughts is turned by seeing some one—thank Heaven, not a footman, this time!—advancing across the sward toward me. Surely I know the nonchalant lounge of that walk—the lazy self-consciousness of that gait, though, when last I saw it, it was not on dewy English turf, but on the baking flags of a foreign town. It is Mr. Musgrave. Until this moment I have ungratefully forgotten his existence, and all the interesting facts he told me connected with his existence—how his lodge faces ours—how he has no father nor mother, and lives by himself at an abbey. Alas! in this latter particular, can I not feel for him? Am *I* not living by myself at a *hall*?

Vick recognizes him at about the same moment as I do. Having first sprung at him with that volubility of small but hostile *yaps*, with which she strikes terror into the hearts of tramps, she has now—having *smelt* him to be not only respectable, but an acquaintance—changed her behavior to a little servile whine and a series of high jumps at his hand.

"It is you, is it?" cry I, springing up and running to meet him with an elate sensation of company and sociability; "I had quite forgotten that you lived near here. I'm *so* glad!"

At my happy remark as to having been hitherto oblivious of his existence, his face falls in the old lowering way I remember so well, and that brings back to me so forcibly the Prager Strasse, the Zwinger, the even sunshine, that favored my honey-moon; but at the heartily-expressed joy at seeing him, with which I conclude, he cheers up again. If he had known that I was in so reduced a state that I should have enjoyed a colloquy with a chimney-sweep, and not despised exchanging opinions with a dustman, he would not have thought my admission worth much.

"So you have come at last," he says, holding my hand, and looking at me with those long dark eyes that I would swear were black had not a conscientious and thorough daylight scrutiny of them assured me long ago that they were hazel.

"Yes," say I, cheerfully; "I told you you would catch sight of us, sooner or later, if you waited long enough."

"And your tenants never dragged you in, after all?"

"No," say I; "we did not give them the chance. But how do *you* know? Were you peeping out of your lodge? If I had remembered that you lived there, I would have been on the lookout for you."

"You had, of course, entirely forgotten so insignificant a fact?" he says, with a tone of pique.

That happy one! how well I recollect it! I feel quite fondly toward it; it reminds me so strongly of the Linkesches Bad, of the brisk band, and of Roger smoking and smiling at me with his gray eyes across our Mai-trank.

"Yes," I say, contritely, "I am ashamed to say I had—*quite*; but you see I have had a good many things to think of lately."

At this point it strikes me that he must have forgotten that he has my hand, so I quietly, and without offense, resume it.

"And you are *alone*—Sir Roger has left you quite *alone* here?"

"Yes," say I, lachrymosely; "is not it *dreadful*? I never was so miserable in my life; I do not think I *ever* was by myself for a *whole* night before, and"—(lowering my voice to a nervous whisper)—"they tell me there is a ghost somewhere about. Did you ever hear of it?—and the furniture gives *such* cracks!"

"And—he has gone *by himself?*" he continues, still harping on the same string, as if unable to leave it.

"Yes," reply I, laconically, hanging my head, for this is a topic on which I feel always guilty, and never diffuse.

"H'm!" he says, ruminatingly, and as if addressing the remark more to himself than to me. "I suppose it *is* difficult to get out of old habits, and into new ones, all of a sudden."

"I do not know what you mean by old habits and new habits," cry I, angrily; "if you think he did not want me to go with him, you are very much mistaken; he would have much rather that I had."

"But *you*," looking at me penetratingly, and speaking with a sort of alacrity, "you did not see it? I remember of old" (with a smile) "your abhorrence of the sea."

"You are wrong again," say I, reddening, and still speaking with some heat, "I *wished* to go—I begged him to take me. However sick I had been, I should have liked it better than being left moping here, without a soul to speak to!"

Silence for a moment. Then he speaks with a rather sarcastic smile.

"I confess myself puzzled; if *you* were dying to go, and *he* were dying to take you, how comes it that you are sitting at the present moment on this bench?"

I can give no satisfactory answer to this query, so take refuge in a smile.

"I see," say I, tartly, "that you have still your old trick of asking questions. I wish that you would try to get the better of it; it is very disadvantageous to you, and very trying to other people!"

He takes this severe set-down in silence.

The trees that surround the garden are slowly darkening. The shadows that intervene between the round masses of the sycamore-leaves deepen, deepen. A bat flitters dumbly by. Vick, to whose faith all things seem possible, runs sharply barking and racing after it. We both laugh at the fruitlessness of her undertaking, and the joint merriment restores suavity to me, and assurance to him.

"And are you to stay here by yourself *all* the time he is away—*all?*"

"God forbid!" reply I, with devout force.

"Not? well, then—I am really afraid this is a question again, but I cannot help it. If you will not volunteer information, I must ask for it—who is to be your companion?"

"I suppose they will take turns," say I, relapsing into dejection, as I think of the precarious nature of the society on which I depend; "sometimes one, sometimes another, whichever can get away best—they will take turns."

"And who is to have the *first* turn?" he asks, leaning back in the corner of the seat, so as to have a fuller view of my lamentable profile; "when is the first installment of consolatory relatives to arrive?"

"Algy and Barbara *were* to have come to-day," reply I, feeling a covert resentment against something of faintly *gibing* in his tone, but being conscious that it is not perceptible enough to justify another snub, even if I had one ready, which I have not.

"And they did not?"

"Now is not that a silly question?" cry I, tartly, venting the crossness born of my desolation on the only person within reach; "if they *had*, should I be sitting moping here with nobody but Vick to talk to?"

"You forget *me*! may I not run in couples even with a *dog*?" he asks, with a little bitter laugh.

"I did not forget you," reply I, coolly; "but you do not affect the question one way or another—you will be gone directly and—when you are—"

"Thank you for the hint," he cries springing up, picking up his little stick off the grass and flushing.

"You are not going?" cry I, eagerly, laying my hand on his coat-sleeve, "do not! why should you? there is no hurry. Let me have some one to help me to keep the ghosts at bay as long as I can!" then, with a dim consciousness of having said something rather *odd*, I add, reddening, "I shall be going in directly, and you may go then."

He reseats himself. A tiny air is ruffling the flower-beds, giving a separate soft good-night to each bloom.

"And what happened to Algy and Barbara?" he says presently.

"Happened? Nothing!" I answer, absently.

"Very brutal of Algy and Barbara, then!" he says, more in the way of a reflection than a remark.

"Very brutal of *father*, you should say!" reply I, roused by the thought of my parent to a fresh attack of active and lively resentment.

"I have no doubt I should if I knew him."

"He would not let them come!" say I, explanatorily, "for what reason? for *none*—he never has any reasons, or if he has, he does not give them. I sometimes think" (laughing maliciously) "that *you* will not be unlike him, when you grow old and gouty."

"Thank you."

"*You* have no father, have you?" continue I, presently; "no, I remember your telling me so at the Linkesches Bad. Well" (laughing again, with a certain grim humor), "I would not fret about it *too* much, if I were you—it is a relationship that has its disadvantages."

He laughs a little dryly.

"On whatever other heads I may quarrel with Providence, at least no one can accuse me of ever murmuring at its decrees in this respect."

We have risen. The darkness creeps on apace, warmly, without damp or chillness; but still, on it comes! I have to face the prospect of my great and gloomy house all through the lagging hours of the long black night!

"They will come to-morrow, *certainly*, I suppose?" (interrogatively).

"Not *certainly*, at all!" reply I, with an energetic despondence in my voice; "quite the contrary! most likely not! most likely not the day after either, nor the day after that—"

"And if they do not" (with an accent of sincere compassion), "what will you do?"

"What I have done to-day, I suppose," I answer dejectedly; "cry till my cheeks are *sore*! You may not believe me" (passing my bare fingers lightly over them as I speak), "but they feel quite *raw*. I wonder" (with a little dismal laugh) "why tears were made *salt*!—they would not blister one half so much if they were fresh water."

He has drawn a pace or two nearer to me. In this light one has to look closely at any object that one wishes specially and narrowly to observe; and I myself have pointed out the peculiarities of my countenance to him, so I cannot complain if he scrutinizes me with a lengthy attention.

"It is going to be such a *dark* night!" I say, with a slight shiver; "and if the wind gets up, I know that I shall lie awake all night, thinking that the gen— that Roger is drowned! Do you not think" (looking round apprehensively) "that it is rising already? See how those boughs are waving!"

"Not an atom!" reassuringly.

We both look for an instant at the silent flower-beds, at the sombre bulk of the house.

"If they do not come to-morrow—" begins Frank.

"But they *will*!" cry I, petulantly; "they *must*! I cannot do without them! I believe some people do not *mind* being alone—not even in the evenings, when the furniture cracks and the door-handles rattle. I dare say *you* do not;

but I hate my own company; I have never been used to it. I have always been used to a great deal of noise—too much, I have sometimes thought, but I am sure that I never shall think so again!"

"Well, but if they do not—"

"You have said that three times," I cry, irritably. "You seem to take a pleasure in saying it. If they do not—well, what?"

"I will not say what I was going to say," he answers, shortly. "I shall only get my nose bitten off if I do."

"Very well, do not!" reply I, with equal suavity.

We walk in silence toward the house, the wet grass is making my long gown drenched and flabby. We have reached the garden-door whence I issued, and by which I shall return.

"You must go now, I suppose," say I, reluctantly. "You will be by yourself too, will not you? Tell me" (speaking with lowered confidential tone), "do your chairs and tables ever make odd noises?"

"Awful!" he answers, laughing. "I can hardly hear myself speak for them."

I laugh too.

"You might as well tell me before you go what the remark that I quenched was? One always longs to hear the things that people are going to say, and do not! Have no fear! your nose is quite safe!"

"It is nothing much," he answers, with self-conscious stiffness, looking down and poking about the little dark pebbles with his cane; "nothing that you would care about."

"Care about!" echo I, leaning my back against the dusk house-wall, and staring up at the sombre purple of the sky. "Well, no! I dare say not! What should I care to hear now? I am sure I should be puzzled to say! But, as I have been so near it, I may as well be told."

"As you will!" he answers, with an air of affected carelessness. "It is only that, if they do not come to-morrow—"

"Fourth time!" interject I, counting on my fingers and smiling.

"If you wish—if you like—if it would be any comfort to you—I shall be happy—I mean I shall be very glad to come up again about the same time to-morrow evening."

"Will you?" (eagerly, with a great accession of exhilaration in my voice). "Are you serious? I shall be so much obliged if you will, but—"

"It is *impossible* that any one can say any thing," he interrupts, hastily. "There *could* be no harm in it!"

"*Harm!*" repeat I, laughing. "Well, *hardly*! I cannot fancy a more innocent amusement."

Though my speech is in agreement with his own, the coincidence does not seem to gratify him.

"What did you mean, then?" he says, sharply. "You said 'but' — "

"Did I?" answer I, again throwing back my head, and looking upward, as if trying to trace my last preposition among the clouds; "but — but — where could I have put a *'but'*? — oh, I know! *but* you will most likely forget! Do not!" I continue, bringing down my eyes again, and speaking in a coaxing tone. "If you do, it will be play to you, but *death* to me; the thought of it will keep me up all the day!"

"Will it?" in a tone of elated eagerness. "You are not *gibing*, I suppose? it does not sound like your gibing voice!"

"Not it!" reply I, gloomily. "My gibing voice is packed away at the bottom of my imperial. I do not think it has been out since we left Dresden. Well, good-night! What do you want to shake hands *again* for? We have done that *twice* already. You are like the man who, the moment he had finished reading prayers to his family, began them all over again. *Mind* you do not forget! and" (laughing) "if you cannot come yourself, *send some one else! any one* will do — I am not particular, but I *must* have *some one* to speak to!"

Almost before my speech is finished, Frank is out of sight. With such rapid suddenness has he disappeared round the house-corner. I stand for a moment, marveling a little at his hurry. Five minutes ago he seemed willing enough to dawdle on till midnight. Then I go in, and forget his existence.

CHAPTER XXII

Suppose that in all this world, during all its ages, there never was a case of a person being *always* in an ill-humor. I believe that even Xantippe had her lucid intervals of amiability, during which she fondled her Socrates. At all events, father has. On the day after my disappointment, one such interval occurs. He relents, allows Algy and Barbara to have the carriage, and sends them off to Tempest.

Either Mr. Musgrave becomes aware of this fact, or, as I had anticipated, he forgets his promise, for he never appears, and I do not see him again till Sunday. By Sunday my cheeks are no longer *raw*; the furniture has stopped cracking—seeing that no one paid any attention to it, it wisely left off—and the ghosts await a fitter opportunity to pounce.

I have heard from Sir Roger—a cheerful note, dated Southampton. If *he* is cheerful, I may surely allow myself to be so too. I therefore no longer compunctiously strangle any stray smiles that visit my countenance. I have taken several drives with Barbara in my new pony-carriage—it is a curious sensation being able to order it without being subject to fathers veto—and we have skirted our own park, and have peeped through his close wooden palings at Mr. Musgrave's, have strained our eyes and stretched our necks to catch a glimpse of his old gray house, nestling low down among its elms. (Was there ever an abbey that did not live in a hollow?) With bated breath, lest the groom behind should overhear me, I have slightly sketched to Barbara the outline of an idea for establishing her in that weather-worn old pile—an idea which I think was born in my mind as long ago as the first evening that I saw its owner at the Linkesches Bad, and heard that he *had* an abbey, and that it was over against my future home.

Barbara does not altogether deny the desirability of the arrangement; she is not, however, so sanguine as I as to its feasibility, and she positively declines to consent to enter actively into it until she has seen him. This will be on Sunday. To Sunday, therefore, I look forward with pious haste.

Well, it is Sunday now—the Sunday of my first appearance as a bride at Tempest church. A bride without her bridegroom! A pang of mortification and pain shoots through me, as this thought traverses my soul. I look at myself dissatisfiedly in the glass. Alas! I am no credit to his taste. If, for this once. I could but look taller, personabler, *older*!

"They will all say that he has made a fool of himself," I say, half aloud.

It is a sultry day, without wind or freshness, and with a great deal of sun; but in spite of this, I put on a silk gown, rich and heavy, as looking more *married* than the cobweb muslins in which I have hitherto met the summer heat. On my head I place a sedately feathered bonnet, which would not have misbecome mother. I meet Algy and Barbara in my boudoir. They are already dressed. I examine Barbara with critical care, and with a discontented eye, though to a stranger her appearance would seem likely to inspire any feeling rather than dissatisfaction, for she looks as clean and fair and chastely sweet as ever maiden did. Ben Jonson must have known some one like her when he wrote:

> "Have you seen but a bright lily grow
> Before rude hands have touched it?
> Have you marked but the fall of the snow
> Before the soil hath smutched it?
> Have you felt the wool of the beaver
> Or swan's-down ever?
> Or have smelled of the bud of the brier,
> Or the nard in the fire?
> Or have tasted the bag of the bee?
> Oh so white, oh so soft, oh so sweet is she?"

But all the same, having a bonnet on, she is distinctly less like Palma Vecchio's St. Catherine, to which in my talk with Frank I compared her, than she was bareheaded this morning at breakfast. Who in the annals of history ever heard of a saint in a *bonnet*?

"I wish that people might be allowed to go to church without their bonnets these hot Sundays," I say, grumblingly. "*You* especially, Barbara."

She laughs.

"I should be very glad, but I am afraid the beadle would turn me out."

"For Heaven's sake," says Algy, gravely, putting back his shoulders and throwing out his chest, as he draws on a pair of exact gray gloves, "do not let us make ourselves to stink in the nostrils of the inhabitants by any eccentricities of conduct, on this our first introduction to them. If we consulted our own comfort, there is no doubt that we should reduce our toilets by a good many more articles than a bonnet—in fact—" (with an air of reflection), "I shudder to think *where* we should stop!"

We are in church now. I have run the gantlet of the observation of all the parishioners, and have been unable to look calmly unaware of it; on the contrary, have grown consciously rosy red, and have walked over hastily between the open sittings. But now I have reached the shelter of our own seat, near the top of the church, with all the gay bonnets behind me, and only the pulpit, the spread-eagle reading-desk, and the gaudy stained window in front. As soon as I am established—almost sooner, perhaps—I turn my eyes in search of Mr. Musgrave. I know perfectly where to look for him, as he drew a plan of Tempest church and the relative position of our sittings, with the point of his stick on the gravel in the gardens close to the Zwinger at Dresden, while we sat under the trees by the little pool, feeding the pert sparrows and the intimate cock-chaffinch that resort thither. He is not there!

Barbara may be crowned with any abomination, in the way of a bonnet, that ever entered into the grotesque imagination of a milliner to conceive—coal-scuttle, cottage, spoon—for all that it matters. The organ strikes up, a file of chorister-boys in dirty surplices—Tempest is a more pretentious church than ours—and a brace of clergy enter. All through the Confession I gape about with vacant inattention—at the grimy whiteness of the choir; at the back of the organist's head; at the parson, a mealy-mouthed fledgling, who, with his finger on his place in the prayer to prevent his losing it, is taking a stealthy inventory of my charms.

Suddenly I hear the door, which has been for some time silent, creak again in opening. Footsteps sound along the aisle. I look up. Yes, it is he! walking as quickly and noiselessly as he can, and looking rather ashamed of himself, while patches of red, blue, and golden light, from the east window, dance on his Sunday coat and on the smooth darkness of his hair. I glance at Barbara, to give her notice of the approach of her destiny, but my glance is lost. Barbara's stooped head is hidden by her hands, and her pure thoughts are away with God. As a *pis aller*, I look at Algy. No absorption in prayer on *his* part baffles me. He is leaning his elbow on his knee, and wearily biting the top of his prayer-book. He returns my look by another, which, though wordless, is eloquent. It says, in raised eyebrow and drooped mouth, "Is that all? I do not think much of him?"

The church is full and hot. The windows are open, indeed, but only the infinitesimally small chink that church-windows ever do open. The pew-opener sedulously closes the great door after every fresh entrance. I kneel simmering through the Litany. Never before did it seem so long! Never did the chanted, "We beseech Thee to hear us, good Lord!" appear so endlessly numerous.

Under cover of my arched hands, shading my eyes, I peep at one after another of the family groups. Most of them are behind me indeed, but there are still a good many that I can get a view of sideways. Among these, the one that oftenest engages my notice is a small white woman, evidently a lady—and, at the moment I first catch sight of her, with closed eyes and drawn-in nostrils, inhaling smelling-salts, as if to her, too, church was up-hill work this morning—in a little seat by herself. At the other pews one glance a piece satisfies me, but, having looked at *her* once, I look again. I could not tell you *why* I do it. There is nothing very remarkable about her in the matter of either youth or beauty, and yet I look.

The service is ended at length, but eagerly as I long for the fresh air, we are—whether to mark our own dignity, or to avoid further scrutiny on the part of our fellow-worshipers—almost the last to issue from the church. At the porch we find Mr. Musgrave waiting. A sort of *mauvaise honte* and a guilty conscience combine to disable me from promptly introducing him to my people, and before I recover my presence of mind, Algy has walked on with Barbara, and I am left to follow with Frank.

He does not seem in one of his most sunshiny humors, but perhaps the long morning service, so trying in its present arrangement of lengthy prayers, praises, and preaching, to a restless and irritable temper, is to blame for that.

"I suppose," he says, speaking rather stiffly, "that I must congratulate you on the arrival of the first detachment."

"First detachment of what?"

"Of your family. I understood you to say that there were to be *relays* of them during all Sir Roger's absence."

"It is to be hoped so, I am sure," I say, devoutly; "especially" (looking up at him with mock reproach) "considering the way in which my friends neglect me. You never came, after all! No!" (seeing the utter unsmilingness of his expression, and speaking hastily), "I am not serious; I am only joking! No doubt you heard that they had come, and thought that you would be in the way. But, indeed you would not. We had no secrets to talk; we should not have minded you a bit."

"I *did* hear that they had arrived," he answers, still speaking ungraciously, "but even if I had not, I should not have come!"

I look up in his face, and laugh.

"You *forgot*? Ah, I told you you would!"

"I did *not* forget."

Again I look up at him, this time in honest astonishment, awaiting the solution of his enigma.

"There is no particular use in making one's self *cheap*, is there?" he says, with a bitter little laugh. "What is the use of going to a place where you are told that *any one else* will do as well?"

A pause. I walk along in silent wonderment. So he actually was happy again! We have left the church-yard. We are in the road, between the dusty quicks of the hedgerows. The carriages bowl past us, whirling clouds of dust down our throats. One is trotting by now, a victoria and pair of grays, and in it, leaning restfully back, and holding up her parasol, is the lady I noticed in church. Musgrave knows her apparently. At least, he takes off his hat.

"Who is she?" I say, with a slightly aroused interest. "I was wondering in church. I suppose she is delicate, as she sat down through the psalms."

At the moment I address him, Mr. Musgrave is battling angrily with an angrier wasp, but no sooner has he heard my question than he ceases his warfare, and allows it to buzz within half an inch of his nose, as he turns his hazel eyes, full of astonished inquiry, upon me.

"You *do not know*?"

"Not I," reply I lightly. "How should I? I know nobody in these parts."

"That is Mrs. Huntley."

"You do not say so!" reply I, ironically. "I am sure I am very glad to hear it, but I am not very much wiser than I was before."

"Is it possible," he says, looking rather nettled at my tone, and lowering his voice a little, as if anxious to confine the question to me alone—a needless precaution, as there is no one else within hearing—"that you have *never* heard of her?"

"Never!" reply I, in some surprise; "why should I?—has she ever done any thing very remarkable?"

He laughs slightly, but disagreeably.

"Remarkable! well, no, I suppose not!"

The victoria is quite out of sight now—quite out of sight the delicately poised head, the dove-colored parasol.

"You are joking, of course," says Frank, presently, turning toward me, and still speaking in that needlessly lowered key. "It is so long since I have seen you, that I have got out of the habit of remembering that you never speak seriously; but, *of course*, you have heard—I mean Sir Roger has mentioned her to you!"

"He has not!" reply I, speaking sharply, and raising my voice a little. "Neither has he mentioned any of the other neighbors to me! He had not time." No rejoinder. "Most likely," continue I, speaking with quick heat, for something in his manner galls me, "he did not recollect her existence."

"Most likely."

He is looking down at the white dust which is defiling his patent-leather boots, and smiling slightly.

"How do you know—what reason have you for thinking that he was aware that was such a person?" I ask, with injudicious eagerness.

"I have no reason—I think nothing," he answers, coldly, with an air of ostentatious reserve.

I walk on in a ruffled, jarred silence. Presently Frank speaks again.

"Are those two"—(slightly indicating by a faint nod the figures in front of us)—"the two you expected?—Are these—what are their names?— *Algy* and *Barbara*?"

"Yes," say I, smiling, with recovered equanimity; "Algy and Barbara." A little pause. "You can judge for yourself now," say I, laughing rather nervously, "whether I spoke truth—whether Barbara is as like the St. Catherine as I told you." For a moment he does not answer. "Of course," I say, rather crestfallen, "the bonnet makes a difference; the likeness is much more striking when it is off."

"The St. Catherine!" he repeats, with a puzzled air, "*what* St. Catherine? I am afraid you will think me very stupid, but I really am quite at sea."

"Do you mean to say," cry I, reddening with mortification, "that you forget—that you do not remember that St. Catherine of Palma Vecchio's in the Dresden Gallery that I always pointed out to you as having such a look of Barbara? Well, you *have* a short memory!"

"Have I?" he answers, dryly; "perhaps for *some* things; for *others*, I fancy that mine is a good deal longer than yours."

"It might easily be that," I answer, recovering from my temporary annoyance and laughing; "I suppose you mean for books and dates, and things of that kind. Well, you may easily beat me there. The landing of William the Conqueror, and the battle of Waterloo, were the only two dates I ever succeeded in mastering, and that was only after the struggle of years."

"Dates!" he says, impatiently, "pshaw! I was not thinking of *them*! I was thinking of Dresden!"

"Are you so sure that you could beat me there?" ask I, thoughtfully; "I do not know about that! I think I could stand a pretty stiff examination; but perhaps you are talking of the pictures and the names of the artists. Ah, yes! there you are right; with *me* they go in at one ear, and out at another. Only the other day I was racking my brain to think of the name of the man that painted the *other* Magdalen—not Guido's—I was telling Algy about it. Bah! what is it? I know it as well as my own."

His head is turned away from me. He does not appear to be attending.

"What is it?" I repeat; "have *you* forgotten too?"

"*Battoni!*" he answers, laconically, still keeping his face averted.

"*Battoni!* oh, yes! thanks—of course! so it is!—Algy" (raising my voice a little)—"*Battoni!*"

"Well, what about him?" replies Algy, turning his head, but not showing much inclination to slacken his speed or to join Frank and me.

"The Magdalen man—you know—I mean the man that painted the Magdalen, and whose name I could not recollect last night, Algy. Barbara! how fast you are walking!" (speaking rather reproachfully)—"stop a moment! I want to introduce you to Mr. Musgrave."

Thus adjured, they have come to a halt, and the presentation is made.

"Surely," think I, glancing at Barbara's face, slightly flushed by the heat, and still gently grave with the sobriety of expression left by devotion, "he *must* see the likeness now!" To insure his having the chance of telling her that he does, I fall behind with Algy.

CHAPTER XXIII

Claret cup has washed the dust from our throats; cold lamb and mayonnaise have restored the force of body and equanimity of mind which the exhausted air and long-drawn Gregorian chants of Tempest Church destroyed. Frank is lunching with us. He had accompanied us to our own gates, and had then made a feint of leaving, but I had pressed him, with an eagerness proportioned to the seriousness of my design upon him, to accompany us, and he had yielded with a willing ease.

I cannot help thinking that Algy does not look altogether pleased with the arrangement, but after all, it is *my* house, and not Algy's. It is the first time that I have entertained a guest since the far-off childish birthdays, when the neighbors' little boys and girls used to be gathered together to drink tea out of the doll's tea service. In the afternoon, we all walk to church again, and in the same order. Barbara and Algy in front, Frank and I behind. I had planned differently, but Algy is obtuse, Barbara will come into the manœuvres, and Frank seems simply indifferent. So it happens, that all through the park, and up the bit of dusty white road we are out of ear-shot of the other two.

"A sky worthy of Dresden!" says Mr. Musgrave, throwing back his head and looking up at the pale blue sultriness above our heads—the waveless, stormless ether sea—as we pace along, with the church-bells' measured ding-dong in our ears, and the cool ripe grasses about our feet.

"*Dear* Dresden!" say I, pensively, with a sigh of mixed regret and remorse, as I look back on the sunshiny hours that at the time I thought so long, in that fair, white foreign town.

"Dear Linkesches Bad!" says Frank, sighing too.

"Dear Groosegarten!" cry I, thinking of the long pottering stroll that Roger and I had taken one evening up and down its green alleys, and that *then* I had found so tedious.

"Dear Zwinger!" retorts Frank.

"Dear Weisserhirsch!" say I, half sadly. "Dear white acacias! dear drives under the acacias!"

"Drives under the acacias!" echoes Frank, dropping his accent of sentimentalism, and speaking rather sharply. "We never had any drives under the acacias! We never had any drives at all, that I recollect!"

"You had not, I dare say," reply I, carelessly, "but *we* had. They are the things that I look back at with the greatest pleasure of any thing that happened there!"

Frank does not apostrophize as *"dear"* any other public resort; indeed, he turns away his head, and we walk on without uttering a word for a few moments.

"By-the-by," say I, with a labored and not altogether successful attempt at appearing to speak with suddenness and want of premeditation, "what did you mean this morning, about that la—about Mrs. Huntley?"

"I meant nothing," he answers, but the faint quiver of a smile about his mouth contradicts his words.

"That is not true!" reply I, with impatient brusqueness; "why were you surprised at my not having heard of her?"

"I was not surprised."

"What is the use of so many falsehoods?" cry I, indignantly; "at least I would choose some better time than when I was going to church for telling them. What reason have you for supposing that—that Roger knows more about her than I—than Barbara do?"

"How persistent you are!" he says, with that same peculiar smile— not latent now, but developed—curbing his lips and lightening in his eyes. "There is no baffling you! Since you dislike falsehoods, I will tell you no more. I will own to you that I made a slip of the tongue; I took it for granted that you had been told a certain little history, which it seems you have *not* been told."

The blood rushes headlong to my face. It feels as if every drop in my body were throbbing and tingling in my cheeks, but I look back at him hardily.

"I don't believe there *is* any such history."

"I dare say not."

More silence. Swish through the buttercups and the yellow rattle; a lark, miles above our heads, singing the music he has overheard in heaven. Frank does not seem inclined to speak again.

"Your story is *not* true," say I, presently, laughing uncomfortably, and unable to do the one wise thing in my reach, and leave the subject alone—"but untrue stories are often amusing, more amusing than the true ones. You may tell yours, if you like."

"I have not the slightest wish."

A few steps more. How quickly we are getting through the park! We shall reach the church, and I shall not have heard. I shall sit and stand and kneel all through the service with the pain of that gnawing curiosity—that hateful new vague jealousy aching at my heart.

It is *impossible*! I stop. I stand stock-still in the summer grass.

"I *hate* your hints! I hate your innuendoes!" I say, passionately. "I have always lived with people who spoke their thoughts straight out! Tell me this moment! I will not move a step from this spot till you do."

"I have nothing worth speaking of to tell," he answers, slightly. "It is only that never having had a wife myself, I have taken an outsider's view; I have taken it for granted that when two people marry each other they make a clean breast of their past history—make a mutual confession of their former—"

He pauses, as if in search of a word.

"But supposing," cry I, eagerly, "that they have nothing to tell, nothing to confess—"

He shrugs his shoulders.

"That is so likely, is it not?"

"Likely or not," cry I, excitedly, "it was true in *my* case. If you had put me on the rack, I could have confessed nothing!"

"I do not see the analogy," he answers, coldly; "*you* are—what did you tell me? nineteen?—It is to be supposed"—(with a rather unlovely smile)—"that your history is yet to come; and he is—*forty-seven*! We shall be late for church!"—with a glance at Algy's and Barbara's quickly diminishing figures.

"I do not care whether we are late or not!" cry I, vehemently, and stamping on the daisy-heads as I speak. "I will not *stir* until you tell me."

"There is really no need for such excitement!" returns he with a cold smile; "since you will have it, it is only that rumor—and you know what a liar *rumor* is—says that once, some years ago, they were engaged to marry each other."

"And why did not they?" speaking with breathless panting, and forgetting my stout asseveration that the whole tale is a lie.

"Because—mind, I *vouch* for nothing, I am only quoting rumor again—because—she threw him over."

"*Threw him over!*" with an accent of most unfeigned astonishment.

"You are surprised!" he says, quickly, and with what sounds to me like a slightly annoyed inflection of voice; "it *does* seem incredible, does not it? But at that time, you see, he had not all the desirables—not quite the pull over other men that he has now; his brother was not dead or likely to die, and he was only General Tempest, with nothing much besides his pay."

"*Threw—him—over!*" repeat I, slowly, as if unable yet to grasp the sense of the phrase.

"We shall *certainly* be late; the last bell is beginning," says Frank, impatiently.

I move slowly on. We have reached the turnstile that gives issue from the park to the road. The smart farmers' wives, the rosy farmers' daughters, are pacing along through the powdery dust toward the church-gate.

"Is she a *widow*?" ask I, in a low voice.

He laughs sarcastically.

"A widow indeed, and desolate, eh? No! I believe she has a husband somewhere about, but she keeps him well out of sight—away in the colonies. He is there now, I fancy."

"And why is not she with him?" cry I, indignantly; but the moment that the words are out of my mouth, I hang my head. Might not *she* ask the same question with regard to *me*?

"She did not like the *sea*, perhaps," answers Frank, demurely.

CHAPTER XXIV

A day—two days pass.

"More callers," say I, hearing the sound of wheels, and running to the window; "I thought we *must* have exhausted the neighborhood yesterday and the day before!" I add, sighing.

"*Whoever they are*," says Barbara, anxiously, lifting her head from the work over which it is bent, "mind you do not ask after their relations! Think of the man whose wife you inquired after, and found that she had run away with his groom not a month before!"

"That certainly was one of my unlucky things," answer I, gravely; then, beginning to laugh—"and I was so *determined* to know what had become of her, too."

I am still looking out. It is a soft, smoke-colored day; half an hour ago, there was a shower—each drop a separate loud patter on the sycamore-leaves—but now it is fair again. A victoria is coming briskly up the drive; servants in dark liveries; a smoke-colored parasol that matches the day.

"Shall I ring, and say 'not at home?'" asks Barbara, stretching out her hand toward the bell.

"No, no!" cry I, hurriedly, in an altered voice, for the parasol has moved a little aside, and I have seen the face beneath.

In two minutes the butler enters and announces "Mrs. Huntley," and the "plain woman—not very young—about thirty—who cannot be very strong, as she sat down through the Psalms," enters.

At first she seems uncertain *which* to greet as bride and hostess; indeed, I can see that her earliest impulse is to turn from the small insignificance in silk, to the tall little loveliness in cotton, and as I perceive it, a little arrow—not of jealousy, for, thank God, I never was jealous of our Barbara—never—but of pain at my so palpable inferiority, shoots through all my being. But Barbara draws back, and our visitor perceives her error. We sit down, but the brunt of the talk falls on Barbara. I am never glib with strangers, and I throw in a word only now and then, all my attention and observation having passed into my eyes. A plain woman, indeed! I have always been convinced of the unbecomingness of church, but *now* more than ever am I fully persuaded of it. And yet she is not pretty! Her mouth is very wide, that is perhaps why she so rarely laughs; her nose cannot say much for itself; her cheeks are thin, and I *think*—nay, let me tell truth—I *hope* that in a low gown she would be *scraggy*, so slight even to meagreness is she! But how thoroughly made the most of! What a shapeless pin-cushion fit my gown seems beside the admirable French sit of hers! How hard, how metallic its tint beside the indefinite softness of that sweep of smoke-color! What a stiff British erection my hair feels beside the careless looseness of these shining twists! What a fine, slight hand, as if cut in faint gray stone!

At each fresh detail that I note, Musgrave's anecdote gains ever more and more probability; and my heart sinks ever lower and more low.

One hope remains to me. Perhaps she may be stupid! Certainly she is not *affording*.

How heavily poor Barbara is driving through the fine weather and the *Times*! and how little more than "yes" and "no" does she get! I take heart. Roger loves people who talk—people who are merry and make jests. It was my most worthless gabble that first drew him toward me. Cheered and emboldened by this thought, I swoop down like a sudden eagle to the rescue.

"You know Rog—, my husband, do not you?" I say, with an abrupt bluntness that contrasts finely with the languid gentleness with which her little remarks steal out like mice. *Mine* rushes forth like a desolating bomb-shell.

"A little—yes."

"You knew him in India, did not you?" say I, unable to resist the temptation of seizing this opportunity to gratify my curiosity, drawing my chair a little nearer hers, and speaking with an eagerness which I, in vain, try to stifle.

"Yes," smiling sweetly, "in India."

"He was there a long time," continue I, communicatively.

"Yes."

(Well, she *is* baffling! when she does not say "yes" affirmatively, she says it interrogatively.)

"All the same he did not like it," I go on, with amicable volubility; "but I dare say you know that. They say—" (reddening as I feel, perceptibly, and nervously twisting my pocket-handkerchief round my fingers)—"that people are so sociable in India: now, I dare say you saw a good deal of him."

"Yes; we met several times."

She is smiling again. There is not a shade of hesitation or unreadiness in her low voice, nor does the faintest tinge of color stain the fine pallor of her cheeks.

(It *must* have been a lie!)

"*Your* husband, too, is out—" I pause; not sure of the locality, but she does not help me, so I add lamely, "*somewhere*, is not he?"

"He is in the West Indies."

"In the West Indies!" cry I, with animation, drawing my chair yet a little nearer hers, and feeling positively friendly; "why, that is where *mine* is too!"

"Yes?"

"We are companions in misfortune," cry I, heartily; "we must keep up each other's spirits, must not we?"

Another smile, but no verbal answer.

A noise of feet coming across the hall—of manly whistling makes itself heard. The door opens and Algy enters. It is clear that he is unaware of there being any stranger present, for his hat is on his head, his hands are in his pockets, and he only stops whistling to observe:

"Well, Nancy! any more aborigines?" then he breaks suddenly off, and we all grow red—he himself beaming of as lively a scarlet as the new tunic that he tried on last night. I make a hurried and confused presentation, in which I manage to slur over into unintelligibility and utter doubtfulness the names of the two people made known to one another.

"One more aborigine, you see!" says Mrs. Huntley, to my surprise—after the experience I have had of her fine taste in monosyllables—beginning the conversation. I took at her with a little wonder. Her voice is quite as low as ever, but there is an accent of playfulness in it; and on her face a sparkle of *esprit*, whose possible existence I had not conjectured. Certainly, she showed no symptom of playfulness or *esprit* during our late talk. I have yet to learn that to some women, the presence of a man—not *the* man, but *a* man—any man—is what warm rain is to flowers athirst. I am still marveling at this metamorphosis, when the door again opens, and another guest is announced—an old man, as great a stranger to us as is the rest of the neighborhood, but of whom we quickly discover that he is deadly, deadly deaf. For five minutes, I bawl at him a series of remarks, each and all of which he misunderstands. He does it so invariably, that I come at length to the conclusion that he is doing it on purpose, and stop talking in a huff. Then Barbara takes her turn—Barbara can always make deaf people hear better than I do, though she does not speak to them nearly so loud, and I rest on my oars. Owing to my position between the two couples, I can hear what is passing between Algy and Mrs. Huntley.

To tell the truth, I do not take much pains to avoid hearing it, for surely they can have no secrets. They are sitting rather close together, and speaking in a low key, but I am so used to *his* voice, and her articulation is so distinct, that I do not miss a word.

"I think I had the pleasure of seeing you in church, last Sunday," Algy says, rather diffidently; not having yet quite recovered from the humiliation engendered by his unfortunate remark.

She nods.

"And I you," with a gently reassuring smile.

"Did you, really? did you see me—I mean us?"

"Yes, I saw you," with a delicate inflection of voice, which somehow confines the application of the remark to him. "I made up my mind—one takes ideas into one's head, you know—I made up my mind that you were a *soldier*; one can mostly tell."

He laughs the flattered, fluttered laugh, that *my* rough speech was never known to provoke in living man.

"Yes, I am; at least, I am going to be; I join this week."

"Yes?" with a pretty air of attention and interest.

"We—we—found out who *you* were," he says, laughing again, with a little embarrassment, and edging his chair nearer hers; "we asked Musgrave!"

"Mr. Musgrave!" (with a little tone of alert curiosity)—"oh! you know *him*?"

"I know him! I should think so: he is quite a tame cat here."

"Yes?"

"Have you any *children*?" cry I, suddenly, bundling with my usual fine tact head-foremost into the conversation (where I am clearly not wanted, and altogether forgetting Barbara's warning injunction) with my unnecessary and malapropos query. For a moment she looks only astonished; then an expression of pain crosses her face, and a slight contraction passes over her features. Evidently, she *had* a child, and it is *dead*. She is going to *cry*! At this awful thought, I grow scarlet, and Algy darts a furious look at me. What *have* I said? I have outdone myself. How far worse a case than the fugitive wife whose destiny I was so resolute to learn from her injured husband!

"I am so sorry," I stammer—"I never thought—I did not know—"

"It is of no consequence," she answers, speaking with some difficulty, and with a slight but quite musical tremor in her voice—very different from the ugly gulpings and catchings of the breath which always set off *my* tears—"but the fact is, that I *have* one little one—and—and—she no longer lives with me; my husband's people have taken her; I am sure that they meant it for the best; only—only—I am afraid I cannot quite manage to talk of her yet" (turning away from me, and looking up into Algy's face with a showery smile). Then, as if unable to run the risk of any other further shock to her feelings, she rises and takes her leave; Algy eagerly attending her to the door.

The old deaf gentleman departs at the same time, loading Barbara with polite parting messages to her husband, and bowing distantly to *me*. Algy reënters presently, looking cross and ruffled.

"You really are *too* bad, Nancy!" he says, harshly, throwing himself into the chair lately occupied by Mrs. Huntley. "You grow worse every day—one would think you did it on purpose—riding rough-shod over people's feelings."

I stand aghast. Formerly, I used not to mind rough words; but I think Roger must have spoilt me; they make me wince now.

"But—but—it was not *dead*!" I say, whimpering; "it had only gone to visit its grandmother."

"Never you mind, my Nancy!" says Barbara, in a whisper, drawing me away to the window, and pressing her soft, cool lips, to the flushed misery of my cheeks; "she was not hurt a bit! her eyes were as dry as a bone!"

CHAPTER XXV

One more day is gone. We are one day nearer Roger's return. This is the way in which I am growing to look at the flight of time; just as, in Dresden, I joyfully marked each sunset, as bringing me twenty-four hours nearer home and the boys. And now the boys are within reach; at a wish I could have them all round me; and still, in my thoughts, I hurry the slow days, and blame them for dawdling. With all their broad, gold sunshine, and their rainbow-colored flowers, I wish them away.

Alas! that life should be both so quick and so lagging! It is afternoon, and I am lying by myself on a cloak at the bottom of the punt—the *unupsettable*, broad-bottomed punt. My elbow rests on the seat, and a book is on my lap. But, in the middle of the pool, the glare from the water is unbearably bright, but *here*, underneath those dipping, drooped trees, the sun only filters through in little flakes, and the shade is brown, and the reflections are so vivid that the flags hardly know which are themselves—they, or the other flags that grow in the water at their feet.

A while ago I tried to read; but a private vexation of my own—a small new one—interleaved with its details each page of the story, and made nonsense of it. I have shut the volume, therefore, and, with my hat tilted over my eyes, and my cheek on my hand, am watching the long blue dragon-flies, and the numberless small peoples that inhabit the summer air. All at once, I hear some one coming, crashing and pushing through the woody undergrowth. Perhaps it is Algy come to say that he has changed his mind, and that he will not go after all! No! it is only Mr. Musgrave. I am a little disappointed, but, as my fondness for my own company is always of the smallest, I am able to smile a sincere welcome.

"It is you, is it?" I say, with a little intimate nod. "How did you know where I was?"

"Barbara told me."

"*Barbara*, indeed!" (laughing). "I wish father could hear you."

"I am very glad he does not."

"And so you found her at home?" I say, with a feeling of pleased curiosity, as to the details of the interview. (He cannot well have volunteered the abbey *already*, can he?)

"I suppose I may come in," he says, hardly waiting my permission to jump into the punt, which, however, by reason of the noble broadness of its bottom, is enabled to bid defiance to any such shock. "She was making a flannel petticoat for an old woman," he goes on, sitting down opposite me, and looking at me from under his hat-brim, with gravely shining eyes; "*herring-boning*, she called it. She has been teaching me how to herring-bone. I like Barbara."

"How kind of you!" I say, ironically, and yet a little gratified too. "And does she return the compliment, may I ask?"

He nods.

"Yes, I think so."

"She would like you better still if you were to lose all your money, and one of your legs, and be marked by the small-pox," I say, thoughtfully; "to be despised, and out at elbows, and down in the world, is the sure way to Barbara's heart."

I had meant to have drawn for him a pleasant and yet most true picture of her sweet disinterestedness, but his uneasy vanity takes it amiss.

"As it entails being enrolled among the blind and lame," he says, smiling sarcastically, and flushing a little, "I am afraid I shall never get there."

A moment ago I had felt hardly less than sisterly toward him. Now I look at him with a disgustful and disapprobative eye. What a very great deal of alteration he needs, and, with that face, and his abbey, and all his rooks to back it, how very unlikely he is to get it! Well, *I* at least will do my best!

We both remain quiet for a few moments. Vick sits at the end of the punt, a shiver of excitement running all over her little white body, her black nose quivering, and one lip slightly lifted by a tooth, as she gazes with eager gravity at the distant wild-ducks flying along in a row, with outstretched necks, making their pleasant quacks. How low they fly; so low that their feet splash in the water, that makes a bright spray-hue in the sun!

"Algy is going away to-morrow!" say I, presently.

"So he told me."

"This is his last evening here!" (in a rather dolorous tone).

"So I should gather," laughing a little at the obviousness of my last piece of information.

"And yet," say I, looking down through the clear water at a dead tree-bough lying at the bottom, and sighing, "he is going to dine out to-night—to dine with Mrs. Huntley."

"With Mrs. Huntley! when?" with a long-drawn whistle of intelligence.

"Tell me," cry I, impulsively, raising myself from my reclining pose, and sitting upright, "you will understand better than I do—perhaps it is my mistake—but, if you had seen a person only *once* for five or ten minutes, would you sign yourself 'Yours very sincerely' to them?"

He laughs dryly.

"Not unless I was writing *after dinner*—why?"

"Nothing—no reason!"

Again he laughs.

"I think I can guess."

"Her name is Zéphine," say I again, leaning over the boat-side and pulling my forefinger slowly to and fro through the warm brown water.

"I am well aware of that fact" (smiling).

How near the swans are drawing toward us! One, with his neck well thrown back, and his wings raised and ruffled, sailing along like a lovely snow-white ship; another, with less grace and more homeliness, standing on his head, with black webs paddling out behind.

"You were quite wrong on Sunday—*quite*," say I, speaking with sudden abruptness, and reddening.

"On Sunday!" (throwing his luminous dark eyes upward to the light clouds and faint blue of the August sky above us, as if to aid his recollection), "nothing more likely—but what about?"

"About—Roger," I answer, speaking with some difficulty ("and Mrs. Huntley," I was going to add, but some superstition hinders me from coupling their names even in a sentence).

"I dare say"—carelessly—"but what new light have you had thrown upon the matter?"

"I asked her," I say, looking him full in the face, with simple directness.

"*Asked her!*" repeats he, with an accent of profound astonishment. "Asked the woman whether she had been engaged to him, and jilted him? Impossible!"

"No! no!" cry I, with tremulous impatience, "of course not; but I asked her whether she used not to know him in India, and she said, 'Yes, we met several times,' just like *that*—she no more blushed and looked confused than *I* should if any one asked me whether I knew you!"

He is still leaning over the punt, and has begun to dabble as I did.

"You certainly have a way of putting things very strongly," he says in a rather low voice, "*convincingly* so!"

"She did not even know what part of the world he was in!" I cry, triumphantly.

"Did she say so?" (lifting up his face, and speaking quickly).

"Well, no—o—" I answer, reluctantly; "but I said, 'He is in the West Indies,' and she answered 'Yes,' or 'Indeed,' or 'Is he?' I forget which, but at any rate it implied that it was news to her."

A pike leaps not far from us, and splashes back again. I watch to see whether the widening faint circles will have strength to reach us, or whether the water's smile will be smoothed and straightened before it gets to us.

"Did Mrs. Huntley happen to say" (leaning lazily back, and speaking carelessly), "how she liked her house?"

"No; why?"

"She has only just got into it," he answers, slightly; "only about a fortnight, that is."

"I wonder," say I, ruminatingly, "what brought her to this part of the world, for she does not seem to know anybody."

He does not answer.

"We *ought* to be friends, ought not we?" say I, beginning to laugh nervously, and looking appealingly toward him, "both of us coming to sojourn in a strange land! It is a curious coincidence our both settling here in such similar circumstances, at almost the same time, is not it?"

Still he is silent.

"*Is not it?*" cry I, irritably, raising my voice.

Again he has thrown his head back, and is perusing the sky, his hands clasped round one lifted knee.

"What *is* a coincidence?" he says, languidly. "I do not think I quite know—I am never good at long words—two things that happen accidentally at the same time, is not it?"

He lays the faintest possible stress on the word accidentally.

"And you mean to say that this in not accidental?" I cry, quickly.

"I mean nothing; I only ask for information."

How still the world is to-day! The feathery water-weeds sway, indeed, to and fro, with the motion of the water, but the tall cats'-tails, and all the flags, stand absolutely motionless. I feel vaguely ruffled, and take up my forgotten book. Holding it so as to hide my companion's face from me, I begin to read ostentatiously. He seems content to be silent; lying on the flat of his back, at the bottom of the punt, staring at the sky, and declining the overtures, and parrying the attacks, of Vick, who, having taken advantage of his supine position to mount upon his chest, now stands there wagging her tail, and wasting herself in efforts, mostly futile, but occasionally successful, to lick the end of his nose. A period of quiet elapses, during which, for the sake of appearances, I turn over a page. By-and-by, he speaks.

"Algy is your eldest brother, is not he?—get away, you little beast!"— (the latter clause, in a tone of sudden exasperation, is addressed, not to me, but to Vick, and tells me that my pet dog's endeavors have been crowned with a tardy prosperity.)

"Yes" (still reading sedulously).

"I thought so," with a slight accent of satisfaction.

"Why?" cry I, again letting fall my volume, and yielding to a curiosity as irresistible as unwise; for he had meant me to ask, and would have been disobliged if I had not.

"We all have our hobbies, don't you know?" he says, shifting his eyes from the sky, and fixing them on the less serene, less amiable object of my face—"some people's is old china—some Elzevir editions—I have a mania for *clocks*—I have one in every room in my house—by-the-by, you have never been over my house—Mrs. Huntley's—she is a dear little woman, but she has her fancies, like the rest of us, and hers is—*eldest sons!*"

"But she is married!" exclaim I, stupidly. "What good can they do her, now?"—then, reddening a little at my own simplicity, I go on, hurriedly: "But he is such a boy!—younger than *you*—young enough to be her *son*— it *can* be only out of good-nature that she takes notice of him."

"Yes—true—out of good-nature!" he echoes, nodding, smiling, and speaking with that surface-assent which conveys to the hearer no impression less than acquiescence.

"Boys are not much in her way, either," he pursues, carelessly; "generally she prefers such as are of *riper* years—*much* riper!"

"How spiteful you are!" I say, glad to give my chafed soul vent in words, and looking at him with that full, cold directness which one can employ only toward such as are absolutely indifferent to one. "How she *must* have snubbed you!"

For an instant, he hesitates; then—

"Yes," he says, smiling still, though his face has whitened, and a wrathy red light has come into his deep eyes; "in the pre-Huntley era, I laid my heart at her feet—by-the-way, I must have been in petticoats at the time—and she kicked it away, as she had, no doubt, done—*others*."

The camel's backbone is broken. This last innuendo—in weight a straw—has done it. I speak never a word; but I rise up hastily, and, letting my novel fall heavily prone on the pit of its stomach at the punt-bottom, I take a flying leap to shore—*toward* shore, I should rather say—for I am never a good jumper—Tou Tou's lean spider-legs can always outstride me—and now I fall an inch or two short, and draw one leg out booted with river-mud. But I pay no heed. I hurry on, pushing through the brambles, and leaving a piece of my gown on each. Before I have gone five yards—his length of limb and freedom from petticoats giving him the advantage over me—he overtakes me.

"What *has* happened? at this rate you will not have much gown left by the time you reach the house."

To my excited ears, there seems to be a suspicion of laughter in his voice. I disdain to answer. The path we are pursuing is not the regular one; it is a short cut through the wood. At its widest it is very narrow; and, a little ahead of us, a bramble has thrown a strong arm right across it, making a thorny arch, and forbidding passage. By a quick movement, Mr. Musgrave gets in advance of me, and, turning round, faces me at this defile.

"What *has* happened?"

Still I remain stubbornly silent.

"We are not going to fight, at this time of day, such old friends as we are?"

The red-anger light has died out of his eyes. They look softer, and yet less languid, than I have ever seen them before; and there is subdued appeal and entreaty in his lowered voice. At the present moment, I distinctly dislike him. I think him altogether trying and odious, and I should be glad—yes, *glad*, if Vick were to bite a piece out of his leg; but, at the same time, I cannot deny that I have seldom seen any thing comelier than the young man who now stands before me, with the green woodland lights flickering about the close-shorn beauty of his face—he is well aware that his are not features that need *planting out*—while a lively emotion quickens all his lazy being.

"We are *not* old friends! Let me pass!"

"*New* friends, then—*friends*, at all events!" coming a step nearer, and speaking without a trace of sneer, sloth, or languor.

"Not friends at all! Let me pass!"

"Not until you tell me my offense—not until you own that we are friends!" (in a tone of quick excitement, and almost of authority, that, in him, is new to me).

"Then we shall stay here all night!" reply I, with a fine obstinacy, plumping down, as I speak, on the wayside grass, among the St. John's-worts, and the red arum-berries. In a moment he has stepped aside, and is holding the stout purple bramble-stem out of my way.

"Pass, then!" he says, in a tone of impatience, frowning a little; "as you have said it, of course you will stick to it—right or wrong—or you would not be a woman; but, whether you confess it or not, we *are* friends!"

"We are NOT!" cry I, resolute to have the last word, as I spring up and fly past him, with more speed than dignity, lest he should change his mind, and again detain me.

CHAPTER XXVI

The swallows are gone: the summer is done: it is October. The year knows that I am in a hurry, and is hasting with its shortened days—each day marked by the loss of something fair—toward the glad Christmas-time—Christmas that will bring me back my Roger—that will set him again at the foot of his table—that will give me again the sound of his foot on the stairs, the smile in his fond gray eyes. So I thought yesterday, and to-day I have heard from him; heard that though he is greatly loath to tell me so, yet he cannot be back by Christmas; that I must hear the joy-bells ring, and see the merry Christmas cheer *alone*. It is true that he earnestly and insistantly begs of me to gather all my people, father, mother, boys, girls, around me. But, after all, what are father, mother, boys, girls, to me? Father never *was* any thing, I will do myself that justice, but at this moment of sore disappointment as I lean my forehead on the letter outspread on the table before me, and dim its sentences with tears, I *belittle* even the boys. No doubt that by-and-by I shall derive a little solace from the thought of their company; that when they come I shall even be inveigled into some sort of hilarity with them; but at present, "No."

There are some days on which all ills gather together as at a meeting. This is one. Barbara is prostrated by a violent headache, and is in such thorough physical pain that even she cannot sympathize with me. Mr. Musgrave never makes his now daily appearance—he comes, as I jubilantly notice, as regularly as the postman—until late in the afternoon. All day, therefore, I must refrain myself and be silent. And I am never one for brooding with private dumbness over my woes. I much prefer to air them by expression and complaint. About noon it strikes me that, *faute de mieux*, I will go and see Mrs. Huntley, tell her *suddenly* that Roger is not coming back, and see if she looks vexed or confused or grieved. Accordingly, soon after luncheon, I set off in the pony-carriage. It is a quiet sultry-looking unclouded day. One uniform livery of mist clothes sky and earth, dimming the glories of the dying leaves, and making them look dull and sodden. Every thing has a drenched air: each crimson bramble-leaf is clothed in rain-drops, and yet it is not raining. The air is thick and heavy, and one swallows it like something solid, but it is not raining: in fact, it is an English fine day.

Under the delusive idea that it is warm, or at least not cold, I have protected my face with no veil, my hands with no mittens; so that, long before I reach the shelter of the Portugal laurels that warmly hem in and border Mrs. Huntley's little graveled sweep, the end of my nose feels like an icy promontory at a great distance from me, and my hands do not feel at all. Mrs. Huntley *is* at home. Wise woman! I knew that she would be. I suppose that I follow on the footsteps of the butler more quickly than is usual, for, as the door opens, and before I can get a view of the inmate or inmates, I hear a hurried noise of scrambling, as of some one suddenly jumping up. For a little airy woman who looks as if one could blow her away—puff!—like a morsel of thistle-down or a snowball, what a heavy foot Mrs. Huntley has! The next moment, I am disabused. Mrs. Huntley has clearly not moved. It was not *she* that scrambled. She is lying back in a deep arm-chair, her silky head gently denting the flowered cushion, the points of two pretty shoes slightly advanced toward the fire, and a large feather fan leisurely waving to and fro, in one white hand. Beyond the *fan* movement she is not *doing* any thing that I can detect.

"How do you do?" say I, bustling in, in a hurry to reach the fire. "How comfortable you look! how cold it is!—Algy!!" For the enigma of the noise is solved. It was Algy who shuffled and scuffled—yes, scuffled up from the low stool which he has evidently been sharing with the pretty shoes—at Mrs. Huntley's feet, on to his long legs, on which he is now standing, not at all at ease. He does not answer.

"Algy!" repeat I, in a tone of the profoundest, accentedest surprise, involuntarily turning my back upon my hostess and facing my brother.

"Well, what about me?" he cries tartly, irritated (and no wonder) by my open mouth and tragical air.

"What *has* brought you here?" I ask slowly, and with a tactless emphasis.

"The fly from the White Hart," he answers, trying to laugh, but looking confused and angry.

"But I mean—I thought you told me, when I asked you to Tempest this week, that you could not get away for an *hour*!"

"No more I could," he answers impatiently, yet stammering; "quite unexpected—did not know when I wrote—have to be back to-night."

"Will not you come nearer the fire?" says Mrs. Huntley, in her slow sugared tones, with a well-bred ignoring of our squabble. "I am sure that you must be perished with cold."

I recollect myself and comply. As I sit down I catch a glimpse of myself in the glass. It is indeed difficult to abstain from the sight of one's self, however little fond one may be of it, so thickly is the room set round with rose-draped mirrors. For the moment, O friends, I will own to you that I appear to myself nothing less than *brutally* ugly. I know that I am not so in reality, that the disfigurement is only temporary, but none the less does the consciousness deeply, deeply depress me. My nose is of a lively scarlet, which the warmth of the room is quickly deepening into a lowering purple. My quick passage through the air has set my hat a little awry, giving me a falsely rakish air, and the wind has loosened my hair—not into a picturesque and comely disorder, but into mere untidiness. And, meanwhile, how admirably small and cool *her* nose looks! What rest and composure in her whole pose! What a neat refinement in the disposition of her hair! What a soft luxury in her dress! Even my one indisputable advantage of *youth* seems to me as dirt. Looking at the completeness of her native grace, I *despise* youth. I think it an ill and ugly thing in its green unripeness. I look round the room. After the thick outside air, saturated with moisture, I think that the warm atmosphere would, were my spirit less disquieted, lull me quickly to sleep. How perfumed it is, not with any meretricious artificial scents, but with the clean and honest smell of sweet live flowers. Yes, though I am aware that Mrs. Huntley has no conservatory, yet hot-house flowers and airy ferns are scattered about the room in far greater profusion than in mine, with all Roger's imposing range of glass—scattered about here, there, and everywhere; not as if they were a rare and holiday treat, but a most common, every-day occurrence. There is not much work to be seen about, and *not a book!* On the other hand, lounging-chairs, suited to the length or shortness of *any* back; rococo photograph stands, framing either a great many men, or a few men in a great many attitudes; soothing pictures—*décolleté* Venuses, Love's *greuze* heads—tied up with rose-ribbon, and a sleepy half-light. On a small table at the owner's elbow, a blue-velvet jeweler's case stands open. On its white-satin lining my long-sighted eyes enable me to decipher the name of Hunt and Roskell; and it does not need any long sight to observe the solid breadth of the gold band bracelet, set with large, dull turquoises and little points of brilliant light, which is its occupant. As I note this phenomenon, my heart burns within me—yea, burns even more hotly than my nose. For father keeps Algy very tight, and I know that he has only three hundred pounds a year, besides his pay.

"I have had such bad news to-day," I say, suddenly, looking my *vis-à-vis* full and directly in the face.

"Yes?"

So far she certainly shows no signs of emotion. Her fan is still waving with slow steadiness. I see the diamonds on her hands (whence did *they* owe their rise, I wonder?) glint in the fire-light.

"Roger is not coming back!"

"Not at all?" with a slight raising of the eyebrows.

"Not before Christmas, certainly."

"Really! how disappointing! I am very sorry!"

There is not a particle of sorrow in face or tone: only the counterfeit grief of an utterly indifferent acquaintance. My heart feels a little lightened.

"And have *you* no better luck, either?" I say, more cheerfully. "Is there no talk of your—of Mr. Huntley coming back?"

Her eyelids droop: her breast heaves in a placid sigh.

"Not the slightest, I am afraid."

What to say next? I have had enough of asking after her child. I will not fall into *that* error again. Ask who all the men in the rococo frames are?—which of them, or whether any, is *Mr.* Huntley? On consideration, I decide not to do this either; and, after one or two more stunted attempts at talk, I take my leave. I ask Algy to accompany me just down the drive, and with a most grudging and sulky air of unwillingness he complies. Alas! he always used to like to be with us girls. The ponies are fresh, and we have almost reached the gate before I speak, with a difficult hesitation.

"Algy," say I, "did you happen to notice that—that *bracelet?*"

He does not answer. He is looking the other way, and turns only the back of his head toward me.

"It was from Hunt and Roskell," I say.

"Oh!"

"It must have—must have—*come to* a good deal," I go on, timidly.

He has turned his face to me now. I cannot complain, but indeed, as it now is, I prefer the back of his head, so white and headstrong does he look.

"I wish to God," he says, in a voice of low anger, "that you would be so obliging as to mind your own business, and allow me to mind mine!"

"But it *is* mine!" I cry, passionately; "what right has she to be sitting all day with young men on stools at her feet?—she, a married woman, with her husband—"

"This comes extremely well from *you*," he says, in a voice of concentrated anger, with a bitterly-sneering tone; "*how is Musgrave?*"

Before I can answer, he has jumped out, and is half-way back to the house. But indeed I am dumb. Is it possible that *he* makes such a mistake?—that he does not see the difference?

For the next half-mile, I see neither ponies, nor misty hedges, nor wintry high-road, for tears. I *used* to get on so well with the boys!

CHAPTER XXVII

When I return home, I find that Barbara is still no better. She is still lying in her darkened room, and has asked not to be disturbed. And even *my* wrongs are not such as to justify my forcing myself upon the painful privacy of a sick-headache. How much the better am I then than I was before my late expedition? I have brought home my old grievance quite whole and unlightened by communication, and I have got a new and fresh one in addition, with absolutely no one to whom to impart it; for, even when Frank comes, I will certainly not tell *him*. I am too restless to remain in-doors over the fire, though thoroughly chilled by my late drive, and resolve to try and restore my circulation by a brisk walk in the park.

The afternoon is still young, and the day is mending. A wind has risen, and has pulled aside the steel-colored cloud-curtain, and let heaven's eyes—blue, though faint and watery—look through. And there comes another strong puff of autumnal wind, and lo! the sun, and the leaves float down in a sudden shower of amber in his light. I march along quickly and gravely through the long drooped grass—no longer sweet and fresh and upright, in its green summer coat—through the frost-seared pomp of the bronze bracken, till I reach a little knoll, whose head is crowned by twelve great brother beeches. From time immemorial they have been called the Twelve Apostles, and under one apostle I now stand, with my back against his smooth and stalwart trunk.

How *beaming* is death to them! Into what a glorious crimson they decline! My eyes travel from one tree-group to another, and idly consider the many-colored majesty of their decay. Over all the landscape there is a look of plaintive uncontent. The distant town, with its two church-spires, is choked and effaced in mist: the very sun is sickly and irresolute. All Nature seems to say, "Have pity upon me—I die!"

It is not often that our mother is in sympathy with her children. Mostly when we cry she broadly laughs; when we laugh and are merry she weeps; but to-day my mood and hers match. The tears are as near my eyes as hers—as near hers as mine.

"'See the leaves around us falling!'"

say I, aloud, stretching out my right arm in dismal recitation. We had the hymn last Sunday, which is what has put it into my head:

"'See the leaves around us falling,
    Dry and withered to the ground—'"

Another voice breaks in:

"'Thus to thoughtless mortals calling—.'"

"How you made me jump!" cry I, descending with an irritated leap to prose, and at least making the leaves say something entirely different from what they had ever been known to say before.

"Why did not you bring your sentinel, Vick?"

He—it is Musgrave, of course—has joined me, and is leaning his flat back also against the apostle, and, like me, is looking at the mist, at the red and yellow leaves—at the whole low-spirited panorama.

"She is ill," say I, lamentably, drawing a portrait in lamp-black and Indian-ink of the whole family; "we are *all* ill—Barbara is ill!"

"Poor Barbara!"

"She has got a headache."

"Poor Barbara!"

"And I have got a heartache," say I, more for the sake of preserving the harmony of my sketch, and for making a pendant to Barbara, than because the phrase accurately describes my state.

"Poor *you!*"

"*Poor me, indeed!*" cry I, with emphasis, and to this day I cannot make up my mind whether the ejaculation were good grammar or no.

"I have had *such* bad news," I continue, feeling, as usual, a sensible relief from the communication of my grief. "Roger is not coming back!"

"*Not at all?*"

The words are the same as those employed by Mrs. Huntley; but there is much more alacrity and liveliness in the tone.

"*Not at all!*" repeat I, scornfully, looking impatiently at him; "that is so likely, is not it?"—then "No not *at all*"—I continue, ironically, "he has run off with some one else—some one *black!*" (with a timely reminiscence of Bobby's happy flight of imagination).

"Not till *when*, then?"

"Not till after Christmas," reply I, sighing loudly, "which is almost as bad as not at all."

"I knew *that!*" he says, rather petulantly; "you told me *that* before!"

"*I told you that before?*" cry I, opening my eyes, and raising my voice; "why, how could I? I only heard it myself this morning!"

"It was not you, then," he says, composedly; "it must have been some one else!"

"It *could* have been no one else," retort I, hastily. "I have told no one— no one at least from whom *you* could have heard it."

"All the same, I *did* hear it" (with a quiet persistence); "now, who could it have been?" throwing back his head, elevating his chin, and lifting his eyes in meditation to the great depths of burning red in the beech's heart, above him—"ah!"—(overtaking the recollection)—"I know!"

"Who?" say I, eagerly, "not that it *could* have been any one."

"It was Mrs. Huntley!" he answers, with an air of matter-of-fact indifference.

I laugh with insulting triumph. "Well, that *is* a bad hit! What a pity that you did not fix upon some one else! I have once or twice suspected you of drawing the long bow—*now* I am sure of it! As it happens, I have just come from Mrs. Huntley, and she knew no more about it than the babe unborn!"

I am looking him full in the face, but, to my surprise, I cannot detect the expression of confusion and defeat which I anticipate. There is only the old white-anger look that I have such a happy knack of calling up on his features.

"I *am* a consummate liar!" he says, quietly, though his eyes flash. "Every one knows *that*; but, all the same, she *did* tell me."

"I do not believe a word of it!" cry I, in a fury.

He makes no answer, but, lifting his hat, begins to walk quickly away. For a hundred yards I allow him to go unrecalled; then, as I note his quickly-diminishing figure and the heavy mists beginning to fold him, my resolution fails me; I take to my heels and scamper after him.

"Stop!" say I, panting as I come up with him, "I dare say—perhaps— you *thought* you were speaking truth!—there must, must be some *mistake!*"

He does not answer, but still walks quickly on.

"Tell me!" cry I, posting on alongside of him, breathless and distressed— "when was it? where did you hear it? how long ago?"

"I never heard it?"

"Yes, you did," cry I, passionately, asseverating what I have so lately and passionately denied. "You know you did; but when was it? how was it? where was it?"

"It was *nowhere*," he answers with a cold, angry smile. "I was *drawing the long bow!*"

I stop in baffled rage and misery. I stand stock-still, with the long, dying grass wetly and limply clasping my ankles. To my surprise he stops too.

"I wish you were *dead!*" I say tersely, and it is not a figure of speech. For the moment I do honestly wish it.

"Do you?" he answers, throwing me back a look of hardly inferior animosity; "I dare say I do not much mind." A little pause, during which we eye each other, like two fighting-cocks. "Even if I *were* dead," he says, in a low voice—"mind, I do not blame you for wishing it—sometimes I wish it myself—but even if I *were*, I do not see how that would hinder Sir Roger and Mrs. Huntley from corresponding."

"They *do not* correspond," cry I, violently; "it is a falsehood!" Then, with a quick change of thought and tone: "But if they do, I—I—do not mind! I—I—am very glad—if Roger likes it! There is no harm in it."

"Not the slightest."

"Do you *always* stay at home?" cry I, in a fury, goaded out of all politeness and reserve by the surface false acquiescence of his tone; "do you *never* go away? I *wish* you would! I wish"—(speaking between laughing and crying)—"that you could take your abbey up on your back, as a snail does its shell, and march off with it into another county."

"But unfortunately I cannot."

"What have I done to you?" I cry, falling from anger to reproach, "that you take such delight in hurting me? You can be pleasant enough to—to other people. I never hear you hinting and sneering away any one else's peace of mind; but as for me, I never—*never* am alone with you that you do not leave me with a pain—a tedious long ache *here*"—(passionately clasping my hands upon my heart).

"Do not I?"—(Then half turning away in a lowered voice)—"*nor you me!*"

"*I!*" repeat I, positively laughing in my scorn of this accusation. "*I* hint! *I* imply! why, I *could* not do it, if I were to be shot for it! it is not *in* me!"

He does not immediately answer; still, he is looking aside, and his color changes.

"Ask mother, ask the boys, ask Barbara," cry I, in great excitement, "whether I ever *could* wrap up any thing neatly, if I wished it ever so much? Always, *always*, I have to blurt it out! *I* hint!"

"Hint! no!" he repeats, in a tone of vexed bitterness. "Well, no! no one could accuse you of *hinting*! Yours is honest, open cut and thrust!"

"If it is," retort I, bluntly, still speaking with a good deal of heat, "it is your own fault! I have no wish to quarrel, being such near neighbors, and—and—altogether—of course I had rather be on good terms than bad ones! When you *let* me—when you leave me alone—I *almost*—sometimes I *quite* like you. I am speaking seriously! I *do*."

"You do not say so?" again turning his head aside, and speaking with the objectionable intonation of irony.

"At home," pursue I, still chafing under the insult to my amiability, "I never was reckoned quarrelsome—*never*! Of course I was not like Barbara—there are not many like her—but I did very well. Ask *any one* of them—it does not matter which—they will all tell you the same—whether I did not!"

"You were a household angel, in fact?"

"I was nothing of the kind," cry I, very angry, and yet laughing: the laughter caused by the antagonism of the epithet with the many recollected blows and honest sounding cuffs that I have, on and off, exchanged with Bobby.

A pause.

The sun has quite gone now: sulky and feeble, he has shrunk to his cold bed in the west, and the victor-mist creeps, crawls, and soaks on unopposed.

"Good-night!" cry I, suddenly. "I am going!" and I am as good as my word.

With the triple agility of health, youth, and indignation, I scurry away through the melancholy grass, and the heaped and fallen leaves, home.

CHAPTER XXVIII

Ding-dong bell! ding-dong bell! The Christmas bells are ringing. Christmas has come—Christmas as it appears on a Christmas card, white and hard, and beset with puffed-out, ruffled robins. Only Nature is wise enough not to express the ironical wish that we may have a "merry one."

For myself, I have but small opinion of Christmas as a time of jollity. Solemn—*blessed*, if you will—but no, not jovial. At no time do the dead so clamor to be remembered. Even those that went a long time ago, the regret for whose departure has settled down to a tender, almost pleasant pain; whom at other times we go nigh to forget; even they cry out loud, "Think of us!"

When all the family is gathered, when the fire burns quick and clear, and the church-bells ring out grave and sweet, neither will *they* be left out. But, on the other hand, to one who has paid his bills, and in whose family Death's cannon have as yet made no breaches, I do not see why it may not be a season of moderate, placid content.

Festivity! jollity! *never!* I have paid my bills, and there are no gaps among my people. Sometimes I tremble when I think how many we are; one of us must go soon. But, as yet, when I count us over, none lacks. Father, mother, Algy, Bobby, the Brat, Tou Tou. Slightly as I have spoken of them to myself, and conscientiously as I have promised myself to derive no pleasure from their society, and even to treat them with distant coolness, if they are, any of them, and Bobby especially—it is he that I most mistrust—more joyfully disposed than I think fitting, yet my heart has been growing ever warmer and warmer at the thought of them, as Christmas-time draws nigh; and now, as I kiss their firm, cold, healthy cheeks—(I declare that Bobby's cheeks are as hard as marbles), I know how I have lied to myself.

Father is not in quite so good a humor as I could have wished, his man having lost his hat-box *en route*, and consequently his nose is rather more aquiline than I think desirable.

"Do not be alarmed!" says Bobby, in a patronizing aside, introducing me, as if I were a stranger, to father's peculiarities; "a little infirmity of temper, but the *heart* is in the right place."

"Bobby," say I, anxiously, in a whisper, "has he—has he brought the *bag*?"

Bobby shakes his head.

"I *knew* he would not," cry I, rather crestfallen. Then, with sudden exasperation: "I wish I had not given it to him; he always *hated* it. I wish I had given it to Roger instead."

"Never you mind!" cries Bobby, while his round eyes twinkle mischievously; "I dare say he has got one by now, a nice one, all beads and wampums, that the old Begum has made him."

I laugh, but I also sigh. What a long time it seems since I was jealous of Bobby's Begum! We are a little behind father, whispering with our heads together, while he, in his raspingest voice, is giving his delinquent a month's warning. That tone! it still makes me feel sneaky.

"Bobby," say I, putting my arm through his substantial one, and speaking in a low tone of misgiving, "how is he? how has he been?"

"We have been a little fractious," replies Bobby, leniently—"a little disposed to quarrel with our bread-and-butter; but, as you may remember, my dear, from *your* experience of our humble roof, Christmas never was our happiest time."

"No, never," reply I, pensively.

The storm is rising: at least father's voice is. It appears that the valet is not only to go, but to go without a character.

"Never you mind," repeats Bobby, reassuringly, seeing me blench a little at these disused amenities, pressing the hand that rests on his arm against his stout side; "it is nothing to *you*! bless your heart, you are the apple of his eye."

"Am I?" reply I, laughing. "It has newly come to me, if I am."

"And I am his 'good, brave Bobby!'—his 'gallant boy!'—do you know why?"

"No."

"Because I am going to Hong-Kong, and he hears that they are keeping two nice roomy graves open all the time there!"

"You are *not*?" (in a tone of keen anxiety and pain); then, with a sudden change of tone to a nervous and constrained amenity: "Yes, it *is* a nice-sized room, is not it? My only fault with it is, that the windows are so high up that one cannot see out of them when one is sitting down."

For father, having demolished his body-servant, and reduced mother to her usual niche-state, now turns to me, and, in his genialest, happiest society-manner, compliments me on my big house.

That is a whole day ago. Since then, I have grown used to seeing father's austere face, unbent into difficult suavity, at the opposite end of the dinner-table to me, to hearing the well-known old sound of Tou Tou's shrieks of mixed anguish and delight, as Bobby rushes after her in headlong pursuit, down the late so silent passages; and to looking complacently from one to another of the holiday faces round the table, where Barbara and I have sat, during the last noiseless month, in stillest dialogue or preoccupied silence.

I *love* noise. You may think that I have odd taste; but I *love* Bobby's stentor laugh, and Tou Tou's ear-piercing yells. I even forget to think whether their mirth passes the appointed bounds I had set it. I have mislaid my receipt of cold repression. My heart goes out to them.

I have been a little disturbed as to how to dispose of father during the day, but he mercifully takes that trouble off my hands. Providence has brought good out of evil, congenial occupation out of the hat-box. He has spent all the few daylight-hours in telegraphing for it to every station on the line; in telling several home-truths to the porters at our own station, which—it being Christmas-time, and they consequently all more or less tipsy—they have taken with a bland playfulness that he has found a little trying; and, lastly, in writing a long letter to the *Times*. And I, meanwhile, being easy in my mind on his score, knowing that he is happy, am at leisure to be happy myself. In company with my brother, I have spent all the little day in decorating the church, making it into a cheerful, green Christmas bower. We always did it at home.

The dusk has come now—the quick-hurrying, December dusk, and we have all but finished. We have had to beg for a few candles, in order to put our finishing touches here and there about the sombre church. They flame, throwing little jets of light on the glossy laurel-leaves that make collars round the pillars' stout necks; on the fresh moss-beds, vividly green, in the windows; on the dull, round holly-berries. In the glow, the ivy twines in cunning garlands round the rough-sculptured font, and the oak lectern; and, above God's altar, a great white cross of hot-house flowers blooms delicately, telling of summer, and matching the words of old good news beneath it, that brought, as some say, summer, or, at least, the hope of summer, to the world.

Yes, we have nearly done. The Brat stands on the top of a step-ladder, dexterously posing the last wintry garland; and all we others are resting a moment—we and our coadjutors. For we have *two* coadjutors. Mr.

Musgrave, of course. Now, at this moment, through the gray light, and across the candles, I can see him leaning against the font, while Barbara kneels with bent head at his feet, completing the ornamentation of the pedestal. I always knew that things would come right if we waited long enough, and *coming* right they are—*coming*, not *come*, for still, he has not spoken. I have consulted each and all of my family, father excepted, as to the average length of time allotted to *unspoken* courtship, and each has assigned a different period; the *longest*, however, has been already far exceeded by Frank. Tou Tou, indeed, adduces a gloomy case of a young man, who spent two years and a half in dumb longing, and broke a blood-vessel and died at the end of them; but this is so discouraging an anecdote, that we all poo-poohed it as unauthentic.

"Perhaps he does not mean to speak at all!" says the Brat, starting a new and hazardous idea; "perhaps he means to take it for granted!"

"Walk out with her, some fine morning," says Algy, laughing, "and say, like Wemmick, 'Hallo! here's a church! let's have a wedding!'"

"It would be a good thing," retorts the Brat, gravely, "if there were a printed form for such occasions; it would be a great relief to people."

This talk did not happen in the church, but at an evening *séance* overnight. Our second coadjutor is Mrs. Huntley.

"I am afraid I am not very efficient," she says, with a pathetic smile. "I can't *stand* very long, but, if I might be allowed to sit down now and then, I might perhaps be some little help."

And sat down she has, accordingly, ever since, on the top pulpit-step. It seems that Algy cannot stand very long, either; for he has taken possession of the step next below the top one, and there he abides. Thank Heaven! they are getting dark now! If *legitimate* lovers, whose cooing is desirable and approved, are a sickly and sickening spectacle, surely the sight of illegitimate lovers would make the blood boil in the veins of Moses, Miriam, or Job.

Bobby, Tou Tou, and I, having no one to hang over us, or gawk amorously up at us, are sitting in a row in our pew. Bobby has garlanded Tou Tou preposterously with laurel, to give us an idea, as he says, of how he himself will look by-and-by, after some future Trafalgar. Now, he is whispering to me—a whisper accompanied by one of those powerful and painful nudges, with which he emphasizes his conversation on his listener's ribs.

"Look at him!" indicating his elder brother, and speaking with a tone of disgust and disparagement; "did you ever see such a *beast* as he looks?"

"Not often!" reply I, readily, with that fine intolerance which one never sees in full bloom after youth is past.

"I say, Nancy!" with a second and rather lesser nudge, "if ever you see any symptoms of—of *that*—" (nodding toward the pulpit) "in me—"

"If—" repeat I, scornfully, "of course I shall!"

"Well, that is as it may be, but if you *do*, mind what I tell you—do not say any thing to anybody, but—*put an end to me*! it does not matter *how*; smother me with bolsters; run your bodkin up to its hilt in me—"

"Even if I *did*," interrupt I, laughing, "I should never reach any vital part—you are *much* too fat!"

"I should not be so fat then," returns he, gravely, amiably overlooking the personality of my observation; "love would have pulled me down!"

The Brat has nearly finished. He is nimbly descending the ladder, with a long, guttering dip in his right hand.

"The other two—" begins Bobby, thoughtfully, turning his eyes from pulpit to font.

"I do not mind *them* half so much," interrupt I, indulgently; "they are not half so disgusting."

"Has he done it yet?" (lowering his cheerful loud voice to an important whisper).

I shake my head.

"Not unless he has done it since luncheon! he had not *then*; I asked her."

"I am beginning to think that *your* old man's plan was the best, after all," continues Bobby, affably. "I thought him rather out of date, at the time, for applying to your parents, but, after all, it saved a great deal of trouble, and spared us a world of suspense."

I am silent; swelling with a dumb indignation at the epithet bestowed on my Roger; but unable to express it outwardly, as I well know that, if I do, I shall be triumphantly quoted against myself.

"Who will break it to Toothless Jack?" says Bobby, presently, with a laugh; "after all the expense he has been at, too, with those teeth! it is not as if it were a beggarly two or three, but a whole complete new set—thirty-two individual grinders!"

"Such beauties, too!" puts in Tou Tou, cackling.

"It is a thousand pities that they should be allowed to go out of the family," says Bobby, warmly. "Tou Tou, my child—" (putting his arm round her shoulders)—"a bright vista opens before you!—your charms are approaching maturity!—with a little encouragement he might be induced to lay his teeth—two and thirty, mind—at your feet!"

Tou Tou giggles, and asserts that she will "kick them away, if he does." Bobby mildly but firmly remonstrates, and points out to her the impropriety and ingratitude of such a line of conduct. But his arguments, though acute and well put, are not convincing, and the subject is continued, with ever-increasing warmth, all the way home.

CHAPTER XXIX

It is Christmas-day—a clean white Christmas, pure and crisp. Wherever one looks, one's eyes water cruelly. For my part, I am very thankful that it did not occur to God to make the world always white. I hate snow's blinding livery. Each tiniest twig on the dry harsh trees is overladen with snow. It is a wonder that they do not break under it; nor is there any wind to shake down and disperse it. Tempest is white; the church is white: the whole world colorless and blinding. I have been in the habit of looking upon Vick as a white dog; to-day she appears disastrously dark—dirty brunette. Soap-and-water having entirely failed to restore her complexion. Bobby kindly proposes to *pipeclay* her.

We have all been to church, and admired our own decorations. And through all the prayer and the praise, and the glad Christmas singing, my soul has greatly hungered for Roger. Yes, even though all the boys are round me—Bobby on this side, the Brat on that—Algy directly in front; all behaving nicely, too; for are not they right under father's eyes? Yes, and, for the matter of that, under the rector's too, as he towers straight above us, under his ivy-bush—the ivy-bush into which Bobby was so anxious yesterday to insert some mistletoe.

Church is over now, and the short afternoon has also slipped by. We are at dinner; we are dining early to-night—at half-past six o'clock, and we are to have a dance for the servants afterward. Any hospitality to my equals I have steadily and stoutly declined, but it seems a shame to visit my own loneliness on the heads of the servants, to whom it is nothing. They have always had a Christmas-dance in Roger's reign, and so a dance they are to have now. We have religiously eaten our beef and plum-pudding, and have each made a separate little blue fire of burnt brandy in our spoon.

It is dessert now, and father has proposed Roger's health. I did not expect it, and I never was so nearly betrayed into feeling fond of father in my life. They all drink it, each wishing him something good. As for me, I have been a fool always, and I am a fool now. I can wish him nothing, my voice is choked and my eyes drowned in inappropriate tears; only, from the depths of my heart, I ask God to give him every thing that He has of choicest and best. For a moment or two, the wax-lights, the purple grapes, the gleaming glass and shining silver, the kindly, genial faces swim blurred before my vision. Then I hastily wipe away my tears, and smile back at them all. As I raise my glistening eyes, I meet those of Mr. Musgrave fixed upon me—(he is the only stranger present). His look is not one that wishes to be returned; on the contrary, it is embarrassed at being met. It is a glance that puzzles me, full of inquiring curiosity, mixed with a sort of mirth. In a second—I could not tell you why—I look hastily away.

"I wonder what he is doing *now, this very minute!*" says Tou Tou, who is dining in public for the first time, and whose conversation is checked and her deportment regulated by Bobby, who has been at some pains to sit beside her, and who guides her behavior by the help of many subtle and unseen pinches under the table; from revolting against which a fear of father hinders her, a fact of which Bobby is most basely aware.

"Had not you better telegraph?" asks Algy, with languid irony (Algy certainly is not quite so nice as he used to be). "Flapping away the blue-tailed fly, with a big red-and-yellow bandana, probably."

"Playing the banjo for a lot of little niggers to dance to!" suggests the Brat.

"They are all wrong, are not they, Nancy?" says Bobby, in a lowered voice, to me, on whose left hand he has placed himself; "he is sitting in his veranda, is not he? in a palm hat and nankeen breeches, with his arm around the old Wampoo."

"I dare say," reply I, laughing. "I hope so," for, indeed, I am growing quite fond of my dusky rival.

The ball is to be in the servants' hall; it is a large, long room, and thither, when all the guests are assembled, we repair. We think that we shall make a greater show, and inspire more admiration, if we appear in pairs. I therefore make my entry on father's arm. Never with greater trepidation have I entered any room, for I am to open the ball with the butler, and the prospect fills me with dismay. If he were a venerable family servant, a hoary-headed old seneschal, who had known Roger in petticoats, it would have been nothing. I could have chattered filially to him; but he is a youngish man, who came only six months ago. On what subjects can we converse? I feel small doubt that his own sufferings will be hardly inferior in poignancy to mine.

The room is well lit, and the candles shine genially down from the laurel garlands and ivy festoons which clothe the walls. They light the faces and various dresses of a numerous assembly—every groom, footman, housemaid, and scullion, from far and near. The ladies seem largely to preponderate both in number and *aplomb*; the men appearing, for the more part, greatly disposed to run for shelter behind the bolder petticoats; particularly the stablemen. The footmen, being more accustomed to ladies' society, are less embarrassed by their own hands, and by the exigencies of chivalry. This inversion of the usual attitude of the sexes, will, no doubt, be set more than right when we have retired. The moment has arrived. I quit father's arm—for the first time in my life I am honestly sorry to drop it—and go up to my destined partner.

"Ashton," say I, with an attempt at an easy and unembarrassed smile, "will you dance this quadrille with me?"

"Thank you, my lady."

How calm he is! how self-possessed. Oh, that he would impart to me the secret of his composure! I catch sight of the Brat, who is passing at the moment.

"Brat!" cry I, eagerly, snatching at his coat-sleeve, like a drowning man at a straw. "Will *you* be our *vis-à-vis*?"

"All right," replies the Brat, gayly, "but I have not got a partner yet."

Off he goes in search of one, and Ashton and I remain *tête-à-tête*. I suppose I ought to take his arm, and lead him to the top of the room. After a moment of hot hesitation, I do this. Here we are, arrived. Oh, why did I ask him so soon? Two or three minutes elapse before the Brat's return.

"How nicely you have all done the decorations!"

"I am glad you think so, my lady."

"They are better than ours at the church."

"Do you think so, my lady?"

A pause. Everybody is choosing partners. Tou Tou, grinning from ear to ear, is bidding a bashful button-boy to the merry dance. Father—do my eyes deceive me?—father himself is leading out the housekeeper. Evidently he is saying something dignifiedly humorous to her, for she is laughing. I wish that he would sometimes be dignifiedly humorous to us, or even humorous without the dignity. Barbara, true to her life-long instincts, is inviting the clergyman's shabby, gawky man-of-all-work, at whom the ladies'-maids are raising the nose of contempt. Mr. Musgrave is soliciting a kitchen-wench.

"Are there as many here as you expected?"

"Quite, my lady."

Another pause.

"I hope," with bald affability, in desperation of a topic, "that you will all enjoy yourselves!"

"Thank you, my lady!"

Praise God! here is the Brat at last! Owing, I suppose, to the slenderness and fragile tenuity of his own charms, the Brat is a great admirer of fine women, the bigger the better; quantity, not quality; and, true to his colors, he now arrives with a neighboring cook, a lady of sixteen stone, on his arm.

We take our places. While chassezing and poussetting, thank Heaven, a very little talk goes a very long way. My mind begins to grow more easy. I am even sensible of a little feeling of funny elation at the sound of the fiddles gayly squeaking. I can look about me and laugh inwardly at the distant sight of Tou Tou and the button-boy turning each other nimbly round; of father, in the fourth figure, blandly backing between Mrs. Mitchell and a cook-maid.

We have now reached the fifth. At the few balls I have hitherto frequented it has been a harmless figure enough; hands all round, and a repetition of *l'été*. But *now*—oh, horror! what do I see? Everybody far and near is standing in attitude to gallopade. The Brat has his little arm round the cook's waist—at least not all the way round—it would take a lengthier limb than his to effect *that*; but a bit of the way, as far as it will go. An awful idea strikes me. Must Ashton and I gallopade too? I glance nervously toward him. He is looking quite as apprehensive at the thought that I shall expect him to gallopade with me, as I am at the thought that he will expect me to gallopade with him. I do not know how it is that we make our mutual alarm known to each other, only I know that, while all the world is gallopading round us, we gallopade not. Instead, we take hands, and jig distantly round each other.

The improvised valse soon ends, and I look across at the Brat. Gallant boy! the beads of perspiration stand on his young brow, but there is no look of blenching! When the time comes he will be ready to do it again.

As I stand in silent amusement watching him, having, for the moment, no dancing duties of my own, I hear a voice at my elbow, Bobby's, who, having come in later than the rest of us, has not been taking part in the dance.

"Nancy! Nancy!" in a tone of hurried excitement, "for the love of Heaven look at *father*! If you stand on tiptoe you will be able to see him; he has been *gallopading*! When I saw his venerable coat-tails flying, a feather would have knocked me down! You really ought to see it" (lowering his voice confidentially), "it might give you an idea about your own old man, and the old Wam—"

"*Hang* the old Wampoo!" cry I, with inelegant force, laughing.

The duty part of the evening is over now. We have all signalized ourselves by feats of valor. I have scampered through an unsociable country-dance with the head coachman, and have had my smart gown of faint pink and pearl color nearly torn off my back by the ponderous-footed pair that trip directly after me. We have, in fact, done our duty, and may retire as soon as we like. But the music has got into our feet, and we promise ourselves one valse among ourselves before we depart.

The Brat is the only exception. He still cleaves to his cook; dancing with her is a *tour de force*, on which he piques himself. Mrs. Huntley and Algy are already flying down the room in an active, tender embrace. I have been asked as long ago as before dinner by Mr. Musgrave. I was rather surprised and annoyed at his inviting *me* instead of Barbara; but as, with this exception, his conduct has been unequivocally demonstrative, I console myself with the notion that he looks upon me as the necessary pill to which Barbara will be the subsequent jam.

The first bars of the valse are playing when Bobby comes bustling up. Healthy jollity and open mirth are written all over his dear, fat face.

"Come along, Nancy! let us have *one* more scamper before we die!"

"I am engaged to Mr. Musgrave," reply I, with a graceless and discontented curl of lip, and raising of nose.

"All right!" says Bobby, philosophically, walking away; "I am sure I do not mind, only I had a fancy for having *one* more spin with you."

"So you shall!" cry I, impulsively, with a sharp thought of Hong-Kong, running after him, and putting his solid right arm round my waist.

Away we go in mad haste. Like most sailors, Bobby dances well. I am nothing very wonderful, but I suit *him*. In many musicless waltzings of winter evenings, down the lobby at home, we have learned to fit each other's step exactly. At our first pausing to recover breath, I become sensible of a face behind me, of a fierce voice in my ear.

"I had an idea, Lady Tempest, that this was *our* dance!"

"So it was!" reply I, cheerfully; "but you see I have cut you!"

"So I perceive!"

"Had not you better call Bobby out!" cry I, with a jeering laugh, tired of his eternal black looks. "You really are *too* silly! I wish I had a looking-glass here to show you your face!"

"Do you?" (very shortly).

Repartee is never Frank's forte. This is all that he now finds with which to wither me. However, even if he had any thing more or more pungent to say, I should not hear him, for I am beginning to dance off again.

"What a fool he is to care!" says Bobby, contemptuously; "after all, he is an ill-tempered beast! I suppose if one kicked him down-stairs it would put a stop to his marrying Barbara, would not it?"

I laugh.

"I suppose so."

It is over now. The last long-drawn-out notes have ceased to occupy the air. As far as *we* are concerned, the ball is over, for we have quitted it. We have at length removed the *gêne* of our presence from the company, and have left them to polka and schottische their fill until the morning. We have reached our own part of the house. My cheeks are burning and throbbing with the quick, unwonted exercise. My brain is unpleasantly stirred: a hundred thoughts in a second run galloping through it. I leave the others in the warm-lit drawing-room, briskly talking and discussing the scene we have quitted, and slip away through the door, into a dark and empty adjacent anteroom, where the fire lies at death's door, low and dull, and the candles are unlighted.

I draw the curtains, unbar the shutters, and, lifting the heavy sash, look out. A cold, still air, sharp and clear, at once greets my face with its frosty kisses. Below me, the great house-shadow projects in darkness, and beyond it lies a great and dazzling field of shining snow, asleep in the moonlight.

Snow-trees, snow-bushes, sparkle up against the dusk quiet of the sky. No movement anywhere! absolute stillness! perfect silence! It is broken now, this silence, by the church-clock with slow wakefulness chiming twelve. Those slow strokes set me a thinking. I hear no longer the loud and lively voices next door, the icy penetration of the air is unfelt by me, as I lean, with my elbow on the sill, looking out at the cold grace of the night. My mind strays gently away over all my past life—over the last important year. I think of my wedding, of my little live wreath of sweet Nancies, of our long, dusty journey, of Dresden.

With an honest, stinging heart-pang, I think of my ill-concealed and selfish weariness in our twilight walks and scented drives, of the look of hurt kindness on his face, at his inability to please me. I think of our return, of the day when he told me of the necessity for his voyage to Antigua, and of my own egotistic unwillingness to accompany him. I think of our parting, when I shed such plenteous tears—tears that seem to me now to have been so much more tears of remorse, of sorrow that I was not sorrier, than of real grief. In every scene I seem to myself to have borne a most shabby part.

My meditations are broken in upon by a quick step approaching me, by a voice in my ear—Algy's.

"You are *here*, are you? I have been looking for you everywhere! Why, the window is *open*! For Heaven's sake let me get you a cloak! you know how delicate your chest is. For *my* sake, *do*!"

It is too dark to see his face, but there is a quick, excited tenderness in his voice.

"*My* chest delicate!" cry I, in an accent of complete astonishment. "Well, it is news to me if it is! My dear boy, what has put such an idea into your head? and if I got a cloak, I should think it would be for my *own* sake, not yours!"

He has been leaning over me in the dusk. At my words he starts violently and draws back.

"It is *you*, is it?" he says, in an altered voice of constraint, whence all the mellow tenderness has fled.

"To be sure!" reply I, matter-of-factly. "For whom did you take me?"

But though I ask, alas! I know.

—

CHAPTER XXX

How are unmusical people to express themselves when they are glad? People with an ear and a voice can sing, but what is to become of those who have not? Must they whoop inarticulately? For myself, I do not know one tune from another. I am like the man who said that he knew two tunes, one was "God save the Queen," and the other was not. And yet to-day I have as good a heart for singing as ever had any of the most famous songsters. In tune, out of tune, I must lift up my voice. It is as urgent a need for me as for any mellow thrush. For my heart—oh, rare case!—is fuller of joy than it can hold. It brims over. Roger is coming back. It is February, and he has been away nearly seven months. All minor evils and anxieties—Bobby's departure for Hong-Kong, Algy's increasing besotment about Mrs. Huntley, and consequent slight estrangement from me—(to me a very bitter thing)—Frank's continued silence as regards Barbara—all these are swallowed up in gladness.

When *he* is back, all will come right. Is it any wonder that they have gone wrong, while *I* only was at the helm? My good news arrived only this morning, and yet, a hundred times in the short space that has elapsed since then, I have rehearsed the manner of our meeting, have practised calling him "Roger," with familiar ease, have fixed upon my gown and the manner of my coiffure, and have wearied Barbara with solicitous queries, as to whether she thinks that I have grown perceptibly plainer in the last seven months, whether she does not think one side of my face better looking than the other, whether she thinks—(with honest anxiety this)—that my appearance is calculated to repel a person grown disused to it. To all which questions, she with untired gentleness gives pleasant and favorable answers.

The inability under which I labored of refraining from imparting *bad* news is tenfold increased in the case of good. I must have some one to whom to relate my prosperity. It will certainly *not* be Mrs. Huntley this time. Though I have struggled against the feeling as unjust, and disloyal to my faith in Roger, I still cannot suppress a sharp pang of distrust and jealousy, as often as I think of her, and of the relation made to me by Frank, as to her former connection with my husband. Neither am I in any hurry to tell Frank. To speak truth, I am in no good-humor with him or with his unhandsome shilly-shallying, and unaccountable postponement of what became a duty months ago.

Never mind! this also will come right when Roger returns. The delightful stir and hubbub in my soul hinder me from working or reading, or any tranquil in-door occupation; and, as afternoon draws on, fair and not cold, I decide upon a long walk. The quick exercise will perhaps moderately tire me, and subdue my fidgetiness by the evening, and nobody can hinder me from thinking of Roger all the way.

Barbara has a cold—a nasty, stuffy, choky cold; so I must do without her. Apparently I must do without Vick too. She makes a feint, indeed, of accompanying me half-way to the front gate, then sits down on her little shivering haunches, smirks, and when I call her, looks the other way, affecting not to hear. On my calling more peremptorily, "Vick! Vick!" she tucks her tail well in, and canters back to the house on three legs.

So it comes to pass that I set out quite alone. I have no definite idea where to go—I walk vaguely along, following my nose, as they say, smiling foolishly, and talking to myself—now under my breath—now out loud. A strong southwest wind blows steadily in my face: it sounded noisy and fierce enough as I sat in the house; but there is no vice or malevolence in it—it is only a soft bluster.

Alternate clouds and sunshine tenant the sky. The shadows of the tree-trunks lie black and defined across the road—branches, twigs, every thing—then comes a sweep of steely cloud, and they disappear, swallowed up in one uniform gray: a colorless moment or two passes, and the sun pushes out again; and they start forth distinct and defined, each little shoot and great limb, into new life on the bright ground. I laugh out loud, out of sheer jollity, as I watch the sun playing at hide-and-seek with them.

What a good world! What a handsome, merry, sweetly-colored world! Unsatisfying? disappointing?—not a bit of it! It must be people's own fault if they find it so.

I have walked a mile or so before I at length decide upon a goal, toward which to tend—a lone and distant cottage, tenanted by a very aged, ignorant, and feudally loyal couple—a cottage sitting by the edge of a brown common—one of the few that the greedy hand of Tillage has yet spared— where geese may still stalk and hiss unreproved, and errant-tinker donkeys crop and nibble undisturbed—

"Where the golden furze
With its green thin spurs
Doth catch at the maiden's gown."

It is altogether a choice and goodly walk; next to nothing of the tame high-road. The path leads through a deep wooded dell; over purple plough-lands; down retired lanes.

After an hour and a quarter of smartish walking, I reach the door. There are no signs of ravaging children about. Long, long ago—years before this generation was born—the noisy children went out; some to the church-yard; some, with clamor of wedding-bells, to separate life. I knock, and after an interval hear the sound of pattens clacking across the flagged floor, and am admitted by an old woman, dried and pickled, by the action of the years, into an active cleanly old mummy, and whose fingers are wrinkled even more than time has done it, by the action of soapsuds. I am received with the joyful reverence due to my exalted station, am led in, and posted right in front of the little red fire and the singing kettle, and introduced to a very old man, who sits on the settle in the warm chimney-corner, dressed in an ancient smock-frock, and with both knotted hands clasped on the top of an old oak staff. He is evidently childish, and breaks now and then into an anile laugh at the thought, no doubt, of some dead old pot-house jest. A complication arises through his persisting in taking me for a sister of Roger's, who died thirty years ago, in early girlhood, and addressing me accordingly. I struggle a little for my identity, but, finding the effort useless, resign it.

"This poor ould person is quoite aimless," says his wife with dispassionate apology; "but what can you expect at noinety-one?"

(Her own years cannot be much fewer.)

I say tritely that it is a great age.

"He's very fatiguin' on toimes!—that he is!" she continues, eying him with contemplated candor—"he crumbles his wittles to that extent that I 'ave to make him sit upo' the *News of the World*."

As it seems to me that the conversation is taking a painful direction, I try to divert it by telling my news; but the bloom is again taken off it by the old man, who declines to be disabused of the idea that the Peninsular is still raging, and that it is Roger's *grandfather* who is returning from that field of glory. After a few more minutes, during which the old wife composedly tells me of all the children she has buried—she has to think twice before she can recollect the exact number—and in the same breath remarks, "How gallus bad their 'taters were last year," I take my departure, and leave the old man still nodding his weak old head, and chuckling to the kettle.

On first leaving the house, I feel dashed and sobered. The inertness and phlegmatic apathy of dry and ugly old age seem to weigh upon and press down the passionate life of my youth, but I have not crossed a couple of ploughed fields and seen the long slices newly ploughed, lying rich and thick in the sun; I have not heard two staves of the throstle's loud song, before I have recovered myself. I also begin to sing. I am not very harmonious, perhaps, I never am; and I wander now and then from the tune; but it is good enough for the stalking geese, my only audience, except a ragged jackass, who, moved by my example, lifts his nose and gives vent to a lengthy bray of infinite yearning.

I am half-way home now. I have reached the wood—Brindley Wood; henceforth I am not very likely to forget its name. The path dips at once and runs steeply down, till it reaches the bottom of the dell, along which a quick brook runs darkling. In summer, when the leaves are out, it is twilight here at high noonday. Hardly a peep of sky to be seen through the green arch of oak and elm; but now, through the net-work of wintry twigs one looks up, and sees the faint, far blue, for the loss of which no leafage can compensate. Winter brownness above, but a more than summer green below—the heyday riot of the mosses. Mossed tree-trunks, leaning over the bustling stream; emerald moss carpets between the bronze dead leaves; all manner of mosses; mosses with little nightcaps; mosses like doll's ferns; mosses like plump cushions; and upon them here and there blazes the glowing red of the small peziza-cups.

I am still singing; and, as no wind reaches this shadowed hollow, I have taken off my hat, and walk slowly along, swinging it in my hand. It is a so little-frequented place, that I give an involuntary start, and my song suddenly dies, when, on turning a corner, I come face to face with another occupant. In a moment I recover myself. It is only Frank, sitting on a great lichened stone, staring at the brook and the trees.

"You seem very cheerful!" he says, rising, stretching out his hand, and not (as I afterward recollect) expressing the slightest surprise at our unlikely rencontre. "I never heard you lift up your voice before."

"I seem what I am," reply I, shortly. "I *am* cheerful."

"You mostly are."

"That is all that *you* know about it," reply I, brusquely, rather resenting the accusation. "I have not been *at all* in good spirits all this—this autumn and winter, not, that is, compared to what I usually am."

"Have not you?"

"I *am* in good spirits to-day, I grant you," continue I, more affably; "it would be very odd if I were not. I should jump out of my skin if I were quite sure of getting back into it again; I have had *such* good news."

"Have you? I wish *I* had" (sighing). "What is it?"

"I will give you three guesses," say I, trying to keep grave, but breaking out everywhere, as I feel, into badly-suppressed smiles.

"Something about the boys, of course!" —(half fretfully)—"it is always the boys."

"It is nothing about the boys—quite wrong. That is *one*."

"The fair Zéphine is no more!—by-the-by, I suppose I should have heard of that."

"It is nothing about the fair Zéphine—wrong again! That is *two!*"

"Barbara has got leave to stay till Easter!"

"Nothing about Barbara!" —(with a slight momentary pang at the ease and unconcern with which he mentions her name).—"By-the-by, I wish you would give up calling her 'Barbara;' she never calls you 'Frank!' There, you have had your three guesses, and you have never come within a mile of it—I shall have to tell you—*Roger is coming back!*" opening my eyes and beginning to laugh joyously.

"*Soon?*" with a quick and breathless change of tone, that I cannot help perceiving, turning sharply upon me.

"*At once!*" reply I, triumphantly; "we may expect him *any day!*"

He receives this information in total silence. He does not attempt the faintest or slightest congratulation.

"I wish I had not told you!" cry I, indignantly; "what a fool I was to imagine that you would feel the slightest interest in any thing that did not concern yourself personally! Of course" (turning a scarlet face and blazing eyes full upon him), "I did not expect you to *feel* glad—I have known you too long for that—but you might have had the common civility to *say* you were!"

We have stopped. We stand facing each other in the narrow wood-path, while the beck noisily babbles past, and the thrushes answer each other in lovely dialogue. He is deadly pale; his lips are trembling, and his eyes—involuntarily I look away from them!

"I am *not* glad!" he says, with slow distinctness; "often—often you have blamed me for *hinting* and *implying* for using innuendoes and half-words, and once—*once*, do you recollect?—you told me to my face that I *lied*! Well, I will not *lie* now; you shall have no cause to blame me to-day. I will tell you the truth, the truth that you know as well as I do—I am *not* glad!"

Absolute silence. I could no more answer or interrupt him than I could soar up between the dry tree-boughs to heaven. I stand before him with parted lips, and staring eyes fixed in a stony, horrid astonishment on his face.

"Nancy," he says, coming a step nearer, and speaking in almost a whisper, "*you* are not glad either! For once speak the truth! Hypocrisy is always difficult to you. You are the worst actress I ever saw—speak the truth for once! Who is there to hear you but me? I, who know it already—who have known it ever since that first evening in Dresden! Do you recollect?—but of course you do—why do I ask you? Why should you have forgotten any more than I?"

Still I am silent. Though I stand in the free clear air of heaven, I could not feel more choked and gasping were I in some close and stifling dungeon, hundreds of feet underground. I think that the brook must have got into my brain, there is such a noise of bubbling and brawling in it. Barbara, Roger, Algy, a hundred confused ideas of pain and dismay jostle each other in my head.

"Why do you look at me so?" he says, hoarsely. "What have I done? For God's sake, do not think that I blame you! I never have been so sorry for any one in my life as I have been for you—as I was for you from the first moment I saw you! I can see you now, as I first caught sight of you—weariness and depression in every line of your face—"

I can bear no more. At his last words, a pain like a knife, sharp to agony, runs through me. It is the grain of truth in his wicked, lying words that gives them their sting. I *was* weary; I *was* depressed; I *was* bored. I fling out my arms with a sudden gesture of despair, and then, throwing myself down on the ground, bury my face in a great moss cushion, and put my fingers in my ears.

"O my God!" I cry, writhing, "what *shall* I do?—how *can* I bear it?"

After a moment or two I sit up.

"How *shameful* of you!" I cry, bursting into a passion of tears. "What sort of women can you have lived among? what a hateful mind you must have! And I thought that you were a nice fellow, and that we were all so comfortable together!"

He has drawn back a pace or two, and now stands leaning against one of the bent and writhen trunks of the old trees. He is still as pale as the dead, and looks all the paler for the burning darkness of his eyes.

"Is it possible," he says, in a low tone of but half-suppressed fury, "that you are going to *pretend* to be surprised?"

"*Pretend!*" cry I, vehemently; "there is no pretense about it! I never was so horribly, miserably surprised in all my life!"

And then, thinking of Barbara, I fall to weeping again, in utter bitterness and discomfiture.

"It is *impossible!*" he says, roughly. "Whatever else you are, you are no fool; and a woman would have had to be blinder than any mole not to see whither I—yes, and *you*, too—have been tending! If you meant to be *surprised* all along when it came to this, why did you make yourself common talk for the neighborhood with me? Why did you press me, with such unconventional eagerness to visit you? Why did you reproach me if I missed one day?"

"*Why did I?*" cry I, eagerly. "Because—"

Then I stop suddenly. How, even to clear myself, can I tell him my real reason?

"And now," he continues, with deepening excitement, "now that you reap your own sowing, you are *surprised—miserably surprised!*"

"I am!" cry I, incoherently. "You may not believe me, but it is true—as true as that God is above us, and that I never, *never* was tired of Roger!"

I stop, choked with sobs.

"Yes," he says, sardonically, "about as true. But, be that as it may, you must at least be good enough to excuse me from expressing *joy* at his return, seeing that he fills the place which I am fool enough to covet, and which, but for him, *might*—yes, say what you please, deny it as much as you like—*would* have been mine!"

"It *never* would!" cry I, passionately. "If you had been the last man in the world—if we had been left together on a desert island—I *never* should have liked you, *never*! I *never* would have seen more of you than I could help! There is *no one* whose society I grow so soon tired of. I have said so over and over again to the boys."

"Have you?"

"What good reason can you give me for preferring you to him?" I ask, my voice trembling and quivering with a passionate indignation; "I am here, ready to listen to you if you can! How are you such a desirable substitute for him? Are you nobler? cleverer? handsomer? unselfisher?—if you are" (laughing bitterly), "you keep it mighty well hid."

No reply: not a syllable.

"It is a *lie*," I cry, with growing vehemence, "a vile, base, groundless lie, to say that I am not glad he is coming back! Barbara knows—they *all* know how I have been *wearying* for him all these months. I was not *in love*, as you call it, when I married him—often I have told him that—and perhaps at Dresden I missed the boys a little—he knows that too—he understands! but now—*now*—" (clasping my hands upon my heart, and looking passionately upward with streaming eyes), "I want no one—*no one* but him! I wish for nothing better than to have *him*—*him only*!—and to-day, until I met *you*—till you made me loathe myself and you, and every living thing—it seemed to me as if all the world had suddenly grown bright and happy and good at the news of his coming."

Still he is silent.

"Even if I had not liked *him*," pursue I, finding words come quickly enough now, and speaking with indignant volubility, as, having risen, I again face him—"even if I had wanted to flirt with some one, why on earth should I have chosen *you*?" (eying him with scornful slowness, from his wide-awake to his shooting-boots), "*you*, who never even *amused* me in the least! Often when I have been talking to you, I have yawned till the tears came into my eyes! I have been afraid that you would notice it. If I had known" (speaking with great bitterness), "I should have taken less pains with my manners."

He does not answer a word. What answer *can* he make? He still stands under the wintry tree, white to lividness; drops of cold sweat stand on his brows; and his fine nostrils dilate and contract, dilate and contract, in an agony of anger and shame.

"What *could* have put such an idea into your head?" cry I, clasping my hands, while the tears rain down my cheeks, as—my thoughts again flying to Barbara—I fall from contempt and scorn to the sharpest reproach. "Who would have thought of such a thing? when there are so many better and prettier people who, for all I know, might have liked you. What wicked perversity made you fix upon *me* who, even if I had not belonged to any one else, could never, *never* have fancied you!"

"Is that true?" he says, in a harsh, rough whisper; "are you sure that you are not deceiving yourself? are you sure that under all your rude words you are not nearer loving me than you think?—that it is not that—with that barrier between us—you cannot reconcile it to your conscience—"

"Quite, *quite* sure!" interrupt I, with passionate emphasis, looking back unflinchingly into the angry depths of his eyes, "it has nothing to say to conscience! it has nothing to say to the *wrongness* of it" (crimsoning as I speak). "If it were quite right—if it were my *duty*—if it were the only way to save myself from *hanging*" (reaching after an ever higher and higher climax), "I *never*, NEVER could say that I was fond of you! I do not see what there is to be fond of *in* you! before God, I do not!"

"There!" he says, hoarsely stretching out his hand, as if to ward off a blow, "that will do!—stop!—you will never outdo that!"

A moment's pause.

Down in the loneliness of this dell, the twilight is creeping quickly on: when once it begins it tarries not. Out in the open country I dare say that it is still broad daylight; but here, the hues of the moss carpet are growing duller, and the brook is darkening. In a sudden panic, I hastily catch up my hat, which has fallen to the ground, and without a word or look of farewell, begin to run fast along the homeward path. Before I have gone ten yards he has overtaken me. His face is distorted by passion out of all its beauty.

"Nancy," he says, in a voice rendered almost unrecognizable by extreme agitation, walking quickly alongside of me, "we are not going to part like this!"

"Do not call me Nancy!" cry I, indignantly; "it makes me *sick!*"

"What does it matter what I call you?" he cries, impatiently; "of what consequence is such a trifle? I will call you by what name you please, but for this once you *must* listen to me. I know, as well as you do, that it is my last chance!"

"*That* it is!" put in I, viciously.

The path is beginning to rise. After mounting the slope, we shall soon be out of the wood, and in the peopled open again.

"How can I help it, if I have gone mad?" he cries violently, evidently driven to desperation by the shortness of the time before him.

"Mad!" echo I, scornfully, "not a bit of it! you are as sane as I am!"

All this time we are posting along in mad haste. Thank God! the high-road is in sight, the cheerful, populous, light high-road. The trees grow thinner, and the path broadens. Even from here, we can plainly see the carts and carters. He stops, and making me stop, too, snatches both my hands.

"Nancy!" he says, harshly, stooping over me, while his eyes flame with a haggard light. "Yes, I *will* call you so this once—to me now you *are* Nancy! I will *not* call you by *his* name! Is it *possible*? You may say that it is my egotism; but, at a moment like this, what is the use of shamming—of polite pretense? Never, *never* before in all my life have I given love without receiving it, and I *cannot* believe"—(with an accent of passionate entreaty)—"that I do now! Feeling for you as I do, do you feel absolutely *nothing* for me?"

"*Feel!*" cry I, driven out of all moderation by disgust and exasperation. "Would you like to know how I feel? I feel *as if a slug had crawled over me!*"

His face contracts, his eyes darken with a raging pain. He *throws* my hands—the hands a moment ago so jealously clasped—away from him.

"Thank you!" he says, after a pause, in a stiff voice of constraint. "I am satisfied!"

"And a very good thing too!" say I, sturdily, still at boiling-point, and diminishing with quick steps the small space still intervening between me and the road.

"Stay!" he says, overtaking me once again, as I reach it, and laying his hand in detention on my arm. "One word more! I should be sorry to part from you—such friends as we have been"—(with a sneer)—"without *one* good wish. Lady Tempest, I hope"—(smiling with malevolent irony)—"that your fidelity will be rewarded as it deserves."

"I have no doubt of it!" reply I, steadily; but even as I speak, a sharp jealous pain runs through my heart. Thank God! he cannot see it!

CHAPTER XXXI

Yes, here out in the open it is still quite light; it seems two hours earlier than it did below in the dark dingle—light enough as plainly to see the faces of those one meets as if it were mid-day. I suppose that my late companion and I were too much occupied by our own emotions to hear, or at least notice the sound of wheels approaching us; but no sooner have I turned and left him, before I have gone three paces, than I am quickly passed by an open carriage and pair of grays—*quickly*, and yet slowly enough for me to recognize the one occupant. As to her—for it is Mrs. Huntley—she must have seen me already, as I stood with Mr. Musgrave on the edge of the wood, exchanging our last bitter words.

It is impossible that she could have helped it; but even had it been possible—had there been any doubt on the subject, that doubt would be removed by the unusual animation of her attitude, and the interest in her eyes, that I have time to notice, as she rolls past me.

I avert my face, but it is too late. She has seen my hat thrown on anyhow, as it were with a pitchfork—has seen my face swollen with weeping, and great tears still standing unwiped on my flushed cheeks. What is far, *far* worse, she has seen him, too. This is the last drop in an already over-full cup.

There is nothing in sight now—not even a cart—so I sit down on a heap of stones by the road-side, and, covering my hot face with my hands, cry till I have no more eyes left to cry with. Can *this* be the day I called good? Can *this* be that bright and merry day, when I walked elate and laughing between the deep furrows, and heard the blackbird and thrush woo their new loves, nor was able myself to refrain from singing?

My brain is a black chaos of whirling agonies, now together, now parting; so that each may make their separate sting felt, and, in turn, each will have to be faced. Preëminent among the dark host, towering above even the thought of Barbara, is the sense of my own degradation. There must have been something in my conduct to justify his taking me so confidently for the bad, light woman he did. One does not get such a character for nothing. I have always heard that, when such things happen to people, they have invariably brought them on themselves. In incoherent misery, I run over in my head, as well as the confusion of it will let me, our past meetings and dialogues. In almost all, to my distorted view, there now seems to have been an unseemly levity. Things I have said to him; easy, familiar jokes that I have had with him; not that *he* ever had much sense of a jest—(even at this moment I think this incidentally)—course through my mind.

Our many *tête-à-têtes* to which, at the time, I attached less than no importance: through many of which I unfeignedly, irresistibly *gaped*; our meetings in the park—accidental, as I thought—our dawdling saunters through the meadows, as often as not at twilight; all, *all* recur to me, and, recurring, make my face burn with a hot and stabbing shame.

And *Roger*! This is the way in which I have kept things straight for him! This is the way in which I have rewarded his boundless trust! he, whose only fear was lest I should be dull! lest I should not amuse myself! Well, I have amused myself to some purpose now. I have made myself *common talk for the neighborhood*! *He* said so. I have brought discredit on Roger's honored name! Not even the consciousness of the utter cleanness of my heart is of the least avail to console me. What matter how clean the heart is, if the conduct be light? None but God can see the former; the latter lies open to every carelessly spiteful, surface-judging eye. And Barbara! Goaded by the thought of her, I rise up quickly, and walk hastily along the road, till I reach a gate into the park. Arrived there, and now free from all fear of interruption from passers-by, I again sit down on an old dry log that lies beneath a great oak, and again cover my face with my hands.

What care I for the growing dark? the darker the better! Ah! if it were dark enough to hide me from myself! How shall I break it to her—I, who, confident in my superior discernment, have always scouted her misgivings and turned into derision her doubts? If I thought that she would rave and storm, and that her grief would vent itself in *anger*, it would not be of half so much consequence. But I know her better. The evening has closed in colder. The birds have all ceased their singing, and I still sit on, in the absolute silence, unconscious—unaware of any thing round me; living only in my thoughts, and with a resolution growing ever stronger and stronger within me. I will *not* tell her! I will *never* tell *any one*. I, that have hitherto bungled and blundered over the whitest fib, will wade knee-deep in falsehoods, before I will ever let any one guess the disgrace that has happened to me. Oh that, by long silence, I could wipe it out of my own heart—out of the book of unerasable past deeds!

Of course, by the cessation of his visits, Barbara will learn her fate in time. *In time*. Yes! but till then—till the long weeks in their lapse have brought the certainty of disappointment and mistake? How can I—myself knowing—watch her gentle confidence (for latterly her doubts—and whose would not?—have been set at rest) decline through all the suffering stages of uneasy expectation and deferred hope, to the blank, dull sickness of despair? How, without betraying myself, see her daily with wistful eyes looking—with strained ears listening—for a face and a step that come not? If she were one to love lightly, one of the many women who, when satisfied that it is no longer any use to cry and strive for the unattainable, the out of reach, clip and pare their affections to fit the unattainable, the within reach—! But I know differently.

Hitherto, whenever love has been offered to her—and the occasions have been not few—she has put it away from her; most gently, indeed, with a most eager desire to pour balm and not vinegar into the wounds she has made; with a most sincere sorrow and a disproportioned remorse at being obliged to cause pain to any living thing; yet, with a quiet and indifferent firmness, that left small ground for lingering hopes. And now, having once loved, she will be slow to unlove again.

It is quite dark now—as dark, at least, as it will be all night—and two or three stars are beginning to quiver out, small and cold, in the infinite distances of the sky. The sight of them, faintly trembling between the bare boughs of the trees, is the first thing that calls me back to the consciousness of outward things. Again I rise, and begin to walk, stumbling through the long wet knots of the unseen grass, toward the house. But when I reach it—when I see the red gleams shining through the chinks of the window-shutters— my heart fails me. Not yet can I face the people, the lights—Barbara! I turn into the garden, and pace up and down the broad, lonely walks: I pass and repass the cold river-gods of the unplaying fountain. I stand in the black night of the old cedar's shade. On any other day no possible consideration would have induced me to venture within the jurisdiction of its inky arms after nightfall; to-day, I feel as if no earthly or unearthly thing would have power to scare me. How long I stay, I do not know. Now and then, I put up my hands to my face, to ascertain whether my cheeks and eyes feel less swollen and burning; whether the moist and searching night-air is restoring me to my own likeness. At length, I dare stay no longer for fear of being missed, and causing alarm in the household. So I enter, steal up-stairs, and open the door of my boudoir, which Barbara and I, when alone, make our usual sitting-room. The candles are unlit; and the warm fire—evidently long undisturbed—is shedding only a dull and deceiving light on all the objects over which it ranges. So far, at least, Fortune favors me. Barbara and Vick are sitting on the hearth-rug, side by side. As I enter, they both jump up, and run to meet me. One of them gives little raptured squeaks of recognition. The other says, in a tone of relief and pleasure:

"Here you are! I was growing so frightened about you! What can have made you so late?"

"It was so—so—pleasant! The thrushes were singing so!" reply I, thus happily inaugurating my career of invention.

"But, my dear child, the thrushes went to bed two hours ago!"

"Yes," I answer, at once entirely nonplussed, "so they did!"

"Where *have* you been?" she asks, in a tone of ever-increasing surprise. "Did you go farther than you intended?"

"I went—to see—the old Busseys," reply I, slowly; inwardly pondering, with a stupid surprise, as to whether it can possibly have been no longer ago than this very afternoon, that the old man mistook me for the dead Belinda—and that I held the old wife's soapy hand in farewell in mine; "the—old—Busseys!" I repeat, "and it took—me a long—*long* time to get home!"

I shiver as I speak.

"You are cold!" she says, anxiously. "I hope you have not had a chill—" (taking my hands in her own slight ones)—"yes—*starved*!—poor dear hands; let me rub them!" (beginning delicately to chafe them).

Something in the tender solicitude of her voice, in the touch of her gentle hands, gives me an agony of pain and remorse. I snatch away my hands.

"No! no!" I cry, brusquely, "they do very well!"

Again she looks at me, with a sort of astonishment, a little mixed with pain; but she does not say any thing. She goes over to the fire, and stoops to take up the poker.

"Do not!" cry I, hastily, "there is plenty of light!—I mean—" (stammering) "it—it—dazzles me, coming in out of the dark."

As I speak, I retire to a distant chair, as nearly as possible out of the fire-light, and affect to be occupied with Vick, who has jumped up on my lap, and—with all a dog's delicate care not to hurt you *really*—is pretending severely to bite every one of my fingers. Barbara has returned to the hearth-rug. She looks a little troubled at first; but, after a moment or two, her face regains its usual serene sweetness.

"And I have been here ever since you left me!" she says, presently, with a look of soft gayety. "I have had *no* visitors! Not even"—(blushing a little)—"the usual one."

"No?" say I, bending down my head over Vick, and allowing her to have a better and more thorough lick at the bridge of my nose than she has ever enjoyed in her life before.

"*You* did not meet him, I suppose?" she says, interrogatively.

"*I!*" cry I, starting guiltily, and stammering. "Not I! Why—why should I?"

"Why should not you, rather?" she says, laughing a little. "It is not such a *very* unusual occurrence?"

"Do you think not?" I say, in a voice whose trembling is painfully perceptible to myself. "You do not think I—I—" ("You do not think I meet him on purpose," I am going to say; but I break off suddenly, aware that I am betraying myself).

"He will come earlier to-morrow to make up for it"—she says, in a low voice, more to herself than to me—"yes"—(clasping her hands lightly in her lap, while the fire-light plays upon the lovely mildness of her happy face, and repeating the words softly)—"yes, he will come earlier to-morrow!"

I *cannot* bear it. I rise up abruptly, trundling poor Vick, to whom this reverse is quite unexpected, down on the carpet, and rushing out of the room.

It is evening now—late evening, drawing toward bedtime. I am sitting with my back to the light, and have asked for a shade for the lamp, on the plea that the wind has cut my eyes—but, in spite of my precautions, I am well aware that the disfigurement of my face is still unmistakably evident to the most casual eye; and, from the anxious care with which Barbara looks *away from me*, when she addresses me, I can perceive that she has observed it, as, indeed, how could she fail to do? If Tou Tou were here, she would overwhelm me with officious questions—would stare me crazy, but Barbara averts her eyes, and asks nothing.

We have been sitting in perfect silence for a long while; no noise but the click of Barbara's knitting-pins, the low flutter of the fire-flame, and the sort of suppressed choked *inward* bark, with which Vick attacks a phantom tomcat in her dreams.

Suddenly I speak.

"Barbara!" say I, with a hard, forced laugh, "I am going to ask you a silly question: tell me, did you ever observe—has it ever struck you that there was something rather—rather *offensive* in my manner to men?"

Her knitting drops into her lap. Her blue eyes open wide, like dog-violets in the sun; she is *obliged* to look at me now.

"*Offensive!*" she echoes, with an accent of the most utter surprise and mystification. "Good Heavens, no! What has come to the child? Oh!" — (with a little look of dawning intelligence) — "I see! You mean, do not you smite them too much? Are not you sometimes a little too *hard* upon them?"

"No," say I, gravely; "I did not mean that."

She looks at me for explanation, but I can give none. More silence.

Vick is either in hot pursuit of, or hot flight from, the tomcat; all her four legs are quivering and kicking in a mimic gallop.

"Do you remember," say I, again speaking, and again prefacing my words by an uneasy laugh, "how the boys at home used always to laugh at me, because I never knew how to flirt, nor had any pretty ways? Do you think" — (speaking slowly and hesitatingly) — "that boys — one's brothers, I mean — would be good judges of that sort of thing?"

"As good as any one else's brothers, I suppose," she says, with a low laugh, but still looking puzzled; "but why do you ask?"

"I do not know," reply I, trying to speak carelessly; "it came into my head."

"Has any one been accusing you?" she says, a little curiously, "But no! who *could*? You have seen no one, not even —"

"No, no!" interrupt I, shrinking from the sound of the name that I know is coming; "of course not; no one!"

The clock strikes eleven, and wakes Vick. Barbara rises, rolls up her knitting, and, going over to the fireplace, stands with one white elbow resting on the chimney-piece, and slender neck drooped, pensively gazing at the low fire.

"Do you know," she says, with a half-confused smile, that is also tinged with a little anxiety, "I have been thinking — it is the first time for three months that he has not been here at all, either in the morning, the afternoon, or the evening!"

"Is it?" say I, slightly shivering.

"I think," she says, with a rather embarrassed laugh, "that he must have heard *you* were out, and that that was why he did not come. You know I always tell you that he likes you best."

She says it, as a joke, and yet her great eyes are looking at me with a sort of wistfulness, but neither to *them* nor to her words can I make any answer.

CHAPTER XXXII

Next morning I am sitting before my looking-glass—never to me a pleasant article of furniture—having my hair dressed. I am hardly awake yet, and have not quite finished disentangling the real live disagreeables which I have to face, from the imaginary ones from which my waking has freed me. At least, in real life, I am not perpetually pursued, through dull abysses, by a man in a crape mask, from whom I am madly struggling to escape, and who is perpetually on the point of overtaking and seizing me.

It was a mistake going to sleep at all last night. It would have been far wiser and better to have kept awake. The *real* evils are bad enough, but the dream ones in their vivid life make me shiver even now, though the morning sun is lying in companionable patches on the floor, and the birds are loudly talking all together. Do *no* birds ever listen?

Distracted for a moment from my own miseries, by the noise of their soft yet sharp hubbub, I am thinking this, when a knock comes at the door, and the next moment Barbara enters. Her blond hair is tumbled about her shoulders; no white rose's cheeks are paler than hers; in her hand she has a note. In a moment I have dismissed the maid, and we are alone.

"I want you to read this!" she says, in an even and monotonous voice, from which, by an effort whose greatness I can dimly guess, she keeps all sound of trembling.

I have risen and turned from the glass; but now my knees shake under me so much that I have to sit down again. She comes behind me, so that I may no longer see her: and putting her arms round my neck, and hiding her face in my unfinished hair, says, whisperingly:

"Do not fret about it, Nancy!—I do not mind much."

Then she breaks into quiet tears.

"Do you mean to say that he has had the *insolence* to write to you," I cry, in a passion of indignation, forgetting for the moment Barbara's ignorance of what has occurred, and only reminded of it by the look of wonder that, as I turn on my chair to face her, I see come into her eyes.

"Have not you been expecting him every day to write to me?" she asks, with a little wonder in her tone; "but *read!*" (pointing to the note, and laughing with a touch of bitterness), "you will soon see that there is no *insolence* here."

I had quite as lief, in my present state of mind, touch a yard-long wriggling ground-worm, or a fat wood-louse, as paper that his fingers have pressed; but I overcome my repulsion, and unfold the note.

> "Dear Miss Grey:
>
> "Can I do any thing for you in town? I am going up there to-morrow, and shall thence, I think, run over to the Exhibition. I have no doubt that it is just like all the others; but *not* to have seen it will set one at a disadvantage with one's fellows. I am afraid that there is no chance of your being still at Tempest when I return. I shall be most happy to undertake any commissions.
>
> "Yours sincerely,
>
> "F. Musgrave"

The note drops from my fingers, rolls on to my lap, and thence to the ground. I sit in stiff and stupid silence. To tell the truth, I am trying strongly to imagine how I should look and what I should say, were I as ignorant of causes as Barbara thinks me, and to look and speak accordingly.

She kneels down beside me, and softly drawing down my face, till it is on a level with hers, and our cheeks touch, says in a tone of gentle entreaty and compassion, as if *I* were the one to be considered—the prime sufferer:

"Do not fret about it, Nancy! it is of no—no consequence!—there is no harm done!"

I struggle to say *something*, but for the life of me I can frame no words.

"It was my own fancy!" she says, faltering, "I suppose my vanity misled me!"

"It is all my fault!" cry I, suddenly finding passionate words, starting up, and beginning to walk feverishly to and fro—"*all!*—there never was any one in all this world so blind, so ill-judging, so miserably mistaken! If it had not been for me, you never would have thought twice of him—never; and I"—(beginning to speak with weeping indistinctness)—"I thought it would be so nice to have you near me—I thought that there was nothing the matter with him, but his temper; *many* men are ill-tempered—nearly *all*. If" (tightly clinching my hands, and setting my teeth) "I had had any idea of his being the *scoundrel* that he is—"

"But he is not," she interrupts quickly, wincing a little at my words; "indeed he is not! What ill have we heard from him? If you do not mind" (laying her hand with gentle entreaty on my arm), "I had rather, *far* rather, that you did not say any thing hard of him! I was always so glad that you and he were such friends—always—and I do not know why—there is no sense in it; but I am glad of it still."

"We were *not* friends," say I, writhing a little; "why do you say so?"

She looks at me with a great and unfeigned astonishment.

"*Not friends!*" she echoes, slowly repeating my words; then, seeing the expression of my face, stops suddenly.

"Are you *sure*," cry I, feverishly snatching her hands and looking with searching anxiety into her face, "that you spoke truth just now?—that you do not mind much—that you will get over it!—that it will not *kill* you?"

"*Kill* me!" she says, with a little sorrowful smile of derision; "no, no! I am not so easily killed."

"Are you *sure*?" persist I, with a passionate eagerness, still reading her tear-stained face, "that it will not take the taste out of every thing?—that it will not make you hate all your life?—it would me."

"*Quite* sure!—certain!" she says, looking back at me with a steady meekness, though her blue eyes brim over; "because God has taken from me *one* thing—one that I never had any right to expect—should I do well, do you think, to quarrel with all that He has left me?"

I cannot answer; her godly patience is too high a thing for me.

"Even if my life *were* spoilt," she goes on, after a moment or two, her voice gaining firmness, and her face a pale serenity, "even if it were—but it is *not*—indeed it is not. In a very little while it will seem to me as good and pleasant and full as ever; but even if it *were*" (looking at me with a lovely confidence in her eyes), "it would be no such very great matter—*this* life is not every thing!"

"Is not it?" say I, with a doubting shiver. "Who can tell you that? who knows?"

"*No one* has been to blame," she continues, with a gentle persistence. "I should like you to see that! There has been only a—a—*mistake*"—(her voice failing a little again), "a mistake that has been corrected in time, and for which no one—*no one*, Nancy, is the worse!"

CHAPTER XXXIII

So this is the way in which Barbara's hope dies! Our hopes have as many ways of dying as our bodies. Sometimes they pine and fall into a slow consumption, we nursing, cockering, and physicking them to the last. Sometimes they fall down dead suddenly, as one that in full health, with his bones full of marrow, and his eyes full of light, drops wordless into the next world unaware. This last has been Barbara's case. When she thought it healthiest, and most vigorous in its stalwart life, then the death-mark was on it. To most of us, O friends, troubles are as great stones cast unexpectedly on a smooth road; over which, in a dark night, we trip, and grumblingly stumble, cursing, and angrily bruising our limbs. To a few of us, they are ladders, by which we climb to God; hills, that lift us nearer heaven—that heaven, which, however certainly—with whatever mathematical precision—it has been demonstrated to us that it exists not here, nor there, nor yet anywhere, we still dimly, with yearning tears and high longings, grasp at. Barbara has always looked heavenward. In all her mirth, God has mixed. Now, therefore, in this grief that He has sent her—this ignoble grief, that yet cuts the none less deeply for being ignoble, and excluding the solace of human sympathy, she but thrusts her hand with a fuller confidence in his, and fixes her sweet eyes with a more reverent surety on the one prime consoler of humankind, who, from his Cross, has looked royally down the toiling centuries—the king, whom this generation, above all generations, is laboring—and, as not a few think, *successfully*—to discrown. To her, his kingship is as unquestioned as when heretics and paynims burnt to prove it.

Often, since then, in those vain longings that come to each of us, I suppose, I tried in after-days—sometimes I try now, to stretch my arms out wide-backward toward the past—to speak the words that would have been as easily spoken then as any other—that no earthly power can ever make spoken words now, of sympathy and appreciation to Barbara.

I did say loving things, but they seem to me now to have been but scant and shabby. Why did not I say a great many more? Oh, all of you who live with those that are dearer to you than they seem, tell them every day how much you love them! at the risk of *wearying* them, tell them, I pray you: it will save you, perhaps, many after-pangs.

I think that, at this time, there are in me *two* Nancys—Barbara's Nancy, and Roger's Nancy; the one so vexed, thwarted, and humiliated in spirit, that she feels as if she never could laugh quite heartily again; the other, so utterly and triumphantly glad, that any future tears or trials seem to her in the highest degree improbable. And Barbara herself is on the side of this latter. From her hopeful speech and her smiles, you would think that some good news had come to her—that she was on the eve of some long-looked-for, yet hardly-hoped prosperity. Not that she is unnaturally or hysterically lively—an error into which many, making such an effort and struggle for self-conquest, would fall. Barbara's mirth was never noisy, as mine and the boys' so often was. Perhaps—nay, I have often thought since, *certainly*—she weeps as she prays, in secret; but God is the only One who knows of her tears, as of her prayers. She has always been one to go halves in her pleasures, but of her sorrows she will give never a morsel to any one.

Her very quietness under her trouble—her silence under it—her equanimity—mislead me. It is the impulse of any hurt thing to cry out. I, myself, have always done it. Half unconsciously, I am led by this reasoning to think that Barbara's wound cannot be very deep, else would she shrink and writhe beneath it. So I talk to her all day, with merciless length, about Roger. I go through all the old queries. I again critically examine my face, and arrive—not only at the former conclusion, that one side is worse-looking than the other, but also that it looks ten years older.

I have my flax hair built in many strange and differing fashions, and again *un*built: piled high, to give me height; twisted low, in a vain endeavor to liken me to the Greeks; curled, plaited, frizzed, and again unfrizzed. I institute a searching and critical examination of my wardrobe, rejecting this and that; holding one color against my cheek, to see whether my pallor will be able to bear it; turning away from another with a grimace of self-disgust.

And this is the same "I," who thought it so little worth while to win the good opinion of father's blear-eyed old friend, that I went to my first meeting with him with a scorched face, loose hair, tottering, all through prayers, on the verge of a descent about my neck, and a large round hole, smelling horribly of singeing, burnt in the very front of my old woolen frock.

His coming is near now. This *very* day I shall see him come in that door. He will sit in that chair. His head will dent that cushion. I shall sit on a footstool at his feet. The better to imagine the position, I push a footstool into the desired neighborhood to Roger's arm-chair, and already see myself, with the eye of faith, in solid reality occupying it. I rehearse all the topics that will engage my tongue. The better to realize their effect upon him, I give utterance out loud to the many greetings, to the numberless fond and pretty things with which I mean to load him.

He always looked so very joyful when I said any little civil thing to him, and I so seldom, *seldom* did. Ah! we will change all that! He shall be nauseated with sweets. And then, still sitting by him, holding his hand, and with my head (dressed in what I finally decide upon as the becomingest fashion) daintily rested on his arm, I will tell him all my troubles. I will tell him of Algy's estrangement, his cold looks and harsh words. Without any outspoken or bitter abuse of her, I will yet manage cunningly to set him on his guard against Mrs. Huntley. I will lament over Bobby to him. Yes, I will tell him *all* my troubles—all, that is, with one reservation.

Barbara is no longer here. She has gone home.

"You will be better by yourselves," she says, gently, when she announces her intention of going. "He will like it better. I should if I were he. It will be like a new honey-moon."

"*That* it will not," reply I, stoutly, recollecting how much I yawned, and how largely Mr. Musgrave figured in the first. "I have no opinion of honey-moons; no more would *you* if you had *had* one."

"*Should* not I?" speaking a little absently, while her eyes stray through the window to the serene coldness of the sky, and the pallid droop of the snow-drops in the garden-border.

"You are sure," say I, earnestly, taking her light hand in mine, "that you are not going because you think that you are not *wanted* now—that now, that I have my—my own property again" (smiling irrepressibly), "I can do very well without you."

"*Quite* sure, Nancy!" looking back into my eager eyes with confident affection.

"And you will come back *very* soon? *very?*"

"When you quarrel," she answers, her face dimpling into a laugh, "I will come and make it up between you."

"You must come before *then*," say I, with a proud smile, "or your visit is likely to be indefinitely postponed."

Roger and I quarrel! We both find the idea so amusing that we laugh in concert.

CHAPTER XXXIV

"Gertrude. Is my knight come? O the Lord, my band! Sister,
do my cheeks look well? Give me a little box o' the ear, that
I may seem to blush."—Eastward Hoe.

She is gone now. The atmosphere of the house seems less clear, less
pure, now that she has left it. As she drives away, it seems to me, looking
after her, that no flower ever had a modester face, a more delicate bloom. If
I had time to think about it, I should fret sorely after her, I should grievously
miss her; but I have none.

The carriage that takes her to the station is to wait half an hour, and
then bring back Roger. There is, therefore, not more than enough time for
me to make the careful and lengthy toilet, on which I have expended so
much painstaking thought. I have deferred making it till now, so that I
may appear in perfect dainty freshness, as if I had just emerged from the
manifold silver papers of a bandbox, before him when he arrives—that not
a hair of my flax head may be displaced from its silky sweep; that there may
be no risk of Vick jumping up, and defiling me with muddy paws that know
no respect of clothes.

I take a long time over it. I snub my maid more than I ever did in my
life before. But I am complete now; to the last pin I am finished. Perhaps—
though this does not strike me till the last moment—perhaps I am rather,
nay, more than *rather,* overdressed for the occasion. But surely this, in a
person who has not long been in command of fine clothes, and even in that
short time has had very few opportunities of airing them, is pardonable.

You remember that it is February. Well, then, this is the warm splendor
in which I am clad. Genoa velvet, of the color of a dark sapphire, trimmed
with silver-fox fur; and my head crowned with a mob-cap, concerning
which I am in doubt, and should be nervously glad to have the boys here
to enlighten me as to whether it is very becoming or rather ridiculous. The
object of the mob-cap is to approximate my age to Roger's, and to assure all
such as the velvet and fur leave in doubt, that I am entitled to take my stand
among the portly ranks of British matrons.

"Algy was right," say I, soliloquizing aloud, as I stand before the long cheval glass, with a back-hair glass in one hand, by whose aid I correct my errors in the profile, three-quarters or back view; "mine is not the most hopeless kind of ugliness. It is certainly modifiable by dress."

So saying, I lay down the hand-glass, and walk sedately down-stairs, holding my head stiffly erect, and looking over my shoulder, like a child, at the effect of my blue train sweeping down the steps after me.

Arrived in my boudoir, I go and stand by the window, though there are yet ten minutes before he is due. Once I open the casement to listen, but hastily close it again, afraid lest the wintry wind should ruffle the satin smoothness of my hair, or push the mob-cap awry. Then I sit carefully down, and, harshly repulsing an overture on the part of Vick to jump into my lap, fix my eyes upon the dark bare boughs of the tall and distant elms, from between which I shall see him steal into sight. The time ticks slowly on. He is due now. Five more lame, crawling minutes—ten!—no sign of him. Again I rise, unclose the casement, and push my matronly head a little way out to listen. Yes! yes! there is the distant but not doubtful sound of a horse's four hoofs smartly trotting and splashing along the muddy road. Three minutes more, and the sun catches and brightly gleams on one of the quickly-turning wheels of the dog-cart as it rolls toward me, between the wintry trees.

At first I cannot see the occupants; the boughs and twigs interpose to hide them; but presently the dog-cart emerges into the open. There is only one person in it!

At first I decline to believe my own eyes. I rub them. I stretch my head farther out. Alas! self-deception is no longer possible: the groom returns as he went—alone. Roger has *not* come!

The dog-cart turns toward the stables, and I run to the bell and pull it violently. I can hardly wait till it is answered. At last, after an interval, which seems to me like twenty minutes, but which that false, cold-blooded clock proclaims to be *two*, the footman enters.

"Sir Roger has not come," I say more affirmatively than interrogatively, for I have no doubt on the subject. "Why did not the groom wait for the next train?"

"If you please, my lady, Sir Roger *has* come."

"*Has come!*" repeat I, in astonishment, opening my eyes; "then where is he?"

"He is walking up, my lady."

"What! all the way from Bishopsthorpe?" cry I, incredulously, thinking of the five miry miles that intervene between us and that station. "*Impossible!*"

"No, my lady, not all the way; only from Mrs. Huntley's."

I feel the color rushing away from my cheeks, and turn quickly aside, that my change of countenance may not be perceived.

"Did he get out there?" I ask, faintly.

"Mrs. Huntley was at the gate, my lady, and Sir Roger got down to speak to her, and bid James drive on and tell your ladyship he would be here directly."

"Very well," say I, unsteadily, still averting my face, "that will do."

He is gone, and I need no longer mind what color my face is, nor what shape of woeful jealousy my late so complacent features assume.

So *this* is what comes of thinking life such a grand and pleasant thing, and this world such a lovely, satisfying paradise! Wait long enough—(I have not had to wait very long for my part)—and every sweet thing turns to gall-like bitterness between one's teeth! The experience of a few days ago might have taught me *that*, one would think, but I was dull to thick-headedness. I required *two* lessons—the second, oh how far harsher than even the first!

In a moment I have taken my resolution. I am racing up-stairs. I have reached my room. I do not summon my maid. One requires no assistance to enable one to *unbuild*, deface, destroy. In a *second*—in much less time than it takes me to write it—I have torn off the mob-cap, and thrown it on the floor. If I had done what I wished, if I had yielded to my first impulse, I should also have trampled upon it; but from the extremity of petulance, I am proud to be able to tell you that I refrain. With rapid fingers I unbutton my blue-velvet gown, and step out of it, leaving it in a costly heap on the floor. Then I open the high folding-doors of the wardrobe, and run my eye over its contents; but the most becoming is no longer what I seek. For a moment or two I stand undecided, then my eye is caught by a venerable garment, loathly and ill-made, which I had before I married, and have since kept, more as a relic than any thing else—a gown of that peculiar shade of sallow, bilious, Bismarck brown, which is the most trying to the paleness of my skin. Before any one could say "Jack Robinson," it is down, and I am in it. Then, without even a parting smooth to the hair, which the violent off-tearing of my cap must have roughened and disheveled, I go down-stairs and reënter the boudoir. As I do so, I catch an accidental glimpse of myself in a glass. Good Heavens! Can three minutes (for I really have not been longer about it) have wrought such a monstrous metamorphosis? Is every woman as utterly dependent for her charms upon her *husk* as I am?

Can this sad, sallow slip of a girl be the beaming, shapely, British matron I contemplated with so innocently pleased an eye half an hour ago? If, in all my designs, I could have the perfect success which has crowned my efforts at self-disfigurement, I should be among the most prosperous of my species.

I sit down as far from the window as the dimensions of the room will allow, call Vick, who comes at first sneakingly and doubtful of her reception, up on my lap, and take a book. It is the one nearest to my hand, and I plunge into it haphazard in the middle.

This is the sentence that first greets me: "Her whole heart was in her boy. She often feared that she loved him too much—more than God himself—yet she could not bear to pray to have her love for her child lessened."

Not a very difficult one to construe, is it? and yet, having come to the end, and found that it conveyed no glimmering of an idea to my mind, I begin it over again.

"Her whole heart was in her boy. She often feared that she loved him too much—more than God himself—yet she could not bear to pray to have her love for her child lessened."

Still no better! What *is* it all about?

I begin over again.

"Her whole heart was in her boy," etc. I go through this process ten times. I should go through it twenty, or even thirty, for I am resolved to go on reading, but at the end of the tenth, my ear—unconsciously strained—catches the sound of a step at the stair-foot. It is not the footman's. It is firmer, heavier, and yet quicker.

Eight weary months is it since I last heard that footfall. My heart pulses with mad haste, my cheeks throb, but I sit still, and hold the book before my eyes. I will *not* go to meet him. I will be as indifferent as he! When he opens the door, I will not even look round, I will be too much immersed in the page before me.

"Her whole heart was in her boy. She often feared that—"

The door-handle is turning. I *cannot* help it! Against my will, my head turns too. With no volition of my own—against my firmest intention—my feet carry me hastily toward him. My arms stretch themselves out. Thank God! thank God! whatever happens afterward, I shall still thank God, and call him good for allowing it. I am in Roger's embrace. No more mistakes! no more delays! he is here, and I am kissing him as I never kissed any one—as I certainly never kissed *him* in my life before.

Well, I suppose that in every life there are *some* moments that are *absolutely* good—that one could not mend even if one were given the power to try! I suppose that even those who, looking back over their history, say, most distinctly and certainly, "It was a failure," can yet lay the finger of memory on *some* such gold minutes—it may be only half a dozen, only four, only *two*—but still on some.

This is one of my gold moments, one of those misplaced ones that have strayed out of heaven, where, perhaps, they are *all* such—*perhaps*—one can't be *sure*, for what human imagination can grasp the idea of even a *day*, wholly made of such minutes?

I have forgotten Mrs. Huntley—Mr. Musgrave. Every ill suspicion, every stinging remembrance, is dead or fallen into a trance. All bad thoughts have melted away from the earth. Only joyful love and absolute faith remain, only the knowledge that Roger is mine, and I am his, and that we are in each other's arms. I do not know how long we remain without speaking. I do not imagine that souls in bliss ever think of looking at the clock. He is the first to break silence. For the first time for eight months I hear his voice again—the voice that for so many weeks seemed to me no better than any other voice— whose tones I *now* feel I could pick out from those of any other living thing, did all creation shout together.

"Let me look at my wife!" he says, taking my countenance in his tender hands, as if it were made of old china, and would break if he let it fall. "I feel as if I had never *had* a wife before, as if it were quite a new plaything."

I make no verbal answer. I am staring up with all my eyes into his face, thinking, with a sort of wonder, how much goodlier, younger, statelier it is than it has appeared to me in any of those dream-pictures, which yet mostly flatter.

"My wife! my wife!" he says, speaking the words most softly, as if they greatly pleased him, and replacing with carefullest fingers a stray and arrant lock that has wandered from its fellows into my left eye. "What has come to you? Had I forgotten what you were like? How pretty you are! How well you look!"

"Do I?" say I, with a pleasant simper; then, with a sudden and overwhelming recollection of the bilious gingery frock, and the tousled hair, "No, nonsense!" I say, uneasily, "impossible! You are laughing at me! Ah!"—(with a sigh of irrepressible regret and back-handed pride)—"you should have seen me half an hour ago! I *did* look nice *then*, if you like."

"Why nicer than now?"—(with a puzzled smile that both plays about his bearded lips and gayly shines in his steel-gray eyes).

"Oh, never mind! never mind!" reply I, in some confusion, "it is a long story; it is of no consequence, but I *did*."

He does not press for an explanation, for which I am obliged to him.

"Nancy!" he says, with a sort of hesitating joy, a diffident triumph in his voice, "do you know, I believe you have kept your promise! I believe, I *really* believe, that you are a little glad to see me!"

"Are *you* glad to see *me*, is more to the purpose?" return I, descending out of heaven with a pout, and returning to the small jealousies and acerbities of earth, and to the recollection of that yet unexplained alighting at Aninda's gate.

"*Am I?*"

He seems to think that no asseverations, no strong adjectives or intensifying adverbs, no calling upon sun and moon and stars to bear witness to his gladness, can increase the force of those two tiny words, so he adds none.

"I wonder, then," say I, in a rather sneaky and shamefaced manner, mumbling and looking down, "that you were not in a greater hurry to get to me?"

"*In a greater hurry!*" he repeats, in an accent of acute surprise. "Why, child, what are you talking about? Since we landed, I have neither slept nor eaten. I drove straight across London, and have been in the train ever since."

"But—between—this—and the—station?" suggest I, slowly, having taken hold of one of the buttons of his coat; the very one that in former difficulties I used always to resort to.

"You mean about my walking up?" he says readily, and without the slightest trace of guilty consciousness, indeed with a distinct and open look of pleasure; "but, my darling, how could I tell how long she would keep me? poor little woman!" (beginning to laugh and to put back the hair from his tanned forehead). "I am afraid I did not bless her when I saw her standing at her gate! I had half a mind to ask her whether another time would not do as well, but she looked so eager to hear about her husband—you know I have been seeing him at St. Thomas—such a wistful little face—and I knew that she could not keep me more than ten minutes; and, altogether when I thought of her loneliness and my own luck—"

He breaks off.

"Are you so sure she *is* lonely?" I say, with an innocent air of asking for information, and still working hard at the button; "are people always lonely when their husbands are away?"

He looks at me strangely for a moment; then, "Of course she is lonely, poor little thing!" he says, warmly; "how could she help it?"

A slight pause.

"*Most* men," say I, jealously, "would not have thought it a hardship to walk up and down between the laurustinus with Mrs. Zéphine, I can tell you!"

"Would not they?" he answers, indifferently. "I dare say not! she always *was* a good little thing!"

"Excellent!" reply I, with a nasty dryness, "bland, passionate, and deeply religious!"

Again he looks at me in surprise—a surprise which, after a moment's reflection, melts and brightens into an expression of pleasure.

"Did you care so much about my coming that ten minutes seemed to make a difference?" he asks, in an eager voice. "Is it possible that you were *in a hurry* for me?"

Why cannot I speak truth, and say yes? Why does an objectlessly lying devil make its inopportune entry into me? Through some misplaced and crooked false shame I answer, "Not at all! not at all! of course a few minutes one way or the other could not make much difference; I was only puzzled to know what had become of you?"

He looks a shade disappointed, and for a moment we are both silent. We have sat down side by side on the sofa. Vick is standing on her hinder legs, with her forepaws rested on Roger's knee. Her tail is wagging with the strong and untiring regularity of a pendulum, and a smirk of welcome and recognition is on her face. Roger's arm is round me, and we are holding each other's hands, but we are no longer in heaven. I could not tell you *why*, but we are not. Some stupid constraint—quite of earth—has fallen upon me. Where are all those most tender words, those profuse endearments with which I meant to have greeted him?

"And so it is actually true!" he says, with a long-drawn sigh of relief; his eyes wandering round the room, and taking in all the familiar objects; "there is no mistake about it! I am actually holding your real live hand" (turning it gently about and softly considering the long slight fingers and pink palm)—"in mine! Ah! my dear, how often, how often I have held it so in my dreams! Have you ever" (speaking with a sort of doubtfulness and uncertain hope)—"have you ever—no, I dare say not—so held mine?"

The diffident passion in his voice for once destroys that vile constraint, dissipates that idiotic sense of bashfulness.

"*Scores* of times!" I answer, letting my head drop on his shoulder, and not taking the trouble to raise it again.

"I never *used* to think myself of a very nervous turn!" he says, presently, with a smile. "Nancy, you will laugh at me, but I assure you upon my honor that all the way home I have been in the most abject and deadly fright: at every puff of wind I thought we were infallibly going to the bottom: whenever the carriage rocked in the least to-day on the way down, I made up my mind we were going to smash! Little woman, what can a bit of a thing like you have done to me to make me seem so much more valuable to myself than I have ever done these eight-and-forty years?"

I think no answer to this so suitable and seemly as a dumb friction of my left cheek against the rough cloth of the shoulder on which it has reposed itself.

"Talk to me, Nancy!" he says, in a quiet half-whisper of happiness. "Let me hear the sound of your voice! I am sick of my own; I have had a glut of that all these weary eight months; tell me about them all! How are they all? how are the boys?" (with a playful smile of recollection at what used to be my *one* subject, the one theme on which I was wont to wax illimitably diffuse). But now, at the magic name no pleasant garrulity overcomes me; only the remembrance of my worries; of all those troubles that I mean now to transfer from my own to Roger's broad shoulders, swoop down upon me.

I raise my head and speak with a clouded brow and a complaining tone.

"The Brat has gone back to Oxford," I say, gloomily; "Bobby has gone to Hong-Kong, and Algy has gone to *the dogs*—or at least is going there as hard as he can!"

"*To the dogs?*" (with an accent of surprise and concern); "what do you mean? what has sent him there?"

"You had better ask Mrs. Zéphine," reply I, bitterly, thinking, with a lively exasperation, of the changed and demoralized Algy I had last seen—soured, headstrong, and unhinged.

"*Zéphine!*" (repeating the name with an accent of thorough astonishment), "what on earth can *she* have to say to it?"

"Ah, *what?*" reply I, with oracular spite; then, overcome with remorse at the thought of the way in which I was embittering the first moments of his return, I rebury my face in his shoulder.

"I will tell you about that to-morrow," I say; "to-day is a good day, and we will talk only of good things and of good people."

He does not immediately answer. My remark seems to have buried him in thought. Presently he shakes off his distraction and speaks again.

"And Barbara? how is she? *She* has not" (beginning to laugh)—"*she* has not gone to the dogs, I suppose!"

"No," say I, slowly, not thinking of what I am saying, but with my thoughts wandering off to the greatest and sorest of my afflictions, "not yet."

"And" (smiling) "your plan. See what a good memory I have—your plan of marrying her to Musgrave, how does that work?"

"*My* plan!" cry I, tremulously, while a sudden torrent of scarlet pours all over my face and neck. "I do not know what you are talking about! I never had any such plan! Phew!" (lifting up the arm that is round my waist, hastily removing it, rising and going to the window), "how hot this room grows of an afternoon!"

CHAPTER XXXV

So the king enjoys his own again, and Roger is at home. Not yet—and now it is the next morning—has his return become *real* to me. Still there is something phantom and visionary about it: still it seems to me open to question whether, if I look away from him for a moment, he may not melt and disappear into dream-land.

All through breakfast I am dodging and peeping from behind the urn to assure myself of the continued presence and substantial reality of the strong shoulders and bronze-colored face that so solidly and certainly face me. As often as I catch his eye—and this is not seldom, for perhaps he too has his misgivings about me—I smile, in a manner, half ashamed, half sneaky, and yet most wholly satisfied.

The sun, who is not by any means *always* so well-judging, often hiding his face with both hands from a wedding, and hotly and gaudily flaming down on a black funeral, is shining with a temperate February comeliness in at our windows, on our garden borders; trying (and failing) to warm up the passionless melancholy of the chilly snow-drop families, trying (and succeeding) to add his quota to the joy that already fills and occupies our two hearts.

"How fine it is!" I cry, flying with unmatronly agility to the window, and playing a waltz on the pane. "That is right! I should have been so angry if it had rained; let us come out at once—I want to hear your opinion about the laurels; they want cutting badly, but I could not have them touched while you were away, though Bobby's fingers—when he was here—itched to be hacking at them. Come, I have got on my strong boots on purpose!—*at once.*"

"*At once?*" he repeats, a little doubtfully turning over the letters that lie in a heap beside his plate. "Well, I do not know about *that*—duty first, and pleasure afterward. Had not I better go to Zéphine Huntley's *first*, and get it over?"

"To *Zéphine Huntley's?*" repeat I, my fingers suddenly breaking off in the middle of their tune, as I turn quickly round to face him; the smile disappearing from my face, and my jaw lengthening; "you do not mean to say that you are going there *again?*"

"Yes, *again!*" he answers, laughing a little, and slightly mimicking my tragic tone; "why not, Nancy?"

I make no answer. I turn away and look out; but I see a different landscape. It looks to me as if I were regarding it through dark-blue glass.

"I have got a whole sheaf of letters and papers from her husband for her," pursues Roger, apparently calmly, and utterly unaware of my discomfiture, "and I do not want to keep her out of them longer than I can help."

Still I make no rejoinder. My fingers stray idly up and down the glass; but it is no longer a giddy waltz that they are executing—if it is a tune at all, it is some little dirge.

"What has happened to you, Nancy?" says Roger, presently, becoming aware of my silence, rising and following me; "what are you doing—catching flies?"

"No," reply I, with an acrid smartness, "not I! I leave that to Mrs. Zéphine."

Once again he regards me with that look of unfeigned surprise, tinged with a little pain which yesterday I detected on his face. When I look at him, when my eyes rest on the brave and open honesty of his, my ugly, nipping doubts disappear.

"Do not go," say I, standing on tiptoe, so that my hands may reach his neck, and clasp it, speaking in my most beguiling half-whisper; "why should you fetch and carry for her? let John or William take her letters. Are you so sure" (with an irresistible sneer) "that she is in such a hurry for them?—stay with me this *one first* day!—*do, please—Roger.*"

It is the first time in all my history that I have succeeded in delivering myself of his Christian name to his face—frequently as I have fired it off in dialogues with myself, behind his back. It shoots out now with the loud suddenness of a mismanaged soda-water cork.

"*Roger!*" he repeats, in an accent of keen pleasure, catching me to his heart; "what! I am *Roger*, after all, am I? The 'general' has gone to glory at last, has he?—thank God!"

"I will ring and tell John at once," say I, with subtile amiability, disengaging myself from his arms, and walking quickly toward the bell.

"Stay!" he says, putting his hand on me in detention, before I have made two steps; "you must not! it is no use! John will not do, or William either: it is a matter of business. I have" (sighing) "to go through many of these papers with her."

"You?"

"Yes, *I*; why is that so surprising?"

"What possible concern is it of *yours*?" ask I, throwing the reins on the neck of my indignation, and urging that willing steed to a sharp gallop, crimsoning as I speak, and raising my voice, as has ever been our immemorial wont in home-broils. "For my part, I never saw any good come of people putting their fingers into their neighbors' pies!"

"Not even if those neighbors are the oldest friends they have in the world?" he says, gently, yet eying with some wonder—perhaps apprehension, for odd things frighten men—the small scarlet scold who stands swelling with ruffled feathers, and angry eyes, winking to keep the tears out of them, before him.

"I thought *father* was the oldest friend you had in the world!" say I, with a jealous tartness; "you always *used* to tell us so."

"*Some* of my oldest friends, then," he answers, looking a little amused, "since you will have me so exact."

"If Mrs. Huntley is the oldest friend you have in the world," say I, acrimoniously, still sticking to his first and most offensive form of expression, and *heavily* accenting it, "I wonder that you never happened to mention her existence before you went."

"So do I," he says, a little thoughtfully. "I am not much of a friend, am I? but—" (looking at me with that sincere and hearty tenderness which, as long as I am under its immediate influence, always disarms me) "my head was full of other things; and people drop out of one's life so; I had neither seen nor heard of her since—since she married."

("Since she was engaged to you," say I, mentally interlining this statement, "and threw you over because you were not rich enough! why cannot you be honest and say so?") but aloud I give utterance to nothing but a shrewish and disbelieving "Hm!"

A pause. I do not know what Roger is thinking of, but I am following out my own train of thought; the fruit of which is this observation, made with an air of reflection:

"Mr. Huntley is a very rich man, I suppose?"

Roger laughs.

"*Rich!* poor Huntley! that is the very last thing his worst enemy could accuse him of! why, he was obliged to run the constable two years ago."

"But I suppose," say I, slowly, "that he was better off—*well* off once—when she married him, for instance?"

"How did you know that?" he asks, a little surprised. "Who told you? Yes; at that time he was looked upon as quite a *parti*."

"Better off than *you*, I suppose?" say I, still speaking slowly, and reading the carpet. "I mean than you were then?"

Again he laughs.

"He might easily have been that? I had nothing but my younger son's portion and my pay; why, Nancy, I had an idea that I had told you that before."

"I dare say you did," reply I, readily, "but I like to hear it again."

Yet another pause.

"He is badly off *now*, then," say I, presently, with a faintly triumphant accent.

"About as badly off as it is possible to be," answers Roger, very gravely; "that is my business with his wife; she and I are trying to make an arrangement with his creditors, to enable him to come home."

"To come home!" echo I, raising my eyebrows in an artless astonishment; "but if he *does* come home, what will become of Algy and the *rest of them*?"

"The rest of *whom*?" asks Roger, but there is such a severity in his eye as he puts the question that it is not too much to say I *dare not* explain. The one thing hated of Roger's soul—the one thing for which he has no tolerance, and on which he brings to bear all the weight of his righteous wrath, is *scandal*. Not even me will he allow to nibble at a neighbor's fame.

"Is she much changed since you saw her last?" pursue I presently, with infantile guilelessness; "was her hair *red* then? some people say it *used* to be black!"

I raise my eyes to his face as I put this gentle query, in order the better to trace its effect; but the concern that I see in his countenance is so very much greater than any that I had intended to have summoned that I have no sooner hurled my dart than I repent me of having done it.

"Nancy!" he says, putting one hand under my chin, and stroking my hair with the other—"am I going to have a *backbiting* wife? Child! child! there was neither hatred nor malice in the little girl I found sitting at the top of the wall."

I do not answer.

"Nancy," he says again, in a voice of most thorough earnestness, "I have a favor to ask of you—I know when I put it *that way*, that you will not say 'No;' if you do not mind, I had rather you did not abuse Zéphine

Huntley!—for the matter of that, I had rather you did not abuse any one—it does not pay, and there is no great fun in it; but Zéphine *specially* not."

"Why *specially*?" cry I, breathing short and speaking again with a quick, raised voice. "I know that it is a bad plan abusing people, you need not tell me *that*, I know it as well as you do, and I never did it at home, before I married, *never*!—none of them ever accused me of it—I was always quite good-natured about people, *quite*; but why *she specially*? why is she to be more sacred than any one else?"

"It is an old story," he answers, passing his hand across his forehead with what looks to me like a rather weary gesture and sighing, "I do not know why I did not tell you before—did not I ever?—no, by-the-by, I remember I never did; well, I will tell you now, and then you will understand!"

"Do not!" cry I, passionately, putting my fingers in my ears, and growing scarlet, while the tears rush in mad haste to my eyes, for I imagine that I well know what is coming. "I do not want to hear! I had rather not! I *hate* old stories." He looks at me in silent dismay. "I mean," say I, seeing that some explanation is needed, "that I know all about it!—I have heard it already! I have been told it."

"Been told it? By whom?"

"Never mind by whom!" reply I, removing my fingers from my ears, and covering with both hot hands my hotter face. "I *have* been told it! I *have* heard it, and, what is more, I *will not hear it again*!"

CHAPTER XXXVI

When I rose this morning, I did not think that I should have cried before night; indeed, nothing would have seemed to me so unlikely. Cry! on the day of Roger's first back-coming! absurd! And yet now the morning is still quite young, and I have wept abundantly.

I am always rather good at crying. Tears with me do not argue any very profound depth of affliction. My tears have always been somewhat near my eyes, a fact well known to the boys, whom my pearly drops always leave as stolid and unfeeling as they found them. But the case is different with Roger. Either he is ignorant, or he has forgotten the facility with which I weep, and his distress is proportioned to his ignorance.

My eyes are dried again now, though they and my nose still keep a brave after-glow; and Roger and I are at one again. But, for my part, on this first day, I think it would have been pleasanter if we had never been at two. However, smiling peace is now again restored to us, and no one, to look at us, as we sit in my boudoir after breakfast, would think that we, or perhaps I should say I, had been so lately employed in chasing her away. As little would any one, looking at the blandness of Vick's profile, as she slumbers on the window-seat in the sun, conjecture of her master-passion for the calves of strangers' legs.

"So you see that I *must* go, Nancy," says Roger, with a rather wistful appeal to my reason, of whose supremacy he is not, perhaps, quite so confident as he was when he got up this morning. "You understand, don't you, dear?"

I nod.

"Yes, I understand."

I still speak in a subdued and snuffly voice, but the wrath has gone out of me.

"Well, you—would you mind," he says, speaking rather hesitatingly, as not quite sure of the reception that his proposition may meet with—"would you mind coming with me as far as Zéphine's?"

"Do you mean come all the way, and go in with you, and stay while you are there?" cry I, with great animation, as a picture of the strict supervision which, by this course of conduct, I shall be enabled to exercise over Mrs. Zéphine's oscillades, poses, and little verbal tendernesses, flashes before my mind's eye.

Roger looks down.

"I do not know about *that*," he says, slowly. "Perhaps she would not care to go into her husband's liabilities before a—a str—before a third person!"

"Two is company and three is none, in fact," say I, with a slight relapse into the disdainful and snorting mood.

He looks distressed, but attempts no argument or explanation.

"How far did you mean me to come, then?" say I, half ashamed of my humors, but still with an after-thought of pettishness in my voice. "Escort you to the hall-door, I suppose, and kick my heels among the laurestines until such time as all Mr. Huntley's bills are paid?"

He turns away.

"It is of no consequence," he says, with a slight shade of impatience, and a stronger shade of disappointment in his voice. "I see that you do not wish it, but what I meant was, that you might have walked with me as far as the gate, so that on this first day we might lose as little of each other's society as possible."

"And so I will!" cry I, impulsively, with a rush of tardy repentance. "I—I—*meant* to come all along. I was only—only—*joking*!"

But to both of us it seems but a sorry jest. We set forth, and walk side by side through the park. Both of us are rather silent. Yes, though we have eight months' arrears of talk to make up, though it seemed to me before he came that in a whole long life there would scarce be time for all the things I had to say to him, yet, now that we are reunited, we are stalking dumbly along through the withered white grass, pallid from the winter storms. Certainly, we neither of us could say any thing so well worth hearing as what the lark, in his most loud and godly joy, is telling us from on high. Perhaps it is the knowledge of this that ties our tongues.

The sun shines on our heads. He has not much power yet, but great good-will. And the air is almost as gentle as June. We have left our own domain behind us, and have reached Mrs. Huntley's white gate. Through the bars I see the sheltered laurestines all ablow.

"May I wait for you here?" say I, with diffident urgency, reflecting hopefully, as I make the suggestion, on the wholesome effect, on the length of the interview that the knowledge of my being, flattening my nose against the bars of the gate all through it, must necessarily have.

Again he looks down, as if unwilling to meet my appealing eyes.

"I think not, Nancy," he answers, reluctantly. "You see, I cannot possibly tell how long I might be obliged to keep you waiting."

"I do not mind waiting at all," persist I, eagerly. "I am not very impatient; I shall not expect you to be very quick, and" (going on very fast, to hinder him from the second refusal which I see hovering on his lips), "and it is not at all cold; just now you yourself said that you had felt many a chillier May-day, and I am so warmly wrapped up, pet!" (taking hold of one of his fingers, and making it softly travel up and down the fur of my thick coat).

He shakes his head, with a gesture unwilling, yet decided.

"No, Nancy, it could not be! I had rather that you would go home."

"I have no doubt you would!" say I, turning sharply and huffily away; then, with a sudden recollecting and repenting myself, "May I come back, then?" I say, meekly. "Come and fetch you, I mean, after a time—any long time that you like!"

"*Will* you?" he cries, with animation, the look of unwilling refusal vanishing from his face. "Would you *like*? would not it be too much trouble?"

"Not at all! not at all!" reply I, affably. "How soon, then?" (taking out my watch); "in half an hour?"

Again his face falls a little.

"I think it must be longer than *that*, Nancy."

"An hour, then?" say I, lifting a lengthened countenance wistfully to his; "people may do a good deal in an hour, may not they?"

"Had not we better be on the safe side, and say an hour and a half?" suggests he, but somewhat apprehensively—or I imagine so. "I shall be sure not to keep you a minute then—I do not relish the notion of my wife's tramping up and down this muddy road all by herself."

"And I do not relish the notion of my husband—" return I, beginning to speak very fast, and then suddenly breaking off—"Well, good-by!"

"Say, good-by, Roger," cries he, catching my hand in detention, as I turn away. "Nancy, if you knew how fond I have grown of my own name! In despite of Tichborne, I think it *lovely*."

I laugh.

"Good-by, *Roger!*"

He has opened the gate, and turned in. I watch him, as he walks with long, quick steps, up the little, trim swept drive. As I follow him with my eyes, a devil enters into me. I cry—

"Roger!"

He turns at once.

"Ask her to show you Algy's bracelet," I say, with an awkward laugh; and then, thoroughly afraid of the effect of my bomb-shell, and not daring to see what sort it is, I turn and run quickly away.

The end of the hour and a half finds me punctually peering through the bars again. Well, I am first at the rendezvous. This, perhaps, is not very surprising, as I have not given him one moment's law. For the first five minutes, I am very fairly happy and content. The lark is still fluttering in strong rapture up in the heights of the sky; and for these five minutes I listen to him, soothed and hallowed. But, after they are past, it is different. God's bird may be silent, as far as I am concerned: not a verse more of his clear psalm do I hear. An uneasy devil of jealousy has entered into me, and stopped my ears. I take hold of the bars of the gate, and peer through, as far as my head will go: then I open it, and, stealing on tiptoe up the drive a little way, to the first corner, look warily round it. Not a sign of him! Not a sound! Not even a whisper of air to rustle the glistening laurel-leaves, or stir the flat laurestine-sprays.

I return to the road, and inculcate patience on myself. Why may not I take a lesson in easy-mindedness from Vick? Was not it Hartley Coleridge who suggested that perhaps dogs have a language of smell; and that what to us is a noisome smell, is to them a beautiful poem? If so, Vick is searching for lyrics and epics in the ditch. I stroll along the wintry brown hedge-row, and begin to pick Roger a little, scant nosegay. He shall see how patient I am! how *un*sulky! with what sunny mildness I can wait his leisure! I have already two or three snow-drops in my breast, that I picked as I came through the garden. To these I add a drooping hazel-tassel or two, and a little bit of honeysuckle-leaf, just breaking greenly into life. This is all I can find—all the scentless first-fruits of the baby year.

It is ten minutes past the due time now. Again I listen intently, as I listened yesterday, for his coming. There is a sound now; but, alas! not the right one! It is the rumbling of an approaching carriage. A pony-chaise bowls past. The occupants are acquaintances of mine, and we bow and smile to each other. As long as they are in sight, I affect to be diligently botanizing in the hedge. When they have disappeared, I sit down on a heap of stones, and take out my watch for the hundredth time; a whole quarter of an hour!

"He does not relish the notion of his wife's tramping up and down this muddy road by herself, does not he?" say I, speaking out loud, and gnashing my teeth.

Then I hurl my little posy away from me into the mud, as far as it will go. What has become of my patience? my sunny mildness? Then, as the recollection of the velvet-gown and mob-cap episode recurs to me, I repent me, and, crossing the road, pick up again my harmless catkins and snow-drops, and rearrange them. I have hardly finished wiping the mire from the tender, lilac-veined snow-drop petals, before I hear his voice in the distance, in conversation with some one. Clearly, Delilah is coming to see the last of him! I expect that she mostly escorts them to the gate. In my present frame of mind, it would be physically impossible for me to salute her with the bland civility which society enjoins on people of our stage of civilization. I therefore remain sitting on my heap.

Presently, Roger emerges alone. He does not see me at first, but looks up the road, and down the road, in search of me. When, at last, he perceives me, no smile—(as has ever hitherto been his wont)—kindles his eyes and lips. With unstirred gravity, he approaches me.

"Here you are *at last!*" cry I, scampering to meet him, but with a stress, from which human nature is unable to refrain, on the last two words.

"At last?" he repeats in a tone of surprise; "am I over time?—Yes"— (looking at his watch)—"so I am! I had no idea of it; I hope you have not been long waiting."

"*I* was here to the minute," reply I, curtly; and again my tongue declines to refrain from accentuation.

"I beg your pardon!" he says, still speaking with unnecessary seriousness, as it seems to me, "I really had no idea of it."

"I dare say not," say I, with a little wintry grin; "I never heard that they had a clock in paradise."

"*In paradise!*" he repeats, looking at me strangely with his keen, clear eyes, that seem to me to have less of a caress in them than they ever had before on meeting mine. "What has *paradise* to say to it? Do you imagine that I have been in *paradise* since I left you here?"

"I do not know, I am sure!" reply I, rather confused, and childishly stirring the stiff red mud with the end of my boot, "I believe *they* mostly do; Algy does—" then afraid of drawing down the vial of his wrath on me a second time for my scandal-mongering propensities, I go on quickly; "Were you talking to yourself as you came down the drive? I heard your voice as if in conversation. I sometimes talk to myself when I am by myself, quite loud."

"Do you? I do not think I do; at least I am not aware of it; I was talking to Zéphine."

"Why did not she come to the gate, then?" inquire I, tartly; "did she know I was there? did not she want to see me?"

"I do not know; I did not ask her."

I look up at him in strong surprise. We are in the park now—our own unpeopled, silent park, where none but the deer can see us; and yet he has not offered me the smallest caress; not once has he called me "Nancy;" he, to whom hitherto my homely name has appeared so sweet. It is only an hour and three-quarters since I parted from him, and yet in that short space an indisputable shade—a change that exits not only in my imagination, but one that no most careless, superficial eye could avoid seeing—has come over him. Face, manner, even gait, are all altered, I think of Algy—Algy as he used to be, our jovial pet and playfellow, Algy as he now is, soured, sulky, unloving, his very beauty dimmed by discontent and passion. Is this the beginning of a like change in Roger?

A spasm of jealous agony, of angry despair, contracts my heart as I think this.

"Well, are all Mr. Huntley's debts paid?" I ask, trying to speak in a tone of sprightly ease; "is there a good hope of his coming back soon?"

"Not yet a while; in time, perhaps, he may."

Still there is not a vestige of a smile on his face. He does not look at me as he speaks; his eyes are on the long, dead knots of the colorless grass at his feet; in his expression despondency and preoccupation strive for supremacy.

"Have you made your head ache?" I say, gently stealing my hand into his; "there is nothing that addles the brains like muddling over accounts, is there?"

Am I awake? *Can* I believe it? He has dropped my hand, as if he disliked the touch of it.

"No, thanks, no. I have no headache," he answers, hastily.

Another little silence. We are marching quickly along, as if our great object were to get our *tête-à-tête* over. As we came, we dawdled, stood still to listen to the lark, to look at the wool-soft cloud-heaps piled in the west—on any trivial excuse indeed; but now all these things are changed.

"Did you talk of business *all* the time?" I ask, by-and-by, with timid curiosity.

It is *not* my fancy; he does plainly hesitate.

"Not quite *all*," he answers, in a low voice, and still looking away from me.

"About *what*, then?" I persist, in a voice through whose counterfeit playfulness I myself too plainly hear the unconquerable tremulousness; "may not I hear?—or is it a secret?"

He does not answer; it seems to me that he is considering what response to make.

"Perhaps," say I, still with a poor assumption of lightness and gayety, "perhaps you were talking of—of old times."

He laughs a little, but *whose* laugh has he borrowed? in that dry, harsh tone there is nothing of my Roger's mellow mirth!

"Not we; old times must take care of themselves; one has enough to do with the new ones, I find."

"Did she—did she say any thing to you about—about *Algy*, then?"— hesitatingly.

"We did not mention his name."

There is something so abrupt and trenchant in his tone that I have not the spirit to pursue my inquiries any further. In deep astonishment and still deeper mortification, I pursue my way in silence.

Suddenly Roger comes to a stand-still.

"Nancy!" he says, in a voice that is more like his own, stopping and laying his hands on my shoulders; while in his eyes is something of his old kindness; yet not quite the old kindness either; there is more of unwilling, rueful yearning in them than there ever was in that—"Nancy, how old are you?—nineteen, is it not?"

"Very nearly twenty," reply I, cheerfully, for he has called me "Nancy," and I hail it as a sign of returning fine weather; "we may call it twenty; will not it be a comfort when I am well out of my teens?"

"And I am forty-eight," he says, as if speaking more to himself than to me, and sighing heavily; "it is a *monstrous*, an *unnatural* disparity!"

"It is not nearly so bad as if it were *the other way*," reply I, laughing gayly; "I forty-eight, and *you* twenty, is it?"

"My child! my child!"—speaking with an accent of, to me, unaccountable suffering—"what possessed me to *marry* you? why did not I *adopt* you instead? It would have been a hundred times more seemly!"

"It is a little late to think of that now, is not it?" I say, with an uncomfortable smile; then I go on, with an uneasy laugh, "that was the very idea that occurred to us the first night you arrived; at least, it never struck us as possible that you would take any notice of *me*, but we all said what a good thing it would be for the family if you would adopt Barbara or the Brat."

"Did you?" (very quickly, in a tone of keen pain); "it struck you all in the same light then?"

"But that was before we had seen you," I answer, hastily, repenting my confession as soon as I see its effects. "When we *had*, we soon changed our tune."

"*If* I *had* adopted you," he pursues, still looking at me with the same painful and intent wistfulness, "if I had been your father, you would have been fond of me, would not you? Not *afraid* of me—not afraid to tell me any thing that most nearly concerned you—you would perhaps"—(with a difficult smile)—"you would perhaps have made me your *confidant*, would you, Nancy?"

I look up at him in utter bewilderment.

"What are you talking about? Why do I want a confidant? What have I to confide? What have I to tell any one?"

Our eyes are resting on each other, and, as I speak, I feel his go with clean and piercing search right through mine into my soul. In a moment I think of Musgrave, and the untold black tale now forever in my thought attached to him, and, as I so think, the hot flush of agonized shame that the recollection of him never fails to call to my face, invades cheeks, brow, and throat. To hide it, I drop my head on Roger's breast. Shall I tell him *now*, this instant? Is it possible that he has already some faint and shadowy suspicion of the truth—some vague conjecture concerning it, as something in his manner seems to say? But no! it is absolutely impossible! Who, with the best will in the world, could have told him? Is not the tale safely buried in the deep grave of Musgrave's and my two hearts?

I raise my head, and twice essay to speak. Twice I stop, choked. How can I put into words the insult I have received? How can I reveal to him the slack levity, the careless looseness, with which I have kept the honor confided to me?

As my eyes stray helplessly round in a vain search for advice or help from the infinite unfeeling apathy of Nature, I catch sight of the distant chimneys of the abbey! How near it is! After all, why should I sow dissension between such close neighbors? why make an irreparable breach between two families, hitherto united by the kindly ties of mutual friendship and good-will?

Frank is young, very young; he has been—so Roger himself told me—very ill brought up. Perhaps he has already repented, who knows? I try to persuade myself that these are the reasons—and sufficient reasons—of my silence, and I take my resolution afresh. I will be dumb. The flush slowly dies out of my face, and, when I think it is almost gone, I venture to look again at Roger. I think that his eyes have never left me. They seem to be expecting me to speak, but, as I still remain silent, he turns at length away, and also gently removes his hands from my shoulders. We stand apart.

"Well, Nancy," he says, sighing again, as if from the bottom of his soul, "my poor child, it is no use talking about it. I can never be your father now."

"And a very good thing too!" rejoin I, with a dogged stoutness. "I do not see what I want with *two* fathers; I have always found *one* amply enough—quite as much as I could manage, in fact."

He seems hardly to be listening to me. He has dropped his eyes on the ground, and is speaking more to himself than to me.

"Husband and wife we are!" he says, with a slow depression of tone, "and, as long as God's and man's laws stand, husband and wife we must remain!"

"You are not very polite," I cry, with an indignant lump rising in my throat; "you speak as if you were *sorry* for it—*are* you?"

He lifts his eyes again, and again their keen search investigates the depths of my soul; but no human eye can rightly read the secrets of any other human spirit; they find what they expect to find, not what is there. Clear and cuttingly keen as they are, Roger's eyes do not read my soul aright.

"Are *you*, Nancy?"

"If *you* are, I am," I reply, with a half-smothered sob.

He makes no rejoinder, and we begin again to walk along homeward, but slowly this time.

"We have made a mistake, perhaps," he says, presently, still speaking with the same slow and ruminating sadness in his tone. "The inscrutable God alone knows why He permits his creatures to mar all their seventy years by one short false step—yes—a *mistake!*"

(Ah me! ah me! I always mistrusted those laurestines! They sent me back my brother churlish and embittered, but oh! that in my steadfast Roger they should have worked such a sudden deadly change!)

"Is it more a mistake," I cry, bursting out into irrepressible anger, "than it was two hours ago, when I left you at that gate? You did not seem to think it a mistake *then*—at least you hid it very well, if you did"—(then going on quickly, seeing that he is about to interrupt me)—"have you been *comparing notes*, pray? Has *she* found it a mistake, too?"

"Yes, *that* she has! Poor soul! God help her!" he answers, compassionately.

Something in the pity of his tone jars frightfully on my strung nerves.

"If God has to help all the poor souls who have made mistakes, He will have his hands full!" I retort, bitterly.

Another silence. We are drawing near the pleasure-grounds—the great rhododendron belt that shelters the shrubbery from the east wind.

"Nancy," says Roger, again stopping, and facing me too. This time he does not put his hands on my shoulders; the melancholy is still in his eyes, but there is no longer any harshness. They repossess their natural kindly benignity. "Though it is perhaps impossible that there should be between us that passionate love that there might be between people that are nearer each other in age—more fitly mated—yet there is no reason why we should not *like* each other very heartily, is there, dear? why there should not be between us absolute confidence, perfect frankness—that is the great thing, is not it?"

He is looking with such intense wistfulness at me, that I turn away. Why should not there be passionate love between us? Who is there but himself to hinder it? So I make no answer.

"I dare say," he says, taking my right hand, and holding it with a cool and kindly clasp, "that you think it difficult—next door to impossible—for two people, one at the outset, one almost on the confines of life, to enter very understandingly into each other's interests! No doubt the thought that I—being so much ahead of you in years"—(sighing again heavily)—"cannot see with your eyes, or look at things from your stand-point—would make it harder for you to come to me in your troubles; but indeed, dear, if you believe me, I will *try*, and, as we are to spend our lives together, I think it would be better, would not it?"

He speaks with a deprecating humility, an almost imploring gentleness, but I am so thoroughly upset by the astounding change that has come over the tone of his talk—by the clouds that have suddenly darkened the morning sunshine of my horizon—that I cannot answer him in the same tone.

"Perhaps we shall not have to spend all our lives together!" I say, with a harsh laugh. "Cheer up! One of us may *die*! who knows?"

After that we neither of us say any thing till we reach the house.

CHAPTER XXXVII

"Yea, by God's rood, I trusted you too well!"

In the hall we part without a word, and I, spiritlessly, mount the staircase alone. How I flew down it this morning, three steps at a time, and had some ado to hinder myself from sliding down the banisters, as we have all often, with dangerous joy, done at home! Now I crawl up, like some sickly old person. When I reach my bedroom, I throw myself into the first chair, and lie in it—

"... quiet as any water-sodden log
Stayed in the wandering warble of a brook."

I do not attempt to take off my hat and jacket. Of what use is it to take them off more than to leave them on, or to leave them on more than to take them off? Of what use is *any thing*, pray? What a weary round life is! what a silly circle of unfortunate repetitions! eating only to be hungry again; waking only to sleep; sleeping only to wake!

At first I am too inert even to think, even to lift my hand to protect my cheek from Vick's muddy paws, who, annoyed at my evident inattention to her presence, is sitting on my lap, making little impatient *clawings* at my defenseless countenance. But gradually on the river of recollection all the incidents of the morning flow through my mind. In more startling relief than ever, the astounding change in Roger, wrought by those ill-starred two hours, stands out. Is it possible that I may have been attributing it to a wrong cause? Doubtless, the first interview with the woman he had loved, and who had thrown him over (by-the-by, how forgiving men are!)—yes, the first, probably, since they had stood in the relation of betrothed people to each other—must have been full of pain. Doubtless, the contrast between the crude gawkiness of the raw girl he has drifted into marrying—for I suppose it was more accident than any thing else—with the mature and subtle grace, the fine and low-voiced sweetness of the woman whom his whole heart and soul and taste chose and approved, must have struck him with keen force. I expected *that*: it would not have taken me by surprise. If he had emerged from among the laurestines, depressed, and vainly struggling for a factitious cheerfulness, I think I could have understood it. I think I could have borne with it, could have tried meekly to steal back into his heart again, to win him back, in despite of ignorance, gawkiness, and all other my drawbacks, by force of sheer love.

But the change was surely too abrupt to be accounted for on this hypothesis. Would *Roger*, my pattern of courtesy—Roger, who shrinks from hurting the meanest beggar's feelings—would he, in such plain terms, have deplored and wished undone our marriage, if it were only suffering to *himself* that it had entailed? Has his unselfish chivalry gone the way of Algy's brotherly love? Impossible! the more I think of it, the more unlikely it seems—the more certain it appears to me that I must look elsewhere for the cause of the alteration that has so heavily darkened my day.

I have risen, and am walking quickly up and down. I have shaken off my stolid apathy, or, rather, it has fallen off of itself. Can she have told him any ill tales of me? any thing to my disadvantage? Instantly the thought of Musgrave—the black and heavy thought that is never far from the portals of my mind—darts across me, and, at the same instant, like a flash of lightning, the recollection of my meeting her on the fatal evening, just as (with tear-stained, swollen face) I had parted from Frank—of the alert and lively interest in her eyes, as she bowed and smiled to me, flames with sudden illumination into my soul. Still I can hardly credit it. It would, no doubt, be pleasant to her to sow dissension between us, but would even *she* dare to carry ill tales of a wife to a husband? And even supposing that she had, would he attach so much importance to my being seen with wet cheeks? I, who cry so easily—I, who wept myself nearly blind when Jacky caught his leg in the snare? If he thinks so much of that part of the tale, *what would he think of the rest?*

As I make this reflection I shudder, and again congratulate myself on my silence. For beyond our parting, and my tears, it is *impossible* that she can have told him aught.

Men are not prone to publish their own discomfitures; even *I* know that much. I exonerate Mr. Musgrave from all share in making it known—and have the mossed tree-trunks lips? or the loud brook an articulate tongue? Thank God! thank God! *no!* Nature never blabs. With infinite composure, with a most calm smile she *listens*, but she never tells again.

A little reassured by this thought, I resolve to remain in doubt no longer than I can help, but to ascertain, if necessary, by direct inquiry, whether my suspicions are correct. This determination is no sooner come to than it puts fresh life and energy into my limbs. I take off my hat and jacket, smooth my hair, and prepare with some alacrity for luncheon.

It is evening, however, before I have an opportunity of putting my resolve in practice. At luncheon, there are the servants; all afternoon, Roger is closeted with his agent: before we set off this morning, he never mentioned the agent: he never figured at all in our day's plan—(I imagined that he was to be kept till to-morrow); and at dinner there are the servants again. Thank God, they are gone now! We are alone, Roger and I. We are sitting in my boudoir, as in my day-dreams, before his return, I had pictured us; but, alas! where is caressing proximity which figured in all my visions? where is the stool on which I was to sit at his feet, with head confidently leaned on his arm? As it happens, Vick is sitting on the stool, and we occupy two arm-chairs, at civil distance from each other, much as if we had been married sixty years, and had hated each other for fifty-nine of them. I am idly fiddle-faddling with a piece of work, and Roger—is it possible?—is stretching out his hand toward a book.

"You do not mean to say that you are going to *read*?" I say, in a tone of sharp vexation.

He lays it down again.

"If you had rather talk, I will not."

"I am afraid," say I, with a sour laugh, "that you have not kept much conversation *for home use*! I suppose you exhausted it all, this morning, at Laurel Cottage!"

He passes his hand slowly across his forehead.

"Perhaps!—I do not think I am in a very talking vein."

"By-the-by," say I, my heart beating thick, and with a hurry and tremor in my voice, as I approach the desired yet dreaded theme, "you have never told me what it was, besides Mr. Huntley's debts, that you talked of this morning!—you owned that you did not talk of business *quite* all the time!"

"Did I?"

He has forgotten his book now; across the flame of the candles, he is looking full and steadily at me.

"When I asked you, you said it was not about old times?—of course—" (laughing acridly)—"I can imagine your becoming illimitably diffuse about *them*, but you told me, that, 'No,' you did not mention them."

"I told truth."

"You also said," continue I, with my voice still trembling, and my pulses throbbing, "that it was not *Algy* that you were discussing!—if *I* had been in your place, I could, perhaps, have found a good deal to say about *him*; but you told me that you never mentioned him."

"We did not."

"Then what *did* you talk about?" I ask, in strong excitement; "it must have been a very odd theme that you find such difficulty in repeating."

Still he is looking, with searching gravity, full in my face.

"Do you *really* wish to know?"

I cannot meet his eyes: something in me makes me quail before them. I turn mine away, but answer, stoutly:

"Yes, I *do* wish. Why should I have asked, if I did not?"

Still he says nothing: still I feel, though I am not looking at him, that his eyes are upon me.

"Was it—" say I, unable any longer to bear that dumb gaze, and preferring to take the bull by the horns, and rush on my fate—"was it any thing about *me*? has she been telling you any tales of—of—*me*?"

No answer! No sound but the clock, and Vick's heavy breathing, as she peacefully snores on the footstool. I *cannot* bear the suspense. Again I lift my eyes, and look at him. Yes, I am right! the intense anxiety—the overpowering emotion on his face tell me that I have touched the right string.

"Are there—are there—are you aware that there are any tales that she *could* tell of you?"

Again I laugh harshly.

"Ha! ha! if we came to mutual anecdotes, I am not quite sure that I might not have the best of it!"

"That is not the question," he replies, in a voice so exceedingly stern, so absolutely different from any thing I have ever hitherto contemplated as possible in my gentle, genial Roger, that again, to the depths of my soul, I quail; how could I ever, in wildest dreams, have thought I should dare to tell him?—"it is nothing to me what tales *you* can tell of *her*!—*she* is not my wife!—what I wish to know—what I *will* know, is, whether there is any thing that she *could* say of you!"

For a moment, I do not answer. I cannot. A coward fear is grasping my heart with its clammy hands. Then—

"*Could!*" say I, shrugging my shoulders, and feebly trying to laugh derisively; "of course she could! it would be difficult to set a limit to the powers of a lady of her imagination!"

"What do you mean?" he cries, quickly, and with what sounds like a sort of hope in his voice; "have you any reason—any grounds for thinking her inventive?"

I do not answer directly.

"It is true, then," I cry, with flashing eyes, and in a voice of great and indignant anguish. "I have not been mistaken! I was right! Is it possible that *you*, who, only this morning, warned me with such severity against backbiting, have been calmly listening to scandalous tales about me from a stranger?"

He does not interrupt me: he is listening eagerly, and that sort of hope is still in his face.

"I *knew* it would come, sooner or later," I continue, speaking excitedly, and with intense bitterness, "sooner or later, I knew that it would be a case of Algy over again! but I did not—did not think that it would have been quite so soon! Great Heaven!" (smiting my hands sharply together, and looking upward), "I *have* fallen low! to think that I should come to be discussed by *you* with *her*!"

"I have *not* discussed you with her," he answers, very solemnly, and still looking at me with that profound and greedy eagerness in his eyes; "with *no* living soul would I discuss my wife—I should have hardly thought I need tell you that! What I heard, I heard by accident. She—as I believe, in all innocence of heart—referred to—the—the—circumstance, taking it for granted that I knew it—that *you* had told me of it, and I—*I*—" (raising his clinched right hand to emphasize his speech)—"I take God to witness, I had no more idea to what she was alluding—as soon as I understood—she must have thought me very dull—" (laughing hoarsely)—"for it was a long time before I took it in—but as soon as I understood to what manner of anecdote it was that she was referring—then, *at once*, I bade her be silent!—not even with *her*, would I talk over my wife!"

He stops. He has risen from his chair, and is now standing before me. His breath comes quick and panting; and his face is not far from being as white as mine.

"But what I have learned," he continues presently, in a low voice, that, by a great effort, he succeeds in making calm and steady, "I cannot again unlearn! I would not if I could!—I have no desire to live in a fool's paradise! I tried hard this morning—God knows what constraint I had to put upon myself—to induce you to tell me of your own accord—to *volunteer* it—but you would not—you were *resolutely* silent. Why were you? Why were you?" (breaking off with an uncontrollable emotion). "I should not have been hard upon you—I should have made allowances. God knows we all need it!"

I sit listening in a stony silence: every bit of me seems turned into cold rock.

"But *now*," he says, regathering his composure, and speaking with a resolute, stern quiet; "I have no other resource—you have left me none—but to come to you, and ask point-blank, is this true, or is it false?"

For a moment, my throat seems absolutely stopped up, choked; there seems no passage for my voice, through its dry, parched gates. Then at length I speak faintly: "Is *what* true? is what false? I suppose you will not expect me to deny it, before I know what it is?"

He does not at once answer. He takes a turn once or twice up and down the silent room, in strong endeavor to overcome and keep down his agitation, then he returns and speaks; with a face paler, indeed, than I could have imagined any thing so bronzed could be; graver, more austere than I ever thought I should see it, but still without bluster or hectoring violence.

"Is it true, then?" he says, speaking in a very low key. "Great God! that I should have to put such a question to my wife; that one evening, about a week ago, on the very day, indeed, that the news of my intended return arrived, you were seen parting with—with—*Musgrave*" (he seems to have an intense difficulty in pronouncing the name) "at or after nightfall, on the edge of Brindley Wood, *he* in a state of the most evident and extreme agitation, and *you* in floods of tears!—is it true, or is it false?—for God's sake, speak quickly!"

But I cannot comply with his request. I am *gasping*. His eyes are upon me, and, at every second's delay, they gather additional sternness. Oh, how awful they are in their just wrath! When was father, in his worst and most thunderous storms, half so dreadful? half so awe-inspiring?

"What sort of an interview could it have been to which there was such a close?" he says, as if making the reflection more to himself than to me; "speak! is it true?"

I can no longer defer my answer. One thing or another I must say: both eyes and lips imperatively demand it. Twice, nay *thrice* I struggle—struggle mightily to speak, and speak well and truly, and twice, nay, three times, that base fear strangles my words. Then, at length—O friends! do not be any harder upon me than you can help, for indeed, *indeed* I have paid sorely for it, and it is the first lie that ever I told; then, at length, with a face as wan as the ashes of a dead fire—with trembling lips, and a faint, scarcely audible voice, I say, "No, it is not true!"

"*Not true?*" he echoes, catching up my words quickly; but in his voice is none of the relief, the restored amenity that I had looked for, and for the hope of which I have perjured myself; equally in voice and face, there is only a deep and astonished anger.

"*Not true!*—you mean to say that it is *false!*"

"Yes, false!" I repeat in a sickly whisper. Oh, why, if I *must* lie, do not I do it with a bold and voluble assurance? whom would my starved pinched falsehood deceive?

"You mean to say," speaking with irrepressible excitement, while the wrathful light gathers and grows intenser in the gray depths of his eyes, "that this—this *interview* never took place? that it is all a delusion; a mistake?"

"Yes."

I repeat it mechanically now. Having gone thus far, I must go on, but I feel giddy and sick, and my hands grasp the arms of my chair. I feel as if I should fall out of it if they did not.

"You are *sure?*" speaking with a heavy emphasis, and looking persistently at me, while the anger of his eyes is dashed and crossed by a miserable entreaty. Ah! if they had had that look at first, I could have told him. "Are you *sure?*" he repeats, and I, driven by the fates to my destruction, while God hides his face from me, and the devil pushes me on, answer hazily, "Yes, quite sure!"

Then he asks me no more questions; he turns and slowly leaves the room, and I know that I have lied in vain!

CHAPTER XXXVIII

And thus I, ingenious architect of my own ruin, build up the barrier of a lie between myself and Roger. It is a barrier that hourly grows higher, more impassable. As the days go by, I say to myself in heart-sickness, that I shall never now cross it—never see it leveled with the earth. Even when we too are dead it will still rise between us in the other world; if—as all the nations have agreed to say—there *be* another. For my part, I think at this time that, if there is any chance of its bearing aught of resemblance to this present world, I had far fainer there were none.

With all due deference to Shakespeare—and I suppose that even the one supreme genius of all time must, in his day, have made a mistake or two—I have but faint belief in the "sweet uses of adversity." I think that they are about as mythical as the jewels in the toad's ugly skull, to which he likened them. It is in *prosperity* that one looks up, with leaping heart and clear eyes, and through the clouds see God sitting throned in light. In adversity one sees nothing but one's own dunghill and boils.

At least such has been my experience. I think I could have borne it better if I had not looked forward to his return so much—if he had been an austere and bitter tyrant, to *whose coming* I had looked with dread, I could have braced my nerves and pulled myself together, to face with some stoutness the hourly trials of life. But when one has counted the days, hours, and moments, till some high festival, and, when it comes, it turns out a drear, black funeral, one cannot meet the changed circumstances with any great fortitude.

It is the horrible contrast between my dreams and their realization that gives the keenest poignancy to my pangs.

To his return I had referred the smoothing of all my difficulties, the clearing up of all my doubts, the sweeping of all clouds from my sky; and now he is back! and, oh, how far, *far* gloomier than ever is my weather! What a sullen leaden sky overhangs me!

I never tell him about Algy after all! I do not often laugh now; but I *did* laugh loudly and long the other day, although I was quite alone, when I thought of my wily purpose of setting Roger on his guard against Mrs. Huntley's little sugared unveracities.

No, I never tell him about Algy! Why should I? it would be wasted breath—spent words. He would not believe me. In the more important case has not he taken her word in preference to mine? Would not he in *this* too? For I know that he knows, as well as I know it myself, that in that matter I lied.

Sometimes, when I am by myself, a mighty yearning—a most constraining longing seizes me to go to him—fall at his feet, and tell him the truth even yet. After all, God knows that I have no ugly fault to confess to him—no infidelity even of thought. But as soon as I am in his presence the desire fades; or at least the power to put it in practice melts away. For he never gives me an opening. After that first evening never does he draw nigh the subject: never once is the detested name of Musgrave mentioned between us. If he had been one most dear to us both and had died untimely, we could not avoid with more sacred care any allusion to him. And, even if, by doing infinite violence to myself, I could bring myself to overcome the painful steepness of the hill of difficulty that lies between me and the subject, and tell the tardy truth, to what use, pray? Having once owned that I had lied, could I resent any statement of mine being taken with distrust? Would he believe me? Not he! He would say, "If you were as innocent as you say, why did you *lie*? If you were innocent, what had you to fear?" So I hold my peace. And, as the days go, and the winter wanes, it seems to me that I can plainly see, with no uncertain or doubtful eyes, Roger's love wane too.

After all, why should I wonder? I may be sorry, for who ever saw gladly love—the one all-good thing on this earth, most of whose good things are adulterated and dirt-smirched—who ever saw it *gladly* slip away from them? But I cannot be surprised.

With Roger, love and trust must ever go hand-in-hand; and, when the one has gone, the other must needs soon follow.

After all, what he loved in me was a delusion—had never existed. It was my blunt honesty, my transparent candor, the open-hearted downrightness that in me amounted to a misfortune, that had at first attracted him. And now that he has found that the unpolished abruptness of my manners can conceal as great an amount of deception as the most insinuating silkiness of any one else's, I do not see what there is left in me to attract him. Certainly I have no beauty to excite a man's passions, nor any genius to enchain his intellect, nor even any pretty accomplishment to amuse his leisure.

Why *should* he love me? Because I am his wife? Nay, nay! who ever loved because it was their duty? who ever succeeded in putting love in harness, and *driving* him? Sooner than be the object of such up-hill conscientious affection, I had far rather be treated with cold indifference—active hatred even. Because I am young? That seems no recommendation in his eyes! Because I love him? He does not believe it. Once or twice I have tried to tell him so, and he has gently pooh-poohed me.

Sometimes it has occurred to me that, perhaps, if I had him all to myself, I might even yet bring him back to me—might reconcile him to my paucity of attractions, and persuade him of my honesty; but what chance have I, when every day, every hour of the day if he likes to put himself to such frequent pain, he may see and bitterly note the contrast between the woman of his choice and the woman of his fate—the woman from whom he is irrevocably parted, and the woman to whom he is as irrevocably joined. And I think that hardly a day passes that he does not give himself the opportunity of instituting the comparison.

Not that he is unkind to me; do not think that. It would be impossible to Roger to be unkind to any thing, much more to any weakly woman thing that is quite in his own power. No, no! there is no fear of that. I have no need to be a grizzle. I have no cross words, no petulances, no neglects even, to bear. But oh! in all his friendly words, in all his kindly, considerate actions, what a *chill* there is! It is as if some one that had been a day dead laid his hand on my heart!

How many, *many* miles farther apart we are now, than we were when I was here, and he in Antigua; albeit then the noisy winds roared and sung, and the brown billows tumbled between us! If he would but *hit* me, or box my ears, as Bobby has so often done—a good swinging, tingling box, that made one see stars, and incarnadized all one side of one's countenance—oh, how much, *much* less would it hurt than do the frosty chillness of his smiles, the uncaressing touch of his cool hands!

I have plenty of time to think these thoughts, for I am a great deal alone now. Roger is out all day, hunting or with his agent, or on some of the manifold business that landed property entails, or that the settlement of Mr. Huntley's inextricably tangled affairs involves. Very often he does not come in till dressing-time. I never ask him where he has been—never! I think that I know.

Often in these after-days, pondering on those ill times, seeing their incidents in that duer proportion that a stand-point at a little distance from them gives, it has occurred to me that sometimes I was wrong, that not seldom, while I was eating my heart out up-stairs, with dumb jealousy picturing to myself my husband in the shaded fragrance, the dulcet gloom of the drawing-room at Laurel Cottage, he was in the house with me, as much alone as I, in the dull solitude of his own room, pacing up and down the carpet, or bending over an unread book.

I will tell you why I think so. One day—it is the end of March now, the year is no longer a swaddled baby, it is shooting up into a tall stripling—I have been straying about the brown gardens, *alone*, of course. It is a year to-day since Bobby and I together strolled among the kitchen-stuff in the garden at home, since he served me that ill turn with the ladder. Every thing reminds me of that day: these might be the same crocus-clumps, as those that last year frightened away winter with their purple and gold banners. I remember that, as I looked down their deep throats, I was humming Tou Tou's verb, "J'aime, I love; Tu aimes, Thou lovest; Il aime, He loves."

I sigh. There was the same purple promise over the budded woods; the same sharpness in the bustling wind. Since then, Nature has gone through all her plodding processes, and now it is all to do over again. A sense of fatigue at the infinite repetitions of life comes over me. If Nature would but make a little variation! If the seasons would but change their places a little, and the flowers their order, so that there might be something of unexpectedness about them! But no! they walk round and round forever in their monotonous leisure.

I am stooping to pick a little posy of violets as these languid thoughts dawdle through my mind—blue mysteries of sweetness and color, born of the unscented, dull earth. As I pass Roger's door, having reëntered the house, the thought strikes me to set them on his writing-table. Most likely he will not notice them, not be aware of them: but even so they will be able humbly to speak to him the sweet things that he will not listen to from me. I open the door and listlessly enter. If I had thought that there was any chance of his being within, I should not have done so without knocking; indeed, I hardly think I should have done it at all, but this seems to me most unlikely. Nevertheless, he is.

As I enter, I catch sudden sight of him. He is sitting in his arm-chair, his elbows leaned on the table before him, his hand passed through his ruffled hair, and his gray eyes straying abstractedly away from the neglected page before him. I see him before he sees me. I have time to take in all the dejection of his attitude, all its spiritless idleness. At the slight noise my skirts make, he looks up. I stop on the threshold.

"I—I thought you were out," say I, hesitatingly, and reddening a little, as if I were being caught in the commission of some little private sin.

"No, I came in an hour ago."

"I beg your pardon," I say, humbly; "I will not disturb you; I would have knocked if I had known!"

He has risen, and is coming toward me.

"Knock! why, in Heaven's name, *should* you knock?" he says, with something of his old glad animation; then, suddenly changing his tone to one of courteous friendly coldness, "Why do you stand out there? will not you come in?"

I comply with this invitation, and, entering, sit down in another arm-chair not far from Roger's, but, now that I am here, I do not seem to have much to say.

"You have been in the gardens?" he says, presently, glancing at my little nosegay, and speaking more to hinder total silence from reigning, than for any other reason.

"Yes," I reply, trying to be cheerful and chatty, "I have been picking *these*; the Czar have not half their perfume, though they are three times their size! *these* smell so good!"

As I speak, I timidly half stretch out the little bunch to him, that he, too, may inhale their odor, but the gesture is so uncertain and faint that he does not perceive it—at least, he takes no notice of it, and I am sure that if he had he would; but yet I am so discouraged by the failure of my little overture that I have not resolution enough to tell him that I had gathered them for him. Instead, I snubbedly and discomfortedly put them in my own breast.

Presently I speak again.

"Do you remember," I say—"no, I dare say you do not, but yet it is so—it is a year to-day since you found me sitting on the top of the wall!—such a situation for a person of nineteen to be discovered in!"

At the recollection I laugh a little, and not bitterly, which is what I do not often do now. I can only see his profile, but it seems to me that a faint smile is dawning on his face, too.

"It was a good jump, was not it?" I go on, laughing again; "I still wonder that I did not knock you down."

He is certainly smiling now; his face has almost its old, tender mirth.

"It will be a year to-morrow," continue I, emboldened by perceiving this, and beginning to count on my fingers, "since Toothless Jack and the curates came to dine, and you staid so long in the dining-room that I fell asleep; the day after to-morrow, it will be a year since we walked by the river-side, and saw the goslings flowering out on the willows; the day after that it will be a year since—"

"Stop!" he cries, interrupting me, with a voice and face equally full of disquiet and pain; "do not go on, where is the use?—I hate anniversaries."

I stop, quenched into silence; my poor little trickle of talk effectually dried. After a pause, he speaks.

"What has made you think of all these dead trivialities?" he asks in a voice more moved—or I think so—less positively steady than his has been of late; "at your age, it is more natural to look on than to look back."

"Is it?" say I, sadly, "I do not know; I seem to have such a great deal of time for *thinking* now; this house is so *extraordinarily* silent! did you never notice it?—of course it is large, and we are only two people in it, but at home it never seemed to me so *deadly* quiet, even when I was alone in the house."

"*Were* you ever alone?" he asks, with a smile. He is thinking of the noisy multitude that are connected in his memory with my father's mansion; that, during all his experience of it, have filled its rooms and passages with the hubbub of their strong-lunged jollity.

"Yes, I have been," I reply; "not often, of course! but several times, when the boys were away, and father and mother and Barbara had gone out to dinner; of course it seemed still and dumb, but not—" (shuddering a little)—"not so *aggressively loudly* silent as this does!"

He looks at me, with a sort of remorseful pain.

"It *is* very dull for you!" he says, compassionately; "shut up in endless duet, with a person treble your age! I ought to have thought of that; in a month or so, we shall be going to London, *that* will amuse you, will not it? and till then, is there any one that you would like to have asked here?—any friend of your own?—any companion of your own age?"

"No," reply I, despondently, staring out of the window, "I have no friends."

"The boys, then?" speaking with a sudden assurance of tone, as one that has certainly hit upon a pleasant suggestion.

I shake my head.

"I could not have Bobby and the Brat, if I would, and I would not have Algy if I could!" I reply with curt dejection.

"Barbara, then?"

Again I shake my head. Not even Barbara will I allow to witness the failure of my dreams, the downfall of my high castles, the sterility of my Promised Land.

"No, I will not have Barbara!" I answer; "last time that she was here—" but I cannot finish my sentence. I break away weeping.

CHAPTER XXXIX

"I think you hardly know the tender rhyme
Of 'Trust me not at all or all in all!'"

There are some wounds, O, my friends, that Time, by himself, with no clever physician to help him, will surely cure. You all know that, do not you? some wounds that he will lay his cool ointment on, and by-and-by they are well. Among such, are the departures hence of those we have strongly loved, and to whom we have always been, as much as in us lay, tender and good. But there are others that he only worsens—yawning gaps that he but widens; as if one were to put one's fingers in a great rent, and tear it asunder. And of these last is mine.

As the year grows apace, as the evenings draw themselves out, and the sun every day puts on fresh strength, we seem to grow ever more certainly apart. Our bodies, indeed, are nigh each other, but our souls are sundered. It never seems to strike any one, it is true, that we are not a happy couple; indeed, it would be very absurd if it did. We never wrangle—we never contradict each other—we have no tiffs; but we are *two* and not *one*. Whatever may be the cause, whether it be due to his shaken confidence in me, or (I myself assign this latter as its chief reason) to the constant neighborhood of the woman whom I know him to have loved and coveted years before he ever saw me; whatever may be the cause, the fact remains; I no longer please him. It does not surprise me much. After all, the boys always told me that men would not care about me; that I was not the sort of woman to get on with them! Well, perhaps! It certainly seems so.

I meet Mrs. Huntley pretty often in society nowadays, at such staid and sober dinners as the neighborhood thinks fit to indulge in, in this lenten season; and, whenever I do so, I cannot refrain from a stealthy and wistful observation of her.

She is ten—twelve years older than I. Between her and me lie the ten years best worth living of a woman's life; and yet, how easily she distances me! With no straining, with no hard-breathed effort, she canters lightly past me. So I think, as I intently and curiously watch her—watch her graceful, languid silence with women, her pretty, lady-like playfulness with men. And how successful she is with them! how highly they relish her! While

I, in the uselessness of my round, white youth, sit benched among the old women, dropping spiritless, pointless "yeses" and "noes" among the veteran worldliness of their talk, how they crowd about her, like swarmed bees on some honeyed, spring day! how they scowl at each other! and *finesse* as to who shall approach most nearly to her cloudy skirts!

Several times I have strained my ears to catch what are the utterances that make them laugh so much, make them look both so fluttered and so smoothed. Each time that I succeed, I am disappointed. There is no touch of genius, no salt of wit in any thing she says. Her utterances are hardly more brilliant than my own.

You will despise me, I think, friends, when I tell you that in these days I made one or two pitiful little efforts to imitate her, to copy, distantly and humbly indeed, the fashion of her clothes, to learn the trick of her voice, of her slow, soft gait, of her little, surprised laugh. But I soon give it up. If I tried till my death-day, I should never arrive at any thing but a miserable travesty. Before—ere Roger's return—I used complacently to treasure up any little civil speeches, any small compliments that people paid me, thinking, "If such and such a one think me pleasing, why may not Roger?" But now I have given this up, too.

I seem to myself to have grown very dull. I think my wits are not so bright as they used to be. At home, I used to be reckoned one of the pleasantest of us: the boys used to laugh when I said things: but not even the most hysterically mirthful could find food for laughter in my talk now.

And so the days pass; and we go to London. Sometimes I have thought that it will be better when we get there. At least, *she* will not be there. How can she, with her husband gnashing his teeth in lonely discomfiture at his exasperated creditors, and receiptless bills, in sultry St. Thomas? But, somehow, she is. What good Samaritan takes out his twopence and pays for her little apartment, for her stacks of cut flowers, for her brougham and her opera-boxes, is no concern of mine. But, somehow, there always *are* good Samaritans in those cases; and, let alone Samaritans, there are no priests or Levites stonyhearted enough to pass by these dear, little, lovely things on the other side.

We go out a good deal, Roger and I, and everywhere he accompanies me. It bores him infinitely, though he does not say so. One night, we are at the play. It is the Prince of Wales's, the one theatre where one may enjoy a pleasant certainty of being rationally amused, of being free from the otherwise universal dominion of *Limelight* and *Legs*. The little house is very full; it always is. Some of the royalties are here, laughing "*à gorge déployée!*" I have been laughing, too; laughing in my old fashion; not in Mrs. Zéphine's little rippling way, but with the thorough-paced, unconventional violence with which I used to reward the homely sallies of Bobby and the Brat. I am laughing still, though the curtain has fallen between the acts, and the orchestra are fiddling gayly away, and the turned-up gas making everybody look pale. My opera-glasses are in my hand, and I am turning them slowly round the house, making out acquaintances in the stalls, prying into the secrets of the boxes, examining the well-known features of my future king.

Suddenly my smile dies away, and the glasses drop from my trembling hands into my lap. Who is it that has just entered, and is slipping across the intervening people in the stalls to his own seat, one of the few that have hitherto remained vacant beneath us? Can I help recognizing the close-shorn, cameo-like beauty—to me *no* beauty; to me deformity and ugliness—of the dark face that for months I daily saw by my fireside? Can there be *two* Musgraves? No! it is *he*! yes, *he*! though now there is on his features none of the baffled passion, none of the wrathful malignity, which they always wear in my memory, as they wore in the February dusk of Brindley Wood. Now, in their handsome serenity, they wear only the look of subdued sadness that a male Briton always assumes when he takes his pleasure. Do you remember what Goldsmith says?—"When I see an Englishman laugh, I fancy I rather see him hunting after joy than having caught it."

As soon as my eyes have fallen upon, and certainly recognized him, by a double impulse I draw back behind the curtain of the box, and look at Roger. He, too, has seen him; I can tell it in an instant by his face, and by the expression of his eyes, as they meet mine. I try to look back unflinchingly, indifferently, at him. I would give ten years of my life for an unmoved complexion, but it is no use. Struggle as I will against it, I feel that rush, that torrent of vivid scarlet, that, retiring, leaves me as white as my gown. Oh! it *is* hard, is not it, that the lying changefulness of a deceitful skin should have power to work me such hurt?

"Are you faint?" Roger asks, bending toward me, and speaking in a low and icy voice; "shall I get you a glass of water?"

"No, thank you!" I reply, resolutely, and with no hesitation or stammer in my tone, "I am not at all faint."

But, alas! my words cannot undo what my false cheeks, with their meaningless red and their causeless white, have so fully done.

The season is over now; every one has trooped away from the sun-baked squares, and the sultry streets of the great empty town. I have never *done* a season before, and the heat and the late hours have tired me wofully. Often, when I have gone to a ball, I have longed to go to bed instead. And, now that we are home again, it would seem to me very pleasant to sit in leisurely coolness by the pool, and to watch the birth, and the prosperous short lives, of the late roses, and the great bright gladioli in the garden-borders. Yes, it would have seemed very pleasant to me—if—(why is life so full of *ifs*? "Ifs" and "Buts," "Ifs" and "Buts," it seems made up of them! Little ugly words! in heaven there will be none of you!)—if—to back and support the outward good luck, there had been any inward content. But there is none! The trouble that I took with me to London, I have brought back thence whole and undiminished.

It is September now; so far has the year advanced! We are well into the partridges. Their St. Bartholomew has begun. Roger is away among the thick green turnip-ridges and the short white stubble all the day. I wish to Heaven that I could shoot, too, and hunt. It would not matter if I never killed any thing—indeed, I think—of the two—I had rather not; I had rather have a course of empty bags and blank days than snuff out any poor, little, happy lives; but the occupation that these amusements would entail would displace and hinder the minute mental torments I now daily, in my listless, luxurious idleness, endure. I am thinking these thoughts one morning, as I turn over my unopened letters, and try, with the misplaced ingenuity and labor one is so apt to employ in such a case, to make out from the general air of their exteriors—from their superscriptions—from their post-marks, whom they are from. About one there is no doubt. It is from Barbara. I have not heard from Barbara for a fortnight or three weeks. It will be the usual thing, I suppose. Father has got the gout in his right toe, or his left calf, or his wrist, or all his fingers, and is, consequently, fuller than usual of hatred and malice; mother's neuralgia is very bad, and she is sadly in want of change, but she cannot leave him. Algy has lost a lot of money at Goodwood, and they are afraid to tell father, etc., etc. Certainly, life is rather up-hill! I slowly tear the envelope open, and languidly throw my eyes along the lines. But, before I have read three words, my languor suddenly disappears. I sit upright in my chair, grasp the paper more firmly, bring it nearer my eyes, which begin greedily to gallop through its contents. They are not very long, and in two minutes I have mastered them.

"My Dearest Nancy:

"I have *such* a piece of news for you! I cannot help laughing as I picture to myself your face of delight; I would make you guess it, only I cannot bear to keep you in suspense. *It has all come right! I am going to marry Frank, after all!* What *have* I done to deserve such luck! How can I ever thank God enough for it? Do you know that my very first thought, when he asked me, was, '*How* pleased Nancy will be!' You dear little soul! I think, when he went away that time from Tempest, that you took all the blame of it to yourself! O Nancy, do you think it is wrong to be so *dreadfully* happy? Sometimes I am afraid that I love him *too* much! it seems so hard to help it. I have no time for more now; he is waiting for me; how little I thought, a month ago, that I should be ending a letter to you for such a reason! When all is said and done, what a pleasant world it is! Do not think me quite mad. I know I *sound* as if I were!

"Yours, Barbara."

My hand, and the letter with it, fall together into my lap; my head sinks back on the cushion of my chair; my eyes peruse the ceiling.

"Engaged to Musgrave! engaged to Musgrave! engaged to Musgrave!"

The words ring with a dull monotony of repetition through my brain. Poor Barbara! I think she would be surprised if she were to see my *"face of delight!"*

CHAPTER XL

My eyes are fixed on the mouldings of the ceiling, while a jumble of thoughts mix and muddle themselves in my head. Was Brindley Wood a dream? or is this a dream? Surely one or other must be, and, if this is not a dream, what is it? Is it reality, is it truth? And, if it is, how on earth did any thing so monstrous ever come about? How did he dare to approach her? How could he know that I had not told her? Is it possible that he cares for her really?—that he cared for her all along?—that he only went mad for one wicked moment? Is he sorry? how soon shall I have to meet him? On what terms shall we be? Will Roger be undeceived at last? Will he believe me? As my thoughts fall upon him, he opens the door and enters.

"Well, I am off, Nancy!" he says, speaking in his usual cool, friendly voice, to which I have now grown so accustomed that sometimes I could almost persuade myself that I had never known any lovinger terms; and standing with the door-handle in his hand.

He rarely kisses me now; never upon any of these little temporary absences. We always part with polite, cold, verbal salutations. Then, with a sudden change of tone, approaching me as he speaks.

"Is there any thing the matter? have you had bad news?"

My eyes drop at length from the scroll and pomegranate flower border of the ceiling. I sit up, and, with an involuntary movement, put my hand over the open letter that lies in my lap.

"I have had news," I answer, dubiously.

"If it is any thing that you had rather not tell me!" he says, hastily, observing my stupid and unintentional gesture, and, I suppose, afraid that I am about to drift into a second series of lies—"please do not. I would not for worlds thrust myself on your confidence!"

"It is no secret of mine," I answer, coldly, "everybody will know it immediately, I suppose: it is that Barbara—" I stop, as usual choked as I approach the abhorred theme. "Will you read the letter, please? that will be better!—yes—I had rather that you did—it will not take you long; yes, *all* of it!" (seeing that he is holding the note in his hand and conscientiously looking away from it as if expecting limitation as to the amount he is to peruse).

He complies. There is silence—an expectant silence on my part. It is not of long duration. Before ten seconds have elapsed the note has fallen from his hand; and, with an exclamation of the profoundest astonishment, he is looking with an expression of the most keenly questioning wonder at me.

"To Musgrave!"

I nod. I have judiciously placed myself with my back to the light, so that, if that exasperating flood of crimson bathe my face—and bathe it it surely will—is not it coming now?—do not I feel it creeping hotly up?—it may be as little perceptible as possible.

"It must be a great, great *surprise* to you!" he says, interrogatively, and still with that sound of extreme and baffled wonder in his tone.

"Immense!" reply I.

I speak steadily if low; and I look determinedly back in his face. Whatever color my cheeks are—I believe they are of the devil's own painting—I feel that my eyes are honest. He has picked up the note, and is reading it again.

"She seems to have no doubt"—(with rising wonder in face and voice)—"as to its greatly pleasing *you!*"

"So it would have done at one time," I answer, still speaking (though no one could guess with what difficulty), with resolute equanimity.

"And does not it now?" (very quickly, and sending the searching scrutiny of his eyes through me).

"I do not know," I answer hazily, putting up my hand to my forehead. "I cannot make up my mind, it all seems so sudden."

A pause. Roger has forgotten the partridges. He is sunk in reflection.

"Was there ever any talk of this before?" he says, presently, with a hesitating and doubtful accent, and an altogether staggered look. "Had you any reason—any ground for thinking that he cared about her?"

"Great ground," reply I, touching my cheeks with the tips of my fingers, and feeling, with a sense of self-gratulation, that their temperature is gradually, if slowly, lowering, "*every* ground—at *one* time!"

"At *what* time!"

"In the autumn," say I, slowly; my mind reluctantly straying back to the season of my urgent invitations, of my pressing friendlinesses, "and at Christmas, and after Christmas."

"Yes?" (with a quick eagerness, as if expecting to hear more).

"The boys," continue I, speaking without any ease or fluency, for the subject is always one irksome and difficult to me, "the boys took it quite for granted—looked upon it as a certain thing that he meant seriously until—"

"Until what?" (almost snatching the words out of my mouth).

"Until—well!" (with a short, forced laugh), "until they found that he did not."

"And—do you know?—but of course you do—can you tell me how they discovered that?"

He is looking at me with that same greedy anxiety in his eyes, which I remember in our last fatal conversation about Musgrave.

"He went away," reply I, unable any longer to keep watch and ward over my countenance and voice, rising and walking hastily to the window.

The moment I have done it, I repent. *However* red I was, *however* confused I looked, it would have been better to have remained and faced him. For several minutes there is silence. I look out at the stiff comeliness of the variously tinted asters, at the hoary-colored dew that is like a film along the morning grass. I do not know what *he* looks at, because I have my back to him, but I think he is looking at Barbara's note again. At least, I judge this by what he says next—"Poor little soul!" (in an accent of the honestest, tenderest pity), "how happy she seems!"

"Ah!" say I, with a bitter little laugh, "she will mend of *that*, will not she?"

He does not echo my mirth; indeed, I think I hear him sigh.

"'Romances paint at full length people's wooings,
   But only give a bust of marriages!'"

say I, in soft quotation, addressing rather myself and my thoughts than my companion.

He has joined me; he, too, is looking out at the serene aster-flowers, at the glittering glory of the dew.

"Since when you have learned to quote 'Don Juan?'" he asks, with a sort of surprise.

"Since *when*?" I reply, with the same tart playfulness—"oh! since I married! I date all my accomplishments from then!—it is my anno Domini."

Another silence. Then Sir Roger speaks again, and this time his words seem as slow and difficult of make as mine were just now.

"Nancy!" he says, in a low voice, not looking at me, but still facing the flowers and the sunshiny autumn sward, "do you believe that—that—*this fellow* cares about her really?—she is too good to be made—to be made—a mere *cat's-paw* of!"

"A *cat's-paw!*" cry I, turning quickly round with raised voice; the blood that so lately retired from it rushing again headlong all over my face; "I do not know—what you mean—what you are talking about!"

He draws his breath heavily, and pauses a moment before he speaks.

"God knows," he says, looking solemnly up, "that I had no wish to broach this subject again—God knows that I meant to have done with it forever—but now that it has been forced against my will—against both our wills—upon me, I must ask you this one question—tell me, Nancy—tell me truly *this* time"—(with an accent of acute pain on the word "*this*")—"can you say, *on your honor—on your honor*, mind—that you believe this—this man loves Barbara, as a man should love his wife?"

If he had worded his interrogation differently, I should have been sorely puzzled to answer it; as it is, in the form his question takes, I find a loop-hole of escape.

"As a man should love his wife?" I reply, with a derisive laugh, "and how is that? I do not think I quite know!—very dearly, I suppose, but not quite so dearly as if she were his neighbor's—is that it?"

As I speak, I look up at him, with a malicious air of pseudo-innocence. But if I expect to see any guilt—any conscious shrinking in his face—I am mistaken. There is pain—infinite pain—pain both sharp and long-enduring in the grieved depths of his eyes; but there is no guilt.

"You will not answer me?" he says, in an accent of profound disappointment, sighing again heavily. "Well, I hardly expected it—hardly hoped it!—so be it, then, since you will have it so; and yet—" (again taking up the note, and reading over one of its few sentences with slow attention), "and yet there is one more question I must put to you, after all—they both come to pretty much the same thing. Why"—(pointing, as he speaks, to the words to which he alludes)—"why should *you* have taken on yourself the blame of—of his departure from Tempest? what had *you* to say to it?"

In his voice there is the same just severity; in his eyes there is the same fire of deep yet governed wrath that I remember in them six months ago, when Mrs. Huntley first threw the firebrand between us.

"I do not know," I reply, in a half whisper of impatient misery, turning my head restlessly from side to side; "how should I know? I am *sick* of the subject."

"Perhaps!—so, God knows, am I; but *had* you any thing to say to it?"

He does not often touch me now; but, as he asks this, he takes hold of both my hands, more certainly to prevent my escaping from under his gaze, than from any desire to caress me.

It is my last chance of confession. I little thought I should ever have another. Late as it is, shall I avail myself of it? Nay! if not before, why *now?* Why *now?*—when there are so much stronger reasons for silence—when to speak would be to knock to atoms the newly-built edifice of Barbara's happiness—to rake up the old and nearly dead ashes of Frank's frustrated, and for aught I know, sincerely repented sin? So I answer, faintly indeed, yet quite audibly and distinctly:

"Nothing."

"Nothing?" (in an accent and with eyes of the keenest, wistfulest interrogation, as if he would wring from me, against my will, the confession I so resolutely withhold).

But I turn away from that heart-breaking, heart-broken scrutiny, and answer:

"Nothing!"

CHAPTER XLI

"She dwells with beauty—beauty that must die,
And joy whose hand is ever at his lips
Bidding adieu!"

Thus I accomplished my second lie: I that, at home, used to be a proverb for blunt truth-telling. They say that "*facilis descensus Averni.*" I do not agree with them. I have not found it easy. To me it has seemed a very steep and precipitous road, set with sharp flints that cut the feet, and make the blood flow.

I think the second falsehood was almost harder to utter than the first: but, indeed, they were both very disagreeable. I cannot think why any one should have thought it necessary to invent the doctrine of a future retribution for sin.

It appears to me that, in this very life of the present, each little delinquency is so heavily paid for—so exorbitantly overpaid, indeed. Look, for instance, at my own case. I told a lie—a lie more of the letter than the spirit—and since then I have spent six months of my flourishing youth absolutely devoid of pleasure, and largely penetrated with pain.

I have stood just outside my paradise, peeping under and over the flaming sword of the angel that guards it. I have been near enough to smell the flowers—to see the downy, perfumed fruits—to hear the song of the angels as they go up and down within its paths; but I have been outside.

Now I have told another lie, and I suppose—nay, what better can I hope?—that I shall live in the same state of weary, disproportioned retribution to the end of the chapter.

These are the thoughts, interspersed and diversified with loud sighs, that are employing my mind one ripe and misty morning a few days later than the incidents last detailed.

Barbara is to arrive to-day. She is coming to pay us a visit—coming, like the lady mentioned by Tennyson, in "In Memoriam"—not, indeed, "to bring her babe," but to "make her boast." And how, pray, am I to listen with complacent congratulation to this boast? For the first time in my life I dread the coming of Barbara. How am I, whose acting, on the few occasions when

I have attempted it, has been of the most improbably wooden description—how am I, I say, to counterfeit the extravagant joy, the lively sympathy, that Barbara will expect—and naturally expect—from me?

I get up and look at myself in the glass. Assuredly I shall have to take some severe measures with my countenance before it falls under my sister's gaze. Small sympathy and smaller joy is there in it now—it wears only a lantern-jawed, lack-lustre despondency. I practise a galvanized smile, and say out loud, as if in dialogue with some interlocutor:

"Yes, *delightful!*—I am *so* pleased!" but there is more mirth in the enforced grin of an unfleshed skull than in mine.

That will never take in Barbara. I try again—once, twice—each time with less prosperity than the last. Then I give it up. I must trust to Providence.

As the time for her coming draws nigh, I fall to thinking of the different occasions since my marriage, on which I have watched for expected comings from this window—have searched that bend in the drive with impatient eyes—and of the disappointment to which, on the two occasions that rise most prominently before my mind's eye, I became a prey.

Well, I am to be subject to no disappointment—if it *would* be a disappointment—to-day.

Almost before I expect her—almost before she is due—she is here in the room with me, and we are looking at one another. I, indeed, am staring at her with a black and stupid surprise.

"Good Heavens!" say I, bluntly; "what *have* you been doing to yourself? *how* happy you look!"

I have always known theoretically that happiness was becoming; and I have always thought Barbara most fair.

> "Fairer than Rachel by the palmy well,
> Fairer than Ruth among the fields of corn,
> Fair as the angel that said, 'Hail!' she seemed,"

but *now*, what a lovely brightness, like that of clouds remembering the gone sun, shines all about her! What a radiant laughter in her eyes! What a splendid carnation on her cheeks! (How glad I am that I did not tell!)

"Do I?" she says, softly, and hiding her face, with the action of a shy child, on my shoulders. "I dare say."

"*Good* Heavens!" repeat I, again, with more accentuation than before, and with my usual happy command and variety of ejaculation.

"And *you?*" she says, lifting her face, and speaking with a joyful confidence of anticipation in her innocent eyes, "and *you?* you are pleased too, are not you?"

"Of course," reply I, quickly calling to my aid the galvanized smile and the unnatural tone in which I have been perfecting myself all the forenoon, "*delighted!* I never was so pleased in my life. I told you so in my letters, did not I?"

A look of nameless disappointment crosses her features for a moment.

"Yes," she says, "I know! but I want you to tell me again. I thought that you—would have such a—such a great deal to say about it."

"So I have!" reply I, uncomfortably, fiddling uneasily with a paper-knife that I have picked up, and trying how much ill-usage it will bear without snapping, "an immensity! but you see it is—it is difficult to begin, is not it? and you know I never was good at expressing myself, was I?"

We have sat down. I am not facing her. With a complexion that serves one such ill turns as mine does, one is not over-fond of *facing* people. I am beside her. For a moment we are both silent.

"Well," say I, presently, with an unintentional tartness in my tone, "why do not you begin? I am waiting to hear all about it! Begin!"

So Barbara begins.

"I am afraid," she says, smiling all the while, but growing as red as the bunch of late roses in my breast, "that I looked horribly *pleased!* One ought to look as if one did not care, ought not one?"

"Ought one?" say I, with interest, then beginning to laugh vociferously. "At least you were not as bad as the old maid who late in life received a very wealthy offer, and was so much elated by it that she took off all her clothes, and kicked her bonnet round the room!"

Barbara laughs.

"No, I was not quite so bad as that."

"And how did he do it?" pursue I, inquisitively. "Did he write or speak"

"He spoke."

"And what did he say? How did he word it? Ah!"—(with a sigh)—"I suppose you will not tell me *that?*"

She has abandoned her chair, and has fallen on her knees before me, hiding her face in my lap. Delicious waves of color, like the petals of a pink sweet-pea, are racing over her cheeks and throat.

"Was ever any one known to tell it?" she says, indistinctly.

"Yes," reply I, "*I* was. I told you what Roger said, word for word—all of you!"

"*Did* you?"—(with an accent of astonished incredulity).

"Yes," say I, "do not you remember? I promised I would before I went into the drawing-room that day, and, when I came out, I wanted the boys to let me off, but they would not."

A pause.

"I wish," say I, a little impatiently, "that you would look up! Why need you mind if you *are* rather red? What do *I* matter? and so—and so—you are *pleased!*"

"*Pleased!*"

She has raised her head as I bid her, and on her face there is a sort of scorn at the poverty and inadequacy of the expression, and yet she replaces it with no other; only the sapphire of her eyes is dimmed and made more tender by rising tears.

Clearly we were never meant to be joyful, we humans! In any bliss greater than our wont, we can only hang out, to demonstrate our felicity, the sign and standard of woe.

"Nancy!"—(taking my hand, and looking at me with wistful earnestness)—"do you think it *can* last? Did ever any one feel as I do for *long?*"

"I do not know—how can I tell?" reply I, discomfortably, as I absently eye the two halves of my paper-knife, which, after having given one or two warning cracks, has now snapped in the middle. Then Roger enters, and our talk ends.

CHAPTER XLII

"God made a foolish woman, making me!"

"Have you any idea whom we shall meet?"

It is Barbara who asks this one morning at breakfast. The question refers to a three days' visit that it has become our fate to pay to a house in the neighborhood—a house not eight miles distant from Tempest, and over which we are grumbling in the minute and exhaustive manner which people mostly employ when there is a question of making merry with their friends.

I shake my head.

"I have not an idea, that is to say, except Mrs. Huntley, and she goes without saying!"

"Why?"

"We are known to be such inseparables, that she is always asked to meet us," reply I, with that wintry smile, which is my last accomplishment. "We pursue her round the country, do not we, Roger?"

Barbara opens her great eyes, but, with her usual tact, she says nothing. She sees that she has fallen on stony ground.

"She is *the oldest friend that we have in the world!*" continue I, laughing pleasantly.

Roger does not answer, he does not even look up, but by a restless movement that he makes in his chair, by a tiny contraction of the brows, I see that my shot has told. I am becoming an adept in the infliction of these pin-pricks. It is one of the few pleasures I have left.

The day of our visit has come. We have relieved our feelings by grumbling up to the hall-door. Our murmuring must per force be stilled now, though indeed, were we to *shout* our discontents at the top of our voices, there would be small fear of our being overheard by the master of the house, he being the boundlessly deaf old gentleman who paid his respects at Tempest on the day of Mrs. Huntley's first call, and insisted on mistaking Barbara for me. Whether he is yet set right on that head is a point still enveloped in Cimmerian gloom.

It is a bachelor establishment, as any one may perceive by a cursory glance at the disposition of the drawing-room furniture, and at the unfortunate flowers, tightly jammed, packed as thickly as they will go in one huge central bean-pot.

As we arrived rather late and were at once conducted to our rooms, we still remain in the dark as to our co-guests. Personally, I am not much interested in the question. There cannot be anybody that it will cause me much satisfaction to meet. It would give me a faint relief, indeed, to find that there were some matron of exalteder rank than mine to save me from my probable fate of bowling dark sayings at our old host, General Parker, from the season of clear soup to that of peaches and nuts. I dress quickly. The toilet is never to me a work of art. It is not that from my lofty moral stand-point I look down upon meretricious aids to faulty Nature. If I thought that it would set me on a fairer standing with Mrs. Zéphine, I would paint my cheeks an inch thick; would prune my eyebrows; daub my eyes, and make my hair yellower than any buttercups in the meadow; but I know that it would be of no avail. I should still be, compared to her, as a sign-painting to a Titian. For a long time now I have cared naught for clothes. I used greatly to respect their power, but they have done *me* no good; and so my reverence for them is turned into indifference and contempt.

I think that I must be late. Roger went down some minutes ago, at my request, so that there might be *one* representative of the family in time.

I hasten down-stairs, fastening my last bracelet as I go, and open the drawing-room door. I was wrong. There is no one down yet: even Roger has disappeared. I am the first. This is my impression for a moment: then I perceive that there is some one in the bow-window, half hidden by the drooped curtains; some one who, hearing my entry, is advancing to meet me. It is Musgrave! My first impulse, a wrong one, I need hardly say, is to turn and flee. I have even laid hold of the just abandoned handle, when he speaks.

"Are you going?" he says in a low voice, marked by great and evidently ungovernable agitation; "do not! if you wish, I will leave the room."

I look at him, and our eyes meet. He always was a pale young man— no bucolic beef-and-beer ruddiness about him—always of a healthy swart pallor; but now he is deadly white!—so, by-the-by, I fancy am I! His dark eyes burn with a shamed yet eager glow.

With the words and tones of our last parting ringing in our ears, we both feel that it would be useless affectation to attempt to meet as ordinary acquaintance.

"No," say I, faintly, almost in a whisper, "it—it does not matter! only that I did not know that you were to be here!"

"No more did I, until this morning!" he answers, eagerly; "this morning—at the last moment—young Parker asked me to come down with him—and I—I knew we must meet sooner or later—that it could not be put off forever, and so I thought we might as well get over it here as anywhere else!"

Neither of us has thought of sitting down. He is speaking with rapid, low emotion, and I stand stupidly listening.

"I suppose so," I answer lazily. I cannot for the life of me help it, friends. I am back in Brindley Wood. He has come a few steps nearer me. His voice is always low, but now it is almost a whisper in which he is so rapidly, pantingly speaking.

"I shall most likely not have another opportunity, probably we shall not be alone again, and I *must* hear, I *must* know—have you forgiven me?"

As he speaks, the recollection of all the ill he has done me, of my lost self-respect, my alienated Roger, my faded life, pass before my mind.

"*That* I have not!" reply I, looking full at him, and speaking with a distinct and heavy emphasis of resentment and aversion, "and, by God's help, I never will!"

"You will *not*!" he cries, starting back with an expression of the utmost anger and discomfiture. "You will *not*! you will carry vengeance for one mad minute through a whole life! It is *impossible! impossible!* if *you* are so unforgiving, how do you expect God to forgive you your sins?"

I shrug my shoulders with a sort of despairing contempt. God has seemed to me but dim of late.

"He may forgive them or leave them unforgiven as He sees best; but—*I will never forgive you!*"

"What!" he cries, his face growing even more ash-white than it was before, and his voice quivering with a passionate anger; "not for *Barbara's* sake?"

I shudder. I hate to hear him pronounce her name.

"No," say I, steadily, "not for Barbara's sake!"

"You will have to," he cries violently; "it is nonsense! think of the close connection, of the *relationship* that there will be between us! think of the remarks you will excite! you will defeat your own object!"

"I will excite no remark!" I reply resolutely. "I will be quite civil to you! I will say 'good-morning' and 'good-evening' to you; if you ask me a question I will answer it; but—I will *never* forgive you!"

We are standing, as I before observed, close together, and are so wholly occupied—voices, eyes, and ears—with each other, that we do not perceive the approach of two hitherto unseen people who are coming dawdling and chatting up the conservatory that opens out of the room; two people that I suppose have been there, unknown to us, all along. They have come quite close now, and we must needs perceive them.

In a second our eager talk drops into silence, and we look with involuntary, startled apprehension toward them. They are Roger and Mrs. Huntley. This is why he acceded with such alacrity to my request. This is why he was so afraid of being late. He has been helping her to smell the jasmine, and to look down the datura's great white trumpet-throats.

Even at this agitated moment I have time to think this with a jeering pain. The next instant all other feelings are swallowed up in breathless dread as to how they will meet. My fears are groundless. On first becoming aware, indeed, whose *tête-à-tête* it is that he has interrupted, whose low, quick voices they are that have dropped into such sudden, suspicious silence at his approach—I can see him start perceptibly, can see his gray eyes dart with lightning quickness from Musgrave to me, and from me to Musgrave; and in his voice there is to me an equally perceptible tone of ice-coldness; but to an ordinary observer it would seem the greeting, neither more nor less warm, exchanged between two moderately friendly acquaintances meeting after absence.

"How are you, Musgrave? I had no idea that you were in this part of the world!"

"No more had I!" answers Musgrave, with an exaggerated laugh. "No more I was, until—until *to-day.*"

He has not caught the infection of Roger's stately calm. His face has not recovered a *trace* of even its usual slight color, and his eyes are twitching nervously. Mrs. Huntley appears unaware of any thing. Her artistic eye has been caught by the tight bean-pot, and her fingers are employed in trying to give a little air of ease and liberty to its crowded inmates. Then, thank God, the others come in, and dinner is announced, and the situation is ended.

The old host, still under the influence of his hallucination, is bearing down like a hawk (with his old bent elbow extended) on Barbara, until intercepted and redirected by a whispered roar and graphic pantomime on the part of his nephew. Then, at last, he realizes Roger's bad taste, and we go in.

As soon as we are seated, I look about me. It is a round table. For my part, I hate a round table. There is no privacy in it. Everybody seems eavesdropping on everybody else.

There are only eight of us in all—those I have enumerated, and Algy. Yes, he is here. Bellona is a goddess who can always spare her sons when there is any chance of their getting into mischief. Roger has taken Mrs. Huntley. *That*, poor man, he could hardly help, his only alternative being his own sister-in-law. Musgrave has taken Barbara. He is still as white as the table-cloth, and hardly speaks. It is clear that *he* will not get up his conversation again, until after the champagne has been round. Algy has taken no one; and, consequently, a bear is an amiable and affable beast in comparison of him. I am placed between our host and his nephew. The latter comes in for a good deal of my conversation, as most of my remarks have to be taken up and rebellowed by him with a loud emphasis, that contrasts absurdly with their triviality; and even then they mostly miscarry, and turn into something totally different.

Talking to the old man is not a dialogue, but a couple of soliloquies, carried on mostly on different subjects, which in vain try to become the same, between two interlocutors. Through soup we prospered—that is to say, we talked of the weather; and though I said several things about it that surprised me a good deal, yet we both knew that we *were* talking of the weather. But since then we have been diverging ever more and more hopelessly. *He* is at the shah's visit, and so he imagines am I. I, on the contrary, am at the Bishop of Winchester's death, and, for the last five minutes have been trying, with all the force of my lungs, and with a face rendered scarlet by the double action of heat and of the consciousness of being the object of respectful attention to the whole company, to convey to him that, in my opinion, the deceased prelate ought to have been buried in Westminster Abbey. I have at last succeeded, at least in so far as to make him understand that I wish *somebody* to be buried in Westminster Abbey; but, as he still persists in thinking it the shah, we are perhaps not much better off than we were before. I lean back with a sense of despairing defeat, and, behind my fan, turn to the young man on the other side. He is a jolly-looking fellow, with an aureole of fiery red hair.

"Would you mind," say I, with panting appeal, "trying to make him understand that it *is not* the shah?"

He complies, and, while he is trying to make it clear to his uncle that he wrongs me in crediting me with any wish to thrust the Persian monarch among the ashes of the Plantagenets, I take breath, and look round again. Algy is eating nothing, and is drinking every thing that is offered to him. His face is not much redder than Musgrave's, and he is glancing across the table at Mrs. Huntley, with the haggard anger of his eyes. Of this, however, she seems innocently unaware. She is leaning back in her chair; so is Roger. They are talking low and quickly, and looking smilingly at each other. When does his face ever light up into such alert animation when he is talking to me? There can be no doubt of it! Why blink a thing because it is unpleasant? *I bore him.*

I have no intention of listening, and yet I hear some of their words—enough to teach me the drift of their talk. "Residency!" "Cawnpore!" "Simlah!" "*Cursed* Simlah!" "*Cursed* Cawnpore!" My attention is recalled by the voice of my old neighbor.

"Talking of that—" he says—(talking of *what*, in Heaven's name?)—"I once knew a man—a doctor, at Norwich—who did not marry till he was seventy-eight, and had four as fine children as any man need wish to see."

By the extraordinary irrelevancy of this anecdote, I am so taken aback that, for a moment, I am unable to utter. Seeing, however, that some comment is expected from me, I stammer something about its being a great age. He, however, imagines that I am asking whether they were boys or girls.

"Three boys and a girl, or three girls and a boy!" he answers, with loud distinctness—"I cannot recollect which; but, after all—" (with an acrid chuckle)—"that is not the point of the story!"

I sink back in my chair, with a slight shiver.

"Give it up!" says my other neighbor, with a compassionate smile, and speaking in a voice not a whit lower than usual—"*I* would!—it really is no good!"

"Why does not he have a *trumpet*?" ask I, with a slight accent of irritation, for I have suffered much, and it is hot.

"He had one once," replies my companion, still pityingly regarding the flushed discomposure of my face; "but people *would* insist on bawling so loudly down it, that they nearly broke the drum of his ear, and so *he* broke *it*."

I laugh a little, but in a puny way. There is not much laugh in me. Again I look round the table. Musgrave is better; he is a better color than he was. Under the influence of Barbara's gentle talk, his features have reassumed almost serenity. Algy is *no* better. I see him lean back, and speak to the servant behind him. He is asking for more champagne. I wish he would not. He has had quite enough already. Roger and Mrs. Huntley are much as they were. They are still leaning back in their chairs—still looking with friendly intimacy into each other's eyes—still smiling. Again a few words of their talk reach me.

"Do you recollect?"

"Do you remember?"

"Have you forgotten?"

Clearly, they have fallen upon old times. I wish—I dearly wish—that I might bite a piece out of somebody.

CHAPTER XLIII

"I saw pale kings, and princes, too;
Pale warriors, death-pale were they all,
They cried, 'La Belle Dame, sans merci,'
Hath thee in thrall."

The long penance of dinner is over at last, thank God! I may intermit my hopeless roarings, melancholy as those of any caged zoological beast. Roger and Zéphine must also fain suspend their reminiscences. There being no lady of the house, I have taken upon myself to hasten the date of our departure. Before Mrs. Zéphine has finished her last grape, I have swept her incontinently away into the drawing-room. But I might as well have let it alone: almost before you could say "Knife" they are after us. I suppose that when three are eager to come, and only two anxious to stay—(I acquit my old friend and his nephew of any over-hurry to rejoin us)—the three must needs get their way. Anyhow, here they all five are! I am so hot! so hot! Nothing heats one like bellowing and being miserable and a failure. I have again taken advantage of the mistressless condition of the establishment, have drawn back the window-curtains, and lifted the heavy sash. The night always soothes me. There is something so stilling in the far placidity of the high stars—in the sweet sharpness of the night winds. I have sat down on a couch in the embrasure, alone.

When the men come in, I remain alone. It does not at all surprise or much vex me. I have nothing pleasant to say to any one. Also, I think I must be almost hidden by the droop of the curtains. Roger, indeed, sent his eyes round the room on his first entry, as if searching for something or somebody. It cannot be Mrs. Huntley, who is right under his nose, and who is, indeed, saying something playful to him over the top of her black fan. For once, he does not hear her. He is still looking. Then he catches a glimpse of my skirts, and comes straight toward me. Thank God! it *was* me he was looking for. I feel a little throb of disused gladness, as I realize this.

"Are not you cold?" he says, perceiving the open window.

"Not I!" reply I, brusquely—"naught never comes to harm."

"I wish you would have a shawl!" he says, as the evening wind comes, with the tartness of autumn, to his face.

"Why do not you say, '*do, for my sake!*' as Algy once said to me, when he mistook me in the dark for Mrs. Huntley?" reply I, with a mocking laugh— "I am not sure that he did not add *darling*, but I will excuse *that*!"

At the mention of Algy, a shade crosses his face, and his eye travels to where, in the dignified solitude of a corner, my eldest brother is sitting, biting his lips, and reading "Alice Through the Looking-glass," upside down.

"Foolish fellow! I wish he had not come!"

"I dare say he returns the compliment."

"I wish she would leave him alone!" he says, with an accent of impatience, more to himself than to me.

"That is so likely," say I, quickly, "so much her way, is not it?"

I suppose that something in the exceeding bitterness of my tone strikes him, for his eyes return from Algy to me.

"Nancy," he says, speaking with a sort of hesitating impulse, while a dark flush crosses his face, "it has occurred to me once or twice—if the idea had been less unspeakably absurd, it would have occurred to me many times—that you are—are *jealous* of Zéphine and me!—You jealous of ME!!"

There is such a depth of emphasis in his last words—such a wealth of reproachful appeal in the eyes that are bent on me—that I can answer nothing. I say neither yea nor nay. He has sat down on the couch beside me.

"Tell me," he says, with low, quick excitement—"and for God's sake do not grow scarlet, and turn your head aside as you mostly have done—did you, or did you not know that—that *Musgrave* was to be here to-day?"

"I *did not*—indeed I *did not*!" I cry, with passionate eagerness; thankful for once to be able to tell the truth; "we none of us did—not even Barbara!"

He repeats my last words with a slightly sarcastic inflection, "*not even Barbara!*"

A moment's pause.

"Why did you stop talking so suddenly, the moment that we interrupted you?" he asks, with an abruptness that is almost harsh—"what were you talking about?"

Phew! how hot it is! even though one is by the open window!—even despite the cool moistness of the night wind.

"I was—I was—I was—congratulating him!" I say, doing the very thing he has forbidden me, reddening and turning half away. He makes no rejoinder; only I hear him sigh, and put his hand with a quick, impatient movement to his head.

"You believe me?" I ask, timidly, laying my hand on his arm.

"No, _I do not!_" he replies, shaking off my touch, and turning his stern and glittering eyes full upon me. "I should be a _fool_ and an _idiot_ if I did!"

Then he rises hastily and leaves me. I watch him as he joins the other men. They are _all_ round her now—all but Musgrave.

Algy has left his corner and his reversed picture-book, moved thereto by the unparalleled audacity of young Parker, who has pulled one of the sofa-cushions down on the floor, and is squatting on it, like a great toad at her feet, examining a gnat-bite on her sacred arm.

Even the old host is doing the agreeable according to his lights. In a very loud voice he is narrating a long anecdote about a pretty girl that he once saw at a windmill near Seville, during the Peninsular. With a most unholy chuckle he is trying to hint that there was more between him and the young lady than it well beseems him to tell; but fortunately no one, but I, is listening to him.

I turn away my head, and look out of the window up at Charles's Wain, and all my other bright old friends. No one is heeding me—no one sees me; so I drop my hot cheek on the sill.

Suddenly I start up. Some one is approaching me: some one has thrown himself with careless freedom on the couch beside me. It is Algy.

Having utterly failed in dislodging Mr. Parker from his cushion—having had a suggestion on his part, on the treatment of the gnat-bite, passed over in silent contempt—he has retired from the circle in dudgeon.

"This is lively, is not it?" he says, in an aggressively loud voice, as if he were quarrelsomely anxious to be overheard.

I say "Hush!" apprehensively.

"As no one makes the slightest attempt to entertain _us_, we must entertain each other, I suppose!"

"Yes, dear old boy!" I say, affectionately, "why not?—it would not be the first time by many."

"That does not make it any the more amusing!" he says, harshly.—"I say, Nancy"—his eyes fixing themselves with sullen greediness on the central figure of the group he has left—on the slight round arm (after all, not half so round or so white as Barbara's or mine)—which is still under treatment, "*is* eau de cologne good for those sort of bites?—her arm *is* bad, you know!"

"*Bad!*" echo I, scornfully; "*bad!* why, I am *all* lumps, more or less, and so is Barbara! who minds *us!*"

"You ought to make your old man—'*auld Robin Gray*'—mind you," he says, with a disagreeable laugh. "It is *his* business, but he does not seem to see it, does he? ha! ha!"

"I *wish!*" cry I, passionately; then I stop myself. After all, he is hardly himself to-night, poor Algy!

"By-the-by," he says, presently, with a wretchedly assumed air of carelessness, "is it true—it is as well to come to the fountain-head at once—is it true that *once*, some time in the dark ages, he—he—thought fit to engage himself to, to *her?*" (with a fierce accent on the last word).

A pain runs through my heart. Well, that is nothing new nowadays. He too has heard it, then.

"I do not know!" I answer, faintly.

"What! he has not told you? *Kept it dark!* eh?" (with the same hateful laugh).

"He has kept nothing dark!" I answer, indignantly. "One day he began to tell me something, and I stopped him! I would not hear; I did not want to hear, I believe; I am sure that they are—only—only—old friends."

"*Old friends!*" he echoes, with a smile, in comparison of which our host's satyr-leer seems pleasant and chaste. "*Old friends!* you call yourself a woman of the world" (indeed I call myself nothing of the kind), "you call yourself a woman of the world, and believe *that!* They looked like *old friends* at dinner to-day, did not they? A little less than kin, and more than kind! Ha! ħa!"

CHAPTER XLIV

Partridges are not General Parker's strong point, and the few he ever had his nephew has already shot. Roger must, therefore, for one day abstain from the turnip-ridges. To amuse us, however, and keep us all sociably together, and bridge the yawning gulf between breakfast and dinner, we are to be sent on an expedition. Not only an expedition, but a picnic. This is perhaps a little risky in such a climate as ours, and in a month so doubtfully hovering on the borders of winter as September; but the sun is shining, and we therefore make up our minds, contrary to all precedent, that he must necessarily go on shining.

Some ten miles away there is a spot whence one can see seven counties, not to speak of the sea, a mountain or two, and some other trifles; and thither Mr. Parker is kindly going to bowl us down on his coach.

A drive on a coach is always to me a most doubtful joy; the ascent, labor; the drive itself, long anxiety and peril; the descent, agony, and sometimes shame. However, that is neither here nor there. I am going. It is still half an hour till the time appointed for our departure, and I am sitting alone in my room when Roger enters.

"Nancy," he says, coming quickly toward me, "have you any idea what sort of a whip that boy is?"

"Not the slightest!" reply I, shortly.

I feel as hard as a flint to-day. Algy's words last night seem to have confirmed and given a solider reality to my worst fears. He has walked to the window and is looking out.

"Are you *nervous*?" say I, with a slightly sarcastic smile.

He does not appear to notice the sarcasm.

"Yes," he says, "that is just what I am. He is a mad sort of fellow, and a coach is not a thing to play tricks with!"

"No," say I, indifferently. It seems to me of infinitely little consequence whether we are upset or not.

"That is what I came to speak to you about!" he says, still looking out of the window.

"Zéphine—"

"Is nervous, too?" ask I, smiling disagreeably. "What a curious coincidence!"

"I do not know whether she is nervous or not!" he answers, quickly; "I never asked her, but it seems that Huntley never would let her go on a drag; he had seen some bad accident, and it had given him a fright—"

"And so you and she are going to stay at home?" say I, coldly, but breathing a little heavily, and whitening.

"Stay at home!" he echoes, impatiently, "of course not; why should we? The fact is" (beginning to speak quickly in clear and eager explanation) "that I heard them talking of this plan yesterday, and so I thought I would be on the safe side, and send over to Tempest for the pony-carriage, and it is here now, and—"

"And you are going to drive her in it?" I say, still speaking quietly, and smiling. "I see! nothing could be nicer!"

"I wish to Heaven that you would not take the words out of my mouth," he cries, losing his temper a little; while his brows contract into a slight and most unwonted frown. "What I wish to know is, will *you* drive her?"

"I!!"

"Yes, *you*; I know—" (speaking with a sort of hurried deprecation) "I know that you are not fond of her; she is not a woman that other women are apt to get on with; but it would not be for long! I tell you candidly" (with a look of sincere anxiety) "I do not half like trusting you to Parker!—I think you are as likely as not to come to grief."

"To come to grief!" repeat I, with a harsh, dry laugh; "ha! ha! perhaps I have done that already!"

"But will you?" he asks, eagerly; not heeding my sorry mirth, and taking my hand. "I would drive you myself, if I could, and if—" (almost humbly) "if it would not bore you; but you see—" (rather slowly) "about the carriage, she—she *asked* me, and one does not like to say 'No' to such an old friend!"

Old friend! At the phrase, Algy's sneering white face rises before my mind's eye.

"Will you?" he repeats, looking pleadingly at me, with the gray darkness of his eyes.

"No, I will not!" I reply, resolutely, and still with that unmirthful mirth; "what ever else I may be, I will not be a *spoil-sport!*"

"A *spoil-sport!*" he echoes, passionately, while his face darkens, and hardens with impatient anger; "good God! will you *never* understand?"

Then he hastily leaves the room. And so it comes to pass that, half an hour later, I am crawling up with a sick heart to the box-seat, piteously calling on all around me to hold down my garments during my ascent. The grooms have let go the horses' heads, and have climbed up in dapper lightness at the back: we are through the first gate! Bah! that was a near shave of the post; yes, we are off, off for a long day's pleasuring! The very thought is enough to put any one in low spirits, is not it?

Barbara and Musgrave are behind us; and at the back, our old host and Algy. The two latter are, I think, specially likely to enjoy themselves; as the raw morning air has got down the old gentleman's throat, and he is coughing like a wheezy old squirrel; and Algy is in a dumb frenzy. I am no great judge of coachmanship, but we have not gone a quarter of a mile, before it is borne in on my mind that Mr. Parker has about as much idea of driving as a tomcat. The team do what is good in their eyes; we must throw ourselves on their clemency and discretion, for clearly our only hope is in them. He has not an idea of keeping them together; they are all over the place; the wheelers' reins are all loose on their backs. We seem to have an irresistible tendency toward bordering to the right which keeps us hovering over the ditch. However, fortunately, the road is very broad—one of the old coach-roads—and the vehicles we meet are few and anxious to get out of our way. Such as they are, I will do ourselves the justice to say that we try our best to run down each and all of them.

It is September, as I have before said. The leaves are still all green, only a stray bramble reddening here and there; but most of the midsummer hedge-row peoples are gathered to their rest. Only a lagging few, the slight-throated blue-bell, the uncouth ragwort, the little, tight scabious, remain. At least, the berries are here, however. While each red hip shows where a faint rose blossomed and fell; while the elder holds stoutly aloft her flat, black clusters; while the briony clasps the hawthorn-hedge, we cannot complain. Not only the *main* things of Nature, but all her odds and ends, are so exceedingly fair and daintily wrought.

It is one of those days that look charming, when seen through the window; bright and sunny, with lights that fly, and shadows that pursue; but it is a very different matter when one comes to *feel* it. There is a bleak, keen wind, that sends the clouds racing through the heavens, and that blows right in our teeth; nearly strangling me by the violence with which it takes hold of my head.

There has been no rain for a week or two, and it is a chalky country. The dust is waltzing in white whirlwinds along the road. High up as we are, it reaches us, and thrusts its fine and choking powder up our noses.

"I suppose," say I, doubtfully, looking up at the shifting uncertainty of the heavens, and trying to speak in a sprightly tone, a feat which I find rather hard of accomplishment, with such a blast cutting my eyes, and making me gasp—"I suppose that it will not rain!"

"*Rain!* not it!" replies our coachman, with contemptuous cheerfulness.

"The glass was going down!" I say, humbly, "and I think I felt a drop just now!"

"*Impossible!* it *could* not rain with this wind."

He says this with such a jovial and robust certainty of scorn, that I am half inclined to distrust the sky's evidence—to disbelieve even in the big drop that so indisputably splashed into my eye just now. "But in case it *does* rain," continue I, pertinaciously, "I suppose that there is a house near, or some place where we can take refuge?"

"No, there is no house nearer than a couple of miles"—making the statement with the easiest composure—"but it will not rain."

"Perhaps"—say I, with a sinking heart—"there is a wood—trees?"

"Well, no, there is not much in the way of trees—except Scotch firs—there are plenty of them—it is a bare sort of place—that is the beauty of it, you know"—(with a tone of confident pride)—"there is a monstrously fine view from it!—one can see *seven* counties!"

"Yes," say I, faintly, "so I have heard!"

At this point, the old gentleman is understood to be bawling something from the back. By the utter morosity of Algy's face—faintly seen in the distance—I conjecture that it is a joke; and, by the chuckling agony of zest with which the old man is delivered of it, I further conclude that it is something slightly unclean, but, thanks to the wind, none of us overtake a word of it. The wind's spirits are rising. Its play is becoming ever more and more boisterous. It would be difficult to imagine any thing disagreeabler than it is making itself; but perhaps it *will* keep off the rain. Thinking this, I try to bear its blows and buffets—its slaps on the face—its boxes on the ear—with greater patience. We have left the broad and safe high-road; Mr. Parker having, in an evil moment, bethought himself of a short-cut. We are, therefore, entangled in a labyrinth of cross-roads—finger-postless, guideless, solitary. *So* solitary, indeed, that we meet only one vacant boy of tender years, of whom, when we inquire the way, the wind absolutely refuses to allow us to hear a word of the broad Doric of his answer. At last—after many bold and stout declarations on the part of Mr. Parker, that he *will not* be beaten—that he knows the way as well as he does his A B C—and that he will find it if he stays till midnight—he is compelled, by the joint and miserable clamor of us all, to turn back—(a frightful process, as the road is narrow, and the coach will not lock)—to retrace our steps, and take up again the despised high-road, where we had left it. These manœuvres have naturally taken some time. It is three o'clock in the afternoon before we at length reach the great spread of desolate, broad, moorland, which is our destination. For more than an hour, absolute silence has fallen upon us. Like poor Yorick, we are "quite, quite chapfallen!" Even the gallant old gentleman could not make a dirty jest if he were to be shot for it. Mr. Parker alone maintains his exasperating good spirits. We find Roger and Mrs. Huntley sitting on the heather waiting for us. There is a good deal of relief—as it seems to me—in the former's eye, as he sees us appear on the scene; and a good deal of another expression, as he watches the masterly manner in which we pull up: all the four horses floundering together on their haunches; the leaders, moreover, exhibiting a mysterious desire to turn round and look in the wheelers' faces.

"Here we are!" cries Mr. Parker, joyously; "I have brought you along capitally, have not I?—but I am afraid we are a little late—eh, Mrs. Huntley? I hope we have not kept you long."

"*Is* it late?" she replies, with a smile and a fine hypocrisy—for she *looks* hungry—"I did not know; we have been quite happy!"

Roger has risen, and is coming to help me down, but I say, crossly, "Do not, please; Algy manages best!" Algy, however, has no intention of helping anybody down. He has helped *himself* down; and, without a word or a look to any of his fellow-travellers, has thrown himself down on the heather at Mrs. Huntley's feet, and is relieving his mind by audible animadversions on our late triumphal progress. I am therefore left to the tender mercies of the grooms; at least, I should have been, if Mr. Musgrave had not taken pity on me, and guided my uncertain feet and the petticoats, which Zephyr is doing his playful best to turn over my head, down the steep declivity of the ladder. This, as you may guess, does not help to restore my equanimity. However, I am down now, on firm ground; and, at least, we are rid of the dust. My eyes are still full of grit, but I suppose they will get over that. I turn them disconsolately about.

On a fine sunny day—with butterflies hovering over the heather-flowers, and bees sucking honey from the gorse—with little mild airs playing about, and a torquoise sky shining overhead—it might be a spot on which to lie and dream dreams of paradise; but *now*! The sun has finally retired, and hid his sulky face for the day; the heather is over; and, though the gorse is not, yet it gives no fragrance to the raw air. All over the great rolling expanse there is a heavy, leaden look, caught from the angry heavens above. The great clouds are gathering themselves together to battle; and the mighty wind, with nothing to check its progress, is sweeping over the great plain, and singing with eerie, loud mournfulness.

I shudder.

"Where are the Scotch firs?" (I say, querulously, to Mr. Parker, who by this time had joined me); "you said there were plenty of them! where are they?"

"*Where?*" (looking cheerfully round), "oh, *there*!" (pointing to where one lightning-riven little wreck bends its sickly head to the gale). "Ah! I see there is only *one*, after all. I thought that there had been more."

My heart sinks. Is that one withered, scathed little stick to be our sole protection against the storm, so evidently quickly coming up?

"Fine view, is not it?" pursues my companion, not in the least perceiving my depression, and complacently surveying the prospect. "Of course it might have been clearer, but, after all, you get a very good idea of it."

I turn my faint eyes in the same direction as his. Down on the horizon the sullen rain-clouds are settling, and, to meet them, there stretches a dead, colorless flat, dotted with little round trees, little church-spires, little houses, little fields, little hedges—one of those mappy views, that lack even the beauties of a map—the nice pink and green and blue lines which so gayly define the boundaries of each county.

"Very extensive, is not it?" he says, proudly; "you know you can see—"

"Seven counties!" interrupt I, sharply, snapping the words out of his mouth. "Yes, I know; you told me."

The horses have been led away to the distant ale-house. The coach stands forlorn and solitary on the moor. Some of us, looking at the threatening aspect of the weather, have suggested that *we* too should make for shelter; but this suggestion is indignantly vetoed by Mr. Parker.

"*Rain!* not a bit of it! It is not *thinking* of raining! The wind! what is the matter with the wind? Nice and fresh! Much better than one of those muggy days, when you can hardly breathe!"

CHAPTER XLV

The cloth is therefore laid, with the dead heather-flowers beneath it, and the low leaden sky above. As large stones as can be found have to be sought on the moorland road to weight it, and hinder our banquet from flying bodily away. It is at last spread—cold lamb, cold partridges, chickens, *mayonnaise*, cakes, pastry—they have just been arranged in their defenceless nakedness under the eye of heaven, when the rain begins. And, when it begins, it begins to some purpose. It deceives us with no false hopes—with no breakings in the serried clouds—with no flying glimpses of blue sky. Down it comes, straight, *straight* down, on the lamb, on the *mayonnaise*, splash into the bitter. Each of us seizes the viand dearest to his or her heart, and tries to shelter it beneath his or her umbrella. But in vain! The great slant storm reaches it under the puny defense. Even Mr. Parker has to change the *form* of his consolation, though not the spirit. He can no longer deny that it is raining; but what he now says is that it will not last—that it is only a shower—that he is very glad to see it come down so hard at first, as it is all the more certain to be soon over.

Nobody has the heart to contradict him, though everybody knows that it is a lie. Mrs. Huntley, at the first drop, has made for the coach, and now sits in it, serene and dry. Algy follows her, with a chicken and a champagne bottle. I sit doggedly still, where I am, on the cold moor.

Roger has not spoken to me since my rude reception of him on arriving, but he now comes up to me.

"Had not you better follow her example?" he asks, speaking rather formally, and looking toward the coach, where with smiling profile and neat hair, my rival is sitting, reveling among the flesh-pots.

Something in the sight of her sleek, smooth tidiness, joined to the consciousness of my own miserable, blowsed disorder, stings me more even than the rain-drops are doing.

"Not I!" I answer, brusquely; "that is what I trust I shall never do!"

He passes by my sneer without notice.

"In this rain you will be drenched in two minutes."

"Après!"

"*Après!*" he repeats, impatiently, "*après?* you will catch your death of cold!"

"And you will be a widower!" reply I, with a bitter smile.

Barbara is as obstinate as I am. She, too, seems to prefer the spite of the elements to disturbing the *tête-à-tête* in the coach. Musgrave has made her as comfortable as he can, with her back against the poor little Scotch fir, and a plaid over both their heads.

The feast proceeds in solemn silence. Even if we had the heart to talk, the difficulty of making ourselves heard would quite check the inclination.

There are little puddles in all our plates—the bread and cakes are *pap*—the lamb is damp and flabby, and the *mayonnaise* is reduced to a sort of watery whey.

Mr. Parker is the only one who, under these circumstances, makes any attempt to pretend that we are enjoying ourselves.

"This is not so bad, after all," he says, still with that same unconquerable accent of joviality. He has to say it three times, and to put up his hands to his mouth like a speaking-trumpet, before any one hears him. When they do, "answer comes there none!"

I, indeed, am not in a position for conversation at the exact moment that the demand is made upon me. I have just come to the end of a long wrestle with my umbrella. It has at last got its wicked will, and has turned right inside out! All its whalebones are aspiring heavenward. It is transformed into a melancholy *cup*—like a great ugly flower, on a bare stalk. I lay the remains calmly down beside me, and affront the blast and the tempest alone! I have a brown hat on—at least it *was* brown when we set off—I am just wondering, therefore, with a sort of stupid curiosity, why the *rill* that so plenteously distills from its brim, and so madly races down my cold nose, should be *sky blue*, when I perceive that Barbara has left her shelter, and her lover, and is standing beside me.

"Poor Nancy!" she says, with a softly compassionate laugh, "how wet you are! come under the plaid with me! you have no notion how warm it keeps one; and the tree, though it does not *look* much, saves one a bit, too—and Frank does not mind being wet—come quick!"

I am too wretched to object. No water-proof could stand the deluge to which mine has been subjected. My shoulder-blades feel moist and *sticky*: my hair is in little dismal ropes, and dreadful runlets are coursing down my throat, and under my clothes.

Without any remonstrance, I snuggle under the plaid with Barbara— with a little of the feeling of soothing and dependence with which, long ago, in the dear old dead days at home, I used, when I was a naughty child, or a bruised child—and I was very often both—to creep to her for consolation.

Thanks to the wind, and to our proximity, we are able to talk without a fear of being overheard.

"You are wrong!" Barbara says, glancing first toward the coach, and then turning the serene and limpid gravity of her blue eyes on me; "you are making a mistake!"

I do not affect to understand her.

"*Am I?*" I say, indignantly; "I am doing nothing of the kind! it is not only my own idea!—ask Algy!"

"*Algy!*" (with a little accent of scorn), "poor Algy!—he is in such a fit state for judging, is not he?"

We both involuntarily look toward him.

It is *his* turn now, and his morosity is exchanged for an equally uncomfortable hilarity. His cheeks are flushed; he is laughing loudly, and going in heavily for the champagne. The next moment he is scowling discourteously at his old host, who, with his poor old chuckle entirely drowned, and overcome by an endless sort of choking monotony of cough, is clambering on tottery old legs into the coach, to try and get his share of shelter.

We both laugh a little; and then Barbara speaks again.

"Nancy, I want to say something to you. Just now I heard Roger ask whether there was a fly to be got at the public-house where the horses are put up, and it seems there *is*; and he has sent for it. You may think that it is for *her*, but it is not—it is for *you!* Will you promise me to go home in it, if he asks you?"

I am silent.

"Will you?" she repeats, taking hold of one of my froggy hands, while her eyes shine with a soft and friendly urgency; "you know you always used to take my advice when we were little—will you?"

Somehow, at her words, a little warmth of comfortable reassurance steals about my heart. At home she always used to be right: perhaps she is right now—perhaps *I* am wrong. I will be even better than her suggestion.

Roger is standing not far from us. The rain has drenched his beard and his heavy mustache: the great drops stand on his eyelashes, and on his straight brows. Perhaps I only imagine it, but to me he looks sad and out of heart. It is not the weather that makes him so, if he is. Much he cares for that!

I call him "Roger!" My voice is small and low, and the wind is large and loud, but he hears me.

"Yes?" (turning at the sound with a surprised expression).

"May I go home in the fly?" I ask impulsively, yet humbly, "I mean with—with *her!*" (a gulp at the pronoun), then, under the influence of a fear that he may think that I am driven by a hankering after creature comforts to this overture, I go on quickly, "it is not because I want to be kept dry—if I were to be dragged through the sea I could not be wetter than I am—but if you wish—Barbara thought—Barbara said—"

I mumble off into shy incoherency.

"*Will* you?" he says, with a tone of eagerness and pleasure, which, if not real, is at least admirably feigned. "It is what I was just wishing to ask you, only" (laughing with a sort of constraint and a touch of bitterness) "I really was *afraid!*"

"Am I such a *shrew?*" I say, looking at him with a feeling of growing light-heartedness. "Ah! I always was! was not I, Barbara?" Then, a moment after, in a tone that is almost gay, I say, "May Barbara come, too? is there room?"

"Of course!" he answers readily; "surely there is plenty of room for all!"

While the words are yet on his lips, while I am still smiling up at him, under the soaked tartan there comes a voice from the coach.

"Roger!"

He obeys the summons. It is just five paces off, and I hear each of the slow and softly-enunciated words that follow.

"I hear that you have sent for a fly! how very thoughtful of you! did you ever forget *any thing*, I wonder? I was—no—not *dreading* my drive home; but now I am *quite* looking forward to it. Why did you not bring a pack of cards? we might have had a game of bézique."

"I think we have made another arrangement," he answers, quietly. "I think Nancy will be your companion instead of me."

"*Lady Tempest!*" (with a slight but to me quite perceptible raising of eyebrows, and accenting of words).

"Yes, Nancy."

I can see her face, but not his. To my acutely listening, sharply jealous ears there sounds a tone of faint and carefully hidden annoyance in his voice. It seems to me, too, that her features would not dare to wear such an expression of open disappointment if they were not answered and meeting something in his. I therefore take my course. I jump up hastily, flinging off the plaid, and advance toward the interlocutors.

She is just saying, "Oh, I understand! very nice!" in a little formal voice when I break in.

"I am going to do nothing of the kind!" I cry, hurriedly. "I have altered my mind; I shall keep to the coach, that is" (with a nervous laugh, and a miserable attempt at coquetry), "if Mr. Parker is not tired of me."

This is the way in which I take Barbara's advice. The fly arrives presently, and the original pair depart in it. Roger neither looks at nor speaks to me again; in fact, he ignores my existence; although, under the influence of one of those speedy and altogether futile repentances which always follow hard on the heels of my tantrums, I have waylaid him once or twice in the hope that he would be induced to recognize it. But no! this time I have outdone myself. I have tried his patience a little too far. I am in disgrace.

It is long, *long* after their departure before *we* get under way. The grooms have either misunderstood Mr. Parker's directions, or are enjoying their mulled beer over the pot-house fire too much to be in any violent haste again to meet the raw air and the persisting deluge.

It is past six o'clock before the horses arrive on the ground; it is half-past before we are off.

And meanwhile Mr. Parker has been rivaling Algy in the ardor with which he calls in the aid of the champagne to keep out the wet. At each fresh tumbler his joviality goes up a step, until at length it reaches a pitch which produces an opposite effect on me, and engenders a depressed fright.

"Barbara," say I, in a low voice, when at length the moment of departure draws near, and only Musgrave is within ear-shot—"Barbara, has it struck you? do not you think he is rather—"

Barbara, however, is diffident of her own opinion, and repeats my question to her lover.

He shrugs his shoulders.

"Is he? I have not noticed him; nothing more likely; last time I saw him he was *flying*! It was in India at a great pig-sticking meeting, and after dinner he got up to the top of a big mango-tree, and tried to *fly*! Of course he fell down, but he was so drunk that he was not in the least hurt."

Mr. Musgrave seems to think this an amusing anecdote; but we do not.

"Why do not *you* drive?" I ask, contrary to all my resolutions addressing my future brother-in-law, and indeed forgetting in my alarm that I had ever made such. I am reminded of it, however, by the look of gratification that flashes—for only one moment and is gone—but still flashes into the depths of his great dark eyes.

"It is so likely that he would let me!" he says, laughing.

"I would not mind so much if I were at the *back*!" I say, piteously, turning to Barbara. "At the back one does not know what is coming, but on the box one sees whatever is happening."

"That is rather an advantage I think," she answers, laughing. "I do not mind; I will go on the box."

"Will you?" say I, eagerly. "*Do!* and I will take care of the old general at the back."

So it is settled. We are on the point of starting now. Mr. Parker is up and is already beginning to struggle with the hopeless muddle of his reins. I think we have perhaps done him an injustice; at all events, his condition is not at all what it must have been when he mounted the mango. Algy's morosity has returned tenfold, and he is performing the evolution familiarly known as "pulling your nose to vex your face." That is to say, he is standing about in the pouring rain utterly unprotected from it. He entirely declines to put on any mackintosh or overcoat. Why he does this, or how it punishes Mrs. Huntley, I cannot say, but so it is.

We are off at last. I, in accordance with my wishes, up at the back, facing the grooms; but not at all in accordance with my wishes, Mr. Musgrave, and not the old host, is my companion.

"This is all wrong!" I cry, with vexed abruptness, as I see who it is that is climbing after me. "Where is the general? We settled that he—"

"I am afraid you will have to put up with me!" interrupts Musgrave, coldly, with that angry and mortified darkening of the whole face, and sudden contraction of the eye-balls that I used so well to know. "We could not make him hear; we all tried, but none of us could make him understand." So I have to submit.

Well, we are off now. The night is coming quickly down: it will be *quite* dark an hour sooner than usual to-night, so low does the great black cloud-curtain stoop to the earth's wet face. Ink above us, so close above us, too, that it seems as if one might touch it with lifted hand; ink around us; a great stretch of dull and sulky heather; and, maddening around us with devilish glee, hitting us, buffeting us, bruising us, taking away our breath, and making our eyelids smart, is a wind—such a wind! I should have laughed if any one had told me an hour ago that it would rise. I should have said it was impossible, and yet it certainly has.

The wind which turned my umbrella inside out was a zephyr compared to that which is now *thundering* round us. Sometimes, for one, for two false moments, it lulls (the lulls are almost awfuller than the whirlwind that follows them), then with gathered might it comes tearing, howling, whooping down on us again, gnashing its angry teeth; bellowing with a voice like ten million lost devils. And on its pinions what rain it brings; what stinging, lacerating, bitter rain! And now, to add to our misfortunes, to pile Pelion on Ossa, we *lose our way.* Mr. Parker cannot be persuaded to abandon the idea of the short-cut. The natural result follows.

If we were hopelessly bewildered—utterly at sea among the maze of lonely roads into which he has again betrayed us at high noon—what must we be now in the angry dark of the evening? This time we have to go into a field to turn, a field full of tussocks, which in the dark we are unable to see, and over which the horses flounder and stumble. However, now at length—now that we have wasted three-quarters of an hour, and that it is quite pitch dark—(I need hardly say that we have no lamps)—we have at length regained the blessed breadth of the high-road, and I think that not even our coachman, to whose faith most things seem possible, will attempt to leave it a second time. I give a sigh of relief.

"It is all plain sailing now!" Musgrave says, reassuringly.

"There is one bad turn," reply I, gloomily—"very bad, at the bottom of the village by the bridge."

We relapse into silence, and into our unnatural battle with the elements. I have to grasp my hat firmly with one hand, and the side of the coach with the other, to prevent being blown off. If my companion were any one else, I should grasp *him.*

We are only a mile and a half from our haven now; the turn I dread is nearing.

"Are you frightened?" asks Musgrave, in a pause of the storm.

"*Horribly!*" I answer.

I have forgotten Brindley Wood—have forgotten all the mischief he has done. I recollect only that he is human, and that we are sharing what seems to me a great and common peril.

"Do not be frightened!" he says, in an eager whisper—"you need not. I will take care of you!"

Even through all the preoccupation of my alarm something in his tone jars upon and angers me.

"*You* take care of me!" I cry, scornfully. "How could you? I wish you would not talk nonsense."

We have reached the turn now! Shall we do it? One moment of breathless anxiety. I set my teeth and breathe hard. No, we shall not! We turn too sharp, and do not take a wide-enough sweep. The coach gives a horrible lurch. One side of us is up on the hedge-bank!—we are going over! I give a little agonized yell, and make a snatch at Frank, while my fingers clutch his nearest hand with the tenacity of a devil-fish. If it were his hair, or his nose, I should equally grasp it. Then, somehow—to this moment I do not know how—we right ourselves. The grooms are down like a shot, pulling at the horses' heads, and in a second or two—how it is done I do not see, on account of the dark—but with many bumpings, and shouts and callings, and dreadful jolts, we come straight again, and I drop Frank's hand like a hot chestnut.

In ten minutes more we are briskly and safely trotting up to the hall-door. Before we reach it, I see Roger standing under the lit portico, with level hand shading his eyes, which are intently staring out into the darkness.

"All right? nothing happened?" he asks, in a tone of the most poignant anxiety, almost before we have pulled up.

"All right!" replies Barbara's voice, softly cheerful. "Are you looking for Nancy? She is at the back with Frank."

Roger makes no comment, but this time he does not offer to lift me down.

"Well, here we are!" cries Mr. Parker, coming beaming into the hall, with his mackintosh one great drip, laughing and rubbing his hands. "And though I say it that should not, there are not many that could have brought you home better than I have done to-night, and, I declare, in spite of the rain, we have not had half a bad day, have we?"

But we are all strictly silent.

CHAPTER XLVI

"... Peace, pray you, now,
No dancing more. Sing sweet, and make us mirth.
We have done with dancing measures; sing that song
You call the song of love at ebb."

Yesterday it had seemed impossible that we could ever be dry again, and yet to-day we are. Even our hair is no longer in dull, discolored ropes. A night has intervened between us and our sufferings. We have at last got the sound of the hissing rain and the thunder of the boisterous wind out of our ears. We have all got colds more or less. I am among the *less*; for rough weather has never been an enemy to me, and at home I have always been used to splashing about in the wet, with the native relish of a young duck. Mrs. Huntley is (despite the fly) among the *more*. She does not appear until late—not until near luncheon-time. Her cold is in the head, the *safest* but unbecomingest place, producing, as I with malignant joy perceive, a slight thickening and swelling of her little thin nose, and a boiled-gooseberry air in her appealing eyes.

The old gentleman is—with the exception, perhaps, of Algy—the most dilapidated among us. He has not yet begun one anecdote, whose point was not smothered and effaced by that choking, goat-like cough. This is perhaps a gain to *us*, as one is not expected to laugh at a *cough*; nor does its *dénoûment* ever put one to the blush.

Mr. Parker has no cold at all, and has even had the shameless audacity to propose *another* expedition to-day. But we all rise in such loud and open revolt that he has perforce to withdraw his suggestion.

He must save his superfluous energy for the evening, when the neighbors are to come together, and we are to dance. This fact is news to most of us, and I think we hardly receive it with the elation he expects. There seems to be more of rheumatism than of dance in many of our limbs, and our united sneezes will be enough to drown the band. However, revolt in this case is useless. We must console ourselves with the notion that at least in a ballroom there can be neither rain nor wind—that we cannot lose our way or be upset, at least not in the sense which had such terror for us yesterday. Roger has gone over to Tempest on business, and is away all day. Mrs. Huntley sits by the fire, with a little fichu over her head, sipping a tisane; while Algy, in undisturbed possession, and with restored but feverish amiability, stretches his length on the rug at her feet, and looks injured if Barbara or I, or even the footman with coals, enters the room.

As the day goes on, there is not much to do; a new idea takes possession of Mr. Parker's active mind.

Why should not we all be in fancy-dress to-night? Well, not all of us, then—not his uncle, of course, nor Sir Roger, but any of us that liked. *Trouble!* Not a bit of it. Why, the ladies need only rouge a bit, and put some flour on their heads, and there they are; and, as for the men, there is a heap of old things up in the lumber-room that belonged to his great-grandfather, and among them there is sure to be something to fit everybody. If they do not believe him, they may come and see for themselves.

Such is the force of a strong will, that he actually carries off the deeply unwilling Musgrave to inspect his ancestor's wardrobe. At first we have treated his proposal only with laughter, but he is so profoundly in earnest about it, and dwells with such eagerness on the advantage of the fact that not a soul among the company will recognize us—he can answer for *himself* at least—it is always by his *hair* (with a laugh) that people know *him*—that we at length begin to catch his ardor.

To tell truth, from the beginning the idea has approved itself to Barbara and me, only that we were ashamed to say so—carrying us back in memory as it does to the days when we dressed the Brat up in my clothes as *me*, and took in all the maid-servants. I think, too, that I have a little of the feeling of faint hope that inspired Balak when he showed Balaam the Israelites from a fresh point of view. Perhaps, in carmine cheeks and a snow-white head, I may find a little of my old favor in Roger's eyes.

Human wills are mostly so feeble and vacillating, that if one thorough-going determined one sticks to *any* proposition, however absurd, he is pretty sure to get the majority round to him in time; and so it is in the present case. Mr. Parker succeeds in making us all, willing and unwilling, promise to travesty ourselves. We are not to dress till after dinner; that is over now, and we are all adorning ourselves.

For once I am taking great pains, and—for a wonder—pleasant pains with my toilet. It is slightly delayed by a variety of unwonted interruptions— knocks at the door, voices of valets in interrogation, and dialogue with my maid.

"If you please, Mr. Musgrave wants to know has Lady Tempest done with the rouge?"

(There is only one edition of rouge, which is traveling from room to room.)

Five minutes more, another knock.

"If you please, Mr. Parker's compliments, and will Lady Tempest lend him a hair-pin to black his eyelashes?"

I am finished now, quite finished—metamorphosed. I have suffered a great deal in the process of powdering, as I fancy every one must have done since the world began; the powder has gone into my eyes, up my nose, down into my lungs. I have breathed it, and sneezed it, and swallowed it, but "*il faut souffrir pour être belle*," and I do not grumble; for I *am* belle! For once in my life I know what it feels like to be a pretty woman. My uninteresting flax-hair is hidden. Above the lowness of my brow there towers a great white erection, giving me height and dignity, while high aloft a little cap of ancient lace and soft pink roses daintily perches. On my cheeks there is a vivid yet delicate color; and my really respectable eyes are emphasized and accentuated by the dark line beneath them. To tell you the truth, I cannot take my eyes off myself. It is *delightful* to be pretty! I am simpering at myself over my left shoulder, and heartily joining in my maid's encomiums on myself, when the door opens, and Roger enters. For the first instant I really think that he does not recognize me. Then—

"*Nancy!*" he exclaims, in a tone of the most utter and thorough astonishment—"*is* it Nancy?"

"*Nancy*, at your service!" reply I, with undisguised elation, looking eagerly at him, with my blackened eyes, to see what he will say next.

"But—what—*has*—happened—to you?" he says, slowly, looking at me exhaustively from top to toe—from the highest summit of my floured head to the point of my buckled shoes. "What have you got yourself up like this for?"

"To please Mr. Parker," reply I, breaking into a laugh of excitement. "But I have killed two birds with one stone; I have pleased *myself*, too! Did you ever see any thing so nice as I look?" (unable any longer to wait for the admiration which is so justly my due).

"Not often!" he answers, with emphasis.

We had parted rather formally—rather *en délicatesse*—this morning, but we both seem to have forgotten this.

"I must not dance *much!*" say I, anxiously turning again to the glass, and closely examining my complexion—"must I?—or my rouge will *run!*"

After a moment—

"You must be sure to tell me if I grow to look at all *smeary*, and I will run up-stairs at once, and put some more on."

He is looking at me, with an infinite amusement, and also commendation, in his eyes.

"Why, Nancy," he says, smiling—"I had no idea that you were so vain!"

"No," reply I, bubbling over again into a shamefaced yet delighted laughter—"no more had I! But then I had no idea that I was so pretty, either."

My elation remains undiminished when I go down-stairs. Yes, even when I compare myself with Mrs. Huntley, for, *for once*, I have beaten her! I really think that there can be no two opinions about it! indeed, I have the greatest difficulty in refraining from asking everybody whether there can.

She is not in powder. Her hair, in its present color, is hardly dark enough to suit the high comb, and black lace mantilla which she has draped about her head, and the red rose in her hair is hardly redder than the catarrh has made her eyelids. A cold always comes on more heavily at night; and no one can deny that her whole appearance is stuffy and choky, and that she speaks through her nose.

As for me, I am not sure that I do not beat even *Barbara*. At least, the idea has struck me; and, when she herself suggests, and with hearty satisfaction, and elation not inferior to my own, insists upon it, I do not think it necessary to contradict her.

None of the three young men have as yet made their appearance; and the guests are beginning quickly to arrive. All the neighbors—all the friends who are staying with the neighbors to shoot their partridges—some soldiers, some odds and ends, *bushels* of girls—there always are bushels of girls somehow; here they come, smiling, settling their ties, giving their skirts furtive kicks behind, as their different sex and costume bid them.

All the duties of reception fall upon the poor old gentleman, and drive him to futile wrath, and to sending off many loud and desperate messages to his truant heir. However, to do him justice, the poor old soul is hospitality itself, and treats his guests, not only to the best food, drink, and fiddling in his power, but also to all his primest anecdotes. No less than *three* times in the course of the evening do I hear him go through that remarkable tale of the doctor at Norwich, of the age of seventy-eight, and the four fine children.

To my immense delight, hardly anybody recognizes me. Many people look *hard*—really *very* hard—at me, and I try to appear modestly unconscious.

We are all in the dancing-room. The sharp fiddles are already beginning to squeak out a gay galop, and I am tapping impatient time with my foot to that brisk, emphasized music which has always seemed to Barbara and me exhilarating past the power of words to express.

I think that Roger perceives my eagerness, for he brings up a, to me, strange soldier, who makes his bow, and invites me.

I comply, with contained rapture, and off we fly. For I have pressingly consulted Roger as to whether I may, with safety to my complexion, take a turn or two, and he has replied strongly in the affirmative. He has, indeed, maintained that I may dance all night without seeing my rosy cheeks dissolve, but I know better.

The room is almost lined with mirrors. I can even perceive myself over my partner's shoulder as I dance. I can ascertain that my loveliness still continues.

How pleasant it is, after all, to be young! and how *delightful* to be pretty!

Does Barbara *always* feel like this? It seems to me as if I had never danced so lightly—on so admirably slippery and springy a floor, or with any one whose step suited mine better. His style of dancing is, indeed, very like Bobby's. I tell him so. This leads to an explanation as to who Bobby is, which makes us extremely friendly.

We are standing still for a moment or two to take breath—we are long-winded, and do not *often* do it; but still, once in a way, it is unavoidable—and everybody else is whirling and galloping, and prancing round us, like Bacchantes, or tops, or what you will, when, looking toward the door, I catch a glimpse of the three missing young men. They are dodging behind one another, and each nudging and pushing the other forward. Clearly, they are horribly ashamed of themselves; and, from the little I see of them, *no wonder!*

"Here they are!" I cry, in a tone of excitement. "Look! do look!" for, having at length succeeded in urging Mr. Parker to the front, they are making their entry, hanging as close together as possible, and with an extremely hang-dog air.

My partner has opened his eyes and his mouth.

"*What* are they?" he says, in a tone of extreme disapprobation. "*Who* are they? Are they *Christy Minstrels?*"

"Oh, do not!" cry I, in a choked voice, "I do not want to laugh, it will make them so angry—at least not Mr. Parker, but the others."

As I speak, they reach me, that is, Algy and Mr. Parker do. Musgrave has slunk into a corner, and sits there, glaring at whoever he thinks shows a disposition to smile in his direction.

I have done Mr. Parker an injustice in accrediting him with any *mauvaise honte*. On the contrary, he clearly glories in his shame.

"Not half so bad, after all, are they?" he says in a voice of loud and cheerful appeal to me, as he comes up. "I mean considering, of course, that they were not *meant* for one, they really do very decently, do not they?"

I have put up my fan to hide the irresistible contortions which lips and mouth are undergoing.

"Very!" I say, indistinctly.

Almost everybody has stopped dancing, and is staring with unaffected wonder at them. Their heads are heavily floured, and their cheeks rouged. They have also greatly overdone the burnt hair-pin, as a huge smouch of black under each of their eyes attests.

They have all three got painfully tight knee-breeches, white stockings, and enormously long, broad-skirted coats, embroidered in tarnished gold. Algy's is plum-color. The arms of all three are very, *very* tight. Had our ancestors indeed such skinny limbs, and such prodigious backs?

Algy is a tall young man, but the waist of his coat is somewhere about the calves of his legs. It has told upon his spirits; he looks supernaturally grave.

Mr. Parker is differently visited. He has an apparently unaccountable reluctance to turning his back to me. I put it down at first to an exaggerated politeness; but, when, at last, in walking away, he unavoidably does it, I no longer wonder at his unwillingness, as his coat-tails decline to meet within half a mile. His forefathers must have been oddly framed.

"*Poor fellows!*" says my partner, in a tone of the profoundest compassion, as he puts his arm round me, and prepares to whirl me again into the throng, "*how* I pity them! What on earth did they do it for?"

"Oh, I do not know," I reply; "for *fun* I suppose!"

But I think that except in the case of Mr. Parker, who really enjoys himself, and goes about making jovial jests at his own expense, and asking everybody whether he is not immensely improved by the loss of his red hair, that there is not much fun in it.

Algy is as sulky and shamefaced as a dog with a tin kettle tied to his tail, and Mr. Musgrave has altogether disappeared.

The evening wears on. I forget my cheeks, and dance every thing. *How* I *am* enjoying myself! Man after man is brought up to me, and they all seem pleased with me. At many of the things I say, they laugh heartily, and I do not wonder—even to myself my speeches sound pleasant. What a comfort it is that, for once in his life, Roger may be honestly proud of me! And he is.

It is surely pride, and also something better and pleasanter than pride, that is shining in the smile with which he is watching me from the doorway. At least, during the first part of the evening he *was* watching me.

Is not he still? I look round the room. No, he is not here! he has disappeared! By a sudden connection of ideas I turn my eyes in search of the high comb and mantilla. Neither are they here. Last time I saw them, they were sitting on the stairs, pathetically observing to their companion how hard it was that one might not feel cool without looking as if one were flirting.

Perhaps they are on the stairs still; perhaps she has gone to bed as she threatened. Somehow my heart misgives me. I become rather absent: my partners grow seldomer merry at my speeches. Even my feet feel to fly less lightly, and I forget to look at myself in the glass. Then it strikes me suddenly that I will not dance any more. The sparkle seems to have gone out of the evening since I missed Roger's face from the door-way.

I decline an overture on the part of my first friend to trip a measure with me—we have already tripped several—and, by the surprise and slight mortification which I read on his face as he turns away, I think I must have done it with some abruptness.

I decline everybody. I stand in the door-way, whence I can command both the ballroom and the passages. They are not on the stairs.

A moment ago Mr. Parker came up to me, and told me in his gay, loud voice how much he would like to have a valse with me, but that his clothes are so tight, he really *dare not*. Then he disappears among the throng, with an uncomfortable sidelong movement, which endeavors to shield the incompleteness of his back view.

I am still smiling at his dilemma, when another voice sounds in my ears.

"You are not dancing?"

It is Musgrave. He has had the vanity to take off his absurd costume, and to wash the powder from his hair, and the rouge from his cheeks. He stands before me now, cool, pale, and civilized, in the faultless quietness of his evening dress.

"No," reply I, shortly, "I am not!"

"Will you dance with me?"

I am not looking at him; indeed, I never look at him now, if I can help; but I hear a sort of hesitating defiance in his tone.

"No, thank you"—(still more shortly)—"I might have danced, if I had liked: it is not for want of asking"—(with a little childish vanity)—"but I do not wish."

"Do not you mean to dance any more this evening, then?"

"I do not know; that is as may be!"

I have almost turned my back upon him, and my eyes are following—not perhaps quite without a movement of envy—my various acquaintances, scampering, coupled in mad embraces. I think that he is gone, but I am mistaken.

"Will you at least let me take you in to supper?" in a tone whose formality is strongly dashed with resentment.

I wish that I did not know his voice so hatefully well: all its intonations and inflections are as familiar to me as Roger's.

"I do not want any supper," I answer, petulantly, turning the back of my head and all my powdered curls toward him; "I never eat supper at a ball; I like to stand here; I like to watch the people—to watch Barbara!"

This at least is true. To see Barbara dance has always given, and does even now give, me the liveliest satisfaction. No one holds her head so prettily as Barbara; no one moves so smoothly, and with so absolutely innocent a gayety. The harshest, prudishest adversary of valsing, were he to see Barbara valse, would be converted to thinking it the most modest of dances. Mr. Musgrave is turning away. Just as he is doing so, an idea strikes me. Perhaps they are in the supper-room.

"After all," say I, unceremoniously, and forgetting for the moment who it is that I am addressing, "I do not mind if I do have something; I—I—am rather hungry."

I put my hand on his arm, and we walk off.

The supper-room is rather full—(when, indeed, was a supper-room known to be empty?)—some people are sitting—some standing—it is therefore a little difficult to make out who is here, and who is not. In total absolute forgetfulness of the supposed cause that has brought me here, I stand eagerly staring about, under people's arms—over their shoulders. So far, I do not see them. I am recalled by Mr. Musgrave's voice, coldly polite.

"Will not you sit down?"

"No, thank you," reply I, bending my neck back to get a view behind an intervening group; "I had rather stand."

"Are you looking for any one?"

Again, I wish that I did not know his voice so well—that I did not so clearly recognize that slightly guardedly malicious intonation.

"Looking for any one?" I cry, sharply, and reddening even through my rouge—"of course not!—whom should I be looking for?—but, after all, I do not think I care about having any thing!—there's—there's nothing that I fancy."

This is a libel at once upon myself and on General Parker's hospitality. He answers nothing, and perhaps the smile, almost imperceptible—which I fancy in his eyes, and in the clean curve of his lips—exists only in my imagination. He again offers me his arm, and I again take it. I have clean forgotten his existence. His arm is no more to me than if it were a piece of wood.

"Where are they? where can they be?" is the thought that engrosses all my attention.

I hardly notice that he is leading me away from the ballroom—down the long corridor, on which almost all the sitting-rooms open. They are, one and all, lit up to-night; and in each of them there are guests. I glance in at the drawing-room: they are not there! We take a turn in the conservatory. We find Mr. Parker sitting very carefully upright, for his costume does not allow of any lolling, or of any tricks being played with it under a magnolia, with a pretty girl—(I wonder, have *my* cheeks grown as streaky as his?)—but they are not there. We go back to the corridor. We peep into the library: two or three bored old gentlemen—martyrs to their daughters' prospects—yawning over the papers and looking at their watches. They are not here. Where *can* they be? Only one room yet remains—one room at the very end of the passage—the billiard-room, shut off by double doors to deaden the sound of the balls. One of the double doors is wide open, the other closed—not absolutely *shut*, but not ajar. Musgrave pushes it, and we look in. I do not know why I do. I do not expect to see any one. I hardly think it will be lit, probably blank darkness will meet us. But it is not so. The lamps above the table are shining subduedly under their green shades; and on a couch against the wall two people are sitting. They *are* here. I found them at last.

Evidently they are in deep and absorbing talk. Roger's elbow rests on the top of the couch. His head is on his hand. On his face there is an expression of grave and serious concern; and she—she—is it *possible?*—she is evidently—

plainly weeping. Her face is hidden in her handkerchief, and she is sobbing quietly, but quite audibly. In an instant, with ostentatious hurry, Musgrave has reclosed the door, and we stand together in the passage.

I am not mistaken now: I could not be: that can be no other expression than triumph that so darkly shines in his great and eager eyes.

"You *knew* they were there!" I cry in a whisper of passionate resentment, snatching my hand from his arm; "you brought me here *on purpose!*"

Then, regardless of appearances, I turn quickly away, and walk back down the passage alone!

CHAPTER XLVII

This is how the ball ends for me. As soon as I am out of sight, I quicken my walk into a run, and, flying up the stairs, take refuge in my bedroom. Nor do I emerge thence again. The ball itself goes on for hours. The drawing-room is directly beneath me. It seems to me as if the sound of the fiddling, of the pounding, scampering feet would never, never end.

I believe, at least I hear afterward, that Mr. Parker, whose spirits go on rising with the steady speed of quicksilver in fine weather, declines to allow his guests to depart, countermands their carriages, bribes their servants, and, in short, reaches the pitch of joyfully confident faith to which all things seem not only *possible*, but extremely desirable, and in whose eyes the mango-tree feat would appear but a childish trifle.

The room is made up for the night; windows closed, shutters bolted, curtains draped. With hasty impatience I undo them all. I throw high the sash, and lean out. It is not a warm night; there is a little frosty crispness in the air, but I am *burning*. I am talking quickly and articulately to myself all the time, under my breath; it seems to me to relieve a little the inarticulate thoughts. I will not wink at it any longer, indeed I will not; nobody could expect it of me. I will not be taken in by that transparent fallacy of old friends! Nobody but me is. They *all* see it; Algy, Musgrave, all of them. At the thought of the victory written in Musgrave's eyes just now—at the recollection of the devilish irony of his wish, as we parted in Brindley Wood—

"I hope that your fidelity may be rewarded as it deserves—"

I start up, with a sort of cry, as if I had been smartly stung, and begin to walk quickly up and down the room. I will not storm at Roger—no, I will not even raise my voice, if I can remember, and, after all, there is a great deal to be said on his side; he has been very forbearing to me always, and I—I have been trying to him; most petulant and shrewish; treating him to perpetual, tiresome tears, and peevish, veiled reproaches. I will only ask him quite meekly and humbly to let me go home again; to send me back to the changed and emptied school-room; to Algy's bills and morosities; to the wearing pricks of father's little pin-point tyrannies.

I have lit the candles, and am looking at myself in the cheval-glass. What has become of my beauty, pray? The powder is shaken from my hair; it no longer rises in a white and comely pile; the motion of dancing has loosened and tossed it; it has a look of dull, gray dishevelment. The rouge has almost disappeared; melted away, or sunk in; there never was a great deal of it, never the generous abundance that adorned Mr. Parker's face. I cannot help laughing, even now, as I think of the round red smouch that so artlessly ornamented each of his cheeks.

I neither ring for my maid, nor attempt to undress myself. I either keep walking restlessly to and fro, or I sit by the casement, while the cold little wind lifts my dusty hair, or blows against my hot, stiff eyes; or I stand stupidly before the glass; bitterly regarding the ruins of my one night's fairness. I do not know for how long; it must be hours, but I could not say how many.

The fiddles' shrill voices grow silent at last; the bounding and stamping ceases; the departing carriage-wheels grind and crunch on the gravel drive. I shall not have much longer to wait; he will be coming soon now. But there is yet another interval. In ungovernable impatience, I open my door and listen. It seems to me that there reaches me from the hall, the sound of voices in loud and angry altercation; it is too far off for me to distinguish to whom they belong. Then there is silence again, and then at last—at last Roger comes. I hear his foot along the passage, and run to the door to intercept him, on his way to his dressing-room. He utters an exclamation of surprise on seeing me.

"Not in bed yet? Not undressed? They told me that you were tired and had gone to bed hours ago!"

"Did they?"

I can say only these two little words. I am panting so, as if I had run hard. We are both in the room now, and the door is shut. I suppose I look odd; wild and gray and haggard through the poor remains of my rouge.

"You are late," I say presently, in a voice of low constraint, "are not you? everybody went some time ago."

"I know," he answers, with a slight accent of irritation; "it is Algy's fault! I do not know what has come to that boy; he hardly seems in his right mind to-night; he has been trying to pick a quarrel with Parker, because he lit Mrs. Huntley's candle for her."

"Yes," say I, breathing short and hard. Has not he himself introduced her name?

"And you know Parker is always ready for a row—loves it—and as he is as screwed to-night as he well can be, it has been as much as we could do to make them keep their hands off each other!" After a moment he adds: "Silly boy! he has been doing his best to fall out with *me*, but I would not let him compass that."

"Has he?"

Roger has begun to walk up and down, as I did a while ago; on his face a look of unquiet discontent.

"It was a mistake his coming here this time," he says, with a sort of anger, and yet compassion, in his tone. "If he had had a grain of sense, he would have staid away!"

"It is a thousand pities that you cannot send us *all* home again!" I say, with a tight, pale smile—"send us packing back again, Algy and Barbara and *me*—replace me on the wall among the broken bottles, where you found me."

My voice shakes as I make this dreary joke.

"Why do you say that?" he cries, passionately. "Why do you *torment* me? You know as well as I do, that it is impossible—out of the question! You know that I am no more able to free you than—"

"You *would*, then, if you *could*?" cry I, breathing short and hard. "You *own* it!"

For a moment he hesitates; then—

"Yes," he says firmly, "I would! I did not think at one time that I should ever have lived to say it, but I *would*."

"You are at least candid," I answer, with a sort of smothered sob, turning away.

"Nancy!" he cries, following me, and taking hold of my cold and clammy hands, while what *looks*—what, at least, I should have once said *looked*—like a great yearning fills his kind and handsome eyes; "we are not very happy, are we? perhaps, child, we never shall be now—often I think so. Well, it cannot be helped, I suppose. We are not the first, and we shall not be the last! (with a deep and bitter sigh). But indeed, I think, dear, that we are unhappier than we need be."

I shrug my shoulders with a sort of careless despair.

"Do you think so? I fancy not. Some people have their happiness thinly spread over their whole lives, like bread-and-scrape!" I say, with a homely bitterness. "Some people have it in a *lump*! that is all the difference! I had mine in a *lump*—all crowded into nineteen years that is, nineteen *very good years*!" I end, sobbing.

He still has hold of my hands. His face is full of distress; indeed, distress is too weak a word—of acute and utter pain.

"What makes you talk like this *now*, to-night?" he asks, earnestly. "I have been deceiving myself with the hope that you were having *one* happy evening, as I watched you dancing—did you see me? I dare say not—of course you were not thinking of me. You looked like the old light-hearted Nancy that lately I have been thinking was gone forever!"

"Did I?" say I, dejectedly, slowly drawing my hands from his, and wiping my wet eyes with my pocket-handkerchief.

"*Any one* would have said that you were enjoying yourself," he pursues, eagerly—"*were* not you?"

"Yes," say I, ruefully, "I was very much." Then, with a sudden change of tone to that sneering key which so utterly—so unnaturally misbecomes me—"And *you*?"

"*I!*" He laughs slightly. "I am a little past the age when one derives any very vivid satisfaction from a ball; and yet," with a softening of eye and voice, "I liked looking at you too!"

"And it was pleasant in the billiard-room, was not it?" say I, with a stiff and coldly ironical smile—"so quiet and shady."

"*In the billiard room?*"

"Do you mean to say," cry I, my factitious smile vanishing, and flashing out into honest, open passion, "that you mean to deny that you were there?"

"Deny it!" he echoes, in a tone of the deepest and most displeased astonishment; "of course not! Why should I? What would be the object? And if there *were* one—have *I* ever told *you* a lie?" with a reproachful accent on the pronouns. "I was there half an hour, I should think."

"And why were you?" cry I, losing all command over myself. "What business had you? Were not there plenty of other rooms—rooms where there were lights and people?"

"Plenty!" he replies, coldly, still with that look of heavy displeasure; "and for my part I had far rather have staid there. I went into the billiard-room because Mrs. Huntley asked me to take her. She said she was afraid of the draughts anywhere else."

"Was it the *draughts* that were making her cry so bitterly, pray?" say I, my eyes—dry now, achingly dry—flashing a wretched hostility back into his. "I have heard of their making people's eyes run indeed, but I never heard of their causing them to sob and moan."

He has begun again to tramp up and down, and utters an exclamation of weary impatience.

"How could I help her crying?" he asks, with a tired irritation in his tone. "Do you think I *enjoyed* it? I *hate* to see a woman weep! it makes me *miserable*! it always did; but I have not the slightest objection—why, in Heaven's name, should I?—to tell you the cause of her tears. She was talking to me about her child."

"Her *child*!" repeat I, in an accent of the sharpest, cuttingest scorn. "And you were taken in! I knew that she made capital out of that child, but I thought that it was only neophytes like Algy, for whose benefit it was trotted out! I thought that *you* were too much of a man of the world, that she knew *you* too well—" I laugh, derisively.

"Would you like to know the true history of the little Huntley?" I go on, after a moment. "Would you like to know that its grandmother, arriving unexpectedly, found it running wild about the lanes, a little neglected heathen, out at elbows, and with its frock up to its knees, and that she took it out of pure pity, Mrs. Zéphine not making the slightest objection, but, on the contrary, being heartily glad to be rid of it—do you like to know *that*?"

"How do *you* know it?" (speaking quickly)—"how did *you* hear it?"

"I was told."

"But *who* told you?"

"That is not of the slightest consequence."

"I wish to know."

"Mr. Musgrave told me."

I can manage his name better than I used, but even now I redden. For once in his life, Roger, too, sneers as bitterly as I myself have been doing.

"Mr. Musgrave seems to have told you a good many things."

This is carrying the war into the enemy's quarters, and so I feel it. For the moment it shuts my mouth.

"Who is it that has put such notions into your head?" he asks, with gathering excitement, speaking with rapid passion. "*Some one* has! I am as sure as that I stand here that they did not come there of themselves. There was no room for such suspicions in the pure soul of the girl I married."

I make no answer.

"If it were not for the *misery* of it," he goes on, that dark flush that colored his bronzed face the other night again spreading over it, "I could *laugh* at the gross absurdity of the idea! To begin such fooleries at *my* age! Nancy, Nancy!" his tone changing to one of reproachful, heart-rending appeal— "has it never struck you that it is a little hard, considering all things, that *you* should suspect *me*?"

Still I am silent.

"Tell me what you wish me to do!" he cries, with passionate emphasis. "Tell me what you wish me to leave undone! I will do it! I will leave it undone! You are a little hard upon me, dear: indeed you are—some day I think that you will see it—but it was not your own thought! I know that as well as if you had told me! It was suggested to you—*by whom* you best know, and whether his words or mine are most worthy of credit!"

He is looking at me with a fixed, pathetic mournfulness. There is in his eyes a sort of hopelessness and yet patience.

"We are *miserable*, are not we?" he goes on, in a low voice— "*most* miserable! and it seems to me that every day we grow more so, that every day there is a greater dissonance between us! For my part, I have given up the hope that we can ever be happier! I have wondered that I should have entertained it. But, at least, we might have *peace*!"

There is such a depth of depression, such a burden of fatigue in his voice, that the tears rise in my throat and choke the coming speech.

"At least you are undeceived about me, are not you?" he says, looking at me with an eager and yet almost confident expectation. "At least, you believe me!"

But I answer nothing. It is the tears that keep me dumb, but I think that he thinks me still unconvinced, for he turns away with a groan.

CHAPTER XLVIII

"I made a posy while the day ran by,
Here will I smell my remnant out, and tie
My life within this band;
But Time did beckon to the flowers, and they
By noon most cunningly did steal away,
And withered in my hand!"

We are home again now; we have been away only three days after all,
but they seem to me like three years—three disastrous years—so greatly
during them has the gulf between Roger and me widened and deepened.
Looking back on what it was before that, it seems to me now to have been
but a shallow and trifling ditch, compared to the abyss that it is now. We
left Mr. Parker standing at the hall-door, his red hair flaming bravely in the
morning sun, loudly expressing his regret at our departure, and trying to
extract an unlikely promise from us that we will come back next week.

During the drive home we none of us hardly speak. Roger and I are
gloomily silent, Barbara sympathetically so. Barbara has the happiest knack
of being in tune with every mood; she never jostles with untimely mirth
against any sadness. I think she sees that my wounds are yet too fresh
and raw to bear the gentlest handling, so she only pours upon them the
balm of her tender silence. There is none of the recognized and allowed
selfishness of a betrothed pair about Barbara. Sometimes I almost forget that
she *is* engaged, so little does she ever bring herself into the foreground; and
yet, if it were not for us, I think that to-day she could well find in her heart
to be mirthful.

After all is said and done, I *still* love Barbara. However much the rest
of my life has turned to Dead Sea apples, I still love Barbara; and, what is
more, I shall always love her now. Is not she to live at only a stone's-throw
from me? I do not think that I am of a very gushing nature generally, but
as I think these thoughts I take hold of her slight hand, and give it a long
squeeze. Somehow the action consoles me.

Two more days pass. It is morning again, and I am sitting in my boudoir,
doing nothing (I never seem to myself to do any thing now), and listlessly
thinking how yellow the great horse-chestnut in the garden is turning,

and how kindly and becomingly Death handles all leaves and flowers, so different from the bitter spite with which he makes havoc of *us*, when Roger enters. It surprises me, as it is the first time that he has done it since our return.

We are on the formalest terms now; perhaps so best; and, if we have to address each other, do it in the shortest little icy phrases. When we are *obliged* to meet, as at dinner, etc., we both talk resolutely to Barbara. He does not look icy now; disturbed rather, and anxious. He has an open note in his hand.

"Nancy," he says, coming quickly up to me, "did you know that Algy was at Laurel Cottage?"

"Not I!" I answer, tartly. "He does not favor me with his plans; tiresome boy. He is more bother than he is worth."

"Hush!" he says, hastily yet gently. "Do not say any thing against him; you will be sorry if you do. He is *ill*."

"*Ill!*" repeat I, in a tone of consternation, for among us it is a new word, and its novelty is awful. "What is the matter with him?"

Then, without waiting for an answer, I snatch the note from his hand. I do not know to this day whether he meant me to read it or not, but I think he *did*, and glance hastily through it. I am well into it before I realize that it is from my rival.

"My dear Roger:
"My hand is trembling so much that I can hardly hold the pen, but, *as usual*, in my troubles, I turn to you. Algy Grey is here. You, who always understand, will know how much against my will his coming was, but he *would* come; and you know, poor fellow, how headstrong he is! I am grieved to tell you that he was taken ill this morning; I sadly fear that it is this wretched low fever that is so much about. It makes me *miserable* to leave him! If I consulted my own wishes, I need not tell *you* that I should stay and nurse him; but alas! I know by experience the sharpness of the world's tongue, and in my situation I dare not brave it; nor would it be fair upon Mr. Huntley that I should. Ah! what a different world it would be if one might follow one's own impulses! but one may not, and so I am leaving at once. I shall be gone before this reaches you."

I throw the letter down on the floor with a gesture of raging disgust.

"Gone!" I say, with flashing eyes and lifted voice; "is it possible that, after having decoyed him there, she is leaving him now to die, *alone*?"

"So it seems," he answers, looking back at me with an indignation hardly inferior to my own. "I could not have believed it of her."

"He will die!" I say a moment after, forgetting Mrs. Huntley, and breaking into a storm of tears. "I *know* he will! I always said we were too prosperous. Nothing has ever happened to us. None of us have ever gone! I *know* he will die; and I said yesterday that I liked him the least of all the boys. Oh, I *wish* I had not said it.—Barbara! Barbara! I *wish* I had not said it."

For Barbara has entered, and is standing silently listening. The roses in her cheeks have paled, indeed, and her blue eyes look large and frightened; but, unlike me, she makes no crying fuss. With noiseless dispatch she arranges every thing for our departure. Neither will she hear of Algy's dying. He will get better. We will go to him at once—all three of us—and will nurse him so well that he will soon be himself again; and whatever happens (with a kindling of the eye, and godly lightening of all her gentle face), is not *God* here—God *our friend*? This is what she keeps saying to me in a soft and comforting whisper during our short transit, with her slight arm thrown round me as I sob in helpless wretchedness on her shoulder. It is very foolish, very childish of me, but I cannot get it out of my head, that I said I liked him the least. It haunts me still when I stand by his bedside, when I see his poor cheeks redder than mine were when they wore their rouge, when I notice the hot drought of his parched lips. It haunts me still with disproportioned remorse through all the weeks of his illness.

For the time stretches itself out to weeks—abnormal, weary weeks, when the boundaries of day and night confound themselves—when each steps over into his brother's territories—when it grows to feel natural, wakefully, to watch the candle's ghostly shadows, flickering at midnight, and to snatch fitful sleeps at noon! to watch the autumnal dawns coldly breaking in the gloom of the last, and to have the stars for companions.

His insane exposure of himself to the rage of the storm, on the night of the picnic, has combined, with previous dissipation, to lower his system so successfully as to render him an easy booty to the low, crawling fever, which, as so often in autumn, is stealing sullenly about, to lay hold on such as through any previous cause of weakness are rendered the more liable to its attacks. Slowly it saps the foundations of his being.

But Algy has always loved life, and had a strong hold on it; neither will he let go his hold on it now, without a tough struggle; and so the war is long and bitter, and we that fight on Algy's side are weak and worn out.

Sometimes the silence of the night is broken by the boy's voice calling strongly and loudly for Zéphine. Often he mistakes me for her—often Barbara—catches our hands and covers them with insane kisses.

Sometimes he appeals to her by the most madly tender names—names that I think would surprise Mr. Huntley a good deal, and perhaps not altogether please him; sometimes he alludes to past episodes—episodes that perhaps would have done as well to remain in their graves.

On such occasions I am dreadfully frightened, and very miserable; but all the same, I cannot help glancing across at Roger, with a sort of triumph in my eyes—sort of *told-you-so* expression, from which it would have required a loftier nature than mine to refrain.

And so the days go on, and I lose reckoning of time. I could hardly tell you whether it were day or night.

My legs ache mostly a good deal, and I feel dull and drowsy from want of sleep. But the brunt of the nursing falls upon Barbara.

When he was well—even in his best days—Algy was never very reasonable—very considerate—neither, you may be sure, is he so now.

It is always Barbara, Barbara, for whom he is calling. God knows I do my best, and so does Roger. No most loving mother could be gentler, or spare himself less, than he does; but somehow we do not content him.

It is not to every one that the gift of nursing is vouchsafed. I think I am clumsy. Try as I will, my hands are not so quick and light and deft as hers—my dress rustles more, and my voice is less soothing.

And so it is always "Barbara! Barbara!" And Barbara is always there—always ready.

The lovely flush that outdid the garden-flowers has left her cheeks indeed, and her eyelids are drooped and heavy; but her eyes shine with as steady a sweetness as ever; for God has lit in them a lamp that no weariness can put out.

Sometimes I think that if one of the lovely spirits that wait upon God in heaven were sent down to minister here below, he would not be very different in look and way, and holy tender speech, from our Barbara.

Whether it be through her nursing, or by the strength of his own constitution, and the tenacious vitality of youth, or, perhaps, the help of all three, Algy pulls through.

I think he has looked Death in the face, as nearly as any one ever did without falling utterly into his cold embrace, but he pulls through.

By very slow, small, and faltering steps, he creeps back to convalescence. His recovery is a tedious business, with many tiresome checks, and many ebbings and flowings of the tide of life; but—he lives. Weak as any little tottering child—white as the sheets he lies on; with prominent cheek-bones, and great and languid eyes, he is given back to us.

Life, worsted daily in a thousand cruel fights, has gained one little victory. To-day, for the first time, we all three at once leave him—leave him coolly and quietly asleep, and dine together in Mrs. Huntley's little dusk-shaded dining-room.

We are quite a party. Mother is here, come to rejoice over her restored first-born son; the Brat is here; he has run over from Oxford. Musgrave is here. I am in such spirits; I do not know what has come to me. It seems to me as if I were newly born into a fresh and altogether good and jovial world.

Not even the presence of Musgrave lays any constraint upon my spirits.

For the first time since the dark day in Brindley Wood, I meet him without embarrassment. I answer him: I even address him now and then.

All the small civilizations of life—the flower-garnished table; the lamps softly burning; the evening-dresses (for the first time we have dressed for dinner)—fill me with a keen pleasure, that I should have thought such little etceteras were quite incapable of affording.

I seem as if I could not speak without broad smiles. I am tired, indeed, still, and my eyes are heavy. But what does that matter? Life has won! Life has won! We are still all six here!

"Nancy!" says the Brat, regarding me with an eye of friendly criticism, "I think you are *cracked* to-night!—Do you remember what our nurses used to tell us? 'Much laughing always ends in much crying.'"

But I do not heed: I laugh on. Barbara is not nearly so boisterously merry as I, but then she never is. She is more overdone with fatigue than I, I think; for she speaks little—though what she does say is full of content and gladness—and there are dark streaks of weariness and watching under the serene violets of her eyes. She is certainly very tired; as we go to bed at night she seems hardly able to get up the stairs, but leans heavily on the banisters—one who usually runs so lightly up and down.

Yes, *very* tired, but what of that? it would be unnatural, *most* unnatural if she were not; she will be all right to-morrow, after a good long night's rest—yes, all right. I say this to her, still gayly laughing as I give her my last kiss, and she smiles and echoes, "All right!"

CHAPTER XLIX

"So mayst thou die, as I do; fear and pain
Being subdued. Farewell! Farewell! Farewell!"

All right! Yes, for Barbara it *is* all right. Friends, I no more doubt that than I doubt that I am sitting here now, with the hot tears on my cheeks, telling you about it; but oh! not—*not* for us!

"Much laughing will end in much crying." The Brat was right. God knows the old saw has come true enough in my case. I exulted too soon. Too soon I said that the all-victor was vanquished. He might have left us our one little victory, might not he?—knowing that at best it was but a reprieve, that soon or late—soon or late, Algy—we all, every human flower that ever blossomed out in this world's sad garden, must be embraced in the icy iron of his arms.

I always said that we were too many and too prosperous; long ago I said it. I always wondered that he had so long overlooked us. And now that he comes, he takes our choicest and best. With nothing less is he content. Barbara sickens. Not until the need for her tender nursing is ended, not until Algy can do without her, does she go; and then she makes haste to leave us.

On the morning after my mad and premature elation, it is but too plain that the fever has laid hold of her too, and in its parching, withering clasp, our unstained lily fades. We take her back to Tempest at her wish, and there she dies—yes, *dies*.

Somehow, I never thought of Barbara dying. Often I have been nervous about the boys; out in the world, exposed to a hundred dangers and rough accidents, but about Barbara—*never*, hardly more than about myself, safely at home, scarcely within reach of any probable peril. And now the boys are all alive and safe, and Barbara is going. One would think that she had cared nothing for us, she is in such a hurry to be gone; and yet we all know that she has loved us well—that she loves us still—none better.

Alas! we have no long and tedious nursing of her. She has never given any trouble in her life, and she gives none now. Almost before we realize the reality and severity of her sickness, she is gone. Neither does she make any struggle. She never was one to strive or cry; never loud, clamorous, and self-asserting, like the boys and me; she was always most meek, and with a great meekness she now goes forth from among us—meekness and yet valor, for with a full and collected consciousness she looks in the face of Him from whom the nations shuddering turn away their eyes, and puts her slight hand gently into his, saying, "Friend, I am ready!"

And the days roll by; *but* few, *but* few of them, for, as I tell you, she goes most quickly, and it comes to pass that our Barbara's death-day dawns. Most people go in the morning. God grant that it is a good omen, that for them, indeed, the sun is rising!

We are all round her—all we that loved her and yet so lightly—for every trivial thing called upon her, and taxed her, and claimed this and that of her, as if she were some certain common thing that we should always have within our reach. Yes, we are all about her, kneeling and standing in a hallowed silence, choking back our tears that they may not stain the serenity of her departure.

Musgrave is nearest her; her hand is clasped in his; even at this sacred and supreme moment a pang of most bitter earthly jealousy contracts my heart that it should be so. What is he to her? what has he to do with our Barbara?—*ours, not his, not his!* But it pleases her.

She has never doubted him. Never has the faintest suspicion of his truth dimmed the mirror of her guileless mind, nor will it ever now. She goes down to the grave smiling, holding his hand, and kissing it. Now and then she wanders a little, but there is nothing painful or uneasy in her wanderings.

Her fair white body lies upon the bed, but by the smile that kindles all the dying loveliness of her face, by the happy broken words that fall from her sweet mouth, we know that she is already away in heaven. Now and again her lips part as if to laugh—a laugh of pure pleasantness.

"As the man lives, so shall he die!" As Barbara has lived, so does she die—meekly, unselfishly—with a great patience, and an absolute peace. O wise man! O philosophers! who would take from us—who have all but taken from us—our Blessed Land, the land over whose borders our Barbara, at that smile, seems setting her feet—you *may* be right—I, for one, know not! I am weary of your pros and cons! But when you take it away, for God's sake give us something better instead!

Who, while they kneel, with the faint hand of their life's life in theirs, can be satisfied with the *probability* of meeting again? God! God! give us *certainty*.

The night has all but waned, the dawn has come. God has sent his messenger for Barbara. An awful hunger to hear her voice once more seizes me, *masters* me. I rise from my knees, and lean over her.

"Barbara!" I say, in a strangling agony of tears, "you are not *afraid*, are you?"

Afraid! She has all but forgotten our speech—she, who is hovering on the confines of that other world, where our speech is needed not, but she just repeats my word, "*Afraid!*"

Her voice is but a whisper now, but in all her look there is such an utter, tender, joyful disdain, as leaves no room for misgiving.

Nay, friends, our Barbara is not at all afraid. She never was reckoned one of the bravest of us—never—timorous rather! Often we have laughed at her easy fears, we bolder ones. But which of us, I pray you, could go with such valiant cheer to meet the one prime terror of the nations as she is doing?

And it comes to pass that, about the time of the sun-rising, Barbara goes.

"She is gone! God bless her!" Roger says, with low and reverent tenderness, stooping over our dead lily, and, putting his arm round me, tries to lead me away. But I shake him off, and laugh out loud.

"Are you *mad*?" I cry, "she is *not* dead! She is no more dead than *you* are! Only a moment ago, she was speaking to me! Do dead people speak?"

But rave and cry as I may, she *is* dead. In smiling and sweetly speaking, even while yet I said "She is here!" yea, in that very moment she went.

Our Barbara is asleep!—to awake—when?—where?—we know not, only we altogether hope, that, when next she opens her blue eyes, it will be in the sunshine of God's august smile—God, through life and in death, *her friend.*   ⌐

CHAPTER L

"Then, breaking into tears, 'Dear God,' she cried, 'and must we see, All blissful things depart from us, or e'er we go to Thee; We cannot guess Thee in the wood, or hear Thee in the wind: Our cedars must fall round us e'er we see the light behind. Ay, sooth, we feel too strong in weal to need Thee on that road; But, woe being come, the soul is dumb that crieth not on God.'"

I am twenty years old now, barely twenty; and seventy is the appointed boundary of man's date, often exceeded by ten, by fifteen years. During all these fifty—perhaps sixty—years, I shall have to do without Barbara. I have not yet arrived at the *pain* of this thought: *that* will come, quick enough, I suppose, by-and-by!—it is the *astonishment* of it that is making my mind reel and stagger!

I suppose there are few that have not endured and overlived the frightful *novelty* of this idea.

I am sitting in a stupid silence; my stiff eyes—dry now, but dim and sunk with hours of frantic weeping—fixed on vacancy, while I try to think *exactly* of her face, with a greedy, jealous fear lest, in the long apathy of the endless years ahead of me, one soft line, one lovely line, may become faint and hazy to me.

How often I have sat for hours in the same room with her, without one glance at her! It seems to me, now, *monstrous*, incredible, that I should ever have moved my eyes from her—that I should ever have ceased kissing her, and telling her how altogether beloved she was by me.

If all of us, while we are alive, could stealthily, once a year, and during a moment long enough to exchange but two words with them, behold those loved ones whom we have lost, death would be no more death.

But, O friends, that one moment, for whose sake we could so joyfully live through all the other minutes of the year, to us never comes.

I suppose trouble has made me a little light-headed. I think to-day I am foolisher than usual. Thoughts that would not tease other people, tease me.

If I ever see her again—if God ever give me that great felicity—I do not quite know why He should, but if—if—(ah! what an if it is!)—my mind misgives me—I have my doubts that it will not be *quite* Barbara—not the Barbara that knitted socks for the boys, and taught Tou Tou, and whose slight, fond arms I can—now that I have shut my eyes—so plainly feel thrown round my shoulders, to console me when I have broken into easy tears at some silly tiff with the others. Can even the omnipotent God remember all the unnumbered dead, and restore to them the shape and features that they once wore, and by which they who loved them knew them?

The funeral is over now—over two days ago. She lies in Tempest church-yard, at her own wish. The blinds are drawn up again; the sun looks in; and life goes on as before.

Already there has grown a sacredness about the name of Barbara—the name that used to echo through the house oftener than any other, as one and another called for her. Now, it is less lightly named than the names of us live ones.

I shall always *wince* when I hear it. Thank God! it is not a common name. After a while, I know that she will become a sealed subject, never named; but as yet—while my wound is in its first awful rawness, I must speak of her to some one.

I am talking of her to Roger now; Roger is very good to me—very! I do not seem to care much about him, nor about anybody for the matter of that, but he is very good.

"You liked her," I say, in a perfectly collected, tearless voice, "did not you? You were very kind and forbearing to them all, always—I am very grateful to you for it—but you liked *her* of your own accord—you would have liked her, even if she had not been one of us, would not you?"

I seem greedy to hear that she was dear to everybody.

"I was very fond of her," he answers, in a choked voice.

"And you are *sure* that she is happy now?" say I, with the same keen agony of anxiety with which I have put the question twenty times before—"well off—better than she was here—you do not say so to comfort me, I suppose; you would say it even if I were talking—not of her—but of some one like her that I did not care about?"

He turns to me, and clasps my dry, hot hands.

"Child!" he says, looking at me with great tears standing in his gray eyes—"I would stake all my hopes of seeing His face myself, that she has gone to God!"

I look at him with a sort of wistful envy. How is it that he and Barbara have attained such a certainty of faith? He can *know* no more than I do. After a pause—

"I think," say I, "that I should like to go home for a bit, if you do not mind. Everybody was fond of her there. Nobody knew any thing about her, nobody cared for her here."

So I go home. As I turn in at the park-gates, in the gray, wet gloom of the November evening, I think of my first home-coming after my wedding-tour.

Again I see the divine and jocund serenity of the summer evening— the hot, red sunset making all the windows one great flame, and they all, Barbara, Algy, Bobby, Tou Tou, laughing welcome to me from the opened gate. To-night I feel as if they were *all* dead.

I reach the house. I stand in the empty school-room!—I, alone, of all the noisy six. The stains of our cookery still discolor the old carpet; there is still the great ink-splash on the wall, that marks the spot where the little inkstand, aimed by Bobby at my head, and dodged by me, alighted.

How little I thought that those stains and that splash would ever speak to me with voices of such pathos! I have asked to be allowed to sleep in Barbara's and my old room. I am there now. I have thrown myself on Barbara's little white bed, and am clasping her pillow in my empty arms. Then, with blurred sight and swimming eyes, I look round at all our little childish knick-knacks.

There is the white crockery lamb that she gave me the day I was six years old! Poor little trumpery lamb! I snatch it up, and deluge its crinkly back, and its little pink nose, with my scalding tears.

At night I cannot sleep. I have pulled aside the curtains, that through the windows my eyes may see the high stars, beyond which she has gone. Through the pane they make a faint and ghostly glimmer on the empty bed.

I sit up in the dead middle of the night, when the darkness and so-called silence are surging and singing round me, while the whole room feels full of spirit presences. *I alone!* I am accompanied by a host—a bodiless host.

I stretch out my arms before me, and cry out:

"Barbara! Barbara! If you are here, make some sign! I *command* you, touch me, speak to me! I shall not be afraid!—dead or alive, can I be afraid of *you?*—give me some sign to let me know where you are—whether it is worth while trying to be good to get to you! I *adjure* you, give me some sign!"

The tears are raining down my cheeks, as I eagerly await some answer. Perhaps it will come in the cold, *cold* air, by which some have known of the presence of their dead; but in vain. The darkness and the silence surge round me. Still, still I feel the spirit-presences; but Barbara is dumb.

"You have been away such a short time!" I cry, piteously. "You cannot have gone far! Barbara! Barbara! I *must* get to you! If *I* had died, and *you* had lived, a hundred thousand devils should not have kept me from you. I should have broken through them all and reached you. Ah! cruel Barbara! you do not *want* to come to me!"

I stop, suffocated with tears; and through the pane the high stars still shine, and Barbara is dumb!

CHAPTER LI

"The last touch of their hands in the morning, I keep it by
day and by night.
Their last step on the stairs, at the door, still throbs through
me, if ever so light.
Their last gift which they left to my childhood, far off in the
long-ago years, Is now turned from a toy to a relic, and
seen through the crystals of tears.
'Dig the snow,' she said,
'For my church-yard bed;
Yet I, as I sleep, shall not fear to freeze,
If one only of these, my beloveds, shall love with heart-
warm tears, As I have loved these.'"

It seems to me in these days as if, but for the servants, I were quite
alone in the house. Father is ill. We always thought that he never would care
about any thing, or any of us, but we are wrong. Barbara's death has shaken
him very much. Mother is with him always, nursing him, and being at his
beck and call, and I see nothing of her.

Tou Tou has gone to school, and so it comes to pass that, in the late
populous school-room, I sit alone. Where formerly one could hardly make
one's voice heard for the merry clamor, there is now no noise, but the faint
buzzing of the house-flies on the pane, and now and again, as it grows
toward sunset, the loud wintry winds keening and calling.

The Brat indeed runs over for a couple of days, but I am so glad when
they are over, and he is gone. I used to like the Brat the best of all the boys,
and perhaps by-and-by I shall again; but, for the moment, do you know, I
almost hate him.

Once or twice I *quite* hate him, when I hear him laughing in his old
thorough, light-hearted way—when I hear him jumping up-stairs three
steps at a time, whistling the same tune he used to whistle before he went.

Poor boy! He would be always sorrowful if he could, and is very much
ashamed of himself for not being, but he cannot.

Life is still pleasant to him, though Barbara is dead, and so I unjustly hate him, and am glad when he is gone. Have not I come home because here she was loved, here, at least, through all the village—the village about which she trod like one of God's kind angels—I shall be certain of meeting a keen and assured sympathy in my sorrow.

> "... Where indeed
> The roof so lowly but that beam of heaven
> Dawned some time through the door-way?"

And yet, now that I am here, the village seems much as it was. Still the same groups of fat, frolicking children about the doors; still the same busy women at the wash-tub; about the house still the same coarse laughs.

It would be most unnatural, impossible that it should not be so, and yet I feel angry—sorely angry with them.

One day when this sense of rawness is at its worst and sharpest, I resolve that I will pay a visit to the almshouse. There, at least, I shall find that she is remembered; there, out of mere selfishness, they must grieve for her. When will they, in their unlovely eld, ever find such a friend again?

So I go there. I find the old women, some crooning over the fire, half asleep, some squabbling. I suppose they are glad to see me, though not *so* glad when they discover that I have brought no gift in my hand, for indeed I have forgotten—no quarter-pounds of tea—no little three-cornered parcels of sugar.

They begin to talk about Barbara at once. Among the poor there is never any sacredness about the names of the dead, and though I have hungered for sorrowful talk about her, for assurance that by some one besides myself the awful emptiness of her place is felt, yet I wince and shrink from hearing her lightly named in common speech.

They are sorry about her, certainly—quite sorry—but it is more what they have lost by her, than her that they deplore. And they are more taken up with their own little miserable squabbles—with detracting tales of one another—than with either.

"Eh? she's a bad 'un, she is! I says to her, says I, 'Sally,' says I, 'if you'll give yourself hully and whully to the Lord for one week, I'll give you a *hounce* of baccy,' and she's that wicked, she actilly would not."

Is *this* the sort of thing I have come to hear? I rise up hastily, and take my leave.

As I walk home again through the wintry roads, and my eyes fix themselves with a tired languor on the green ivy-flowers—on the little gray-green lichen-cups on the almshouse-wall, I think, "Does *no one* remember her? Is she already altogether forgotten?"

It is still early in the afternoon when I reach home. The dark is *coming* indeed, for it comes soon nowadays, but it has not yet come.

I go into the garden, and begin to pace up and down the gravel walks, under the naked lime-trees that have forgotten their July perfume, and are tossing their bare, cold arms in the evening wind.

Only *one* of my old playfellows is left me. Jacky still stands on the gravel as if the whole place belonged to him; still stands with his head on one side, roguishly eying the sunset.

Thank Heaven, Jacky is still here, sly and nefarious, as when I bent down to give him my tearful good-by kiss on my wedding-morning. I kneel down, half laughing, half crying, on the damp walk, to stroke his round gray head, and hear his dear cross croak. Whether he resents the blackness of my appearance as being a mean imitation of his own, I do not know, but he will not come near me; he hops stiffly away, and stands eying me from the grass, with an unworthy affectation of not knowing who I am. I am still wasting useless blandishments on him, when my attention is distracted by the sound of footsteps on the walk.

I look up. Who is this man that is coming, stepping toward me in the gloaming?

I am not long left in doubt. With a slight and sudden emotion of surprised distaste, I see that it is Musgrave. I rise quickly to my feet.

"It is you, is it?" I say, with a cold ungraciousness, for I have not half forgiven him yet—still I bear a grudge against him—still I feel an angry envy that Barbara died with her hand in his.

"Yes, it is I!"

He is dressed in deep mourning. His cheeks are hollow and pale; he looks dejected, and yet fierce. We walk alongside of each other in silence for a few yards.

"Why do not you ask what has brought me here?" he asks suddenly, with a harsh abruptness. "I know that that is what you are thinking of."

"Yes," I reply, gravely, without looking at him, "it is!—what has?"

"I have come to bid you all good-by," he answers, in a low, quick voice, with his eyes bent on the ground; "you know"—raising them, and beginning to laugh hoarsely—"if—if—things had gone right—you would have been my nearest relation by now."

I shudder.

"Yes," say I, "I know."

"I am going away," he goes on, raising his voice to a louder tone of reckless unrest, "*where?*—God knows!—*I* do not, and do not care either!—going away for good!—I am going to let the abbey."

"To *let* it!"

"You are *glad!*" he cries in a tone of passionate and sombre resentment, while his great eyes, lifted, flash a miserable resentment into mine; "I *knew* you would be! I have not given you much pleasure very often, have I?"—(still with that same harsh mirth).—"Well, it is something to have done it *once!*"

I clasp my down-hanging hands loosely together. I lift my eyes to the low, dark sky.

"*Am* I glad?" I say, hazily. "I do not know!—I do not think I am!—I do not think I care one way or another!"

"Nancy!" he says, presently, in a tone no longer of counterfeit mirth, but of deep and serious earnestness, "I do not know why I told you just now that I had come to bid them all good-by—it was not true—you know it was not. What are they to me, or I to them, now? I came—"

"For what did you come, then?" cry I, interrupting him, pantingly, while my eyes, wide and aghast, grow to his face. What is it that he is going to say? He—from whose clasp Barbara's dead hand was freed!

"Do not look at me like that!" he cries, wildly, putting up his hands before his eyes. "It reminds me—great God! it reminds me—"

He breaks off; then goes on a little more calmly:

"You need not be afraid! Brute and blackguard as I am, I am not quite brute and blackguard enough for *that!*—that would be past *even* me! I have come to ask you once again to forgive me for that—that old offense" (with a shamed red flush on the pallor of his cheeks); "I asked you once before, you may remember, and you answered"—(recalling my words with a resentful accuracy)—"that you *'would not, and, by God's help, you never would'*!"

"Did I?" say I, with that same hazy feeling. Those old emotions seem grown so distant and dim. "I dare say!—I did not recollect!"

"And so I have come to ask you once again," he goes on, with a heavy emphasis—"it will do me no great harm if you say 'No' again!—it will do me small good if you say 'Yes.' And yet, before I go away *forever*—yes"—(with a bitter smile)—"cheer up!—*forever!*—I must have one more try!"

I am silent.

"You may as well forgive me!" he says, taking my cold and passive hand, and speaking with an intense though composed mournfulness. "After all, I have not done you much harm, have I?—that is no credit to me, I know. I would have done, if I could, but I could not! You may as well forgive me, may not you? God forgives!—at least"—(with a sigh of heavy and apathetic despair)—"so they say!—would *you* be less clement than He?"

I am looking back at him, with a quiet fixedness. I no longer feel the slightest embarrassment in his presence; it no longer disquiets me, that he should hold my hand.

"Yes," say I, speaking slowly, and still with my sunk and tear-dimmed eyes calmly resting on the dull despair of his, "yes—if you wish—it is all so long ago—and *she* liked you!—yes!—I forgive you!"

CHAPTER LII

"Love is enough."

And so, as the days go by, the short and silent days, it comes to pass that a sort of peace falls upon my soul; born of a slow yet deep assurance that with Barbara it is well.

One can do with probabilities in prosperity, when to most of us careless ones it seems no great matter whether there be a God or no? When all the world's wheels seem to roll smoothly, as if of themselves, and one can speculate with a confused curiosity as to the nature of the great far cause that moves them; but in grief—in the destitute bareness, the famished hunger of soul, when "one is not," how one craves for *certainties*! How one yearns for the solid heaven of one's childhood; the harping angels, the never-failing flowers; the pearl gates and jeweled walls of God's great shining town!

They may be gone; I know not, but at least *one* certainty remains— guaranteed to us by no outside voice, but by the low yet plain tones that each may listen to in his own heart. That, with him who is pure and just and meek, who hates a lie worse than the sharpness of death, and loves others dearer than himself, it shall be well.

Do you ask where? or when? or how? We cannot say. We know not; only we know that it shall be well.

Never, never shall I reach Barbara's clear child-faith; Barbara, to whom God was as real and certain as I; never shall I attain to the steady confidence of Roger. I can but grope dimly with outstretched hands; sometimes in the outer blackness of a moonless, starless night; sometimes, with strained eyes catching a glimpse of a glimmer in the east. I can but *feel* after God, as a plant in a dark place feels after the light.

And so the days go by, and as they do, as the first smart of my despair softens itself into a slow and reverent acquiescence in the Maker's will, my thoughts stray carefully, and heedfully back over my past life: they overleap the gulf of Barbara's death and linger long and wonderingly among the previous months.

With a dazed astonishment I recall that even then I looked upon myself as one most unprosperous, most sorrowful-hearted.

What in Heaven's name ailed me? What did I lack? My jealousy of Roger, such a living, stinging, biting thing *then*; how dead it is now!

Barbara always said I was wrong; always!

As his eyes, in the patient mournfulness of their reproachful appeal, answer again in memory the shrewish violence of my accusation on the night of the ball—the last embers of my jealousy die. He does not love me as he did; of that I am still persuaded. There is now, perhaps, there always will be, a film, a shade between us.

By my peevish tears, by my mean and sidelong reproaches, by my sulky looks, I have necessarily diminished, if not quite squandered the stock of hearty, wholesome, honest love that on that April day he so diffidently laid at my feet. I have already marred and blighted a year and three-quarters of his life. I recollect how much older than me he is, how much time I have already wasted; a pang of remorse, sharp as my knife, runs through my heart; a great and mighty yearning to go back to him at once, to begin over again *at once, this very minute*, to begin over again—overflows and floods my whole being. Late in the day as it is—doubly unseemly and ungracious as the confession will seem now—I will tell him of that lie with which I first sullied the cleanness of our union. With my face hidden on his broad breast, so that I may not see his eyes, I will tell him—yes, I will tell him. "I will arise, and go to him, and say, 'I have sinned against Heaven and before thee.'"

So I go. I am nearing Tempest: as I reach the church-yard gate, I stop the carriage, and get out.

Barbara was always the one that, after any absence from home, I used first to run in search of. I will go and seek her now.

It is drawing toward dusk as I pass, in my long black gown, up the church-path, between the still and low-lying dead, to the quiet spot where, with the tree-boughs waving over her, with the ivy hanging the loose luxuriance of its garlands on the church-yard wall above her head, our Barbara is taking her rest.

As I near the grave, I see that I am not its only visitor. Some one, a man, is already there, leaning pensively on the railings that surround it, with his eyes fixed on the dark and winterly earth, and on the newly-planted, flagging flowers. It is Roger. As he hears my approaching steps, the swish of my draperies, he turns; and, by the serene and lifted gravity of his eyes, I see that he has been away in heaven with Barbara. He does not speak as I come near; only he opens his arms joyfully, and yet a little diffidently, too, and I fly to then.

"Roger!" I cry, passionately, with a greedy yearning for human love here—at this very spot, where so much of the love of my life lies in death's austere silence at my feet—"love me a little—*ever so little!* I know I am not very lovable, but you once liked me, did not you?—not nearly so much as I thought, I know, but still *a little!*"

"*A little!*"

"I am going to begin all over again!" I go on, eagerly, speaking very quickly, with my arms clasped about his neck, "quite all over again; indeed I am! I shall be so different that you will not know me for the same person, and if—if—" (beginning to falter and stumble)—"if you still go on liking *her* best, and thinking her prettier and pleasanter to talk to—well, you cannot help it, it will not be your fault—and I—I—will try not to mind!"

He has taken my hands from about his neck, and is holding them warmly, steadfastly clasped in his own.

"Child! child!" he cries, "shall I *never* undeceive you? are you still harping on that old worn-out string?"

"*Is* it worn out?" I ask, anxiously, staring up with my wet eyes through the deep twilight into his. "Yes, yes!" (going on quickly and impulsively), "if you say so, I will believe it—without another word I will believe it, but—" (with a sudden fall from my high tone, and lapse into curiosity)—"you know you must have liked her a good deal once—you know you were engaged to her."

"*Engaged to her?*"

"Well, *were not* you?"

"I never was engaged to any one in my life," he answers with solemn asseveration; "odd as it may seem, I never in my life had asked any woman to marry me until I asked you. I had known Zéphine from a child; her father was the best and kindest friend ever any man had. When he was dying, he was uneasy in his mind about her, as she was not left well off, and I promised to do what I could for her—one does not lightly break such a promise, does one? I was fond of her—I would do her any good turn I could, for old sake's sake, but *marry* her—be *engaged* to her!—"

He pauses expressively.

"Thank God! thank God!" cry I, sobbing hysterically; "it has all come right, then—Roger!—Roger!"—(burying my tear-stained face in his breast)—"I will tell you *now*—perhaps I shall never feel so brave again!—do not look at me—let me hide my face; I want to get it over in a hurry! Do you remember—" (sinking my voice to an indistinct and struggling whisper)— "that night that you asked me about—about *Brindley Wood?*"

"Yes, I remember."

Already, his tone has changed. His arms seem to be slackening their close hold of me.

"Do not loose me!" cry I, passionately; "hold me tight, or I can *never* tell you—how could you expect me? Well, that night—you know as well as I do—I *lied*."

"You *did*?"

How hard and quick he is breathing! I am glad I cannot see his face.

"I *was* there! I *did* cry! she *did* see me—"

I stop abruptly, choked by tears, by shame, by apprehension.

"Go on!" (spoken with panting shortness).

"He met me there!" I say, tremulously. "I do not know whether he did it on purpose or not, and said dreadful things! must I tell you them?" (shuddering)—"pah! it makes me sick—he said" (speaking with a reluctant hurry)—"that he loved me, and that I loved him, and that I *hated* you, and it took me so by surprise—it was all so horrible, and so different from what I had planned, that I cried—of course I ought not, but I did—I *roared!*"

There does not seem to me any thing ludicrous in this mode of expression, neither apparently does there to him.

"Well?"

"I do not think there is any thing more!" say I, slowly and timidly raising my eyes, to judge of the effect of my confession, "only that I was so *deadly, deadly* ashamed; I thought it was such a shameful thing to happen to any one that I made up my mind I would never tell anybody, and I did not."

"And is that *all*?" he cries, with an intense and breathless anxiety in eyes and voice, "are you sure that that is *all*?"

"All!" repeat I, opening my eyes very wide in astonishment; "do not you think it is *enough*?"

"Are you sure," he cries, taking my face in his hands, and narrowly, searchingly regarding it—"Child! child!—to-day let us have nothing—*nothing* but truth—are you sure that you did not a little regret that it must be so—that you did not feel it a little hard to be forever tied to my gray hairs—my eight-and-forty years?"

"Hush!" cry I, snatching away my hands, and putting them over my ears. "I will not listen to you!—what do I care for your forty-eight years?—If you were a hundred — two hundred — what is it to me? — what do I care — I love you! I love you! I love you — O my darling, how stupid you have been not to see it all along!"

And so it comes to pass that by Barbara's grave we kiss again with tears. And now we are happy — stilly, inly happy, though I, perhaps, am never quite so boisterously gay as before the grave yawned for my Barbara; and we walk along hand-in-hand down the slopes and up the hills of life, with our eyes fixed, as far as the weakness of our human sight will let us, on the one dread, yet good God, whom through the veil of his great deeds we dimly discern. Only I wish that Roger were not nine-and-twenty years older than I!